Olzanah
HUNTED

R.M.Drost

PARTRIDGE
A Penguin Random House Company

ISBN:	Hardcover	978-1-4828-9689-3
	Softcover	978-1-4828-9688-6
	eBook	978-1-4828-9699-2

To order additional copies of this book, contact
Toll Free 800 101 2657 (Singapore)
Toll Free 1 800 81 7340 (Malaysia)
orders.singapore@partridgepublishing.com

www.partridgepublishing.com/singapore

Art Washes Away From The Soul The Dust Of Everyday Life

He sat watching his child sleep in the hand made crib he spent a long time crafting while he wife's belly was swollen with the small child. The light haired child looked so peaceful sleeping in front of him, such quiet noises escaping those new lips.

"Can you bring her over?" he picked up the child, trying not to wake her and brought her over to his beautiful and strong wife whom lay in bed, tired from the birth of their first child.

"Beautiful, utterly beautiful. She looks just like you," slowly the child opened her eyes and looked around the room, opening her tiny mouth to yawn before closing her eyes again and falling quickly into a deep slumber again.

"She looks just like us," he leaned over and gave his wife a kiss on the forehead. "The Goddess has truly blessed us with this gift," she looked down at her child with such love and admiration.

"Yes, but did that vial creature ruin it for us?"

"Please don't refer to her as that. She did what she was instructed to do and has destroyed herself. If you are to be mad with anyone then be mad with Lucifer, he is the vial creature that commanded her to do the act," she looked down at her child and worried for what might happen in her future.

"We just have to wait and see my love."

"I know."

"We have to leave. It isn't safe here for all of us, not just because of this but people are starting to suspect and the ones that do know are scared now. We have to leave," he walked over to the window that overlook a beautiful sight of the Egyptian landscape. The rolling hills with sand a thick forest that went on for miles, hiding the sun to those who walked underneath.

"How will you explain it to everyone?"

"I don't know. We'll give it a year, two at the maximum and then we will have to go. Go somewhere no one will know where we are, we have to fall off the grid."

"We can't just take everyone away from what they've grown up with, what they know," she protested.

"We may not have a choice soon enough. The fault is neither ours and we must embrace what is to come to us," she had no reason to dispute what the love of her life was saying to her and she knew the day was going to come sooner or later, it was just a matter of how much later.

* * *

She ran through the open field, dodging the trees as fast as her little legs could take her, trying to move away from the predator behind her. She could hear the noises creeping closer and closer to her, making as much noise as to alert her newly forming senses. Everything was so sharp, every leave, every twig breaking on the ground, every animal that ran through the forest along with them.

"I'm coming for you," he called out with a laugh, getting a giggle from her before hearing a thump and approaching the small light haired child lying on the floor of the forest laughing and kicking her legs in the air. He leaned down and rubbed her belly before picking her up and holding her like she was an airplane, flying her around in the air.

"Daddy," she laughed, the childish sound echoing through the forest, hitting the ears of animals, making them run in fear of the unknown.

"Come here my Princess. You are so loved. Never forget that, so loved. Mama loves you. Papa loves. Be safe and be true to yourself," he kissed her cheek before marching out with the girls hand in his and her walking by his side, her small form barely able to be seen against his tall, muscular form.

"Come here my Princess," the girl ran towards her mother, "We love you so much," she let her mother hug her tightly like it was the last time they were going to hug and get to be together. The girl hung onto both her parents, letting their warmth and love seep into her skin, letting her know just how much they loved and her and how strong they thought she was.

His red eyes watched on from the bushes as the two parents said goodbye to their daughter. She wasn't safe and she never would be, not from people wanting what she has and not from people like him.

Tears stained the parents eyes and it was a true sight of glory to see such strong people crying over something they would never see again. His heart filled with satisfaction at watching the two fall and he knew he was always going to be the cause of that pain and those tears.

A smile spread onto his lips as he watched everything unfold and the car drive away, the two mighty people standing, tears streaming down their faces, waving at the empty road that the car had gone down.

"The beginning is here. Let the games begin. I will hunt you and I will get you."

Chapter One

What We Play Is Life

HE CHECKED HER up and down, making sure she looked OK to leave the house. Everything that might draw the wrong kind of attention was covered, although it hurt me, I didn't want to see the bruises exposed and I didn't want people to be staring at them, knowing what was going on behind closed doors.

Young girls ran along the make shift board walk, tossing their arms in the air, trying to get away from their mothers waiting to go home after a long day. Teenagers sat on towels on the fake sand with iPod's in and sunglasses on; ready to get that summer glow before the real December sun came out.

A mop of long thick wavy red hair was pulled into a plait on the side of a young lady's face. A wide brimmed sat on top of the girls head as she let the warmth of the late afternoon sun soak into the skin on her back. Headphones were placed in her ears and bug eyed sunglasses sat over her closed eyes. Summer was just around the corner and she reveled in the fact that her last year of school would be coming to an end.

A man watched from the sidelines, looking very out of place as he sat on a wooden, worn out bench seat in a pair of full length dark wash jeans and a black jumper. The sun was warm today and he would be sweating in that outfit but his eyes were trained on one thing and one thing only.

"Ollie," a loud bubbly voice cut through the peaceful sounds at the makeshift beach set up at Rosewood. The girl ignored the loud incessant voice that called to her, choosing to instead turn the music up in her ears.

The voice got louder as the girl approached and she had no choice but to shut her music off and spin around so she could see who was calling for her. "Olyanah!" the voice called again, getting closer and closer.

"Hey, Lacy" Ollie, the red headed girl, sat up on her beach towel and smiled at her friend. Lacy looked down at Ollie, her blonde hair blowing in the wind and getting in her eyes. Lacy helped Ollie up and waited with her hands on her hips for Ollie to gather her things in her beach bag. Lacy's model like body was seen through a white chiffon style beach dress buttoned up at the front; see-through enough that the floral bathers she wore underneath were to be seen by all those around.

"You better be kidding me. After yelling at you to get your attention for ten minutes all you have to do is say 'hey' and then take your sweet time getting your shit together?" Lacy eyed her best friend before deciding she was going to be the bigger person.

"Pretty much," Ollie conceded with a simple, easy-going wink.

"Well because I am such an amazing friend, I am going to let that one slide. Besides, I have some news that I am sure you are more then willing to hear," Lacy squealed as the two best friend walked along the boardwalk and towards the car park. The squeal was one know to the red headed girl as 'bad news that she needed to know' was coming her way. "Well, your dad is getting in bed with Miss. Collins as we speak right now," Lacy spoke so fast that a normal girl wouldn't be able to understand her, but Ollie was no normal girl; no. She was Lacy's best friend and very used to the theatrical girl she loved so much.

"And I needed to know that information why?" Ollie enquired as they reached their cars. Lacy raised an eyebrow at her friend before letting out a huge sigh that her how body felt.

"Because your mother dearest is shacking up with the principal. Now." Ollie rolled her eyes before pulling the bug-eyed sunglasses off her deep blue eyes. To Ollie, her parents' cheating openly on one another was not new news. In fact there hadn't been a single week in her eighteen years that she could recall when her parents had been faithful to one another.

She had learnt to deal with it by now but interfering with her school, that was where she drew the line.

"I don't need this right now. Exams are in a week, if I suffer because of this, than shit will hit the fan in a way no one will ever expect," Ollie stopped herself from ranting loudly in the filling car park and settled with a loud groan.

"You can crash at mine tonight if you want," Lacy suggested shrugging her shoulders. Some R&R was exactly what Ollie needed but unfortunately for Lacy, her friend was much too school driven and wanted good marks to 'leave her future open'.

"Thanks, Lac, but I have damage control to do and some homework that needs attacking with a knife," Ollie replied pulling out her keys to her blue Hyundai i20, or as she like to call it; her Blue Baby.

"Alright, well I'll catch you tonight or tomorrow," Lacy hugged Ollie before opening her Black Beauty, a black Honda Jazz. The two girls parted ways with a wave before hitting the road.

"You can forget about school for the next few weeks young lady," was the first thing that was said to Ollie as she walked in the door. She looked around the kitchen before placing her bag on the kitchen counter and begging for the strength to get through these next few weeks. Four more weeks, that was all.

"Shut up, Greg," Ollie's mum, Jane, replied to her ranting partner. "Just because you have working class doesn't mean you can tell my daughter what to do!"

"She's my daughter too, Jane," Greg, Ollie's father, yelled back.

"And 'she' is the cats mother," Ollie calmly interjected. "Now shut up and listen," knowing her parents were about to argue with her language, Ollie held up her hand to stop them, effectively telling them she didn't want to hear it. "I have exams next week and I have to study this week. If I have to hear your bullshit fighting then I am going to pack my bags and say goodbye and have a nice life. I am eighteen and stay here because I am your daughter, not because I have to. Got it? Good," Ollie looked at her parents. Normally Ollie wouldn't be so brazen, scared for what they might do to her, but Ollie only had four more weeks, something she felt as though she could handle.

Unfortunately for Ollie, she had young parents, which meant, even though they didn't get along, they usually combined forces when it came to punishing her. Jane stood looking at Greg with a stunned expression on her face. Jane, being only thirty-six, looked a lot younger then that and used that to her advantage whenever it came to hurting Greg. Greg, only three years older then Jane, looked quite fit and kept up appearances to impress younger women. He'd slept with girls younger then Ollie, but never thought much of it; he only wanted to annoy Jane.

It became apparent that Ollie had made a big mistake talking to her parents like that when Greg narrowed his eyes at his daughter and stepped forward, arms crossed over his well-defined chest.

"Who do you think you are to talk to us like that?" those narrowed eyes caused Ollie to shiver involuntary as Greg took another step towards her.

"I just feel as though . . ."

"No, you don't get to talk to us like that. Eighteen or not, we own you and I can prove it," Jane leaned back against the couch as Greg cracked his knuckles like a bad action movie and pulled one arm back, opening his hand as he slapped Ollie across the face.

She fell to the floor, pain tingling on her cheek. She knew it would be turning a red colour and a lot of makeup would be needed.

It wasn't as though the pain in her cheek was pleasant, but it was something Ollie had grown accustom to and knew that when she left, it was something she would be able to say goodbye to forever.

* * *

Ollie pulled out her English book to start on some homework when her phone rang. 'My milkshake brings all the boys to the yard' echoed around her room. Ollie dived onto her bed and answered it, knowing it was Lacy on the other end. The girl seemed determined to embarrass Ollie at every turn and had made her pinky swear not to change the personalized ringtone. Imagine the looks Ollie got when she was out and Lacy called; mothers were not too happy about it.

"Hey, Lac," Ollie felt like a teenager in a bad American movie, sitting on her bed on her stomach with her legs up and twirling her thick red dyed plait around her finger. Ollie looked around her very simple room, white walls with some photos pinned up on them, photos of her, Lacy and their friends at parties, at the shops, at the make-shift beach that was in Rosewood.

Everything else in her room was very simple, her parents refusing to pay for anything and Ollie wanted to save the money she got working for when her and Lacy went away, and for moving out.

"So I hear the rumour mill is grinding out that Miss. Collins already wants to see you tomorrow," Lacy didn't bother with 'hello'.

"Firstly, the rumour mill couldn't have found out Miss. Collins is wanting to bust my chops about god knows what and secondly I don't think running and talking sounds as though it is working," Ollie could hear Lacy puffing as she ran. Lacy was a ball of energy and Ollie didn't know how she did it. Lacy would always come up with crazy ways to burn her energy and Ollie used to be in on it too.

"You used to be fun! What happened to you? You are stuck in a boring old square you know that?" Lacy shot at Ollie as she puffed.

"I had no choice but to," Ollie started shouting, "Grow up because my parents are too childish to act their age," getting that out of her system made Ollie feel a little better. Not a lot, but a little. "I wish I had your energy, Lac," Ollie sighed rolling onto her back.

"You used to but then your fun sucking square came along and wrapped you in its confines. But I know a way in which you could break those walls down."

"I do love a good intrigue."

"Say yes to Alex. I hear he is pinning for his Princess being kept in her room by her fire breathing parents," Ollie could help but let a bark of laughter leave her body. No one at school, or in the world besides Lacy and her family, knew of Ollie's parents' booty calls and that was the way she planned to keep it.

"My answer will be the same as always. He's a sweet kid but not my type, not that I know what that is but I know what it isn't."

"You are so goddamn stubborn! Live a little and have some fun! I mean all you do is study now and you barely breathe because you parents are riding the shit out of other people. Why can't you have some fun? You deserve it out of all people. Come on, Ollie, live a little. What's the worst that could happen if you didn't keep your parents in line for a day?" Lacy had stopped running, Ollie could tell from how fast she was talking, her jaw was going at superman speed, triple zero would be called soon because of the smoke.

"It's not a 'them' thing, it's a 'me' thing," Ollie tried to communicate with Lacy. Lacy knew almost everything about her life since they meet when they were twelve, but there something Ollie had kept to herself for a long time. Ollie couldn't afford to jump out of her boring old square; she didn't know what might happen to her if she did.

"No, it's an overpowering the boring square thing."

"Thanks for the support, Lac," the sarcasm was evident in Ollie's tone. "I have study to do and you have a younger brother to run home and annoy," Ollie hung up the phone and sighed.

Ollie had admired Lacy and Matt's relationship from a very young age, being an only child would do that. Matt was three years younger then Lacy and Ollie and a serial flirt. Although Ollie saw Matt as her own brother and Matt saw Ollie as a hot older sister, it didn't stop him flirting with her and trying to make his 'Joey' move on her.

Ollie, deciding after twenty minutes of trying to do homework, that it wasn't going to work for her, walked out of her room and into the kitchen to find something to eat for dinner. Before making it three steps down the hall all Ollie could hear were her parents screaming at each other. She went back to her room, fed up with the two year old behaviour, and grabbed her car keys, wallet and phone.

Jumping in her car, which she paid for herself, Ollie back out of her drive way and turned on the radio to some pop song that was 'good' at the moment. To her, all these new songs sounded the same. Some originality was needed within the music world that is why she opted for different music.

I pulled my hair out and let my unnatural curls fall down my shoulders, back and rest below my waist at my lower back. I had an almost backless dress with thin straps holding it up at my shoulders.

The silk, red dress was long with a slit on my right side, showing off my skin coloured stocking legs. Small black heels were on my feet as I walked down the hallway, hearing them clip with each step.

I could hear loud, drunk voices at the end of the hallway, happily chatting and laughing as they sat with jugs of beers in their hands. I knew who was over, it was the usual gang of he liked, I didn't bother to learn their names, I preferred to call them by their features.

There was 'Beard', 'Baldy', 'Tubby' and a few others.

Ollie finally arrived at what everyone called 'The Local'. It was a small strip of shops that included a pizza shop, fish and chip shop, small old-fashioned diner, a few boutique shops and a mini grocery store. 'The Local' was where all the kids from school hung out and Ollie was practically there every night chilling with her friends and if she wasn't with them then she was working at the diner with Lacy.

"Hey, Ollie," a few young year ten girls greeted Ollie as she got out of her car. Ollie smiled at the girls before making her way towards the diner where she could already see her friends sitting at a booth. Lacy was seated at the end next to their friend Martha. Martha sat with her chocolate hair pulled back into a tight sock bun, being the fashionista of the group Martha was always supporting the newest trends to hit the racks and today was no disappointment. To Martha everyday was a day to get dressed up; she was wearing a tight long sleeved black dress on her beautiful curvy body.

Next to the beautiful Martha sat Harry, he was sitting with his hair all messed up perfectly like a surfer and clothes that Ollie could only associate with a rich English boy, not that Harry was rich but he and Martha got on well and she was often there to help him dress well.

The fifth addition to the eight friends was Polly, a strawberry blonde girl with a cute pixie cute and light eyes accented with makeup. Polly was very much the artist one of the group and it often showed in her clothing. Paint would cover them and if not paint then they would be rather plain, simple and yet eerie.

Liam sat next to Polly, laughing at a joke that was being told by the animated Lacy. Liam's hair was a bit longer and sat in a ponytail that only held half his hair up, not normally a fan of the look Ollie had to admit that Liam pulled if off well and it showed with all the attention he got from the girls at school.

Sarah and Jay were the last in the group. Jay was a known serial flirt and he and Ollie were often caught flirting in a friendly way. Both never thought of each other as more then friends but it was rather fun to wind the other up; Ollie usually won in their little game. Jay was the classic footy player, as were all the guys when they played. Jay had dark hair, shaved on the sides and shorter on top, he was a rather handsome guy.

Sarah had a pretty face that was shaped by light brown hair that was unruly in its curls, but with the face she had, Sarah was able to pull it off without a worry. Her ambitions to be a reporter were helped by her looks and knowledge of what was always going on in the world.

All eight made up what most people would call the 'popular' group, but none of them considered themselves better then anyone else. Lacy and Ollie were without a doubt the nicest of the group, always making sure they were remembered after they finished school as lovely girls, not 'those bitches'. Although the other six were all brilliant in their own ways, they all had reputations that Ollie and Lacy were happy not to have. They weren't known as horrible people, just people that like to have fun with a lot of different other people, especially at parties.

"Hello there," Ollie cried as she opened the door of the 50's styled diner.

"Look who could turn away from the books for more then a second!" Lacy laughed as everyone moved around for Ollie to sit next to Jay.

"Just because I have expectations of myself," Ollie joked with her friends while taking a seat and ordering a banana smoothie from the young waitress.

"Hey, Ol," Jay started placing his arm around her shoulder and pulling her closer to his chiseled body, "You looked mighty fine today at the beach," Jay winked at the girl under his arm as she tried to wiggle her way out of his iron man grip.

"Thanks, babe," Ollie replied trying to hold back the sarcasm but failing. A few guys from lower years walked past and smiled nervously at the group.

"Hi, Ollie," one of them managed to get out.

"Hey," she smiled back trying to be as friendly as possible around the awkward boys.

"It must be hard being so popular," Sarah said with her serious reporter face on.

"It's a real job no doubt but somehow I manage," Ollie gave her famous wink along with her famous and almost perfect Southern Belle accent. Everyone laughed before being interrupted by Lacy's phone ringing, the theme music for Jaws played loud enough for other tables to have a bit of a snicker too.

"Shit," she cursed as she fumbled for her phone in her bag. Pulling it out she pressed the touch screen and pressed it to her ear. "Hello mother dearest, what do I owe this great pleasure?" she asked into the phone. Ollie loved Lacy's parents along with her younger brother Matt. Charles and Sally were amazing to Ollie as she spent half the time at their house. It was like Ollie was an adopted child, majority of the time calling them 'Mama S' and 'Papa C'.

"Everything good in the hood?" Ollie asked as Lacy hung up and put away her phone.

"In my hood? Yes. In your hood? That would have to be a big fat negative," Lacy and Ollie stepped away from the group and outside, their friends knew how private Ollie was about her home life, they didn't know why but were good enough to respect her privacy. Ollie rarely had them over and if she did her parents were out or going out or only one was home.

"What's up my buttercup?" Ollie asked once they were outside. Taking a seat on a cool metal seat outside the fish and chip shop, Ollie waited for the bomb to hit her head.

"Your parents have called the cops on you and are high on your trail," Lacy replied looking down at her phone to check the time.

"How do you know this stuff so quickly? I've been out of the house for almost ten minutes and already they have the freaking cavalry on my arse," Ollie couldn't believe her parents sometimes. "Why have they called in the troops?" Ollie kept her voice calm and even as she spoke to Lacy but her hands were shaking with fear.

"Because they think you have run away and are freaking out. I think this is the first time I've heard of them getting along in over three years. You truly do bring out the best in people my precious rose," Lacy reached over and grabbed hold of Ollie's cheek, shaking it like an old aunt.

"Let me go," Ollie laughed grabbing her phone from her bag and pressing call on her mother's name. "Catch you inside when I am no longer running from the law," Ollie smiled casually at Lacy but felt anger building up inside her at her parents. Lacy went back inside while Ollie waited for her 'frantic and scared' mother to pick up. The only time Ollie felt confident when it came to her parents was when she was on the phone to them where she couldn't be touched or intimidated.

"Hello? Ollie?" on the last ring Jane's voice rang through the speaker.

"Hello," Ollie put on her posh English accent. She may not have been out of the state of the Northern Territory before but she knew her way around an accent and was quite good at all of them too. "There is no need to worry mum. I'm in town with my friends alright, I'm not on the road with some hairy biker that is going to have his way with me then dump my body on a deserted road," the sarcasm dripped from Ollie's voice as she spoke to her mum.

"You have scared your father and I to death tonight," her mother shot back.

"Cough once for there is a gun at your head or twice for the police being there and making you act like a caring mother," Ollie gave her mother the options.

"I am not playing here, Ollie; this is serious. We didn't know where you were."

"And you haven't cared before, why the change in heart? Is the ice finally melting? Actually don't answer that, I don't want to know because the warmth is weird so go back and turn the heater down on your body and cool your jets and heart again. You can call off the troops as I am fine and I shall see you when I get home," with that Ollie hung up and walked back inside to be with her friends.

Jane and Greg had never gone to this extreme before to try and find Ollie, they usually liked to go with something a little more hidden then straight out with the police.

Even with such a brave response and putting her parents in their place, Ollie was very scared for what might happen when she got home. She was worried that they would go off and try to put her in her place instead.

Ollie looked into the diner and looked at the people that were sitting in there, wondering what their stories were. Ollie was curious person, someone who was very interested in what people and the world had to offer.

Her table of seven friends sat laughing and joking around while another table of younger friends were talking quietly like they were exchanging secrets. There was a table with a man sitting at it, wearing a black suit and dark sunglasses over his eyes, reading the newspaper in the dark light.

The stories these people had hidden amazed Ollie, she would never stop being intrigued by those around her and what they had to offer, not only herself but the world and everyone else in it.

"Oh My God!" Lacy called as Ollie closed the diner door behind her. Lacy's voice sounded nasally and exactly like Janice from *friends*.

"Jan-ice! Jan-ice!" Ollie called back in the same voice as she sat at the booth with a wide smile on her face. "The troops are retreating, the war has been won!" the declaration had everyone laughing as Ollie held her arms in the air in triumph.

"Well now that that has been sorted let's get the party started," Lacy called the waitress over and ordered some alcohol or as the guys liked to call them 'lolly drinks'. The diner originally didn't sell alcohol but with the crowd they were getting they had to adjust to the school kids. ID was always checked but Ollie and all her friends were all over eighteen, which was lucky for them.

The diner was where Ollie and Lacy worked, whenever they weren't there for social gatherings they were either at school, studying or working there. The uniform was a pink poodle skirt with a white shirt and black silk scarf tied around their necks, the guys work brown trousers with a buttoned up white shirt and colourful bow tie. The girls rolled around on old fashioned four wheeled roller-skates while the guys wore simple black and white shoes.

"Hello, beautiful," Ollie tried not to groan out loud as a familiar voice travelled to her ears from behind.

"Hi, Alex," she spun around in her chair to get a look at the year eleven boy. He was a charming young man and although only seventeen had his choice of girls, but he always chose Ollie for a reason that was beyond her.

"Can I talk to you?" he asked. Ollie nodded her head and got out of the booth to walk over to another corner of the diner.

"What can I do for you, Alex?"

"Well I was wondering if you were busy this weekend?"

"Alex, it's exams next week, I have study to do and you know that Lacy and I are leaving pretty soon to go travelling for a year. I'm sorry but there is only so many times I can turn you down before you understand that a relationship is something that is not on my mind," Ollie tried to be nice about the situation but it was hard when Alex was bothering her every few days.

"I know," his face fell, "I was just hoping, as always. Thanks for being so cool about everything all the time, Ollie, I know I'm a real pain but you're awesome," with that Alex smiled and left the diner and Ollie went to sit with her friends, shaking her head in annoyance and guilt, she felt pretty bad about always turning Alex down, but at some point he had to get the message and Ollie wasn't going to be here forever.

"What was that about?" Jay asked, embracing Ollie under his arm as she sat down again at the booth.

"Alex confessing his undying love for me again," Ollie smiled as their drinks were delivered and everyone got stuck into them, Ollie, the only one who didn't drink out of the group, got the smoothie that she ordered. Everyone, knowing the routine, coughed up their keys to Ollie with a groan. Sipping her banana smoothie, Ollie smiled evilly at her friends when they groaned.

"You're too responsible, Ol," Jay laughed as a few beers were delivered for the guys. Ollie just shook her head and started digging into the chips that were in the middle of the table.

"You love me," Ollie sang. It never ceased to amaze Ollie's friends the talents that she possessed. They ranged from singing to art to sport and almost every other area of life. "Anyways, I have to go but I'll see you all tomorrow and please don't get anyone pregnant or get pregnant yourselves, I am so not ready to be an aunty," Ollie joked around as she placed the keys in the middle basket and walked off with a wave, holding her take away cup with her smoothie.

Ollie was not looking forward to seeing her parents at home and worried that they might still be fighting. Ollie had a stack of study to get done and her parents' fighting was a horrible distraction. The six-day block at school wasn't enough for Ollie's eight subjects. Taking on English, art, mathematics, psychology, legal studies, business management, community services and media was something that Ollie thought would leave her future wide open for herself. The world was her oyster and she was prepared to work for the pearl that was sitting in the middle waiting for her.

"I'm home," Ollie opened the front door wide and called out to her parents. Normally she would just walk in quietly but after getting the cops called on her, she didn't want her parents to 'worry'. Ollie knew it was all an act but she thought it might set their minds at ease if she called out to announce her arrival.

"Be quiet!" her father called back as Ollie heard the television on.

"Just letting you know that I am safe and well," Ollie shot back sourly before walking into her bedroom and slamming the door closed.

"Watch your attitude you spoilt brat!" Greg called to his daughter as the door hit the frame and crashed around the house.

"Right! I'm the spoilt little shit!" Ollie screamed back at her father. This new confidence was something that brought a smile to Ollie's face.

"My life would be a hell of a lot easier if you weren't in it! You took a life away from me so yes, you are the spoilt little shit!" Ollie rolled her eyes, letting her father fume in the lounge room and pulled out some books to start on some study.

She had a full day tomorrow at school and after already completing Physical Education and accounting the year before, Ollie just wanted school to be over so she could enjoy schoolies and then her travel with Lacy. Ollie wanted to make sure the Uni would be easy to get into with lots of experience with education. All her friends just thought she was crazy for putting the pressure on herself.

My body moved in motion with the men by me, but my mind was somewhere else, a place that took me away from what was going on in front of me. I didn't want to be here, but I knew the minute I stopped, the minute I left, I would be in trouble and I wouldn't be alive for much longer.

The pain of fear, they say, is the heart of love, but love is not filled with fear; love is filled with passion and emotion. The fear that crossed my heart and my veins when I saw my parents and when I spoke to my parents wasn't normal, it wasn't love and I knew that; but they didn't, not that they cared too much about how I was feeling. I was just some baggage that they were using to make more money on the side of their usual business.

Ollie woke with a start in the middle of the night. Her curtains were open, how she normally slept with the moonlight shinning in through the windows. It made her feel a lot closer to nature; something that she always strived for.

She looked up at the moonlight and smiled. The calm feeling that overcame her whole body was just the best feeling Ollie could ever have. Stars sparkled around and a smile spread across Ollie's lips. She closed her eyes and tried to think of a wish to make.

"First star I see tonight, I wish I may, I wish I might," her eyes opened as a wish popped into her mind. "I wish I could forget my parents and what they have done to me," she whispered before putting her head down on the pillow and dreaming of getting away from school and being able to go and travel the world with Lacy after the went to schoolies in Queensland.

Chapter Two

If You Can't Do Something Smart, Do Something Right

A LOUD OBNOXIOUS SOUND pierced Ollie's ears and she cursed under her breath at the thought of having to endure seven and a half hours of school today. She shut off her alarm and rolled over in bed so she was laying on her back looking up at her ceiling, which was covered with drawings of the full moon, that Ollie had made with water colours, charcoal, pencil and with torn off pieces of magazine articles and ads. Ollie got up off her bed and as her feet hit the plush dark carpet she groaned again at the early morning.

There weren't many things that captured her attention for so long, she was usually just curious about things but the full moon was something Ollie had never been able to get out of her mind.

Once a month, on the full moon, Ollie wouldn't be able to control her need to feel nature so she'd end up walking outside in the middle of the night and everything within her heightened. Eyesight, touch, feel, hearing; everything made her feel as though she was more then what she really was.

The thing that Ollie had kept hidden from everyone, aside from her need to be with nature, was her deep blue eyes glowing in the moon light at night on the full moon when she walked around outside, enjoying nature as it intended to be enjoyed in the Northern Territory.

Ollie stood in front of her full-length mirror, preparing to change into the Ashton High School uniform, which consisted of a black pleated skirt with a white shirt and black tie along with black stockings. The school emblem was sown onto the breast of the blazer and Year 12 hoodies.

Being in Year 12 and having Martha as a friend, none of the girls wore the right school uniform, opting for a black pencil skirt and white shirt with the black tie hanging from her neck, the knot sitting just above her breast in what the guys describe as 'very sexy'. A black cardigan was the next piece of clothing to add to the look and then black tights with black ballet flats. Ollie spun around in the mirror, silently approving what she was wearing before grabbing her big white leather handbag and walking into the kitchen with some of her books in hand.

"You look like a whore," Greg said as he saw his daughter. Most fathers would be joking when they said that to their daughters, Ollie knew Charles, Lacy's dad, would be but her father was different; meaner even though he usually approved of such attire, only when it suited him though of course.

"And you look like a man-whore," Ollie countered. Greg sat with a white buttoned up with the sleeves rolled off his forearms. Being a fit man, Greg liked to show off his body so as to piss Ollie and Jane off.

"Go make some money tonight and sell yourself on the street corners. You owe me anyway," Greg stared at his daughter with narrow eyes.

"For what?"

"Being alive. I've had to fork out money for you and believe me I don't like wasting my money on worthless shit," his reply was gruff.

"Shut up, Glen, she looks hot," Ollie could admit that sometimes her mother was alright, sticking up for her but in general it was a very strained mother and daughter relationship.

"From one whore to another," Greg left the room with that comment, hating that he was being ganged up on.

"What crawled up his arse sideways and decided to set up shop?" Ollie asked buttering her raison toast. Jane just shrugged her shoulders as she turned on the kettle and pulled out a travel mug.

To Ollie a travel mug was a very good sign. Whenever the travel mug was pulled out it meant that Jane was going to be going to work straight away not go and have a quick spin around for a quick bang and then get a takeaway coffee. Ollie always loved when the coffee mug was out and the brief case was set in the entrance.

"No idea but don't take it too heart. I think it has been up there a long time," Jane picked up her travel mug after making the coffee, planted a kiss on Ollie's forehead and waved goodbye.

"Bye," Ollie called, her eyebrows furrowed in confusion. After eating she decided it was time to go and grabbed her books, bag and car keys. Ollie drove the two-minute drive to school and parked her car in the student car park, opposite the L shaped concrete room where the lockers were kept. While Ollie grabbed her things, Lacy's Black Beauty pulled up next to Ollie's car.

"Someone looks happy!" Lacy sang, slamming her car door closed, making Ollie jump.

"Yeah well mum was alright this morning but dad was a complete arse so it's a double edged sword," Ollie replied as the two walked towards the lockers. "I'm over their crap. A new week, a new Ollie," Ollie had to shield her ears when Lacy squealed with excitement.

"Liam! She is back!" Lacy pulled Ollie along to meet Liam at the lockers. "It is time for some much needed energy from our most natural source; Ollie! It's been a while my friend," Lacy couldn't hold back her laughter.

"You bet your sweet arse it's energy time," Ollie opened up her locker with force and pushed her books inside, only grabbing the ones she needed for her first and second periods, English and Psychology.

All seven of the close friends had their lockers together and arriving with five minutes until class started they would hang around and catch up on any gossip that they missed the night before at the diner.

"Good to know that we can rely on the hyper twins to keep the energy swirling," Liam's voice was echoed around the locker, a fun smirk playing on his handsome lips. "And, Ol, that tie looks pretty hot," Liam winked.

"Thank god you like it!" she started fanning her face with her hand like a schoolgirl meeting a celebrity. Ollie's knees bent as she continued fanning her face before righting herself and rolling her eyes. "I was going to die if you didn't approve," sarcasm laced her voice.

"Come here, hot stuff," Jay's deep voice echoed in the locker room as he wrapped his arms around Ollie's waist and rested his head on her shoulder. Being almost two heads taller then the petite girl, resting his head on Ollie's shoulder gave him a hunched back.

"Control yourself, Jay Charleston or someone will have to whip you into shape."

"Are you going to be the one to get me under control?" Jay questioned with a cocky smirk playing on his lips. Jay and Ollie could be pretty flirty with each other but they both knew there was nothing between them, only friendly playfulness.

"You better believe it," Ollie dropped her voice, leaving it low and husky. Known for her 'stripper voice' Ollie loved to pull it out around Jay, just to watch him sweat and suffer. Jay crumbled to the ground, sitting on his knees and grabbed Ollie's hands as though her was proposing to her in the middle of the schools lockers.

"Take me away now and have your way with me," Jay pleaded of Ollie, his eyes begging for her.

"I don't think you can handle all of this," Ollie unwound her hands from Jay's and ran them up and down her body. The loud bell sounded throughout the lockers, making students jump and get a move on to their first class. "Saved by the bell," Ollie waved her English books around in Jay's face and Lacy entwined their arms together and walked off towards the English classroom.

"You have skill, Olyanah Kent," Liam laughed as he walked past.

"Oh yeah baby! If you've got it flaunt it," was Ollie's loud response.

"That voice and that uniform are going to get you in trouble," Jay warned as he caught up to the two best friends. "And I hope to be the one giving you the punishment," Jay swatted Ollie's bum as he jogged off to his first class of the day. All the girls around Jay started melting to the ground as his muscles were highlighted with each powerful leg movement.

"Girls are desperate," Ollie whispered to Lacy.

"Agreed. It is amazing that they haven't mauled you for flirting with Jay yet. I mean look at those eyes. Green isn't a colour that looks good on a lot of people but those younger girls seem to wear it well," Lacy stated, moving away from the group and into the main building.

Lacy and Ollie were the only two of the troublesome eight that had English together first period and pretty much everyone sat in the same seats everyday. Ollie and Lacy took their seats at the back of the room and opened their books. Miss. Collins, the young English teacher, had no control over the year twelve class and everyone just talked throughout, only taking a few notes to pacify their parents and at least understand some things.

"Olyanah Kent," Miss. Collins called out over the noise, "Principal Davis wants to see you. Now," and just like that she started writing notes on the whiteboard. People would write them down without paying attention. Ollie smiled awkwardly at Miss. Collins before giving Lacy the look that meant 'I'm going to kill my parents'.

"Good luck," Lacy mouthed to her best friend as she filed out of the room. Ollie knew she'd need the luck considering her father was bonking her English teacher and her mother was sleeping with the Principal. This wasn't going to be a fun meeting, Ollie rarely went out of her way to have a relationship with teachers, they were stuck in their roles and Ollie wanted no part of it.

She knocked on the door to the Principal's office and when she heard a faint, "Come in," she opened up the wooden door and smiled coldly at the young official man behind the desk. For a principal, Davis' was quite young, probably a little over thirty. Ollie couldn't help observing that he was a bit older then the men her mother usually went for but, each to their own.

"Olyanah," Principal Davis' started but Ollie cut him off.

"Ollie. My name is Ollie," Ollie sat down in the seat opposite Principal Davis desk.

"Ollie, then," he started again, giving Ollie a careful smile. "How are you doing? Enjoying year twelve?" he folded his hands together on the desk. The first thought that came to Ollie's mind was a therapist. He reminded her of a therapist the way he was trying to get her to feel comfortable and open up to him. He probably didn't know she was a psychology student and therefore could read everything he was trying to do.

"I'm fine," in true Ollie form; she mimicked Principal Davis position. "How are you, Principal Davis?" she asked using a professional voice, much like the one he had used on her. Principal Davis cracked a smile before relaxing back in his chair.

"I find it curious that you seem to be taking eight subjects in a six day block," a piece of paper sat squarely in the middle of his desk that his eyes wondered over.

"I find it curious that you are only taking an interest in what I am doing now that you are shagging my mother. Don't you think it's a little late in the year to be bringing such a thought up?" Ollie wasn't in the mood to sit there like a good little girl. She needed something to play with and if Principal Davis was going to play with her mum in bed, then Ollie was going to play with his head at school.

"I don't know if you know this but I studied psychology when I went to Uni. To me it seems as though you are doing all that to impress someone," Ollie resisted the urge to roll her eyes at the pathetic man in front of her.

"I don't know if you know this but I am studying psychology at the moment and to me, this little 'bonding session' or whatever you want to call it, seems as though you are trying to impress someone too. I know that that someone is my mother and I know my mother doesn't give a rats arse about me, so you can stop the games and go back to your computer and looking at students as though they are just numbers again. A little too late, Davis; a little too late," with that Ollie rose from her chair with a sour look on her face and stormed out of the room, slamming the office door closed.

Infuriated at the thought of Principal Davis thinking he can just waltz into her life like that and act as though he cares when he has never muttered so much as a 'hello' to Ollie. Her blood boiled as walked back into her English classroom, where Miss. Collins greeted her student with a cold unforgiving look.

"If you have something to say then say it," Ollie snapped. Taken aback, Miss. Collins just went back to writing on the whiteboard. "That's what I thought," Ollie said under her breath as she went to sit next to a stunned Lacy. With the class never being under control, no one had witnessed her snap at the young teacher.

"Care to explain that fine show?" Lacy asked regaining her composure, a sly smile over taking her lips, surprised and excited at her friends stand.

"She's a twit that needs to be taught a lesson. I am not my dad or my mum and don't treat as though I am. Principal Davis wanted a heart to heart but I told him just because he and my mum bump the uglies in their spare time doesn't mean he has the right to suddenly take an interest in me," Ollie took a deep breath before letting it out and smiling a warm smile at Lacy.

"Good for you girl! Taking a stand against the dark side. I like it," Ollie couldn't help the laugh that over took her body at Lacy's response to her rant.

"Where would I be without you?"

"In the middle of a mental institute begging for the lethal injection because you can't go one day without my dark and dry humour any more. Or my sarcasm," Lacy explained as though it were nothing.

"Guess what?"

"What?" Lacy's eyes widened with intrigue

"Fighting the dark side doesn't give you cookies and they don't have them on their side either," Lacy groaned.

"There go my hopes and dreams at becoming the new Lucifer of Hades."

"Sorry to be a dream dasher."

* * *

Ollie sat down at a table outside and threw her head back so the suns rays could hit her face. She needed and loved the refreshing feeling after the morning she had had. Ollie hated school for the fact that she missed out on such beautiful days stuck inside.

She sat at the lunch table by herself as she waiting for her friends to get their food and join her. Most people felt rather uncomfortable or feel as though they were being judged if they sat at a table by themselves but Ollie was quite content with the feeling. She didn't have a need to be validated with people around her, more so she just wanted people to like her and feel as though they could approach her.

The school didn't have any fences or restrains around it so students were free to come and go as they pleased, which meant so were uninvited guests.

He watched from a distance, sitting in his new car, staring at the girl sitting at the table by herself with her eyes closed and body lying out to soak up as much of the sun as possible. He had been watching her long enough to know what she was like and exactly what he was getting himself into when and if he decided to go through with his plan.

His phone rang, forcing him to tear his gaze from her and pick up the incoming call from his associate.

"Any news?" the female voice asked on the other end.

"No."

"When are we planning?"

"Soon. Very soon."

"I'll let him know what is happening."

"Good," and he slammed his phone closed, looking up again and watching her interact with other people at the previously empty table.

Being at the table alone, two year ten girls took the opportunity to go up and talk to Ollie about the upcoming formal. At Ashton High, formal was held on the day after the last exam and all senior years went; year ten, year eleven and year twelve. Although year tens and elevens had to leave at eleven thirty, year twelve's were allowed to bring out the alcohol at that stage and the formal for them finished at two in the morning. Lacy was organizing to have the after party at her house and that would go until people passed out or decided to leave.

"Hi Ollie," a nervous looking girl said with an anxious smile, forcing Ollie to open her eyes and plaster on a warm smile.

"Hey," so many people went to the school, about a hundred in each year level, and it was hard to remember everyone's names. "What's up?"

"We were wondering if you were going to be going to the school formal?" the nervous girls friend asked.

"Of course. Are you guys thinking of going this year?" The two girls nodded. "It's really fun, I was bloody nervous before my first formal but it's really cool once you get there and calm down. No segregation just a brilliant night. The music, people and dancing of course adds," Ollie winked at the girls. The formal was also a goodbye for the year twelve's at the end of the night when all the other year levels left.

"Do you know what you are going to wear?" Ollie could already see which one of the two girls was more nervous.

"No idea at all but I'll find something all in due time. Don't worry too much about it, try and enjoy it as much as possible because it's over pretty much in a heart beat," Ollie tried to encourage the two nervous year tens. It was a very fun night and everyone deserved to enjoy it as much as the final years.

"Thanks, Ollie," both girls said in unison. As soon as the girls were gone, Ollie's friends walked up to the table with sly smiles on their faces.

"Giving out some bad advice there, Ol?" Martha said with a small laugh. "The formal is a big thing to worry about, don't tell them other wise," Martha's face grew serious before subtly winked at Ollie.

"Leave the poor girls alone, just because you 'set the trends' doesn't mean you can go around freaking younger girls out," friendly banter started around the table about whether formal was a big deal or not. Jay slipped into a seat next to Ollie and wrapped his arm around her shoulder.

"You look so hot today," before Jay could finish Ollie and Lacy cut in at the same time.

"Like a sunrise!" the whole group burst into laughter at the cheesy Aami car insurance ad.

"Moving on, you cannot leave a guy hanging," Jay moved around the little outburst. The whole group shut up to listen in to what happened to keep Jay 'hanging'. It wasn't often Jay would bring up an episode from the day.

"That was a one time thing," Ollie slapped his shoulder in reprimand as she tried to hide her flaming cheeks. Ollie wasn't one to blush but the situation was getting rather promiscuous for her liking.

"Did you two have sex in the lockers and we missed out on the free show?" Lacy cried out. Admitting defeat Ollie decided, 'If you can't beat 'em, join 'em'.

"Yeah we did. Do you want details or . . . ?" Ollie asked in a sensual voice.

"Yes!" Lacy almost fell over with anticipation, "Is he big?" Jay's lips formed into a cocky smile, ready for Ollie to rave about her 'experience'.

"Barely felt a thing," Ollie shut him down. Jay's face paled as he was brought back to reality with a bang.

"That's not what all your screaming said. You were begging for me," Jay pulled Ollie closer as she rolled her eyes and mouthed 'no' to her friends. "Come on Ol, don't deny the passion."

"I know how much your ego means to you and I didn't want to break that," Ollie truthfully said. Before Ollie knew it, her talking back had landed her sandwiched between Lacy and Jay. "Ow! I am not a human punching bag," Ollie tried to cry as her body crumbled in on its self.

"Human punching bags aren't allowed to talk!" Polly said and fist bumped Lacy in the process.

"You people are really mean," Ollie sulked as she crossed her arms when the assault stopped.

"Aw, come here Princess," Liam said standing up and hugging Ollie from behind. Ollie shrugged him off and stood, stuffing her lunch into her bag. "Come on, Ol, we were joking! Where are you going?" Liam objected.

"Library, unlike you people I have to study and do well in my exams."

"Your square is shrinking!" Lacy called after Ollie. Ollie's response was to flash Lacy the bird above her head, not looking back. Ollie loved how playful her friends were, they always managed to put a smile on her face even when she was feeling horrible. Ollie found it hard to be truly angry at her friends, anyway, who would want to be angry around such joyous people?

Chapter Three

The Universe May Not Always Play Fair, But It Has One Hell Of A Sense of Humour

THE LIBRARY HAD slowed down as the day wore on and the people that were studying within and Ollie decided it was time to pack and head to The Local. She'd spent most of the day trying to catch up on her studies as she prepared for the exams coming up.

By her car Jay, Harry, Liam, Sarah, Polly, Martha and Lacy were all talking, leaning up against their cars with 'Footloose' playing through someone's speakers.

Ollie walked up to her friends, ready for them to put some light into her life after studying for so long. They were always able to lighten her day whenever she was feeling day or tired.

"Who's up for some Cold Rock?" Ollie called over the music as they all looked over at their red headed friend.

"Me!" everyone's hands shot up and soon they were pilling into their cars and made their way towards the local where cold rock sat at the end of the strip of shops they all knew so well.

Ollie was the first to arrive and parked her car opposite the shop, getting out a few year twelve's waved at her and she waved back in a friendly way. Ollie walked into *Cold Rock* ready to work out what mix-ins to go with her vanilla ice cream.

"Hi, how can I help you?" Ollie looked up and smiled at the girl behind the counter, whom she recognized from school as the girl who asked her about formal earlier that day and her nervous friend. Her nametag read 'Al' and Ollie was grateful she didn't have to try and work out what her name was.

"Hey, you still thinking of going to the formal?" Ollie asked as Cold Rock started filling up and Al's nervous friend walked out.

"Yeah, Beth and I are actually starting to get excited about it, too bad we have to get through exams first," Al laughed. Al's friend, whose nametag read 'Beth', smiled her usual nervous smile. "Now what can I get for you? On the house of course," Al's smile widened.

"Nope, not on the house. You two need the money to get a dress, they start getting a little but expensive around this time. I know from experience you'll need all the work you can get," with that Ollie ordered a Vanilla ice cream in a waffle cone with mix-ins of m&m's, Tim Tam's and a smashed up Flake. Ollie thanked Al and paid for her ice cream and then went to claim a booth while the rest of her friends.

Harry, Liam and Lacy soon joined Ollie after getting their ice creams and sat with her, eager to hear how excited her was about being voted Queen. Ollie was a modest girl and the thought humbled her as she spoke to her friends.

"Alright, enough school and formal talk before my head explodes," by this time everyone had joined the table and Martha was none stop talk about how the girls should wear their hair and how they should do their makeup.

"OK, Ollie and I are in finalization stage," Lacy announced.

"About?" Harry tried to probe.

"Travel after schoolies," Lacy started. "Mum has a surprise for us in the middle but the plan is Queensland for schoolies then wherever mum has planned for two weeks then America!" Lacy's face lit up with the thought of travelling with her best friend. They were both so excited for the trip ahead that they almost felt as thought exams should be brushed past.

"You are going to love travelling," Jay chimed in, sitting down in the booth. Ollie had never left the town, let alone country. She'd never been on a plane, seen the real bush side of Australia or travelled much at all. The furthest Ollie had ever been was Saint Louis and Burlywood, both were, at the furthest, fifteen minutes away.

"Yeah, Queensland is so warm, plus you'll be there with us," Ollie could see Martha slowly fade away as she thought more and more about schoolies only a few weeks away, this was what everyone had been dreaming about for such a long time that it was almost insane that it was coming true now.

Beach, sand, shopping, sun and boys, that was what they were all waiting for and were all dying to get up to. Exams were going to be over pretty soon and all minds were on what was coming after, not what was between now and schoolies.

"Come on guys! You are making me jealous, plus we have to get me on a plane first and who knows how that is going to go?" Ollie tried to laugh but her fears were already starting to show.

"Come on, Ol, we'll be there for you and don't think we'll let you get out of getting on the plane," Lacy pulled Ollie in for a bone crushing hug.

"Once we get you on the plane you'll never want to come back home, Ol. You'll leave us all in the dust as you go jet setting across the world and meet exotic men. Just make sure they don't have herpes," Harry teased Ollie.

"What can I say? I dream big?" Ollie shrugged her shoulders.

"Yeah, we know. Remember in grade six when you ran away from home?" Lacy asked with a wide smile playing on her lips.

"I packed my blanket and teddy and ran to the park where I met you and my life changed forever. And not in a good way," Lacy took a swing and clipped Ollie behind the ear. "Ow. You practically marched me back home and told me to stay thinking I was obedient. Boy were you in for a shock?" Ollie and Lacy laughed as they remembered the first time they had met.

"What did you want me to do? You didn't even have any cookies with you! What kind of a person runs away without packing cookies?" Lacy tried to defend her actions.

"I didn't think that cookies were pertinent to the situation. I wanted to go somewhere, anywhere and hunger pains weren't at the forefront of my mind at that point in time," Ollie sadly said.

"Well then thank god I found you when I did! You would've starved within a matter of hours and all we would've been left with was one hungry spirit haunting the shit out of us all," Lacy knew her friend well and knew she would take any opportunity, alive or dead, to freak people out.

"You ran away?" the shock on Sarah's face said everything. She seriously underestimated her friend's stubbornness. "God, you must've had some balls as a kid cause the only time I've ever done something like that is when my parents are fighting and me leaving was the only way they would pull their heads in and trying to work as a team to find me," Lacy and Ollie exchanged a very discrete look, Ollie's friends never went around to her house unless her parents were out or only one was home.

"I needed time to think," Ollie slowly defended her actions as a twelve year old.

"Even at twelve you were rational," Harry shook his head, "Amazing how some people never change," he chuckled to himself.

"Rationality is the only way to go. When life gives you lemons then you better make some damn good lemon desserts because lemonade is really gross," Ollie exaggerated her wink at her spin on a cliché.

"That was a bad spin, Ol, even for you," Liam laughed.

"I'll work on it but my mind is fuzzled from study."

"Fuzzled?"

"Yeah, it just proves my point even more that I am completely gone in the intellect department so you can all discount a proper conversation with me," the laughter that exploded within the booth was enough to shake the small ice cream establishment.

"Well even with a 'fuzzled' brain you can still string together a pretty coherent sentence," Martha pointed out with a stern motherly look.

"I'd like to hope so, Miss Collins has assigned me extra homework because she thought study for exams wasn't enough already," Ollie slide out of the booth, Lacy following close behind.

"We'll catch you all tomorrow," Lacy waved goodbye and walked out with Ollie. It was only three thirty and the sun was shinning down on the girls, letting them know summer was just around the corner and to hang in there.

"All this shit is going to kill me. I don't have time to do extra homework," Ollie complained as the two girls reach their cars, which were parked next to each other. Ollie looked over the top of Lacy's Black Beauty.

"You're royalty, you can handle anything," Lacy tilted her head in a royal way before winking. "You'll pull through just call me if you need me and mum said you can sleep any time you want. Mum's sweet with you rocking up unannounced. You're like the daughter she wanted but instead she got stuck with me," Lacy played before opening her door.

"Thanks, Lac. I'll catch you later," with that the two girls, in sync, got in their cars and drove away.

* * *

There are only so many things that one person can handle before they crack, but if I crack then I won't be able to live normally again.

So many things always ran through my mind whenever I had to dress for an event that he had organised. I knew what I was in for but that never stopped the nerves as I stepped into the shower to clean the dirty feeling off myself and the night hadn't even started.

Ollie's usual routine consisted of going home, getting something to eat and then wondering back to her room to knock off a few hours of study then off to the local. But today when she arrived home she was shocked to see her mother standing in the kitchen with a bloodied knife in her hands. Greg stood with a knife of his own in his hand, facing it towards Jane as they stared at each other. To Ollie it felt just like a Western but with knives in her own kitchen, how reality and movie story lines can cross over baffled Ollie.

"I don't want to hear it," Ollie held up her hand, indicating to her parents that she did not have the time, care or patients to give a damn about what they were about to say. "Drop the freaking knives and follow me," although her voice was calm there was a definite authority that had her parents obeying and following Ollie into the lounge room. Ollie placed herself on the coffee table while her parents sat opposite on the couch.

Before Ollie could say anything, Jane interrupted with a crazed rant, "He threatened me first! What do you expect? That I'll let myself be stabbed to death by that freak?" and with that Greg went off. All Ollie could do was roll her eyes and let out a growl to shut her parents up. Their eyes widened but Ollie thought nothing of the animalistic noise that had erupted from the throat, there were bigger things to worry about then that.

"We are your parents," Ollie snorted at that, "And you will respect us," Jane demanded. "I was threatened and I will defend myself."

"Always blame your temper on me! It's not my fault you can't control yourself and your whoring ways! Now Olyanah is taking after you and dressing like a low class streetwalker," Greg exploded.

"Shut up!" Ollie screamed. "I am eighteen and in my final year of school, but I am practically parenting you two! I don't want to come home and hear about who fucked whom because the next time one of you steps out of line I'm gone. I'm over this shit and I don't need it. Act your age or get out of my life, it'll be easier that way to forget I was even born, although you both seem to do a lovely job of it now," Ollie threatened.

Greg gave a snort of derision, "And where would you go?"

"Anywhere but here. Lacy's offered up her house, I'm going to schoolies, oh and I'm not coming back," Ollie hasn't told her parents of her travel plans for the next year. "Lacy and I are gone. Europe, America, Asia, Africa," if this had been a cartoon, Ollie was sure her parents faces would be red with smoke exploding from their ears. "This is what happens when you fuck with not only each other lives but mine too. You aren't parents, your pathetic excuses. I'm here because I'm your daughter, not because I have to be, I'm eighteen and that means I'm can do as I please so count yourselves lucky I'm still here to provide a steady income for you two because I do no enjoy what you do to me or what you make me do," Ollie's eyes narrowed more and more as she spoke to her parents, she wasn't going to let them intimidate her any further, she was a free person.

"You can't do this!" Jane started protesting.

"Oh I believe I can. I've been working since I was fifteen and I'm paying for it all so you can forget about pulling that card out of your arse," Ollie stood from the coffee table and look down at Jane and Greg. "For once think about someone else other then yourself. Just remember the day you met," Ollie walked to the bookshelf and pulled a photo, a photo she loved, of her parents. Jane was dressed in a yellow dress with a fluro pink belt wrapped around her waist. Greg had his arms hanging on her hips as they sway to the music together at the concert they met at. "Just pull your heads out and remember life wasn't always a bitch, she only turned into one because you lost sight of how to live," Ollie placed the photo on the table as a replacement of herself and walked off.

Ollie walked into her room and called Lacy, ready for some much needed laughter and a good outlet for the anger she was feeling right now. It never ceased to amaze Ollie the selfishness people had; it was all about them with no consideration for anyone else.

"Ahoy," Lacy answered.

"I think Principal Davis needs to learn how to be a real psychologist, otherwise he would've been able to sort out my parents like I did just then. Knives and everything and then I'm pretty sure I saw a tear."

"You are a miracle worker," Lacy agreed.

"That I am, Lacy Larkin," Ollie winked knowing Lacy would picture it. "Now I want to get out of here before," Ollie was interrupted with a loud groan from the other end of the house, "That happens. My herpes ridden parents are officially contracting every sexual disease known to man right now," a shudder ran through Ollie's body at the mention of it.

"Come to mine."

"Nah, I think I wanna hit the beach, the real beach. I'll catch you later," Ollie hung up and packed a few things in a bag before grabbing her car keys, school bag and books and got in her car away from the haunting noises of her parents yelling at each other as they screwed.

Ollie plugged her phone into her car and cranked her *Fun.* playlist, her favourite band. She let the lyrics of 'Be Calm' try to relax her mind as she drove the short drive to Saint Louis. Once she could see ocean, it was like the world was telling her everything was going to be alright and she just had to hang in there because the light at the end of the tunnel wasn't as far away as it seemed.

Ollie parked in the beach car park and looked down, realizing that she was still in her school uniform. Lucky for Ollie, her best friend was Lacy and she was good friends with Martha, both insisted that everyone have a spare change of clothes in their car. Ollie reached into the backseat and managed to get changed in her car without getting out, into her leather leggings, floral crop top and denim button vest that she left open.

Ollie stepped out of her car with black ballet flats on her feet. She checked her hair and makeup in the mirror of her car. Her long red hair hung in soft waves down her back with a simple floral headband tied into 'bunny ears' on top of Ollie's head in a very 50's style. A full moon belly ring with a wolf howling could be seen in the sun along with a soft nose piercing.

"Wow," Ollie turned to see a big group of surfer guys coming towards her. They were all checking her out with cocky smirks slowly growing on their faces. Ollie could practically read their minds; they thought she was an easy girl, ready for fun with who ever came along. Were they in for a rude shock? Ollie laughed to herself as she pulled out her wallet, phone and headphones from her car and locked it, holding her keys over her shoulder and winking.

"Rosewood," one of the guys greeted Ollie. Ollie could tell already by the cocky smile that she could have fun with this. This guy was used to girls melting at those eyes, but Ollie was different. Ollie's eyes widened softly as she realized what was happening. The smell of fresh rain in summer on a forest boarding the ocean floated into her nose and she could already tell that it was the handsome guy in front of her that smelt like heaven on earth. She was so mesmerized that she almost forgot to speak, lucky Ollie was able to keep her face straight so that it didn't give anything else away.

"Louis," she replied and noticed that all the guys faulted at her confidence. Saint Louis had a beach and shops and Ollie was really starting to wonder why her and her friends didn't come here more often. Beach, shopping, sexy boys, what more could a girl want out of life? "Cat got your tongue?" Ollie asked when the guy didn't reply to her smart arse retort. There was a clear hierarchy within the group and the 'leader' of the guys just shook his head before walking off.

"Poor guy," Ollie started, "Clearly easily excitable," she added with a subtle wink before walking off and sitting on a bench that was just off the sand. Not long before sitting down, Ollie's phone started ringing and she knew by the ringtone and the fact that everyone around was looking at her, that it was Lacy calling.

"Calmed?"

"Ahoy to you too. You know, I don't know why we don't come to Saint Louis more often," Ollie's eyes followed the tall, tanned, well built surfer that had first greeted her with 'Rosewood'. Those clearly defined muscles that were outlined, even from so far away had Ollie's clear attention as she spoke to Lacy on the phone.

"Because . . . wait, me neither?" Lacy sounded a little bit confused on the other end of the phone. Ollie still couldn't pull her eyes away from the surfer she had nicknamed Louis. He dived in under a wave and as he came up Ollie could see with such intensity the water dripping off his dark skin. Completely ignoring the fact that she could see practically every drop of water on a guy five hundred metres away, she turned her attention back to a hysterical Lacy.

"Calm down and start again you crazed lunatic."

"You totally found someone! Tell me everything!" if Lacy had been there she would've been drooling at the way Louis' muscles tensed ever so slightly as he sat on his board waiting for a wave. "Wait there! I will be there in twenty minutes," without even so much as a goodbye Lacy hung up on Ollie.

Ollie sat with her headphones in, 'The Shins' playing through the small buds as she watched Louis surf above the waves. Every time he crashed or jumped off Ollie could see the water wash over him and coat his deeply tanned body in water beads.

"Who are you trying to impress?" a familiar voice pierced through the music playing in Ollie's head and she turned to see Lacy getting out of her car with a knowing smile on her face. "He better be good because he needs my approval first," Lacy warned. "So, how'd it go with your parents?"

"You don't look too bad yourself. I knew you could scrub up well," Ollie looked over Lacy's outgoing outfit. She had a white chiffon material button top that you could see her black bikini top through and a hot pink skirt that came in at the waist.

"I do try. And don't try and change the topic, spill with the juice."

"They stopped yelling."

"That's good."

"And are now bumping the uglies as we speak."

"Not so good. I mean good that they are getting along but couldn't they wait before you left?"

"Apparently all this bent up sexual frustration needed to be let out; now," Ollie was happy that Jane and Greg were on speaking terms again, but still something didn't feel right to her.

"So does a dot, dot, dot apply here?" Lacy asked quoting the musical 'Mamma Mia'. Being such good friends the two always quoted movies as they frequently had movie marathons together.

"It does in the most perverted way."

"That is so wrong!" Lacy cried leaning back on the wooden bench. The two girls, in a fit of giggles, got up and went to their cars, which were parked next to each other. "I wanna go for a dip," Lacy announced.

"Me too."

"I think you are forgetting the small detail of bathers?" Lacy enquired.

"Bra and undies, duh! I mean guys are always saying how they are the same as bathers so why not go with the flow?" Ollie started taking off her vest and throwing it in the backseat of her car.

"You are insane," Lacy laughed as she undressed too. "I like it though, I missed the insane skinny dipping best friend!" Lacy dumped her clothes in Ollie's car. Ollie pulled off her leather leggings and floral crop top revealing a lacey red bra and lacey black underwear.

"Ready?" Ollie winked at her best friend.

"Always," the two walked onto the sand, attracting attention from the people around as they awkwardly copied the Bay Watch run. "I agree, we should come here a lot more," Lacy said winking at one of the sexy surfer guys who had come out of the water and was setting his surfboard down on the ground, his eyes following Lacy's body and her every movement.

"I completely and utterly agree," the cool water hit Ollie's toes and the two kept walking into the water until it reached their waists. Being only small girls it didn't take long, the two were shorter then most of their friends and therefore it didn't take long for the ocean to become too deep for them.

"This is the life," Lacy sighed and dived under the water. Ollie couldn't help herself and laughed as she saw Lacy twist and turn under the water.

"Looking good, Rosewood," Louis, the sexy surfer guy called out as he paddled over to where Lacy and Ollie bobbed in the water. Ollie winked at the guy and couldn't help it as a smile spread onto her lips.

"Hi, I'm Lacy," Lacy introduced herself, knowing that it was a way to get Ollie really embarrassed.

"Cruze," the guy replied.

"This is my best friend, Ollie, now instead of exchanging heated winks would you please just ask her out whether you want to or not. She needs to out of her boring old square and loosen up a little," Lacy boldly said to Cruze who looked amused sitting on top of his surfboard. Ollie groaned as a blush tinted her cheeks and covered her face with her wet salty hands.

"I'll see what I can do to help her out. I've been told I'm really good at helping people 'loosen up'," Cruze said with a wink directed at Ollie. Ollie could easily admit to herself that Cruze was a damn fine looking guy, but that line showed her that he was such a player and she really couldn't be bothered with that. She'd already turned Alex down more times then she could count, why go for a guy she'd never met before when she was leaving in a few weeks. Especially when he'd go screw someone new the next day. Who knew what diseases he was carrying down there.

"Really," Ollie thought she might as well show Lacy she was out of her square without being treated for herpes. Ollie turned on her sensual voice and walked over to Cruze's surfboard, pushing out her already ample chest and resting her arms on the board. "Maybe you could show me a trick or two," she started to say slowly, seeing that Cruze was getting very interested; in more ways then one, "but, I think you just don't the experience and . . ." her eyes looked him up and down, ". . . Quality I'm looking for. Sorry baby, maybe another time," Ollie winked. She didn't even let Cruze respond before taking off after Lacy to murder her.

"That was mean!" Cruze called out after the small red head.

"Life is mean, baby," Ollie turned and started walking backwards, "You just have to roll with the punches and try not to be knocked out," Ollie turned and tried not to laugh at Lacy who was being attacked by the waves. *'I guess karma is looking out for me today and making sure I don't actually have to kill Lacy myself,'* Ollie thought to herself as she grabbed her friend's arm and pulled her out of the water.

"So?" Lacy asked.

"He's damn sexy, I won't deny that but he needs to tone down on the whole cocky thing because it just told me he thought he was better then me. Not a turn on. It's a real shame too, I could've had some fun with him," Ollie scrunched up her nose as Lacy laughed at her.

"If you don't, I will," Lacy winked at Ollie. Ollie felt a sudden wave of jealously wash over her at the thought of Cruze with Lacy instead of her. Shaking her head to rid herself of those thoughts she tried to remain rational. She'd turned him down; Lacy could do what she wanted, Ollie didn't have a claim over Cruze.

"Go for your life," Ollie replied trying to sound casual. Ollie pulled her crop top back on and her school pencil skirt while Lacy dressed herself in the white chiffon on shirt and pink pencil skirt.

"You should've thrown yourself at him, Ol," Lacy laughed bringing it up again. "I would've, he was pretty hot with a capital 'HOT'!"

"How can you lecture me on my none existent love life when you have less of a love life then me. I mean at least I have Jay to tease," Ollie said as she slammed her car door closed making Lacy jump out of her skin.

"No need to point out the painfully obvious," she pouted. Ollie was about to something else when she could hear her phone start going off with suspense music from every horror film, it was either her mum or her dad calling. "Answer it before the wicked witch of the depths of hell sends out her evil minions of monkeys to come and fly you away to a guarded tower," Lacy dismissed Ollie with a wave of her hand.

"What up, mother dearest," Ollie answered the phone in the sweetest voice she could muster, knowing it would annoy her mum most.

"Hey sweetie," sweetie? Ollie looked over her shoulder at Lacy with worry etched into her usually calm and laid back features, but Lacy was occupied with taking to Cruze and some other surfer. "I was just wondering if you'll be home for dinner?" she asked. Ollie almost forgot to answer her unusually calm mum as jealousy built up inside her. Lacy was only flirting with the guy that Ollie didn't know but the fact that she was still talking to Cruze made Ollie mad for reasons she didn't understand.

"What? Oh yeah probably not why?" Ollie ripped her eyes away from the three friends and towards the pier. There was a railing on one side of the pier with rotted wood everywhere, Ollie knew one day it would collapse but when that day was she had no idea.

"Your father and I are going out for dinner and then dancing so make sure you eat something. Oh and you are a complete marriage savior,

Ollie. I think you should start apply at Uni's to be a marriage therapist," the giggling her mum was doing on the other end of the line was making Ollie's blood boil. "If any of your little friends want to come by then they are more then welcome but make sure they get permission from their parents. Have fun, sweetie," Ollie was just about ready to attack her mother, it was like she didn't know her at all, treating her like she was a five year old not an eighteen year old.

"Whatever, mum, don't go getting any unwanted diseases and make sure you use protection because you wouldn't want another mistake to come along," Ollie heard her mother gasp at her sass but hung up before she could get a lecture. Ollie put her phone in the pocket of her pencil skirt and rested her elbows on the rotting wood. Ollie felt as though this was all too exhausting at the moment and she just couldn't keep up with her parents. One minute they wanted to be good parents and know about her life and make sure she was alright, even if calling the police was over the top, and the next minute they didn't give a crap and thought she was a three year old.

"Ollie!" Ollie looked up and saw Lacy rushing over with Cruze and his friend following slowly behind. "All good on the Western front?" she asked with a smile playing on her lips.

"Peachy," Ollie immediately felt bad for the tone she used against Lacy. "Sorry, I shouldn't take it out on you, mum and dad are going out and I am pretty sure they are bipolar or something," Ollie turned her attention back to the ocean as waves rushed past the mossy wooden poles that kept the pier up.

He watched as she moved around the new town, it wasn't often she wondered out of Rosewood, causing his mind to jump and think of so many different plans to attempt to rectify the situation. His mind jumped quickly enough to call upon his allies and get them to do exactly what he needed them to do, now he sat watching her standing on the pier looking angry, sad almost.

Everything was working to the plan perfectly, almost too perfectly and he was waiting for the speed bump in the road to wake him up from this perfection.

"Isn't it a good thing that they are getting along now?" Lacy asked, confusion written across her face.

"I guess," Ollie sighed, "I'm just over it all," with that anger Ollie grabbed her phone from her pocket and held it tightly in her hand. "I just want them to grow up and act like parents, not like horny twenty year olds!" Ollie practically screamed as she threw her phone into the rushing waves below.

Both Lacy and Ollie's mouths dropped as they realized what happened at the same time. They turned to look at each other with stunned expressions mirroring each other.

"Did I just . . . ?" Ollie managed to squeak out.

"Yup."

"Shit."

"Yup."

"Shit."

"Yup," Lacy kept nodding her head as she tentatively leaned over the edge to see if she could spot Ollie's decorated iPhone 3. "When I said to get out of your boring old square I didn't mean tear the walls down and turn green like the Hulk," Lacy was still looking down at the water as she spoke. By now the top had stopped rippling and there was no way of seeing the phone.

"I'm never leaving the house again. I'm going to be grounded until I am old and grey. I wouldn't even be able to get cats and become a crazy cat lady because I'll be grounded and won't be able to work to afford a cat," Ollie could see her future already.

"Don't worry. I'll help you escape, Ol. I got your back," with that the two friends fell into a fit of giggles. "Alright, we have one more thing we need to do."

"And what is that?"

"Say goodbye. Ollie's phone, you were a good phone, always causing a laugh but how slow and old you were. We will never forget your playful drawings and smashed screen. May you rest in peace," Lacy closed her eyes and rested her hand on her heart.

"You served me well over the years we were together and stuck by me when I graffiti you with my highlighters and sharpies. You survived many falls with only a few scars and loss of glass to show for it. You will forever remain in my heart as the embarrassing phone that would turn off silent in class and play the theme to Jaws. May you rest in pieces," Ollie rested her head on Lacy's shoulder as they stood silently for a few seconds.

"Well now that that is over. Jason and Cruze have offered to take us out for dinner. How sweet is that?" Lacy cried forgetting about the funeral service they just held.

"The sweetest," Ollie plastered on a fake smile, trying to be as happy about the cocky surfers offering to take them to dinner as Lacy was.

"Chill out, Ol, your mum and dad are happy and won't care about it," she tried to assure Ollie. "Plus my mum agreed a long time ago to house a fugitive if need be so you can always come hide out at mine," Lacy linked her arm in Ollie's.

"Thank god because I might just need to take you up on the offer sooner rather then later," Ollie sighed.

"Do you two always talk like . . ." Cruze cut in, struggling to find the words to describe the conversation that had just gone on in front of him.

"Crazy people? Psychos? Freaks? Escaped mental asylum patients?" Ollie offered up a number of suggestions. Cruse just nodded his head to every suggestion.

"All of the above."

"Then the answer to that my good Sir would have to be one big fat giant yes with some icing sugar and mint leaves sprinkled on top," Ollie winked. "Don't worry, people get used to it after a while, if not they usually just ignore us and try to pretend we are normal, which we take as an insult because we most defiantly are not normal," Ollie smiled at Cruze and for the first time since meeting him felt as though it was a real smile. She looked up into his crystal blue eyes as they twinkled in the sunshine and she tried not to blush. Cruze was a good head and a half, if not more, taller then Ollie.

"Well I like it, Rosewood. It's different."

"Oh I bet it is, Louis. I hear it's really dull here, people having normal conversations about normal topics. Who in their right mind would enjoy that?" Ollie rolled her eyes in a very sarcastic way.

"No one comes to mind," Cruze answered as he walked with Ollie back to her car. Lacy and Jason lingered a few metres behind, caught up in each other already. "So are you two good for dinner?" Cruze asked checking Ollie out slyly.

"Shit!" Lacy suddenly cried out grabbing her phone from the backseat of Ollie's car. "Mum is going to drop her shit if I'm not home to look after Matt in half an hour and I'm pretty sure you Knight in shinning amour is pinning for you," Lacy showed Ollie her phone which had message after message from jay on the screen asking about Ollie.

"A real gentleman," Ollie laughed giving Lacy back her phone after a quick reply. "I swear his mind hasn't left the gutter in over three years. All he wants to know is if a booty call is on the tables," Ollie laughed.

"That's because you encourage him."

"You're the one who tells me to have a little fun and I do and now you're yelling at me for it," Ollie defended her actions, holding out her hands in mock surrender. "Plus I would never go there! I mean it's Jay! He's like a brother not a booty call," Ollie's nose scrunched up at the thought of being more then friends with Jay.

"Sorry guys but I think we're going to have to rain check dinner for another less emotional and frantic day," Lacy apologized to an amused looking Cruze and Jason.

"At least can I get your number?" Cruze asked stepping a bit closer and pining Ollie up against her Blue Baby.

"I would say yes but sadly my phone has recently passed away and I am still in the mourning stages," Ollie fake cried. "Just give your number to Lacy and she'll message you my home number," she suggested. Cruze nodded his head and punched in his number into Lacy's phone, Jason followed suit and then the two tanned, tall surfers waved goodbye and left to get their boards.

"I'll catch ya, Rosewood," Cruze called over his shoulder.

"In your dreams you will, Louis," Ollie called back with a goofy smile adorning her rosy lips.

Chapter Four

Wake Up Everyday As If On Purpose

"Good morning, sweetheart," Ollie looked up from the kitchen counter and eyed off her mother as she bounded happily into the kitchen.

"What's so good about it?" Ollie replied grumpily as she lifted her head and rested her elbows on the cool bench top. Jane looked at her daughter in the most parental way she knew as Greg came into the kitchen, wrapping an arm around Jane's waist.

"Everything," Ollie's mum replied in a cheesy, love sick voice.

"Excuse me while I go throw up a little," Ollie said getting out of the chair and dragging her feet back to her room without her mum or dad noticing that she had even left the room.

Ollie had tossed and turned last night with bad sleep because her mind was only thinking of one thing; Cruze. His cocky smile, those crystal blue eyes, that tan that covered his body. Ollie didn't even know why she had this sudden attraction to him but there was something there and she didn't like it. It was like her mind and body weren't even giving her a choice, he fascinated her and that wasn't about to change.

Ollie needed to sleep well last night as well, she had her first exam today; English, and she could only hope it went well. It'd been a whole week since she had met Cruze and while Lacy said he called and was trying to talk to Ollie through Lacy, Ollie couldn't be bothered with a relationship that reminded her of twelve year olds, she was leaving soon and felt that avoiding him would get rid of her feelings and she would be able to deal better when she left.

After a week of not having a phone Ollie was going crazy; she had missed so many opportunities to take embarrassing photos of her friends and her mum had promised to get her one everyday after work but still hadn't; as stupid as it sounded, her whole life was on that pathetic piece of metal and plastic.

Ollie was pulled from her self-loathing thoughts by a knock at her bedroom door. Sitting up off her bed Ollie ground her teeth together. Her mother in a peppy mood was not something Ollie was looking forward to.

"Only come in if you are planning to stick a gun to my head and murder me then dump my lifeless body in the ocean to get rid of all the evidence," Ollie basically plotted the murder for her mother. *'I really need to stop watching those crime shows.'*

"I'm sorry I haven't got you a phone yet but I want you to know I'll get you one soon and we are grateful for you bringing me and your father back together. But I hope you know now that throwing your phone in the water wasn't a very good idea," her mum started lecturing.

"Really? I thought it would be really fun to see what happened. Guess I was wrong about that one, I'll try to remember that next time I have a piece of expensive technology in my hands."

"That would be very helpful, Ollie," Jane tried not to be sarcastic towards her daughter. "Well Greggy and I are going to be out late tonight so if you don't want to stay home alone in the dark then why don't you call up one of your friends? You seem to be very close with that footy player, that's what Simon said at least. Maybe he can come and keep you company?" Ollie's eyebrows furrowed as she looked at her mother.

"Who the hell is Simon?"

"Principal Simon Davis."

"Oh, well have fun with that one," Ollie rolled over on her bed so she was lying on her back.

"Well call your friend so you aren't alone and scared," Ollie's mother started closing the bedroom door.

"While I'm at it why don't I get pregnant with Jay's baby and just say it's yours?" Ollie cried as she heard giggling from her mum and the front door close. "Good to know you have an interest in my life," Ollie couldn't be bothered with her parents so she grabbed some clothes and went to her bathroom, which connected to her bedroom, and had a quick shower to wake herself up for the exam.

Ollie pulled on a pair of black leggings with a loose chiffon floral top with a white singlet underneath. Exams meant free dress and Ollie couldn't be bothered with the stress of looking good so she just went for casual. Ollie pulled her hair into a braid, which ended up being thick because of her thick set hair and lightly put her makeup on. Ollie added her 50's styled sunglasses and smiled at herself in the mirror before grabbing her bag and heading out the door to get and tackle her first exam.

* * *

"If that is your 'causal I don't care, I'm going for comfortable' look then the rest of the female population is in trouble because you look freaking smokin'," Ollie turned to see Martha walking towards her. Martha gave Ollie the look all her friends knew as 'the look of approval'.

"Aren't you just the sweetest thing going 'round?" Ollie turned on her Southern Belle accent.

"Yes I am," Martha replied to Ollie with a smug look on her face.

"Don't you dare let that go to your head, kiddo. You still have a long way to go," Ollie winked and Martha playfully hit her shoulder. "The truth hurts, amigo."

"So where'd you go off to last week. The local missed a bit of flavour and you haven't been back since," Martha fell into step with Ollie as they walked around to the big seminar room that the exam was going to be held in. People had gathered in front of the room with papers out for some last minute studying.

"I needed some time away from studying so I went for a little adventure to Saint Louis."

"You didn't! Were the boys looking as sexy as ever?" Martha asked dreamily. Ollie sighed and put her arm around Martha's shoulder as she thought about Cruze's cocky smile and the way he acted around Ollie the week before. As much as Ollie hated it, she was hung up on him. This had never happened to her before and it was kind of scaring the poor girl.

"Better Marth, much better. They've grown up real well, girl, I mean damn! Those boys know how to work the surfer look," Ollie added, taking her arm back as more people started coming towards the large exam room. "Lacy got herself a man. Jason, not a surfer name but we can roll with it," Ollie winked as Lacy approached, just in earshot.

"Ollie didn't luck out either!" Lacy said as she entered the conversation. "Cruze, baby!" Lacy cried out causing everyone to look over at the three girls. "Take me hard and take me now!" Lacy added a sexy moan at the end of her own little sex show. "Ollie did the flirting nasties last night with our good mate Cruze," Lacy winked.

"Really! I am so mad that I missed out on that! It's not often we get to see 'serious flirting Ollie', it's normally just joking with Jay that we have to endure," Martha gave her input.

"Ollie didn't just step out of her boring square last week, she jumped out with a splash. Olyanah Kent is back. Back and ready to play so any boys who are game enough, form a line," Lacy cried out, causing Ollie's cheeks to go pink with a blush.

"Let me be the first to line up and buy a ticket," Jay said coming in from the lockers. "Or do I get a free ride because it's me and you love me?" he winked.

"I'm back, not a whore so back off buddy. This still costs a damn hell of a lot of trust and love," Ollie rubbed her hands up and down her body. "But keep dreaming sweetheart, I'm sure you won't sleep well tonight."

"You know how to crush a guy, Ol," Jay shook his head.

"You know I only aim to please," Ollie put on her Southern Belle accent again to go with her innocence. "Come now darling," Jay looked deflated, "There are plenty of girls out there looking for a Knight in shinning amour to take them away in the sunset on a white horse riding bareback," Ollie kept on her accent as she painted a rather beautiful picture for Jay to aim for.

"I guess you're right. That girl is one lucky chick, I mean not many girls get to go bareback on a horse with me," Jay teased trying to entice Ollie a little further.

"Honey, you know I'm right," Ollie gave one more look over her book as she waited for her name to be called into the big room to start this exam. After this it was one down and seven more to go. Ollie was stressing out about this exam but she knew she didn't have much of a choice but to go in there and do her best.

* * *

Ollie walked out of the exam room with her friends looking just as defeated as her. Although her mind was in tact, her thoughts were all over the place and it was written on her face just how confused she really was. Jay, Harry and Liam looked utterly deflated as they all walked to their lockers. The only one who wasn't completely buggered was Lacy who was bouncing around the locker room. Being kept in such a silent room for three hours didn't help Lacy's energy levels and now she needed some way to get rid of all the excess energy she had built up.

"My place after the math's exam and then we can party till morning!" Lacy cried out bouncing around.

"We still have the rest of the week to go with exams and then we can party and celebrate and get ready for formal," Ollie said to Lacy and she slowly dialed down her energy and looked a little deflated. *'Maybe the exam killed her a little more then I thought,'* Ollie thought to herself as she grabbed some books for the math's exam all year twelve's had at the end of the day.

"Guess you're right."

"You OK there?" Ollie asked, walking off separately with Lacy.

"Yeah, Matt kept me up most of last night and now I want to murder the little brat," Ollie raised an eyebrow at her friends white lie.

"Matt's fifteen, not one. I don't think he's the one who kept you up all night, Lac. I'm going to put my money on a surfer named Jason," a pink blush covered Lacy's cheeks as the two sat down at the table, opened up their books and started eating.

"Does it really matter? The point is I'm tired and grumpy," Lacy crossed her arms over her chest and attempted to pout, but a smile cracked on her lips when Ollie kept a straight face and raised an eyebrow at Lacy.

"Oh it matters my friend. It is very rare that you are smitten so I am going to enjoy the blush that will continue to stain your chubby little cheeks," Ollie leaned over and gave Lacy a giant bear hug. "I mean finally one of us ins getting some action! I want all the details!"

"We just talked," she insisted.

"All night?"

"Yeah, all night. It's not that big of a deal, Ol!" Lacy shoved her sandwich into her mouth to stop her from saying anything that would incriminate her further in Ollie's eyes.

"You sexted him didn't you! Don't you lie to me, Lacy Larkin!" Ollie accused.

"No! Gross! Hell no! As if! Sexting isn't that bad is it? Maybe? Of course not! A little. No photos! Just sexy talking! Don't look at me like that, Ollie; you'd do the same in my shoes. You should hear his voice on the phone, it's so hot!" Lacy gave a lot of answers, trying to avoid the real one before giving in to her friends stern, yet amused, look. "Any way, Jason, before all the low sexy talking, said Cruze was asking about you. I've given him your number, has he called?" Lacy asked turning the conversation on its head.

"Firstly, you need to make him work for it, Lacy, don't go handing it out for free. Tease him a little first. Secondly, no he hasn't called and I don't really expect that he will so we can drop that conversation idea on its head and kill it. So tell me what happened, Lac! You always want details, not it is your turn to spill!"

"Nothing much happened. We talked for a few hours last night, and would chat in low voices some times. He wants to teach me to surf though, and I am not passing up an opportunity to see him shirtless," Lacy winked.

"Well don't forget we are leaving. You don't want to start something and then leave almost right at the start. Think about it, Lacy. It's fun now but it won't be when you are saying goodbye soon after only so long of knowing each other," Ollie tried to get her friend to see reason.

"I know, but it's hard. Anyway, enough about me, what about you? You do want to talk about him because the mere mention and you are practically weak at the knees for Cruze."

"I just remind myself that I am leaving soon. It's not that big of a deal, you know how I have a weak spot for surfers, and he is the utter epiphany of what I look for. If it had been a few years in the future or some other time then sure, I'd go for it, but timing isn't right," Ollie didn't want to admit it to herself, let alone Lacy, but she had a thing for Cruze and it wasn't going to go away over night.

The time was approaching, patience was the key here; patience and staying hidden for the right amount of time. He was so close he wasn't about to let the plan be ruined now, not after eighteen years of planning.

Chapter Five

The Only Reason To Be Alive Is To Enjoy It

EXAMS WERE OVER now and Ollie really needed to start preparing for the formal in three days time. Her exams finished a few days earlier then most peoples so she had a couple of extra days to get ready. Lacy and Ollie were planning on going to Saint Louis to do some shopping at the little surf and boutique shops that scattered the town. Lacy wanted to go on account of she was meeting up with Jason for lunch while Ollie would go and get herself a phone, something her mother had promised a long time ago and never delivered on.

Although Ollie could see why, it hadn't been all peaches and roses in their house because the minute she got home from her first exam her mum and dad were back to their old ways, yelling, fighting and then sleeping together. They also included a new act of yelling and screaming at Ollie, who had lost her confidence at talking back and would cower in a corner as they yelled at her and sometimes laid a hand on her.

Ollie had spoken to Cruze once since their meeting and it had been a very short somewhat disappointing conversation. Ollie was studying for her last exam when he called and didn't have long to talk so they had to cut a very odd conversation short.

Cruze seemed to have an odd obsession with the supernatural and all the creatures that came under the heading. Ollie had also learnt that Jay and Cruze were friends from way back and Cruze got a few pointers from Jay, it was clear by the way he spoke to Ollie on the phone.

He spoke for a little bit about what he called 'Mystics', which included Werewolves, Vampires, Elves, Fae and everything else he spoke about, but Ollie zoned out, just enjoying the sound of his voice.

"What are you talking about?" Ollie had asked, going through some homework and making sure she knew everything that was going to be on the exam.

"Haven't you ever wondered if we aren't the only ones on Earth?"

"Of course, but it doesn't consume me."

"Who said it consumes me?" Ollie felt as though she wasn't able to concentrate on what was in front of her, hearing his deep voice flow through the phone.

"Sounds like it does though."

"I'm just curious."

"I guess I can understand why, but if you get abducted by those creatures, don't come crying to me that they aren't as nice as you thought they were."

"I never said they were nice."

"Tell me again the purpose of this conversation, because I feel as though it is going no where but you attacking me with other questions that I never asked."

"Hey, hey, calm down OK? Listen, I just want to have a conversation with you."

"I have an exam tomorrow that I am studying for. I'm sorry."

"No big deal. Good luck and I'll let you get back to studying, but I will see you again soon," and he'd hung up after that.

Ollie shook her head as she pulled open her wardrobe door and looked for something to wear shopping. She pulled out a black-based dress with light floral prints on it. The dress was a button up at the front and came in tight at the waist, making Ollie's petite body look even smaller. Ollie added a pair of black ballet flats and looked herself up and down in the mirror. She added white lace gloves, a white brim hat and a military green bag.

"I'm going out!" Ollie called to her mother as she grabbed her car keys.

"Have fun! Make sure you are safe and don't stay out too late or predators will get you. Let me know what you buy. Are you buying for anything in particular?" Ollie resisted the urge to roll her eyes at her mother's naïve comment.

"I'm going out with Lacy and we are trying to find dresses for formal in a few days," Ollie said in a 'duh' type voice. Ollie closed the front door shaking her head and drove to Lacy's house with her iPod blaring out of the speakers.

Once she arrived at Lacy's house, she beeped the horn and saw her friend jump out of her house with a smile plastered on her face. Ollie wasn't disappointed with her colourful friend dressed up in a bright yellow button up shirt with no sleeves, a fluro pink skirt with a lime green belt and black lace up shoes. Lacy took colour blocking to the extreme like it was an art.

"We need a plan of action," Lacy announced as she jumped in Ollie's car. "We can check out the boutique shops for some funky dresses and the surf shops then after that, if it's cool with you, I'll go and have lunch with Jason and then we can check out the shopping centre and look at the mainstream shops," Lacy decided quickly, speaking at a pace only Ollie could understand.

"Go and have fun with Jason. I'm sure I can find something to do while you rock it up with your sex god," Ollie smiled at her bubbly friend.

"You are by far the bestest friend in the whole wide world!" just as Lacy finished talking, the girls favourite song Everybody Talks by Neon Trees came on and Ollie turned up the radio while they sang along.

"God, it's sunny here," Ollie announced as she emerged from the car. The waves were easily heard as they crashed against the sand bank.

"Why don't we come here more often?" Lacy asked as Ollie locked her car and the two started walking towards the long strip of boutique and surf shops that over looked the ocean.

"Because it's far too close to home. Come on, Lac, I wanna get some new clothes and find a killer dress for formal!" Ollie cried as the two friends passed a few shops designed for older women, not teenage girls. "What are you thinking for formal? What style of dress or colour?"

"I want to get some really sex black heels to make me look taller," Lacy decided as the two entered the first surf shop.

"I think the whole idea of heels is to make us short arses look taller to those who are blessed with height. We'll go to some shoe shops because I want to get some red ones, fluro green and fluro pink ones," Ollie told Lacy as she scanned the bathers rack.

"What are you thinking of for a dress?" Lacy asked Ollie, appearing on the other side of the metal bathers rack with a pair of bug eyed sunglasses and a wide brimmed hat on.

"I think you are trying to steal my style," Ollie laughed, as she looked at some 50's styled bathers.

"Yeah, well they suit you a lot better then they suit me," Lacy agreed as Ollie pouted in the mirror with Lacy behind her. "Anyway, dress! What are you thinking you want?" Lacy asked Ollie again.

"Vintage?" Ollie suggested, shrugging her shoulders. "I really have no idea what I'm looking for. I guess it'll jump out at me when I see it. What do you want?"

"Something colourful and fun!" Lacy was practically jumping up and down on the spot as she thought of a beautiful dress to wear to formal.

A deep voice broke the conversation between the two girls, "That's you in a nut shell," forcing them to turn around, a wide smile appearing on Lacy's lips as she saw Jason and he held out his arms for her to jump in for a hug.

Cruze stood behind Jason with a sly smile on his face as he watched his friend standing with the girl that had consumed his mind and life. Standing right behind the two was the girl that Cruze had been obsessing about for far too long but he knew he was never going to get over those deep blue eyes and that fiery hair.

"Hell no!" Ollie cried out outing a hand on Jason's chest. "This is girl time! You get her later but she's mine now! Hands off, big boy!" Ollie commanded and Jason a few steps back, unwinding his arms from Lacy's waist. Jason had a bit of a shocked look in his eyes, but he didn't know Ollie that well but she was just as crazy as Lacy, if not worse; you just had to get to know her first before she opened up and showed just how mental she really was.

"Ollie," Lacy wrapped her arms around Ollie's forearm and dragged her away from prying ears and eyes. "Please let him tag along. I mean come on, he'll tell me if I look hot or not, plus Cruze is here for you," Lacy whispered to Ollie. The only thing going through Ollie's mind was how much this reminded her of an American movie.

"Go on. You two go off and have fun together. I'll try and find some awesome dress that you'll be jealous of because you weren't there when I found it," Ollie threw her arms in the air.

"I love you and owe you!" Lacy said with a squeal as she kissed Ollie on the cheek and skipped off towards Jason.

"No, you more then owe me!" Ollie practically commanded, looking at Lacy with a little bit of boredom. "Now go off and have some fun, I'll be shopping. I'll send you a photo when I find a wonderful dress," Ollie dismissed Lacy.

"Thanks! You are by far the bestest friend-slash-sister a girl could ask for. Ollie, your mum messaged," Ollie waited to hear what her mum had to say but Lacy just handed her friend her phone. Ollie had made the decision to get herself a phone today after already getting herself a SIM in anticipation a few days ago.

'Lacy, please tell Ollie that there is no point in her coming home tonight. We are far too busy to deal with her at the moment and don't need the extra hassle if she comes home because knowing Ollie, she'll be another accident.'

Ollie was fuming as she handed the phone back to Lacy and tried to place a smile on her face.

"Everything alright?" Lacy asked, she hadn't dared to look at the message before Ollie read it because it was from Jane.

"Yeah, fine. You guys go on, I'll be shopping," with that Ollie stormed out of the shop and moved on to one a few doors down. Ollie knew she wasn't planned; her father was always reminding her, but she was over being treated like she wasn't a member of the family. Ollie flicked through the rack of dresses until a lacy black dress caught her eye.

She was a fire; that much he had observed and he knew just how much fun he would have with a firecracker from experience.

He was going to have a lot of fun with this when the time came for it. She'd managed to withstand everything that had been thrown at her but his glowing red eyes were tempted to break her now; then all the planning would go down the drain and he refused to be the one responsible for that.

No, his time to shine was coming and then he could have just as much fun with her as many other men had too.

"You," SMACK, "Pathetic," SLAP, "Piece," PUNCH, "Of," BANG, "Worthless," KICK, "Shit!" a cool sensation of something stick surrounded my mouth and then started pouring out like a water fall.

I have felt pain and I had been in many painful situations before but this was by far the worst and there was no way in hell I was going to let anyone see me this scared and this sad about the life I lived.

People knew me as fun, strong and care free, I wasn't about to break that imagine for anything or anyone.

"You forgot lazy," the squeak came out of my mouth weakly and like I had a drink in my mouth, but I spat up some metallic tasting blood as I spoke, clearing my mouth and my air ways so I could finally breathe.

"This is why I have to work you to the bone, so you can avoid this lazy patch you're going through," he grabbed the top of my hair and pulled my head up so he could look at me in the eyes and try to read my thoughts. "One of these days you will get what you deserve and I sure hope I'm there to witness it and laugh. You ruined my life you disgusting mistake."

"I think you've gone too far this time," she stepped out of the shadows and looked at my damaged body and face, holding her hands timidly in front of her body like she was the one about to be attacked.

He dropped my head, throwing it on the concrete floor and stood up, stalking towards her small body. She may not be the best person in the world, but she wasn't the worst and no one deserved what I could see in his eyes; he'd had that look with me a few times and I wasn't about to have anyone else experience the same pain.

"Pick on someone your own size you barbarian," she gave me an apologetic and sorry look, a look she'd given me a few times before, then hurried away so she wouldn't have to see what she had done to me indirectly.

Lacy looked over the messages on her phone until she landed on the one from Ollie's mum. She hadn't read it before Ollie but now that she had, she was convinced that she was going to hit Ollie's parents in the face. How could Jane say such a thing to Ollie when she was a complete angel?

"I'm going to go after her, I'll call you later and let you know if lunch is on," Lacy stood on her toes and gave Jason a quick kiss on the lips.

"Let me know, don't strain yourself if you need to be with Ollie," Jason assured Lacy.

"Maybe we should come," Cruze intervened. "I mean it's clear she needs support and I can be that support, I mean we call can be that support for her with whatever is going on in her life," Cruze stumbled over his own words.

"You barely know her," Lacy looked skeptically at her 'boyfriends' close friend.

"Just let him go, Lac, it's something he needs to do," Jason tried to reason.

"If she doesn't want to take your calls then she doesn't want to have you in her business. I don't care what you say, she is my best friend and I know what she wants," a look was exchanged between Jason and Cruze that Lacy didn't understand.

"It's a long story, Lacy, something we'll explain another day, but please hear me out for now. He needs to get to know Ollie," Jason took Lacy's hands in his own and looked in her deep blue eyes.

"Don't intimidate me, Jason Bomani Miles! You do not get to tell me or Ollie what to do. Cruze doesn't control her and you don't control me," Lacy turned on her heels and stormed out of the shop and went into the next three surf shops on a search to find an upset Ollie.

* * *

The black lace dress had a plunging v-neck and thick straps that came up over Ollie's shoulders and down the back, criss crossing and leaving majority of her back exposed. The dresses skirt had thick pieces of satin with a layer of chiffon and lace over Ollie's waist as a soft belt. The rest of the dress poofed out with chiffon and a layer of lace over the top, giving a vintage look to the dress that Ollie had fallen in love with.

"Ollie," Ollie could hear Lacy's voice calling out around the shop.

"I'm going to come out, but you cannot laugh at me," Ollie called out.

"No promises," Lacy called back with a laugh at the end. Ollie pulled the long chained with a full moon pendant down, she'd gotten the necklace from her grandpa; at least that is what her mum had told her and something about the way Jane had told her, told Ollie that for once she had been telling the truth.

Ollie stepped out of the changing room and Lacy's jaw hit the floor. Ollie span around in the dress, watching it rise before stopping and smiling shyly at her friend.

"You look amazing!"

"You don't think it's too much?" Ollie asked looking down and seeing her wolf and full moon belly ring. "Do you think it goes down too short? It's a school formal, and maybe the v-neck is too deep?" Ollie started fretting over the dress. She stared at herself in the mirror, patting the dress down as she studied it on her small body.

"If you don't buy it for yourself then I will!" Lacy almost pushed Ollie back into the dressing room. "Now get changed and pay for it!" Lacy demanded. "We can get you a cute hair piece here too for your formal do," Lacy called over the dressing room door.

"OK calm down, Lac, I'll get it," Ollie laughed. "So did you really ditch Jason for me?" Ollie opened the dressing room door and smiled at her best friend.

"Of course! Bros over hoes, or something along those lines for girls," Lacy laughed draping her arm over Ollie's shoulder. "You should've seen them though. Cruze went crazy wanting to see if you were alright and then they started on some mysterious conversation about that it was Cruze's right and they would explain it all later. I got angry and told Jason to shove it because he wanted to tell me what to do. You are my sister-slash-best friend and I know what is best for you and me," Lacy winked.

"I'm thinking we should go to the chemist and buy some chill pills so they will loosen up," Ollie suggested.

"I like that idea," Lacy agreed.

"So, where to now, Captain?" Ollie asked taking her shopping bag and heading towards the car to dump it.

"To infinity and beyond!" Lacy said and both girls started laughing. The two friends took superhero steps forward towards more shops to try and find a dress for Lacy to wear to formal. "How about Forever New? They usually have some wicked colourful and elegant clothes there and I am sure I can find something stylish and Martha approved," Ollie nodded her head in agreement.

Lacy ended up with a beautiful lavender dress with rhinestones on the bust and spaghetti straps with a silk skirt covered in chiffon. Lacy also brought a pair of nude shoes to go with the dress. Ollie also got some fluro pink, yellow and green heels, heels that she had wanted for a very long time. The heel wasn't too tall; Ollie wasn't good at walking in heels so she always got ones that weren't that tall.

"What do you want to do now?" Lacy asked Ollie as they went and put their bags in Ollie's Blue Baby.

"Don't you still want to go to lunch with Jason?" Ollie asked. "Maybe you could get some answers about this 'I'll tell you later' bull shit," Ollie suggested with a big bump to Lacy's side. "Call the poor boy, he's probably crying about you."

"You sure?"

"Yeah, I need to go and get a new phone anyway because mum still hasn't gotten me one and I am in need of a camera so I can take photos of you at your worst," Ollie winked as Lacy pulled her phone out and dialed Jason's number.

"Hey, Jason, we need to have a talk," Lacy walked away a little bit while Ollie waved goodbye as she went to find a phone shop. "Catchya later," Lacy smiled.

"Bye! Have fun with lover boy and enjoy your lunch! Don't pregnant because I ain't ready to be an aunty just yet lovely!" Ollie called out and started walking away with a smile playing on her lips. Ollie walked through the strip she passed a pole with a very handsome man standing against it.

"Hello there," Ollie turned and realized it was Cruze standing in a pair of jean shorts and with a while circular neck t-shirt with a red and blue pattern on it.

"Hi," Ollie smiled at Cruze. Ollie honestly didn't know how to feel about Cruze at the moment. He had been stuck in her mind since she had met him and yet she didn't want to pick up his calls when he called Lacy to talk to her.

"I wanted to say sorry. I don't know what your mum said but you seemed pretty upset and I am sorry that I wasn't able to see if you were alright," Cruze started.

"Cruze, calm down. Lacy told me about the crazy 'it's a secret' look and conversation you all had so I am sure I will get over it. Now if you don't mind, I have to go and get myself a new phone," Ollie didn't know what it was but whenever she was around Cruze it was as though her body was begging her to touch him and be with him, while her mind was just plain angry for no reason at all. That amazing smell of fresh summer rain in a forest by the beach hit Ollie's nose again and she almost melted.

"Can I come with you?"

"It's a free county, at least that is what they say, I've yet to find evidence to support that theory," Ollie replied to Cruze's question as she kept walking. "So, catch any narly waves at the moment?" Ollie asked trying to stray away from an uncomfortable silence.

"Narly waves?" Cruze coughed as he started laughing.

"Shut up! I don't know surfer talk, I'm just making conversation, more then what I can say for you," Ollie pointed out.

"Not really the time at the moment for good waves. When summer hits it'll be rockin'," Cruze explained, "November is just a warm up for the real summer. January usually has the best waves around here."

"I've always wanted to learn to surf," the confession caught both Ollie and Cruze by surprise, neither were expecting the slightest bit of honesty. Cruze pulled his arm around and draped it over Ollie's shoulders, just as Lacy had done not long ago.

"Maybe I can teach you?" Ollie looked up at the tall, she'd like to say boy but Cruze was more of a man, surfer man with crystal blue eyes.

"Maybe," Ollie pulled away from Cruze and walked into a phone store.

"Hi, how can I help you?" a young school guy asked when Ollie walked in.

"I'm looking for a phone, I have a SIM already but no phone to go with it. I don't have a lot of money to spend so what deal can you do for me?" Ollie went straight into business mode.

"Are you looking for a specific type of phone?"

"Is cheap a specific type of phone?"

"I'd have to say no, how about I get a few of the cheaper phones and show you?" Ollie nodded her head at the young man and he grabbed a key to open the glass cabinets, which held all the phones in it. "I've got an *iPhone 3* smartphone which I can get for you for about $100, the sale price without a plan or prepaid SIM as an outright price is usually $150, but I can take $50 off for you," Ollie took the box and opened it up, pulling out her already purchased SIM and put it in the phone.

The phone started with a funny *iPhone* noise, which brought a smile to her face. Playing around with the phone for a few minutes, she placed it on the glass bench and smiled at the young man behind the counter.

"I'll take it, thank you," she pulled out her wallet and handed him $100 in cash.

"Already taken care of, thank you," the young man handed her the receipt and box in a bag.

"How?" Ollie looked around with eyebrows furrowed.

"Consider it an apology for being such an arse all the time and not calling you myself but using Lacy," Cruze grabbed Ollie's forearm and dragged her out of the store. "Come on, you should get some contacts in your phone," Cruze didn't want any backlash from Ollie about buying her a phone.

"What the fuck, Cruze?" Ollie ripped her arm away from his grip and stared at him with wide eyes. "Firstly, don't grab me like that. I'm not an animal. Secondly don't think for a second you can buy me," Ollie trust the phone and bag into Cruze's chest.

"OK, tell me where your phone is then?"

"At the bottom of the ocean, may he rest in peace. Why would you bring up such a horrible memory?" Ollie narrowed her eyes as she stared at Cruze. The way he infuriated her was something she had never experienced before in her life. "If your apology for not calling me directly is to buy me a new phone so you can, then you can forget it because I don't know anyone that will be bought and I can promise you that I won't be," Ollie stared at Cruze in disgust. "I don't want pity."

"This isn't pity Olyanah! This is me being a nice guy, so just take it and be grateful. If you are upset with me buying it for you then you can pay me back," Cruze insisted, handing the bag out in front of him for Ollie to take. "Before you ask, I am bloody sure I want you to have it," Ollie didn't know what else to do but to take the bag with a smile.

"Thanks, Louis," Ollie opening her new touch screen phone and sent a message to Lacy.

"Do you have to go?"

"What else am I meant to do while Lacy is kicking it up with her new sex god somewhere in town?" Ollie was curious to hear Cruze's answer.

"Maybe you could chill with your sex god?" Cruze asked, Ollie would swear that she heard a little bit of insecurity in his voice.

"Well that might be a good idea, but I'd have to go find him and that seems as though it would be too much work for me," Ollie didn't even crack a smile as she stared up at Cruze.

"Don't try and break my confidence here, Rosewood. How about we go out for lunch and you can go on a search for your own love?"

"Where might you have in mind?"

"Somewhere quiet and private," Ollie put her hand up, effectively cutting Cruze off.

"Lunch, that's all."

"Fine, but you're missing out on a really fun experience," Cruze winked at Ollie as he stepped closer to her.

"I think I'll live, thanks all the same Mr. Cocky," Ollie replied and was surprised at how confident and steady her voice sounded when her heart was racing inside her chest, trying to break out and get closer to Cruze.

"There is nothing wrong with a little confidence, I was just blessed with the gift," Cruze winked at Ollie and subtly flexed his muscles.

"You're right, there is nothing wrong with having a bit of confidence, but apparently you got the whole bag thrown over your head and it never came off. Such a shame too, you loose your sex appeal by having such a big head," Ollie started walking away from a completely baffled Cruze. As he gathered his wits, Cruze jogged after the small, yet fast moving young lady.

"Wait, I loose my sex appeal?" he asked, "I thought it would only add to the package that the world was blessed with?"

"Nope, nothing worse then a guy who thinks the world owes him and expects every girl he sees to jump him and ride him like there is no tomorrow," Ollie explained simply with a shrug of her shoulders and a small smile on her tinted red lips.

"How do you do it?"

"Do what?"

"Slip sexual references into a conversation like it is normal and then not even acknowledge that you did it?" Cruze had a confused look on his face and it was then that Ollie realized he wasn't used to such brazen conversations. The realization puzzled Ollie; Cruze was one for slipping his own sexual references into a conversation and seemed to think that he could get any girl he looked at for more then a second.

"I've known Lacy too long I guess," Ollie shrugged her shoulders, "I didn't even know I did it," she laughed.

Cruze stood outside a Mexican restaurant and smiled, "Mexican?"

"After you, Sir," Ollie smiled.

"No, no, after you ma'am," Ollie stepped inside the cute little Mexican restaurant and smiled when a short man with a large belly came up and greeted the two. He led Ollie and Cruze to a table put the back on the balcony. "Do you know what you want?" Cruze asked after only a few seconds of looking at the menu.

"Yeah, but I'm paying this time," Ollie said quickly and put up her hand telling Cruze there was no arguing.

"So do you believe in Mystics?" Cruze sat with his meal in front of him, move it around on his plate and then shoveling some into his mouth.

"I don't know, there is csome compelling evidence that they could be true, but at the same time there is no evidence at all. It would be pretty cool if they were, I'd love to be a Mermaid, always wanted to be one when I was little. Just imagine being able to swim underwater with an amazingly powerful tail and a talent that no one would be able to understand," Ollie's eyes glassed over as she spoke, imagining what she was saying.

Cruze was watching the beautiful red headed girl in front of him; her deep blue eyes glittered in the light that the sun let out. He could see her mind working over time with her over active imagination.

A small rumble erupted from Cruze's chest, showing his contentment with the situation.

"Don't even try and hide that," Ollie held her fork at Cruze.

"Still a bit hungry I guess."

"Fine," Ollie stilled eyed Cruze skeptically, it wasn't an 'I'm hungry' tummy rumble, it was something else entirely.

This wasn't going to plan; the tall man, a man he knew very well but not in a good way, was letting her know information that wasn't in his plan. Those red eyes watched the two at the Mexican place and begged for the bastard he knew as Cruze to stop talking.

He hated all those on this side and all he wanted to do was shot an arrow right into Cruze's heart and stop him from spilling all the secrets.

With every word that left Cruze's lips, he wanted to abandon his plan and jump him, killing him once and for all but he wasn't going to tell her. No way was Cruze stupid enough, not yet.

She would have to learn her past and who she was, but not from Cruze, no. She would learn who she was and what she was while staring into those glowing red eyes with utter fear plastered in her face.

Ollie and Cruze left the little Mexican place with smiles on their lips and laughter in their bellies. The two got along like a house on fire with several hitches. It seemed nothing Cruze did wouldn't press a button and the same with Ollie. They made each other hopelessly angry and bitter and yet there was such an attraction neither could deny but tried to hide.

Ollie went to pull out her phone to see if Lacy was ready, and like clockwork the phone lit up and Lacy's name on it. Ollie winked at Cruze as she clicked the call button and put on her stripper voice.

"Good afternoon, Elegant escorts, Gwen speaking," Ollie smiled at Cruze when he looked a little shocked by her low, slow, husky voice.

"I'd like to book your best dancer. For the whole night."

"At your service," Ollie replied. She could hear Jason laughing on the other end of the phone while Cruze's bewildered expression just turned into a smirk as he draped his arm over Ollie's shoulder.

"I'll be by your car in five, baby. I want a good show for the money I'm paying too," Lacy gave her best impression of a mans voice.

"I'll be there with easily accessible bells on," Ollie replied than hung up on a laughing Lacy.

"Do I want to know?" Cruze asked.

"Probably not," Ollie replied taking the hand that was hanging by her shoulder. Ollie and Cruze walked in comfortable silence through the streets and towards Ollie's blue car where Jason pushed up against Lacy.

"Guys, I washed my car yesterday, I don't want to have to clean it again. Let's keep the baby making to the confines of a bedroom or whatever floats your boat, just off the door of my car," Ollie sighed. She could see the passion between the two and longed for something like that. No matter what, she wanted to deny that it was with Cruze that she felt such passion, but it was getting harder and harder to deny.

"Ready to go?" Lacy asked bouncing around.

"Yeah. I think you need to see Principal Davis about your energy thing. It might benefit Jason, but not the rest of us," Ollie told Lacy as she went to stand next to her, effectively shaking Cruze's arm off her shoulder, leaving her with a cold and empty feeling.

"Why him?"

"He's a psychologist."

"How do you know that?" Lacy stared at Ollie, a little confused at her knowledge.

"He told me when he decided I was worthy of being called into his office for a nice little chat. Miss. Collins pointed it out too when she saw me after English a few weeks ago. I think they think that I'm mentally disturbed," Ollie widened her eyes to prove the point of her former teachers.

"Now where would they pull that conclusion from?" Lacy questioned, tapping her index finger against her chin with thought written across her face.

"No idea. If you ask me they are the ones that need the help," Ollie slowly said.

"Not meaning to break this up," Jason interrupted, "But we have to get going. I'll see you soon though, Lacy. You too, Ollie," Jason pulled Lacy by the waist in for a hug and quick kiss.

"We'll talk," Cruze said walking over to Ollie and placing a hand on her should to emphasis the seriousness of what he was saying. "We need to talk. Soon," with that and a quick kiss on her soft cheek, Cruze hurried away with Jason following him.

"I will never understand those two," Ollie concluded.

"I will," Ollie stared at Lacy but when she didn't elaborate on the muttered comment, Ollie assumed it was a slip of the tongue. "Home again home again jiggity jig?" Lacy asked with a smile, turning on the radio as Ollie started the car.

"I guess. I have nowhere else to be," Ollie yawned.

* * *

"Did you talk to her?" Cruze sat on the sand next to his surfboard and pulled his shirt off, ready to run into the cool water of Saint Louis. He looked up at his best friend when he didn't reply. Jason stood looking out at the water, his shirt scrunched up in his hand.

Black designs covered the right peck and shoulder bone at the back and went halfway down his bicep. Cruze looked at his own designs and sighed. Covering the right peck, his full right arm and his shoulder blade on his back, the black swirls went a bit further down his skin.

"Yeah I did," Jason finally answered.

"And?" Cruze wasn't in the mood for short answers. He needed to know what happened so he could report back.

"She took it exactly how you think she would. Called me crazy and fainted when I showed her. Took a long time to get her to wake up and calm down and then I was able to tell her the full story and everything that was going on. Safe to say Charles and Sally Larkin are about to receive a very angry young daughter when she gets home," Jason let a small chuckle escape his lips before kneeling down to rub some wax onto his board for grip, a small, sad smile playing on his lips; waiting for Cruze to ask the question before he spoke about it further.

"Then what's the problem?"

"She's still leaving."

* * *

Lacy stormed into her house and called her parents to attention almost immediately. Matt, her younger brother, slinked out of his bedroom and leaned against the wall in the lounge room. Lacy sat her parents down on the couch and paced around the lounge room floor, thinking about how to start what she wanted to say.

"Lacy, what's going on?" Sally, her mother, interrupted her thought process. Charles held his wife's hand as he watched his disgruntled daughter stare with wide eye at the pair.

"I know. The name Jason Bomani Miles might ring a bell," Lacy could see her parents tense straight away. "What the hell? Why didn't you tell us? What is your problem?"

"How much did he tell you?" Charles asked.

"Everything. And I think you owe Matt the truth about our lives," Lacy crossed her arms over her chest and started at her parents in disgust. "Or maybe he would like to hear it from me. Or even Cruze," Sally stood up and walked over to her daughter.

"We did it to protect you both. Ollie was apart of your future, that much was known and we couldn't have her knowing. You met young and we couldn't be sure you wouldn't let something slip. We're sorry sweetie but that's the truth. You're right, you are old enough to know and so is Matt," Sally looked at her shirtless son and gave him a small smile. "Sit down, Matt. We have something to tell you."

Chapter Six

It's Only After You've Lost Everything That You are Free To Do Anything

Ollie sat in her room with a small smile on her lips, the cover of *Queen of the Slipstream* by *Fun.* was playing in her room. Ollie's phone vibrated on her bed constantly with messages from Cruze. Ollie didn't want to ignore them but she had travel plans to organize and lists that needed ticks in boxes.

Ollie already had a suitcase packed for America and Europe, another suitcase was ready to be packed for schoolies. Ollie was going to send her schoolies suitcase back home with Lacy's and then only have her one big one when they travelled around the world.

Ollie sat at her desk ticking a few more items off her list as she folded a few jumpers and placed them on her bed. Finally picking up her phone to check her messages from Cruze.

Cruze: We need to talk. Soon. I know you leave in two days but we need to talk.

Cruze: Let me know when you are free for a talk.

Cruze: I know formal is tomorrow night, maybe we could do lunch?

Ollie: Why do we need to talk? I have work today and tomorrow and then I have to get ready for formal, then the actual formal, after party and recovery the day after and then we are going to be leaving the day after. I can maybe do the day after formal but I don't know.

Cruze: Tonight. When do you finish work?

Ollie: 11pm, it's the graveyard shift. Cruze just tell me what's going on.

Cruze didn't reply to Ollie's last message, which left her frustrated and annoyed. With this new anger, Ollie decided going for a walk would be the best idea for her. Grabbing her iPod and pulling on some white canvas shoes, Ollie smiled at her mum as she left the house to clear her head. *Fun.* pumped through her headphones and into her mind to sooth her racing heart. *Barlights* was interrupted by 'My milk shake brings all the boys to the yard.' Ollie unplugged her headphones and answered Lacy's call.

"Elegant escorts please leave your name and number and we'll be sure to call you back with our best girls as soon as possible," Lacy laughed on the other end of the phone.

"It's damage control time," Lacy announced and Ollie could hear the smile on that would be playing on Lacy's face.

"What did you do?" Ollie sighed with a small laugh. Lacy had a frantic tone on the other end of the line, all laughter gone. Ollie could hear the girl laugh pacing around her bedroom.

"I'm not happy with mum and dad and I want you here with me tonight. We get off at eleven together so will you sleep at mine and then we can chill tomorrow at work and get ready together!" Ollie could hear the pain in Lacy's voice, it wasn't often that Lacy didn't get along with her parents and it wasn't really an option for Lacy to stay at Ollie's with such dysfunctional parents.

"I'll come and drop my stuff off now."

"I knew I could count on you, sister!" Lacy hung up without so much as a goodbye and Ollie headed home to get her things for formal and sleeping at Lacy's for a couple of nights. It was almost worth taking her schoolies and Europe suitcases with her.

The kitchen was a complete mess with food splattered everywhere and dirty dishes all over the bench and even some on the floor. Ollie's eyebrows furrowed as she walked into the odd sight of her normally clean house. Ollie made her way into the lounge room and saw her mother and father standing with their arms crossed over their chests, staring at Ollie.

"What's up buttercup?" neither one of her parents found that amusing.

"You're leaving?" Jane asked with a stern expression coating her face.

"Yes?" confusion flooded Ollie's voice.

"Why didn't you tell us?" Greg asked. Ollie was still confused as to what her parents were talking about, catching onto this, Greg elaborated. "With Lacy. You are leaving to travel. Now why wouldn't you tell us? We are your parents!"

"I was going to, when I was in Queensland and away from you psychotic sex craved people. Can you really blame me? The only time I see you is when you're off screwing a teacher or screwing each other or making em screw up my life. Literally," before anything else could be said Greg marched up to his daughter and pulled his closed hand back, slapping her right across the cheek; the sound of skin on skin and bone on bone echoed around the lounge room. Ollie's limp body fell against the carpeted floor of the lounge room as a squeal left Jane's lips. Greg turned to look at the lady he called his wife with narrow eyes and his hand still raised.

Ollie could see little particles of dirt stuck in the carpet, her only thought being that she needed to vacuum, soon. The pain hadn't kicked in yet and all Ollie could feel was numb.

Nothing. There were no feelings floating around in her usually happy body and mind. It was a normal feeling for Ollie, something she had learnt to cover up at a very young age.

"Don't talk to me in that manner," Greg stood over Ollie as she moved slightly on the ground, a moan of pain escaping her lips before Greg kicked Ollie in the stomach and stormed out of the room. A cough erupted out of her lips, a red liquid following and staining the light carpet.

Ollie lay on the floor for a few moments longer, her nose stinging with her fathers closed fisted slap and her stomach cramping as her insides bruised from his steel toed shoes. All Ollie could think about was the fact that Lacy called and needed her as soon as possible, her mind cleared with the pain in her body. She didn't want to think about what had just happened, she hated thinking about it whenever it happened.

Jane didn't know to the extent of Greg's ways, and this being the first time she had seen it and she just let it happen and walked away. Once or twice she'd tried to step in but Ollie could imagine just how scared she was.

She felt as though it was wrong of herself to like her mum. She'd never laid a hand on Ollie and had tried to intervene but Greg was a strong, tall man with a mean streak and that was something Ollie had always excused because otherwise she'd be in a much worse position.

But Jane; Jane had never seen his true dark side. Greg was very good at keeping it hidden from the outside world, only showing his true self to Ollie when he was in a money crazed, drunken rage.

Pulling herself up from the unimaginable pain, Ollie slowly walked to her bedroom and studied the packed suitcase for Europe and the half packed suitcase for schoolies.

Packing everything she owned into the half packed suitcase, Ollie grabbed her keys and wheeled the two large bags out to her car. Striping the house key off her key chain, Ollie said her own goodbye to the house she had grown up in.

Her father had been violent to her before but this was the last straw. Ollie was eighteen and she didn't have to put up with this any more. She was leaving soon and there was no need for her to have to worry about her father's wrath.

Her cheek stung still from the punch, but she tried not to think about the emotional pain and focus on the physical pain that radiated around her stomach and face.

Deciding that she would take a quick detour from Lacy's, she gave her a quick call through the Bluetooth in her car and came up with a quick lie so she wouldn't have to tell Lacy exactly what happened over the phone.

"Fluffy cupcakes dancers at your service, how may I help you?" Lacy answered but Ollie could only manage a small smile.

"I'm going to be a bit late, I'll explain at yours but for the time just trust me," there was no humour in Ollie's voice as she spoke to Lacy on the phone. Looking through the front window, Ollie could see the ocean slowly approaching.

"You got it," Lacy's voice reflected the understanding she had as Ollie's best friend.

"Thanks. See you soon," Ollie hung up just as she pulled into the Saint Louis beach car park. All her hopes were pinned on Cruze going for a surf and being at the beach today.

Pulling down the mirror in her car, Ollie saw for the first time the black eye that was slowly forming across the bridge of Ollie's nose and under her eyes. Green, purple, yellow and black tints that weren't going to be covered by makeup had appeared.

She pulled up her top and saw a large bruise along her stomach as well, realizing it was where her father had kicked her and where the pain was coming from. Slipping the top down, Ollie attempted to hide what she could of her face with makeup.

The laughter of children echoed around outside the blue car as life went on without so much as a care to what had just happened. Violence was an everyday occurrence, something people didn't look twice at anymore.

A knock against the glass of the driver side window startled Ollie and she jumped back in her seat, hand over her heart. Looking up she saw the pained expression of Cruze staring down at her. He opened the door to see the beautiful girl he was slowly getting to know, looking broken and lost.

"Ollie," was all Cruze could manage as she opened the car door and fell into his arms, sobbing slightly, her whole body shaking. "What happened? Who did this?" Ollie couldn't answer as she started choking on her own words. Resting her head against Cruze's strong chest and let everything out. She let all her fears and worries out as Cruze's strong arms wrapped around the small of her back and held her close.

"I'm sorry," Ollie started as she pulled away and looked up into Cruze's light eyes. So much warmth and safety lay within them but Ollie wasn't ready to let herself be safe, let alone let someone else protect her.

"Don't be sorry, tell me what happened. I will kill them," the seriousness in Cruze's tone had shivers running down her spin.

"I shouldn't have come, Cruze, I am sorry," Ollie turned and opened her car door and jumped in, unwinding the window. "I really am sorry," she sobbed before turning on the car and backing out with a sorrowful look in her eyes.

The pain in leaving Cruze was a new pain Ollie had never experienced. It was so much worse then the pain forming in her stomach and on her nose. It was a pain within that had no source, just something that had only one solution; Cruze.

This is what eighteen years of planning got you, the perfect situation that you could use to your advantage. He had his alliances in tact and they were working perfectly, only a few more steps and soon he would be King of his world.

His only problem in his plan was not being seen which was hard for someone with glowing red eyes. He had to cover them constantly and cover his markings so he wouldn't be given away to those around.

The one fault in an otherwise perfect plan; in his mind.

Everything had worked out perfectly for the past eighteen years, but the problem with that was sometimes things worked out too perfectly, not that the man with the glowing red eyes could see that; all he saw was what he had created; a young scared woman who was soon be to at his mercy, but she had been subject to this for too long and she wasn't going to be scared any longer.

Arriving at Lacy's house, Ollie's stomach was filled with nothing but pain and dread. Ollie shuffled around in her car, studying the simple outside of Lacy's house. White painted wooden slats lined the outside with a simple wooden porch and swing out the front along with fairy lights down the beams holding the porch roof up; the American Dream in the middle of Australia.

Ollie was worried that there would be too many questions for her to answer when she walked in, and she wasn't ready to answer those questions just yet, she needed a way to hide everything but makeup wasn't going to cover what Greg had done to her.

Finding the courage to get out of her car, Ollie managed to grab a few of the hand bags out of her back seat and dragged them to the front door, opening the locked door with her own key.

"Is that the only daughter I love?" Ollie could hear Sally's voice through the house.

"It is, my lovely Mama," Ollie called out. "I'll be back in a minute, I've just got to dump my crap in my new room," the Larkin's had two single beds in Lacy's room, for these types of situations. Sally and Charles knew all too well of Ollie's parents and their ways so they always had an open door and spare bed for her. Of course the knowledge of violence and abuse was something no one knew.

"Dinner is ready, you are just in time," Lacy appeared in the doorway of the ensuite from her bedroom.

"Perfect," Ollie kept her back to her best friend, she suspected that her eyes were still puffy and raw from crying and bruised from the beating that she received from her father.

"You OK, Ol? You seemed pretty upset on the phone. Everything OK?"

"I'll explain later," Ollie went through her handbags and found her makeup as Lacy left the room.

A few minutes later, Ollie emerged from Lacy's bedroom into the dining room where everyone was gathered with a big bowl of salad, dressing and chicken schnitzels on the oak table. Sally, Charles, Lacy and Lacy's younger flirtatious brother Matt, all looked up. All mouths dropped and hit the floor beneath at the sight of Ollie's battered face.

"Please don't look at me like that," Ollie sat at her seat on the table and started filling her empty plate. "It's not what it looks like. Let me explain later but I can't, not now. Not just yet," with that understanding, everyone tried to ignore the black eyes and bruised nose on Ollie's face and went about with easy mealtime chatter.

"So Lacy called you?" Sally asked Ollie.

"Yeah, she said you two had gone off the rails and were being annoying as all hell," Charles and Sally let out a nice little laugh and sighed as they looked at their daughter.

"What? We're like sisters. I tell her everything," Lacy shrugged her shoulders and popped a piece of schnitzel in her mouth.

"Come on, Mama, Papa. I'm sure Lacy was just overreacting as usual," Ollie tried to reason, missing the look shared between the family. "Plus, it gave me an excuse to come here and spend the night. I mean I have to leave soon for work and so does Lac so we can carpool and it'll be so much easier," Lacy and Ollie winked at each other.

"We can get ready tomorrow together too, not that we wouldn't have done that but you know, it'll be easier now that you're here," Lacy added, bouncing around on her chair.

"I can help too. You'll probably need someone to help you put your dress on," Matt leaned over the table and winked, not even hiding that he was flirting with his older sisters best friend in front of his parents.

"You're so gross," Lacy threw a tomato at Matt.

"Well, she has to pay rent some how."

"Yeah, she can pay by letting me kick you up the arse," Lacy threatened, holding a piece of chicken out in front of her.

"Maybe Ollie can do the honour's?"

"Maybe the police can do them. I hear you can be a perv no matter what age and they lock you up."

"And I hear making threats in also a jailable offense."

"Jailable isn't a word, smart arse," Ollie sat back watching Lacy and Matt fighting, wishing she had had someone to grow up with like that. Even though she had Lacy, they didn't meet until they were twelve and Ollie had spent all the time before that by herself or in her parents control because of their self-indulgent ways.

"Matt, Lacy, shut up. We are trying to enjoy dinner," Charles threw a carrot at each at his children. "Now tell me how your days have been," Sally got the brunt of the look from her husband and took the hint.

"Well, not much happened to me today, Olyanah?" Ollie looked up at her adoptive mother and gave a slight crumble of her nose.

"Well, if you all must know, I have good for nothing parents with an abusive father who decided to take it to the next level and really start the abuse because he found out that I was going to be travelling. At least it's nice to know I have an adoptive family that loves me. I can always count on you losers," Ollie winked. "But seriously, thanks for bringing me in. I don't know what I would do if I had to stay with my biological parents," it was as though the room tensed at Ollie's last few words.

"Ol, what would you say if you found out your parents weren't really your parents?" Ollie's eyebrows furrowed as she contemplated the question. It was so random, even coming from Lacy, and Ollie had no idea how she was going to respond to that.

"That's weird even for you," Ollie narrowed her eyes at her best friend, trying to see past what she had said.

"Hey, I'm just saying how much better your life would be."

"Yeah, but then I'd also be a little pissed at whoever were my real parents for leaving me with such horrible people in the first place," Ollie's rebuttal had Lacy a little startled. "Although, knowing I didn't share the same genes as those two mutilated freaks, I guess I would be a little bit happy," Sally and Charles exchanged a look but quickly covered it before Ollie could pick it up.

"Well, now that that depressing topic is over and done with, you know you are like a daughter to us, Olyanah and we want nothing more then your happiness, so please stay as long as you need, even when you two get back next year," a smile spread on Ollie's lips at the blessed people that sat around her.

"Thanks, Mama," Ollie and Lacy finished their dinner in a hurry, changed into their poodle skirts for work and then got in Lacy's car and sped away to the local to start their second last shift at the diner.

The black and white checkered floors were polished clean when Lacy and Ollie arrived for their shift and strapped on their old fashioned roller skates. John, their boss, greeted them with open arms, knowing he was going to be losing his best two employees while they travelled. No one made mention of Ollie's eyes, Lacy had covered them expertly with makeup so there was only a slight ting that looked like Ollie had been sleeping badly, most likely due to exam pressure they hoped people would assume.

"My two lovely ladies, ready to start?" John smiled, holding Ollie out at arms length. John knew the diner was the local spot for kids from their school to hang out at and he didn't mind too much if Lacy and Ollie stopped to have a chat with people, especially with their big group of friends, so long as they worked.

Ollie could see Martha, Sarah, Polly, Jay, Harry and Liam walk in and take their usual table, setting their car keys in the middle of the table and waving Ollie and Lacy over impatiently with smiles on their faces. They were always the most difficult customers, just to mess with the two working girls.

"How can I help you?" Ollie asked in her Southern Accent as she skated over to the group. Jay winked at her, ready to give her a really hard order.

"I'll get a strawberry milkshake with no strawberries and whipped cream, but add cherries and the seeds of the strawberries for texture and a cheeseburger with no cheese, no lettuce, no tomatoes, but with cream, chips, olives and yogurt," Ollie raised one eyebrow at Jay before writing down the usual order he had, ignoring the stupid order he had given her. The rest of the table went like that, people would say silly things and Ollie would write down the usual orders they had, normal orders.

"Karma is going to hit you hard, because when we leave and if you say that to other workers, you will get that order," it had been so long since any of them had said their real order they probably didn't remember it.

"Come on, Ol, we know what we are doing," Liam laughed and bumped her shoulder. *'If Karma is going to go on a holiday, then I might have to be her substitute,'* Ollie thought to herself with an evil smile on her lips as she skated away from her friends.

"You're planning something," Lacy said as Ollie came up to punch in the order. It might be a 50's diner, but they still needed to keep up with technology to help things flow better.

"Jay wants a cheeseburger with olives, cream and yogurt, then he'll get one with olives, cream and yogurt," the same sly smile spread onto Lacy's lips as she stood next to her best friend as she punched in the weirdest of orders they could think of.

"Karma is a bitch," Lacy rubbed her hands together.

"No, Karma is a lady. A fair lady that likes to teach people a lesson," Ollie winked at the chef as he got the orders and shook his head.

"These right, Ol?" he asked.

"Of course, they ordered them," the chef shook his head and laughed as he started making the odd concoctions, starting to understand where Ollie and Lacy were going with this weird and whacky plan.

Ollie picked up three plates, resting on her forearm, Lacy copied Ollie and they skated over to the table with smiles on their faces. Placing the plates on the table, the two girls were greeted with looks of dread.

"Just what you ordered," Ollie said with her accent, a wink and then off she went, linking arms with a cackling Lacy. "Enjoy," Ollie called over her shoulder.

"We are bad people," Lacy laughed, winking at Ollie.

At the end of the shift, Ollie and Lacy made their way back to Lacy's house, again ignoring the topic of Ollie's physically abusive father. The ride home was silent except for the radio that was turned down to be background noise. It wasn't often Ollie and Lacy were seated in uncomfortable silence, and they weren't in the car, but it wasn't as though they needed to fill every second with mindless chatter.

"Ol," Lacy broke the somewhat comfortable silence as they turned into the street that Lacy's house was on.

"Yeah?"

"Do you want to talk about it?"

"Not really."

"Well if you do, at any point, you know I am here for you," Ollie was grateful to have such a caring friend, someone that was going to be there for her no matter what. "I know, Lac. I know," Lacy turned off the car and the two slowly walked inside, careful not to wake anyone, and got ready for a good night sleep before their last shift tomorrow morning and then formal.

* * *

Ollie woke first and dressed for work in the uniform she had grown to love. It fitted her personality so well that Ollie didn't feel out of place wearing it at all. Flicking through her *iPhone*, Ollie found the most annoying sound that she could and put it right up to Lacy's ear. The noise blasted through the room, causing Lacy to jump and fall off her bed.

"You're a real bitch," Lacy grumbled as she pulled her tired body off the floor and sat up on the edge of her bed.

"Embrace the bitch," Ollie laughed as Lacy flipped her off. Ollie left the room, letting Lacy get changed and ready for work, going into the kitchen to get something to eat for an early breakfast.

"Morning," Ollie smiled at Charles as he sat at the kitchen table reading the morning Saturday paper.

"Ollie," Charles put the paper down, looking up at the girl he and his wife had practically adopted.

"Papa C, what up?"

"Was that the first time your father had hit you?"

"What do you mean?"

"Please don't avoid the question, Olyanah. Was this the first time that Greg has hit you?" the confronting question had Ollie turning her back to Charles as she robotically started making breakfast for herself.

"Yes," the answered sounded fake and forced even to Ollie, but she knew she had to stick to it.

"I know you aren't telling the truth," Ollie could feel Charles' disappointed look without turning around and the thought of upsetting someone she loved had her heart falling out her chest. Charles was so lovely to her; a real father.

The fire crackled behind the deep hearty laughter in the dark room to the left of the bar. Dark wallpaper covered the walls and small tables with dark velvet covered individual couches.

I stepped into the room; heart racing against my chest, knowing full well everyone in the room could hear it, but not knowing why they could hear it. All eyes fell on my scarcely covered body and I fought the urge to cover it with my arms.

"Step forward," the familiar male voice I had grown up with echoed through the small room, causing all the males in the room to stop talking and look up at me standing in my red see-through dress.

I stepped forward, hands shaking behind my back as rough hands grabbed my upper arm and propelled me into the room, right in the middle so I was on full display for the ten males sitting with cigars hanging from their lips.

"You have a minimum of a thousand," from then on shouting erupted in the room, while I stood with him behind my back, slowly creeping up on me.

"Tell me the truth, Olyanah," the pressure was causing Ollie's hands to shake as she pulled a piece of toast from the toaster.

"No. It's not the first time."

"Why haven't you told anyone?"

"Because it isn't that big of a deal. It's happened before and I can deal with it. I mean I'm leaving soon. I'll never have to see those people again," Ollie hadn't referred to the two who had raised her as her parents in a very long time, refusing to admit that they were even related.

Her hands were still shaking as she waited for her toast to pop, all she wanted was for Charles to drop the topic, she knew he cared about her but that didn't mean he had the right to pressure her into telling him everything about her. Apart from letting her stay at their house, Ollie had no real reason to tell him what had happened to her in her past.

"This isn't something you can just wish away. I love you like you were my own daughter and seeing you in pain; it's not something I want to experience again, or let you experience. Now tell me what he has done to you," as though by some twisted turn of fate, Lacy and Sally walked in, suspending all conversation between Charles and Ollie.

"Come on, Ollie, we have to get to work before John docs our pay," Lacy said, grabbing Ollie's arm and pulling her away, not seeing the tension in the room or the thankful expression on her best friends face.

* * *

Sally looked up at her husband and took a hold of his strong hand in hers. She could see and feel the pain rolling off him in waves, almost knocking her over with the force. Her petite form, so much like her daughters, steadied and held onto Charles, wrapping her small arms around his large muscular waist.

"What's wrong?" her soft voice slowly calmed Charles down, making him remember when he was and who was with him.

"Nothing. We'll talk about it later, I need to go for a drive," Sally accepted that Charles wasn't much of a talker a long time ago and let him go off for a drive to clear his head and let him work out the story so he could tell he her with little emotions, something he preferred doing.

"Drive safely, we have a long day ahead of ourselves. Everyone is coming here first before formal, don't forget that," Sally called after her husband before she heard the door slam shut.

Being alone in the house wasn't something Sally was used to, Lacy and Ollie were at work, Charles was off clearing his head. The only thing she could think to do was turn on the music and start cleaning the house.

"Damn it, mum!" a grumpy voice called out, causing Sally to place a hand against her beating heart as she forgot about Matt still being in bed at nine o'clock on a Saturday morning.

"Sorry, Matty, do you want to come and help me clean?"

"I'm a growing boy, all I want is food and sleep. So that will be a no from me. Where's everyone else?" walking into the kitchen with nothing but track-suit-pants on, Matt gave a small grumpy smile to his mother.

"The girls have gone to work and your father, well he's in need of a bit of TLC," Matt knew what that meant and gave his mum a hug.

* * *

The road rattled the new car in a way no one would've expected, causing a chorus of swear words to come pouring out of Charles' mouth. His distaste for unmade roads in new cars was evident, although a man of nature, he preferred to explore nature on foot, not in a beast of a car.

Slowly he reached the gate where the dark coloured castle like mansion stood on top of the hill, hidden from society. Punching in a number, he was allowed access and soon was parking his car in a car space and walking up the steps, taking two at a time to hurry the process along.

"I need to talk to Enakal," Charles' deep voice said as he entered the place.

"He's busy," a young guy sitting on a living room couch said without looking up. Charles walked over to the tough looking punk and grabbed him by the collar of his shirt, lifting him off the ground.

"I need to speak to Enakal," he said again, his deep voice echoing in the empty hall. "Now." Shivering with fear, the young man hurried away with his tail between his legs.

Chapter Seven

Life Is Too Important To Take Seriously

OLLIE AND LACY danced around their room getting ready for formal, singing loudly to the music that was blasting from the speakers the two girls had taken from the lounge room.

"You know you have a pretty awesome singing voice?" Lacy asked Ollie, turning the music down and rubbing green goo on her face.

"You look like Shrek," Ollie laughed as she started applying her own facemask.

"Well hello, Fiona," Lacy winked, wrapping an arm around her shoulder. "So, your voice. How come I haven't noticed before? I mean I have but it just gets better and better. You might be the new Adele."

"I don't really notice, I know I can hold a tune, but I don't think I'm that good," Ollie laid down on her new bed and looked over at Lacy. Lacy was sitting on her own bed on her stomach with her legs kicked up like a cheesy American teen movie. Ollie was laying on her back, looking up at the poster of Marilyn Monroe that she had put up there last night before she went to work.

"You are good," Lacy pulled a magazine out and threw it at Ollie. "So have you spoken to Cruze recently?" the suggestion was evident in Lacy's tone as she wriggled her eyebrows.

"A few times, messaging and all but not in person since lunch. You? You seemed pretty mad at Jason and then happy and then mad and then called me because you were mad again. Care to explain?"

"He was just being an arse, nothing special," Lacy felt horrible at how easily she was able to lie to Ollie about what had happened between herself and Jason and what she had learnt when she got home. It had taken a while before Lacy had calmed down, it helped that Matt was angry too but when Lacy called Ollie she knew it was a bad idea. Was she a horrible friend for being grateful that Ollie had had something happen to her to take the topic off why Lacy called her, no. She was just thinking of her friend's safety, in a very upside down way.

"You sure? Because you seemed pretty angry on the phone."

"Yeah, we've patched things up. Oh and Jason has booked somewhere with a few friends, Cruze included, in Queensland for next week. I am so excited. I know this may sound stupid, Ol, but I really think he could be the one," Ollie could see by the look on Lacy's face that this wasn't just the honeymoon period, this was something more, something special.

"Hold onto it, Lac, make sure you can talk to him when we are away because you don't want him gravitating away," Ollie was in full support of her friend and that somewhat surprised Lacy.

"You know, I never thought you to be one to believe in love."

"People can surprise you everyday. I've seen you two together, you have something I never saw in parents, but I see it in you two everyday. I know it's there but I have yet to find it. There's more then one love of your life, Lacy, just don't forget that, but love each new time," Lacy tried not to laugh at Ollie thinking there was more then one love, after everything she had learnt it felt like such an odd concept, especially hearing it from Ollie.

"I'll hold onto it. I promise," Lacy got up off her bed and walked over to Ollie's. "But you have to promise me that you will open your eyes when love comes and embrace it, not run because of your parents," Ollie knew Lacy was just looking after her but she felt as though it might have been a bit of an under handed comment in some ways, like there was a second meaning that Lacy wanted Ollie to work out with no help.

"I promise, now let's get this crap off our faces before it hardens and we got to formal looking like The Hulk," Lacy laughed and the two started scrubbing at their faces with a towel in the bathroom.

"You two OK in there?" Sally called over the loud music that was still blasting in Lacy's room.

"Dandy as a rose in summer!" Ollie called back and fell into a fit of giggles.

"Let me know when you are hungry and I'll make you two something to eat," Lacy heard her mother's footsteps walking away and looked at Ollie with a smile.

"I have the best mother in the world."

"That you do."

"Now look at me," Ollie turned herself to face Lacy face on. "What happened last night. You haven't said much about it but I know your dad hurt you again."

"My only worry is that you won't be able to work your magic and cover all of this up," Ollie turned on her sarcastic side, hiding the serious side of things.

"Do you know how to be serious?" Lacy laughed.

"Yes, but I choose not to be because I'm over being the serious boring person my parents turned me into. I want to live life, not just watch it pass by with a nice wave of its chaotic hand," Lacy listened to her hurting friend, trying to see her point of view without seeming like she was judging her.

"I always thought it was a good thing to face your problems."

"Probably, but I am not in the mood for it today so please let's just get on with today."

"OK."

* * *

The waves smashed against the sand as surfers guided their boards in before jumping off and paddling back out. The sound of seagulls flying around above the salty ocean water. People sat on the sand with towels separating themselves from the heated sand that had been warmed up under the afternoon sun.

The sun warmed the wet skin of a tall, strong man who was slowly drying his legs with a dry towel. Not bothering to dry his torso before pulling on a white t-shirt that was adorned with a black and white picture of a girl surfing in the flat ocean. Running his fingers through his light hair with brown rooting, he looked around the beach, spotting his mates.

"You going to the meeting? Apparently Enakal and Arabella want to have a little chat about the little break down your girlfriend had last night. You might want to have a little chat with her about that before you go in blind. You've seen how angry Enakal has gotten on the subject of Olyanah when Jay doesn't have answers," a tall guy, not taller then Cruze but tall nonetheless, with brown hair and light eyes patted Cruze on the back.

"I was going to send her a message once I got back to the house," Cruze pulled out his phone, knowing Josh wasn't going to let it go until Cruze had sent the message.

Cruze: Hey, I just wanted to check you were alright after last night xx

Cruze put his phone on loud and set it in his bag before lifting his surfboard under hit shoulder and throwing his sports bag at Jason. Flipping him the bird, Jason took the bag and walked with Josh behind Cruze as he went to attach the board in the back of his black ute, leaving the tail fins handing out the end.

Ollie: Yeah, I'm alright. Feeling much better. Getting my groove on with Lacy as we dance the night away before dancing the night away at formal

A small smile crept onto Cruze's lips at Ollie's response. Jason and Josh piled into the Ute, it being a four door; they didn't have to squish in the front of the Ute cabin. Jason, sitting shotgun, turned the radio on to *triple j* and let some alternative music blast through the speakers.

"Got answers?" Josh finally asked.

"Nope, but she's a funny girl so it's hard to stay angry with her," Jason nodded his head.

"The exact same as Lacy. No wonder, they are practically sisters," Jason pulled his phone put and started messaging his short time lover for information on the Ollie situation that was slowly unfolding.

"Yeah well if you get any new information then pass it on or I will grill you just as hard as Enakal grills me," Jason just started laughing shaking his head. "You're a dirty bastard," Cruze laughed, shoving his long time friends' shoulder.

"I'd like to see you win in a fight against me," Jason challenged. Immediately Cruze stopped the car, pulling it over to the side of the road and eyed Jason with dark clouded eyes.

"Is that a challenge?" Jason realized his mistake and lowered his head, avoiding eye contact with the strong male sitting in the drivers seat.

"No."

"No?"

"No."

"Good," Cruze's eyes cleared up as his mind opened up as he started seeing clearly again. "Sorry."

"Don't mention it, you saw it as a challenge," Jason kept his head low as he accepted Cruze's apology and soon the three were back on the road heading towards the shared house.

"Enakal is wanting you to come by as soon as possible. He's waiting for you to have that little chat," Josh finally said something after the tense ordeal. "So pedal to the medal buddy before everyone knows about your new connection," Cruze pulled off the main road and onto another dirt road, pushing the accelerator down onto the floor, revving the engine and letting dirt fly up behind the four-wheeled drive. The engine needle tilted the top end of eighty; normally this road would only push to sixty kilometers an hour at most but the situation called for a bit of 4-wheeled driving.

"Calm down, Cruze, you need to chill before you get us all killed," the three boys laughed at that comment, understanding the inside joke.

"I'd like to see that day," Cruze agreed, slowing down the car as they came around a corner, letting the trees open up to a large white castle like mansion. The dark rendered walls blended in with the country that surrounded the place.

A handsome tall man with filled out muscles and silver, knowing eyes stood behind a desk, his arms flexing as he crossed them over his chest. Barely looking a day over thirty, his eyes suggested otherwise, showing age beyond his appearance. The light brown hair that was cut back to suit the classic style on a 1940's young man. The man ran his fingers through his hair in annoyance and pain.

"Cruze," he said before Cruze had even knocked on the door to enter the office like room. "We need to talk."

"Before you say anything, I told you not to do it. I warned you not to trust those two. They were unmated and we knew they weren't exactly friends before this happened," Cruze didn't let the tall powerful man in front of him talk. Cruze was slightly taller then him but intimidation was not an option for Cruze.

"Enough! I want to know what happened to Olyanah last night," the loud booming voice echoed around the room, causing Cruze to lower his eye contact.

"I know as much as you. She came to me in pain and I held her, but then she didn't want to talk about it. I spoke to her today but she seemed happy. Like everything had been forgotten. I don't know what to do about this," Cruze fell into the new leather chain that was on the other side of the office like desk. The fresh leather smell hit Cruze's nose and caused him to scrunch up his nose at the strong scent.

"Cruze, you need to be there for her. If I can't, then you have to be," Cruze looked up at the man he had slowly been seeing as his father. After loosing his own father, Enakal had been the closets thing to a father Cruze had known in years.

"She's still leaving, I don't know what I can do. I know Jason and Brent are going up to Surfers Paradise next week but I feel wrong leaving everyone. It's my role to be your second; be there for you and everyone else here," Enakal rounded the oak office desk and placed a hand on the young man in front of him.

"You are strong. Go and be with her for the final week. I am sure we can trust Lacy Mandisa Larkin. Sweet is her middle name after all," Cruze smiled up at the kind man he had grown to love and soon the two were embraced in a manly hug.

"Thank you, Enakal, I will not let you down," Cruze smiled.

"Oh and Cruze. I suggest you take a detour with Jason to see Charles. There is some important information he has that you need to know," Cruze nodded his head in acknowledgement and left the office with a smile on his face, ready to change and jump into his ute to go for a much needed drive. He threw the surfboard in the storage room where everyone else left their surfboards.

Running up to his room, Cruze threw almost every piece of clothing he owned on the floor in search of the one thing that was on his mind. He needed it by tonight and without it, he was stuffed.

* * *

Ollie turned around so Lacy could lace up the back of her low backed black formal lace dress. Lacy threaded the black silk ribbon around the holes and tied a bow at the top, where it covered Ollie's bra strap at the back.

"You look beautiful," Lacy spun Ollie around and held her at arms length with her hands on her shoulders.

"What about you? Glamour looks good on you," Ollie looked Lacy up and down, admiring the way the lavender chiffon flowed at the skirt and the rhinestone top looked with spaghetti straps. Lacy had curled her hair and stuck it in a very loose bun with pieces flowing around her face, shaping her beautiful features. The light purple and silver eye shadow along with light cream lips finished the new school glamour look off.

Ollie on the other hand looked as though she had stepped off the red carpet in 1954. Light eyeliner coated the top of her eyelids in a thin line, flicking out at the corner; the eyeliner was surrounded by light white eye shadow. Red plump lips with cheekbones with light blush looked at Lacy. The black lace dress fitted the 50's red carpet look at Lacy had achieved on Ollie. Red shiny shoes sat on Ollie's shoes and a smile adorned her bright red lips.

"I think mum wants some photos," Lacy said, pulling Ollie in for a big sisterly hug.

"People will be coming soon too," the two girls walked out into the living room, getting photos with Sally, Charles and Matt before Jay, Harry, Liam, Polly, Martha and Sarah came over and before the limo arrived.

"You two look amazing," Jay gave Ollie and Lacy a hug.

"Thank that one," Ollie thrust her thumb in Lacy's direction over her shoulder. "She's the one who managed to do this," Jay pulled Ollie in for another hug.

"Either way, I'm lucky to have you in my life. Little sis," Ollie smiled at the pet name. The two, although flirty, were like family and it have never crossed Ollie's mind just how much Jay meant to her and how much she could mean to Jay.

"No worries. Damn you're going to miss me next year, brother," Ollie kissed Jay's cheek before wiping away the lipstick she had left.

"I know; I have no idea what I am going to do without you. Maybe find another lovely sexy partner," Jay teased and a snap was taken of the two laughing and having a nice before formal joke.

"Come on you two! We need photos of the group!" Lacy pulled Ollie and Jay towards the group were snaps were taken of the eight close friends. Just as everyone's parents had taken all the photos, a car pulled up and two tall men got out of the car, smoothing out their suits with small, calm smiles on their faces.

The dark haired one walked up towards Lacy and smiled, kissing her cheek before getting down on one knee and opening a velvet red box. A gasp resonated around the group as Lacy's jaw dropped.

"Jason, what are you doing?" Lacy's eyes were almost popping out of her eye sockets as she tried to wrap her head around what her short time boyfriend was doing on one knee in front of her.

"I love you, Lacy Mandisa Larkin," Jason opened the black velvet case and pulled out a beautiful sterling silver chain bracelet with a circular pendent on the end with engraved art work on it. "Be my girlfriend, officially," Lacy put out her hand like royalty with a smile on her lips.

"You may do the honour's," Lacy said with a bad English accent on her lips. Jason clipped the bracelet into place and kissed the top of her hand.

"I just wanted to say how beautiful you look and I'll see you later tonight?" Lacy nodded, inspecting the silver now on her wrist. "I'll see you when you get back here at one to shake the house down for the after party," Jason got to his full height and gave a kiss to his official girlfriend.

"See you later tonight," Lacy blushed.

He watched them all arrive and he watched them all leave in the limo, yes; she was going to be more then satisfactory for him. Far more satisfactory then he has first thought.

A well formed body, something he already knew from watching her dance, and a perfectly symmetrical face that pleased his red eyes and his cold heart.

Cruze stood next to her, slowly chatting to her but he could tell it was an intense conversation. She was trying to ignore what he was saying but the look of determination he had was far too scary for her to back away.

Arriving at the formal building all the eight friends could hear was music blasting from inside, like music had been blasting in the limo on the short drive to the venue. Lacy had asked the driver to take a detour and they ended up going through Saint Louis and Burlywood to make the most of their money and time in the limo drinking, laughing, chatting and singing badly to the music pumping through the speakers.

"We are going to rock this!" Martha called out as she stepped out of the limo in her vibrant red dress. Ollie emerged from the limo with a smile plastered on her lips as she thought about seeing Cruze decked out in his suit at Lacy's house. Although they hadn't spoken, while Jason was giving Lacy her present, Ollie and Cruze exchanged flirty eyes. Ollie's phone beeped with a message and she pulled it out of her clutch bag.

Cruze: You look beautiful. I hope I can see you tonight at Lacy's after party

Ollie: Thank you and only if you're lucky

Ollie couldn't help the smile that emerged on her lips as she closed her phone and put it back in her bag as she walked into the decorated venue. The green and red of Ashton High covered the walls and tables in true school spirit. Ollie rolled her eyes at the bad decorating and headed over to the table her friends had already claimed.

A stage a metre off the ground stood at the front of the venue where the DJ stood and there was also a microphone on stage on a stand. Principal Davis stood with his arms behind his back, hands clasped together, watching over the student body. He approached the microphone and coughed into it to gather everyone's attention. The DJ cut off the music and which was the thing that caught everyone's attention.

"Welcome everyone, it is boarding on nine o'clock now and in an hour we will announce the King and Queen of formal, another hour and we will ask all year elevens and tens to leave before formal finishes at twelve thirty," everyone cheered as Principal Davis stepped away from the microphone and the DJ started up again.

"This night is going to kill me!" Polly laughed as she fell into a seat and poured herself a glass of water. "I'm too old for such late nights," after a few drinks in the limo, most of the girls and guys already had a happy amount of alcohol in their systems, with four hours until they could drink again.

"Ollie," Ollie looked up from her seat and saw Principal Davis. "May I have a word with you?" Ollie stood up, leaving her bag behind on the table and followed Principal Davis to a quieter area.

"What can I do you for, PD?" Ollie asked with a gangster voice and sly eyes.

"Call me Simon, I'm no longer your principal, in fact, and Jane wanted to talk to you about this but seeing as you are leaving and no longer living at home. We are a couple, not just a fling. I am your mothers soul mate, something you'll understand soon enough but I thought I should just tell you," Ollie didn't know how to respond to Principal Davis declaration.

"I don't know what to say, PD," but she was cut off.

"Simon, please call me Simon."

"OK, Simon," it felt weird saying it, foreign almost, "Why are you telling me this? It's not as though I am going to be seeing my parents again in my lifetime," Ollie stared at her ex-principal.

"I just thought you should know because Jane raised you . . ."

"No, I raised myself. Jane and Greg did nothing, don't even pretend that they did," Simon stepped back, not expecting that reaction from Ollie. "Thanks all the same for the information but I don't care too much; I have to admit," a small smiled showed that it was nothing personal against Simon, just Jane and Greg.

Ollie walked away from Simon, re-entering the party part of the venue and started dancing when Jay pulled her by the waist. Dancing in the middle of the dance floor, Ollie swung her arms in the air, singing towards Lacy as Barbie Girl came on.

Cruze pulled up at Lacy's house a few hours early with Jason, eager to know what Enakal wanted him to find out from Charles. His curiosity had been on edge all day and Cruze couldn't stand not knowing what was about to happen or be said.

"Cruze, Jason," Sally opened the door to the two and smiled, letting them in. "I wasn't expecting you so early. Come in and take a load off," Cruze had always like Sally, she was kind and just seemed to want the best for everyone, no matter who they were. "What can we do for you?"

"Enakal suggested I have a talk with Charles today," Cruze could see Sally tense up and Charles lower the book he had in front of his face. Looking at her husband, Sally's suspicions rose.

"This wouldn't have anything to do about the conversation you were having with Ollie this morning would it?" Cruze had never seen such a sheepish look on such a manly face.

"Would you give us a minute?" Charles asked.

"No I will not give you a minute. Don't you dare forget she is my adoptive daughter too and I will know what is going on so you can cut the code talk or quit spy talking because I will know what has happened," Cruze had seen this before, the guy stood no chance at saying no when they were this deeply in love and only wanted to see their better half happy.

"OK, well to put it simply, Ollie admitted to me that this wasn't the first time Greg has hit her," Cruze's face was completely straight and calm as Charles told him the news, but on the inside he was fuming.

"So it was Greg who did that to her?" he asked, his voice reflecting the calm his face was showing.

"Yes, and I fear that it has gone further then that before. I don't know how we have never noticed it before but she was terrified to even admit it was more then this once," Charles, Cruze, Sally and Jason migrated over to the kitchen table when they all sat listening to the news that their strong Ollie was strong for a reason.

"You've only told Enakal of this?"

"Yes."

"Good. Keep it that way."

"Cruze, is what he said true. That you're her . . . ?" Charles let the question hang in the air as he waited for an answer.

"Yes."

Chapter Eight

Your Future Is Created By What You Do Today, Not Tomorrow

AFTER LEAVING, OLLIE had already packed her whole suitcase for schoolies and travelling, so there wasn't much for her to do as she waited for Lacy to pack her bags. Ollie admired the way in which Lacy managed to pack her suitcase and message Jason without missing a beat.

"I cannot believe you waited until now to pack," Ollie commented, laying on her back on her bed with a book in her hands.

"I cannot believe you didn't wait until now to pack," Lacy retorted, poking her tongue out at Ollie. "What are you reading anyway?" Ollie dog eared the book and closed the old yellowed pages, placing it on the bedside table.

"Lady Chatterley's Lover," Lacy got up off the floor and went over to Ollie's bed, sitting on the side causing it to dip a bit under her minimal weight. Grabbing the old book, Lacy examined the worn pages and flipped through them, smelling smells from years ago stuck on the pages.

"Steamy," Lacy commented after reading a few pages.

"It was banned in the 1950's because of that reason."

"Where'd you get it?"

"I don't know. Jane said my grandfather gave it to me before he died. Apparently someone in my family liked me because I seemed to have a lot of things from him," Ollie pulled the long chained engraved full moon pendant from around her neck for Lacy to see and pulled up her top to show her belly button ring that was a wolf in a full moon with deep blue crystal eyes.

"Well they are beautiful," Lacy gave a small, pitiful smile before going back on the floor to finish her packing.

"I know. Makes me feel as though someone out there cares," the room filled with silence as the two girls stopped to think about their lives. "Anyway, enough of the sorrowful conversation. We have three hours, Lacy; get your arse showered and clothes packed so we can start the crying goodbyes," Ollie put her book in her bag that she was taking on the plane and walked out into the lounge room where Charles, Sally and Matt were seated on the couches, watching Wife Swap USA together.

"You ready for this, Olyanah?" Sally asked, making room for her on the couch.

"As ready as I'll ever be."

"You'll be fine. Plane's are fun," Matt said, showing his age in that one sentence. "If you need I can go with you," he winked, "Make sure you are safe in the plane and at the beach," Ollie couldn't help the laugh that erupted from her at that thought.

"I'll be right, Matty, thanks all the same," Ollie winked back at him. "I have Lacy, she's all I need to take my mind off whatever imminent danger I'm placing myself in." "And you are lucky to have me!" Lacy sang as she walked into the room, water dripping from the ends of her hair. Her normally blonde hair looked darkened, as it was wet, sitting flat on top of her head.

"That I am," Ollie got up and embraced Lacy in a warm hug. "Now dry your hair because knowing you, you're going to have a complete cry session when we leave," Lacy nodded her head and went back to the bathroom to finish getting ready before leaving.

Ollie went into the kitchen to get herself something to eat and drink before returning, trying to clear her mind of all fear that was starting to gather from the thought of her first plane ride.

Ollie stood in a pair of blue high waisted jeans and a black top that was tucked in, with a rounded low cut neckline. Her grandfather's necklace hung low, resting below her bust, almost hitting her stomach and banging against the fabric whenever she moved. Ollie had tied her hair into French Twist with an old piece of floral fabric tied around her hair, pulling it all back except for the fringe, which framed her face nicely.

"Are you excited," the low, soft voice behind her echoed around the silent cut off kitchen. Ollie's heart quickened as she heard Charles talk. "About leaving?"

"Yeah I am," Ollie plastered on a smile before turning around.

"You're a daughter to me, Olyanah. I am sorry I wasn't there when Greg was hurting you. I would've stopped it. I would've helped. Sally and Matt too," Ollie could hear the truth behind the words.

"I know," she walked over and pulled him into a hug. "I know."

* * *

"I'm going to miss you two so much," Sally pulled Ollie and Lacy into a bone crushing hug, something such a petite woman shouldn't be able to do but her strength was hidden well.

Charles and Matt both hugged the girls, tears forming in the corners of their eyes. "Be safe, enjoy your trip but remember you cannot leave again because it's too hard for me," Ollie held her tears back, placing a kiss on Sally's cheek.

"You got it, Mama," Lacy did the same, embracing her mum.

"We'll have fun!" Ollie and Lacy jumped into Lacy's car and drove off, waving before they turned off the street.

"This is it. This is really it," Ollie was almost astounded at how excited and scared she was. "I didn't think I would feel so liberated leaving!" Ollie rolled down her window and let the wind wash against her face, refreshing her inside and out.

Soon enough the two girls could smell the salty air of the ocean near by, letting them know that their second goodbye was coming up. Cruze and Jason had promised to say goodbye at the beach, sort of an 'I'll see you again soon,' thing. Lacy pulled into the car park, seeing Jason and Cruze and jumping out of the car, almost forgetting to put it in park.

Jason embraced Lacy in his strong arms, trying to remember the feeling of her in his arms for long enough to let him last while she was away.

Cruze stood to the side, smiling at his friend and the way in which he loved Lacy. Cruze had seen the love before and now that he had it, he was scared. He never thought he'd be scared when it came to him, instead he thought he'd embrace the love, not run from it. But Ollie had him second-guessing everything, second-guessing the life he had been hiding and living and the life she had been forced to live.

"Hey, you," Cruze said, slowly sauntering over to Ollie who was emerging from the car. She looked like a beautiful goddess as she stepped out with a smile on her face. Bare feet slapped against the ground as Ollie slowly walked over to Cruze with a sly smile plastered on her face.

"Hey yourself," she said standing close to him. Her voice was soft and low, almost begging Cruze to give her a memory and reason to come back. "Excited?"

"That seems to be the question of the day," Ollie's eyes flickered over Cruze's face, trying to remember every single detail. His masculine face smiled down at her, letting Ollie see every dimple and detail that sat upon Cruze's skin.

"I need to get more creative with my questions then," he breathed out, resisting the urge to do as Ollie was begging and pull her into a passionate kiss.

"Agreed."

"So, are you excited?"

"Nervous, excited, scared, curious. All of the above," Ollie smiled. Cruze embraced her hands in his, letting his warmth fill her up.

"Don't have too much fun. You might never come back," Cruze leaned down and gave Ollie a soft kiss on her forehead.

"I don't think that will happen."

"Good. Be careful, Olyanah, the world is a dangerous place with predators just looking for inexperienced girls to come walking along. Promise me you'll be careful?" it was almost as thought Cruze was begging Ollie not to go.

"Are you not coming to Queensland?"

"I am, but not for long and not yet. Only a few days, I have things here I need to take care of," Cruze could see the poor choice of words as pain flashed across Ollie's face before she covered it up with her easy going smile.

"OK, well I'll see you up there," she managed to squeak out. "When will you come up?" Ollie was trying to work out how long it would be until she could see Cruze again.

"In a few days. Probably Wednesday," it dawned on Ollie that today was Sunday so it would be four days until Ollie could see Cruze's sun kissed hair and tanned face and body again. "I can't get away from work for long," it occurred to Ollie that she didn't even know how old Cruze was, if he was in school or what he did with his life other then surf.

"Oh, well I guess I'll see you then, maybe," Ollie smiled and walked off trying to contain her pain. Pain and sadness was something Ollie was used to, something she had blocked from herself but this was a new pain, a pain that involved her heart being ripped out of her chest.

Ollie saw Lacy and Jason finally tear themselves from each other and wave before Lacy returned to the car. Jason was going to be joining them tomorrow, Ollie didn't know why he wasn't going up today, she assumed it had something to do with not being able to get a flight today.

"Ready?" Ollie asked.

"Of course," Ollie wound down the window again and watched as the new scenery rolled past. The fast rolling highways and thinning out trees was something Ollie had never seen before. Cars drove past in more then one lane going the same way as buildings started getting higher and higher into the air.

"I can't believe this is happening," Ollie said, poking her head out the window as the car slowed and Lacy unwound her window to get a ticket to enter the car park. Ollie followed the concrete around until they reached level two, parked and got out with their suitcases, ready to start the most amazing holiday of their lives.

He had everything planned. Leaving the day before he missed seeing her leave, he missed the waving goodbye, watching from the shadows.

He left the day earlier so he could make sure everything was sorted and go and see his girls, let them go and bring in new 'entertainment' not just for himself but for his accomplices too.

He drove through the harsh wildlife in the 4-wheeled drive, pushing through the bogs and over grown weeds as he arrived at his second home. Splitting his life in three was a hard concept to gather but for eighteen years he had managed to pull it off without too many questions being asked. Between making sure his plan went off without a hitch, to checking on his girls and accomplices and then his real life that he had, it really took it out of a guy, but soon enough three would become two and then two would become one.

He was just lucky that he had his allies to make it easier for him to work around everything and know where she was going to be and what she was going to be doing as well as people managing things back home.

He arrived safely at the abandoned building and parked the car a few metres away so no one heard a noise. A very familiar lady emerged from the front of the building and smiled at him as he arrived.

"It's time for a new bunch. I'm getting bored."

"How could you get bored when you are barely here?" she asked stepping closer and close to him, showing her deep golden glowing eyes. Her eyes stared into his red glowing eyes and they exchanged a whole conversation.

"How long have we had them?"

"A month, max."

"That's too long. Get rid of them and get some new ones and we'll hold onto them for a week and then they can go to and then we can start collecting again, but I want our kind and only our kind," his commanding tone left no room for argument.

"As you wish it," she nodded her head and went inside to organise what he had asked for.

"And every piece connects."

Chapter Nine

We Cannot Direct The Wind, But We Can Adjust The Sails

OLLIE'S HAND SHOOK as she tried to calm her nervous body. Announcements went over the loudspeaker and people shuffled around the terminal towards whatever gate they needed to be at. Ollie's perfectly done French Twist was in disarray as she pulled at the sides, pulling the cloth out and messing up the bobby pins that had been placed in the hair style.

People moved around carrying small suitcases, hand bags and back packs as they wondered around, making sure they had everything they needed for their flights. Mindless chatter was held between people while others read magazines, books, iPad's, and listening to music.

Ollie sat with her head in her hands, leaning forward in an emergency position as she panicked about her first flight. Watching the planes take off and land made her even more anxious, so she turned her eyes away, trying to think of something else to calm her down.

"Ollie, can you please listen to me instead of just putting your head down?" Lacy's voice penetrated the silence that had engulfed Ollie's mind. "Please," Ollie pulled her head up, pulling the final bobby pins out and letting it flow down in unnatural waves.

"What?" Ollie snapped at Lacy, letting the pressure and fear get to her.

"Let me call Cruze and you can talk to him. He'll calm you down," Ollie let the words wash over her without so much as acknowledging her long time friend. Lacy dialed Cruze's number, understanding just how important he was going to be to Ollie for the rest of her life, especially now.

"Salve," Cruze answered in Latin.

"Cruze my dear friend, I've hit a bit of a snag," Lacy ignored the Latin that she didn't understand and went straight to the root of the problem.

"What happened?"

"Ollie is in panic mode, she's freaking out about flying. Encourage her, boy! Make her feel better and able to do this!" Lacy straight away handed the phone to Ollie. "Talk to Cruze," Ollie took the phone and put it to her ear as she breathed heavily.

"Hey," Cruze casually said. "How was the drive to the airport? Different?"

"Alright. Long," the restriction in her voice was evident to Cruze on the other end of the line.

"Different?"

"Yeah."

"You've never been to the city have you?"

"No. Only seen it all on TV when watching the footy. Jane and Greg didn't really let me watch TV," Ollie's heart rate started to slow down as she spoke calmly with Cruze on the phone. Hearing his voice already had a soothing feel about it.

"Different to what you thought?"

"Very different. So many lanes on the freeway and highway, I don't even know the difference between the two. It's a technicality I think," a small laugh echoed on the other end of the line as Cruze chuckled at Ollie.

"I think it is too. Hey, do you know Latin?" the question struck Ollie as quite odd but it was Cruze and she felt as though it was a normal type of question for him.

"Yes. I didn't get to spend a lot of time with my parents so I took out-of-school-classes. I know Latin, Indonesian, Italian, French, Dutch, Greek, sign language and the language of flowers. Believe me, my parents have been quite absent in my life. I also know ballet, tap, jazz, burlesque and self defense," Ollie rattled off what she had been doing with her minimal spare time for the past eighteen years.

"A woman of many talents. Quomodo refrigerii (How refreshing)," Ollie let out a bark of laughter.

"Ego potest imaginary (I can imagine)," Ollie said to show off that she wasn't joking about her extensive language knowledge.

"OK, now that I know you have many talents, I want you to do something for me. Stay calm. Remember something for me. Do you remember the way the ocean smells after it has rained?" Ollie's mind went straight to one of the first times she had seen Cruze. He was in the water surfing after a quick encounter on the sand. She could smell fresh summer rain after a storm in the forest that stood by the ocean.

"OK," Ollie waited for him to go on.

"Imagine the way it smells after a storm, the way the water hits the sand with such force, trying to rid itself of all foreign contaminants that have been washed in," Ollie's mind stayed on the image of Cruze surfing and the way in which the water ran off his perfectly tanned and sculptured body. "Got it?"

"Yes."

"Whenever you get stressed, scared or just miss home, think of that. Think of home and think of what you are coming back to. Also just relax and have a conversation with someone. The more casual the better you will feel."

"Thank you."

"I'll see you soon. I miss you already, Olyanah," Ollie's heart raced hearing those words from Cruze.

"Ciao," she replied and was left with a chuckle before the line went dead.

"All good?" Lacy asked taking her phone back.

"Yeah, all good," Ollie admitted with a smile.

"So, what did he say?"

"Nothing too exciting, just the usual stuff. Did you know he spoke Latin?" Ollie asked, opening up her bag and pulling out her headphones and a magazine to read. 'Cleo' was written in big bold writing on the front with a few sub-headings on the front with a picture of Emma Stone. Ollie didn't watch many new movies, but loved the classics like *Dirty Dancing* and *Grease.* Emma Stone was a name Ollie wasn't familiar with, but she knew she would learn from Lacy on this trip soon enough. They were going to exotic places and going to watch amazing movies in different theatres.

"What do you think of Cruze?" Lacy asked, leaning back and smiling slyly at Ollie.

"What do you mean?"

"Do you like Cruze? He's a pretty nice guy, cares for you too," Ollie thought about it for a minute.

"I guess but I won't be seeing him for a long time so what can I do about it? Forget about him and just pray that some amazingly handsome guy from another country will ravish me," Lacy barked out in laughter.

"You'd know all about the ravishing," Lacy cackled.

"And you wish you knew more from Jason," Ollie nudged her friend, forgetting the fact that her experiences were less then excitable.

"You know it girl. We might have to come up with a code, a tie on the door knob means someone is getting busy," Lacy winked.

"Problem one; we don't have ties. Problem two; I am not getting busy, not in Queensland. Not while we are still in Australia. I'm waiting for some Bali or American action," Lacy laughed. "How about a hat on the door knob."

"Sounds like a plan," Lacy and Ollie cut their laughter as they heard their call for their flight go out. "Ready to go? Just think about whatever it was Cruze told you to think about."

"Casual conversations help, and some other stuff," Lacy winked at Ollie as she took the suggestive tone.

"You are going to get some when we get back," Lacy laughed, handing Ollie her flight ticket.

* * *

The flight went quickly with Ollie and Lacy laughing, taking the fear off the idea of flying in the air faster then humanly possible. Lacy updated Ollie on new aged actors, letting her know what was hot and wasn't hot at the moment by using the *Cleo* magazine.

Ollie and Lacy stepped off the plane got their bags and went to the hotel they were going to be staying in. Polly, Sarah, Martha, Jay, Harry and Liam were coming in a bit later in the day, letting Lacy and Ollie set up the apartment and pick what room they wanted.

The two friends got in a taxi; ready to go towards their hotel that would be their home for the next week. Ollie admired the way Surfers Paradise was set up and the way in which people moved about in such a casual yet purposeful manner.

Palm trees sat above the paved boardwalk that sat on the edge of the sand that opened up to the wide white beach. Girls in barely anything walked around watching boys looking the same with no tops on, checking the girls out. Ollie's face was plastered against the open window as she studied the way people interacted in a beach side city.

Lacy tugged on Ollie's arm, showing her the other side where the shops lay, people walking in and out with bags on their arms.

"You're like a kid in a candy shop," Lacy laughed at Ollie's wide eyes.

"It's all new to me, I can't say I've seen this before," she laughed as Lacy took hold of her hand.

"A new day, a new chapter. This is the beginning of the rest of our lives," Lacy smiled and hugged her best friend as they sat on the taxi, arriving at the hotel. "Thank you," Lacy thanked the driver as she got the bags and the two hurried inside to check in.

The room was quite large, an apartment like kitchen, lounge room, dinning table in an open planned living with two large master bedrooms with double beds, and two more rooms with two singles in one and three singles in the other. The decorations were rather simple, minimal. Three bathrooms stood in the apartment as well, making sure that everyone would have time to get ready during the day.

"What room do you want?" Lacy asked with excited eyes.

"Master?" Ollie winked.

"Alright but the code?"

"There is a single bed in another room that I can sleep on if need be," Ollie reasoned with a smile.

"This is going to be so much fun! Let's get settled, go shopping for food and then we can shop for clothes and then spend time on the beach," Lacy suggested and Ollie nodded her head.

"Sounds like a plan to me," Ollie and Lacy got to unpacking. A whistled rang through the apartment and Ollie dived on her phone to see who had messaged her.

Cruze: Did you arrive safely?

Ollie: Yeah we did. It is amazing up here.

Cruze: I knew you'd love it.

Ollie: I more then love it. Do you know how close the city is to the beach!

Ollie almost laughed at how childish her message sounded, but she guessed that Cruze knew he well enough not to judge her on her curious ways. Lacy smiled at her friends smitten face, guessing whom she was already talking to.

"How's Cruze?" she asked, nudging her friend.

"Fine, I mean we aren't talking about how we are. That's an 'in person' conversation," Lacy laughed, Ollie's bashful response was something quite different and therefore funny to Lacy. She felt good watching her best friend being able to talk to someone other then herself about things and the fact that Ollie had such strong feelings towards Cruze, not that she would act on them, Ollie was far too reasonable for that when they were going away.

"Yeah, you're right," she agreed, grabbing her bag and taking all the books and things she had used on the plane, leaving only her wallet, sunglasses, headphones and phone in the bag.

"Ready to get some food?"

"You bet."

* * *

Music was blasting around the beach, creating a partying environment for those gathered around on the sand. A bon fire was being started as the light started fading from the sky and the bright stars and moon appeared, creating a more natural and beautiful light. A full moon sat above the crowd that was slowly gathering. Girls stood in small tight dresses where their bikinis could be seen, while guys stood in board shorts, jeans and a top on, everyone had casual or no footwear, showing just how laidback the week was going to be.

A cool, refreshing feeling washed over Ollie as she stood on the balcony with the glass sliding door closed behind her. The feeling wasn't an odd, unfamiliar feeling, in fact Ollie was used to it. Once a month on the full moon this feeling of calm and power washed over her body, almost like the moon was giving her the will to carry on.

She had noticed it only happened when she could see the moon and it almost made her glow in the light. Her skin was clear, leaving Ollie with no makeup on her skin and her hair flowed in the most natural way down her back, finishing at the bottom of her hips. Her body was covered in a pair of high waisted; white-based floral shorts with a white singlet tucked in to the waist of the shorts.

Her deep blue eyes glowed in the moonlight, letting Ollie see unusually good details that littered the beach far below her. The way the white foam collected on the beach, the way small bubbles stuck together in the white foam and the way they were disrupted when people tumbled down onto the ground. A detail in which she shouldn't be able to see was almost natural in the way the world was working. Scars, freckles and marks on peoples skin was noticeable, even from the fourth floor of the building they were on.

"Ollie, are you ready?" the sound of the door opening escaped Ollie's attentive ears and she jumped in shock at hearing Jay's voice behind her.

"Yeah, I'll be in, in a second," she replied, turning with eyes half closed and a smile plastered on her lips.

"You alright?"

"Fine," Jay stepped out into the warm Queensland night air and closed the door behind him. The screeching of the plastic beneath the door closing vibrated within Ollie's ears, causing her to cringe.

"You sure? You always seem to do this. I'm not saying you're on your at your time but it has something to do with the same time every month," Ollie couldn't help the laughter that echoed out of her.

"I'm not on my 'time', don't worry."

"I'm not worried. I just want to make sure you are alright. You always avoid us like this, refusing to meet our eyes, refusing to even look at us," Ollie knew it was all true, she knew that her glowing eyes were something that she couldn't control but admitting that to others was something she wasn't ready for.

"I got new contacts and they kind of freak me out some times," she lied quickly.

"Let's see," Ollie lifted her head reluctantly and opened her eyes wide, revealing the deep blue glow within her eyes. Jay lifted her chin further, placing two fingers under her chin so their eyes met. His eyes widened in shock a bit as he first laid eyes on the glow that sat around Ollie's pupils.

"Do you always wear them?"

"No, I like to try to get used to them slowly. My doctor said once a month but you can see why they freak me out," Ollie saw something in Jay that she had never seen before. He knew she was lying and she knew he knew why her eyes glowed. He was lying to her; he was keeping something from her. Ollie didn't know how to feel about their normally open relationship being turned around with secrets.

"They look really cool," Jay finally concluded. Ollie moved her eyes away from Jay's light hazel eyes and scanned his calm, smooth face.

"Don't lie to me Jay. I couldn't stand it if you out of all people lied to me," reluctance covered Jay's face but he said nothing. "I get it," Ollie walked off and back inside, blocking out the screeching of the sliding door out of her mind.

"Ready to rock this beach party?" Lacy asked, jumping up to her friend.

"You better believe it!" Ollie covered her sad emotions as she saw everyone in the lounge room with smiles on their faces. "Just needed the warm air to get me in the mood. Let me just fix my make up and I'll be out in a second," Ollie walked into the room she was sharing with Lacy and through the room towards the ensuite that they were going to be sharing.

Ollie stood looking in the mirror, staring at her glowing eyes. The hairs on her arms stood on edge as she placed a deep pink hat on her head with a silk ribbon around the base. Ollie couldn't remember the last time she had felt so unsure of herself, so uneven in her thinking.

$200,000. I was worth two hundred thousand dollars. One hour. Two hundred thousand dollars. Turns out I was making up for being born after all.

A man in a dark suit and top hat strolled over out from the dark shadows of the room. The fire crackled beyond the groans of failure and loss. The other men in the room hated the fact that they would have to wait their turn to use me and the fact that I would already have been used at least once before.

The man I knew so well, the man who had pocketed the money, stood over me with a wicked grin on his face. Those dark eyes stared down at me with knowing in them and malice behind the first window the most could see.

"You have one hour. There is a timer and I will not hesitate to stop you if your time is up and you refuse to come out," his deep voice echoed around the room, laying down the rules for everyone to hear. He ran his fingers through his short dark hair, letting it stand up in disarray.

"Come on pretty thing," the man in the top hat had a deep southern accent. He grabbed me by my forearm, dragging me into the already prepared room. He locked the door behind us with an evil grin slowly forming around his cracked and yellowing teeth, tobacco was clear on his breath.

My hairs stood on edge as he pulled the top hat off and started to undo his black tie. Fear came over me as I stared at the man slowly undressing in front of me in the dark mood lighting.

"I want a show. A quick game is a good game."

Composing herself, Ollie shook her head, tapped a little blush on her cheeks and covered her lips in light pink, pale lipstick before heading out with a fake smile on her lips. Everyone sat with a drink in their hands and smiles on their lips as they saw Ollie come out.

"Ready to get your groove on?" she asked. A chorus of 'woo's' boomed around the apartment as everyone placed their drinks down and got ready to go out. The girls grabbed their bags and the guys checked that they had their wallets in their pockets.

"I like to move it move it!" Lacy called out.

"You like to move it move it!" Martha continued.

"We like to," Polly waited.

"Move it!" Sarah finished and everyone laughed as the door closed behind them, locking immediately, causing Ollie's steps to falter.

CHAPTER TEN

Don't You Understand? When You Give Up Your Dream, You Die

CRUZE ARRIVED AT the airport not long after Jason, catching an earlier flight to be with Ollie for longer then a few days before she left. Enakal had been sure that he could handle things without his second there to help him along.

Jason had waited outside in the sun while Cruze got his things from the airport and met him at the taxi rank. Jason's hands were shaking at the thought of seeing Lacy again. It'd only been a day and yet he felt as though he was dying on the inside, he had no idea how he was going to last a year. Maybe he'd follow the two girls on their trip around the world just to make sure they didn't get into any trouble, but knowing those two, they would.

"I think they are going to be hung over," Cruze appeared behind Jason, causing him to jump as he was pulled from his thoughts.

"All but Ollie," Jason and Ollie had formed a good friendship as Lacy's friends. They got along great and used that to find out information about Lacy and each other.

"Why?"

"Ollie doesn't drink," Jason was staring to wonder what Cruze and Ollie spoke about when they were together, but he guessed a lot of talking didn't go on. "Do you talk to her at all?"

"Yes," Cruze punched Jason's shoulder. "I have to keep my distance or she'll suspect something."

"I think something's have already been suspected. You think these emotions are normal?" Jason was almost in shock that Cruze thought it was such an easy thing to push aside. "You really need to get a check. If she is what you say she is, then I think you need to be open about it. She needs to know about all of this Cruze. You cannot keep hiding this. Enakal needs to understand that she had the right to know about her past," Jason waved down a taxi and put the suitcases in the boot before jumping in with Cruze.

"This isn't something you just tell someone."

"Why not? Lacy knows, Matt now knows. I don't see why you cannot tell her. I'd imagine that Ollie would take all this information quite well; she's a bright young girl. At what age do you think she's going to find out if you don't tell her? I give it a year or two before it all unravels. Imagine if you didn't know anything about your life and then it was dropped on you, only because of your age. I'd want to know a lot earlier," Cruze thought about what Jason was saying.

"You want to have the conversation?"

"I've already had that conversation, buddy. It's your turn," Cruze groaned at that thought. "At least you are surprising her today."

"Yeah, but I think she thinks I'm seeing someone else," Jason shook his head.

"You're an idiot."

"And you need to stop stating the obvious."

* * *

Ollie sat on the balcony facing the road and beach with Lady Chatterley's Lover in her hand. A simple pale blue and pink summer dress that was halter neck with a v-neck drop that came in at the waist sat on Ollie's petite body. Her legs were propped up on another chair as the sun soaked into her skin, warming her whole body.

A wide brimmed straw hat sat on top of her head, keeping her dyed red hair off her face. Ollie had tied her hair into a low pony tail at the base of her head, letting it flow down the back of the chair and out of the way.

Ollie could see a bright yellow taxi pull up at the front of the building on the main road and watched two tall, well-built guys get out. Her jaw almost dropped as she realized who it was.

"Lacy!" Ollie called through the open sliding door that led into the master bedroom the two were sharing.

"What?" a grumpy voice called from the bed.

"Come out here."

"No! I'm sleeping!"

"Sleeping Beauty, come here. Now!" Ollie could here the floor boards move as Lacy jumped off the bed and slowly made her way to the balcony. "Now look over the edge and tell me what you see," a few seconds of looking and Ollie could hear Lacy gasp with excitement.

"Oh, my, gosh!" Lacy pulled her hair into a ponytail, grabbed Ollie's hand, the room key and the two ran downstairs to greet Jason and Cruze.

The two guys were barely in the reception area when Lacy and Ollie plowed into them. Lacy attached herself to Jason after letting Ollie's hand go at the elevator. Ollie awkwardly walked up to Cruze, not knowing if she should hug him or what to do.

"Come here," Cruze stalked Ollie and pulled her into his arms. Ollie inhaled the amazing smell that rolled off Cruze; that fresh rain smell in the forest near the beach. It was something Ollie was starting to fall in love with.

Cruze rested his chin on Ollie's head and closed his eyes as he soaked up the feeling of this small girl in his arms. Old books and lavender made it's way up into Cruze's nose and a small smile fell onto his lips; old books along with lavender was suddenly his favourite smell on the world.

"I thought you weren't coming for a few more days?" Ollie asked, pulling away from Cruze's strong hold so she could look up into his light crystal eyes.

"I wasn't but I needed to talk to you and see you. I changed my flight and came to see you earlier," Ollie didn't know how to respond to that. She hadn't expected such honesty from Cruze who was usually very reserved with expressing his emotions.

"Do you have a room here?"

"Yeah, a small apartment for the two of us and two others when they come up tomorrow."

"Who are they?"

"Josh and Drake. Old friends."

"Like the show on Nickelodeon?" Ollie joked with a wink.

"No," Cruze kept a straight face, something Ollie was used to with the emotionless tall guy. Ollie had learnt not to judge on the way people experienced emotions differently, if was something she herself did quite often.

"Well do you want to go unpack and get settled and then we can go out for lunch?"

"Yeah, sounds good to me," Cruze and Jason were on the same level as Ollie and Lacy, making the rest of the week easy. Their apartment was similar to Ollie and Lacy's but only had three bedrooms with two bathrooms, a smaller floor plan.

Ollie left Cruze to settle and half an hour later he was knocking on their door, ready to take her out to lunch somewhere in town. A small café on the beach stood out for the two and Cruze and Ollie took a seat on the sand.

The heated sun sizzled down on the couple as they sipped at some water. Ollie was waiting for Cruze to bring up what he wanted to talk about, while her head was going around what he could possible want to talk to her about. Ollie barely had time to ask before they ordered and waited for Cruze to bring it up.

"OK, so we need to talk."

"I gathered that one. But the real question here it; what do we need to talk about?" Ollie asked being a complete smart arse, which brought a smile to Cruze's lips.

"Us. I want to know what we are and what I mean to you."

"Have you ever watched a fairytale?" the question seemed random to Cruze, but he was used to that when it came to being around Ollie.

"Yes."

"Have you ever noticed that the guy confessed his love first and is always the one to start the 'feelings' conversation," the meaning behind her words finally hit Cruze and he realized Ollie wanted him to be the first to say how he felt.

"I want to give you this," Cruze pulled a silk bag out of his pocket and placed it on the table, slowly pulling the silk ribbon that would open the bag up. Inside, covered in paper, was a sterling silver ring that had a single small, understated diamond in the centre.

"Cruze, what is this?" Ollie didn't know what to think.

"This is me asking you a very specific question, after I tell you something that may make you hate me."

"If you are going to ask me to marry you, then I think you need to realize that I am only eighteen and you are?"

"I'm twenty-two. In your years," Ollie's eyebrows furrowed.

"'My years'? Don't tell me you are some sort of freaky Vampire-Elf thing," her eyes narrowed at she studied Cruze's perfect face. Somehow that didn't seem so far fetched now. A bark of laughter caused Ollie to rethink the idea as Cruze tried to hide his smile.

"I am not an Elf or Vampire, or a cross. Believe me. Elf's are quite, how do I put this, secretive and shady. Vampires are just stupid," the way Cruze spoke about the mythical creatures had Ollie question the sanity of the guy sitting opposite her.

"I am starting to think you have run away from a mental asylum."

"Nope, completely sane and what some would consider 'Mythical'," Ollie shook her head, trying to understand what he was on about.

"You need to be less cryptic in what you are saying."

"OK. You know how Ancient Egyptians worshiped a cross between animals and humans?"

"I did history, so yes," Ollie was getting a bit bored with this.

"Well do you know why?"

"Because they believed those gods were the creators of the world?" her eyebrows furrowed at her own answer because it felt too simple.

"Because they were real. Anubis, the god of death, afterlife and mummification. Anubis was pictured as human with a wolf's head. His daughter Kebeechet was the goddess of purification through water. She was quite helpful to her father with giving water to the spirits while they waited for mummification," Ollie listened as Cruze rattled off a history lesson.

"I don't mean to sound rude, but why are you telling me this?" their food arrived and the two got stuck in, keeping up the conversation.

"Because this relates to you."

"How?"

"Jane and Greg. They belong in this too, but they are not who you think they are."

"No, quite honestly, I think I know them a little bit better then you know them because I've spent eighteen years with them," Ollie started in a matter-of-fact voice.

"You haven't known them for eighteen years. You've known them for sixteen years," Ollie eyed Cruze off sideways. "They aren't your real parents."

Numb. I felt numb. My body was tired, my eyes were heavy and I couldn't believe what I had just been through. The dark room was now empty, the fire was out and the only sounds were those outside the door.

"Get up!" a loud booming voice called through the door as I took a seat on the plush chair that was seated opposite the dead fire.

Numb. I still felt numb. There were no feelings within my body. Nothing.

"I want you out here now. Dancing. You still owe me," I nodded my head in compliance but my whole body was tired along with my mind.

Skin on skin woke me up as I fell on the ground, pain vibrating through my back. I could feel the beat of the slow erotic music through the polished floorboards I was now pressed against.

"You still owe me," he said again as he pulled my long dyed hair and pulled me up off the ground. A sharp stabbing pain was felt through my head as I was raised to my feet. "Now dance," I knew it was an order so I dragged my body to the stage where I changed to a barely there purple sparkling top and purple undies. Chains attached the two together, making them clink every time I moved exotically.

"Are you serious?" Ollie almost didn't believe what Cruze was saying, yet something deep inside her was begging her to listen and believe him. "I know they aren't good people, but you can't just go around saying things like that Cruze. I was not kidnapped as a child," Ollie stood to leave the table, barely touching her meal.

"What features are the same? You don't look anything like them," Cruze put his hand in his pocket, pulling out his wallet and dragging out an old picture. "I never said you were kidnapped either," Ollie turned around and walked back to the table, picking up the picture harshly. "You never had pictures of you when you were a baby," Ollie was struck hard by these facts that came pouring out of Cruze's mouth.

Everything was true. Ollie looked nothing like her parents and had never seen photos of her when she was a baby, two years or younger. There were so many memories of her past that were hazy from a certain age.

"What is this?" Ollie threw the photo of a dark haired man and light haired lady with long locks that feel down her back, the same length as Ollie's. Light eyes stared back at her from the photo, the man with silver eyes and the lady with light blue eyes, much the same as Ollie's when she was younger, from what she could tell.

A little girl stood in the middle of the two, a very small young girl with long light locks that fell down her back. She had a pretty red dress on that stopped at her shins with white lace over the top and white frilly socks and white shoes.

"Who is this?" the young girls deep blue eyes stared at Ollie, reflecting the light from the sun when the photo was taken.

"The man is Enakal and his wife Arabella," Ollie kept staring at the picture, trying to see how this related to her. The little girl at the front stood awkwardly, like standing and walking was something new to her. All three were looking past the camera with large smiles on their faces.

"Who is the little girl?"

"Their daughter, Olyanah," Ollie's world stopped as the words were spoken. She had seen the same blue eyes many times before in old photo albums her 'parents' had kept away in their room. Once Ollie had snuck in, forgetting the wrath from her parents, and found them in a locked box. Getting to see young Ollie for the first time in her life.

"I think you need to really think about your delivery before you talk to me again," Ollie kept the photo in her hand as she walked out on Cruze.

* * *

Ollie slammed the door to the apartment closed and cried out, not even checking to see if anyone else was there. She knelt down on her knees in the lounge room, covering her face with her hands as she dropped the photo on the floor in front of her.

"Ol," Ollie looked up and saw Jay standing topless in his bedroom doorframe. "What's wrong?"

"You!" she stood up, pointing her finger at Jay. "You knew! You knew and you didn't say anything! How long have you known?" the accusing tone in Ollie's voice had Jay stepping back with his hands up in defense. She felt as though the way he had acted the night before had something to do with what Cruze had told her today.

Although she didn't want to believe it, she could see that there was a bit of truth behind everything she had been told. Her mind refused to believe it but her heart and emotions were telling her that everything was true and there was no way around it.

"Knew what?"

"Knew that Jane and Greg aren't my real parents! You knew and you had the chance to say something last night. You lied to me Jay! You lied to me!" Ollie grabbed a pillow off the couch and threw it hard at Jay, with much more force then she had originally thought she had.

"What the fuck?" Jay cried back, thanking his quick reflexes for dodging the pillow.

"You know exactly 'what the fuck'! You could've said something, you could've told me! You had every chance! How long have you known, Jay?" Ollie's voice went from yelling to a low ground out tone. "How long have you known? Answer me," the question was left hanging as Ollie waited for Jay to answer her.

"A while," his soft voice had Ollie's skin boiling.

"A while! That is all you have to say?"

"Fine! Since I was eighty-seven," Ollie picked up another pillow and threw it at Jay.

"I said don't lie to me Jay!" the door to Ollie and Lacy's door opened and Lacy and Jason walked out.

"What the hell is going on here?" Lacy cried out looking at the scene in front of her. Ollie stood with several pillows in her hand while Jay shielded his body with hands up. Lacy's eyes were wide as she tried to understand what was going on. "I asked what was going on. Now tell me!"

"Apparently there is more then one person in the world that knows about my past. Knows that Jane and Greg are not my real parents," Lacy stepped back and stared at Jay.

"Come again," Jason placed a hand on Lacy's shoulder but she yanked it away.

"Do not touch me if you knew about this," Lacy stepped back and walked towards Ollie with evil in her eyes, directed right at Jason. "Did you know about this?" the small nod of his head had her fuming. Lacy stood next to Ollie with her arms crossed over her chest, defying Jason.

"Don't, Lacy," Jason's voice was low and deep, authority dripping from his words.

"Don't you dare try and use that voice on me! You said I was your equal, you said I was the same as you. Don't Jason. Just don't," Jason tried to raise his voice, getting rid of the authority but it seemed almost impossible when he was feeling this angry at Lacy not wanting his touch.

"Lacy."

"Don't 'Lacy' me you son of a bitch!" Lacy cried, grabbing a pillow from Ollie and throwing it with force at Jason. Jason dodged the pillow easily, catching it in his hand and holding it next to his head where he caught it.

"Lacy," Jason warned. The front door of the apartment slammed open and loud noises travelled in, followed by a familiar group of people. Martha stopped everyone as they walked in, taking in the scene in front of them.

"So, what's new?" Polly asked, looking over Martha's shoulder.

"Apparently these people are serial liars!" Ollie cried out.

"Shut up, Olyanah and listen to me!" Ollie turned around as Cruze made his way through the group and stood near her.

"Don't you dare come near me," Ollie warned, holding a couch pillow in front of her body as protection. "Stay away from me, Cruze!" Ollie called.

"Just listen to me!"

"No!"

"Listen to me, Olyanah!"

"No!" Ollie threw the pillow on the ground and marched out of the apartment, avoiding touching everyone else. Lacy was hot on her heels, leaving the apartment so they could clear their heads from everything.

* * *

Ollie and Lacy sat on a bench on the pavement that was overlooking the beach where a volleyball game was on. People cheered every time a point was scored and the two girls admired the fit guys in board shorts as they ran around on the sand.

So many thoughts were running through the girl's minds as they tried to process them all together.

"Did you know Jane and Greg weren't my parents?" Ollie asked, expecting only the truth.

"No. I knew there was something different about you, Jason told me not long after I met him when we were shopping for formal dresses, but I didn't know you were adopted," not once did the two girls look at each other, just stared out at the volleyball game and the ocean.

"What's different about me and don't start talking about Anubis," Ollie warned.

"Well it's all true. I know you don't want to hear it but we are different," Ollie listened quietly as Lacy spoke. "Anubis was half human and half wolf. In Ancient Egypt, long before time was recorded, werewolves were created," Lacy reached into the bag that she had grabbed before leaving and pulled a book out. The book was bound in brown leather with a 3D stone image of Anubis of the front.

"What is this?"

"This is the book of Werewolves. Just read it please. It will explain at lot, Princess," Ollie raised her eyebrows at Lacy as she took the book. It was as though light filled Ollie up and the book glowed in front of her.

"You know I hate it when people are cryptic, Lacy," Ollie wasn't amused by what was going on around her.

"I know, but sometimes it is the only way to get someone to understand. Just understand that you are so special, to yourself and all of us. Be careful, Ol, there are people out there that want to take advantage of what you have, but you cannot let them, no matter what happens, do not give up,"

Lacy got up from the bench, leaving Ollie to think about what he long time friend had just told her.

Worthless. I was worthless. I was completely and utterly worthless. No one cared what happened to me or if I died. No one thought any different if I made it out alive of this. Especially not the man I called father.

"Ollie, please let me explain," Ollie was slowly flipping through the thick old pages of the book in front of her. Every time she touched it, she was scared that the book would break, tear or disappear from her hands.

Cruze stood above her before realizing that she was in her own world for the time being. Ollie's eyes were glassed over as she robotically looked at each page in detail. Cruze knew the book she was holding well. It was history in her hands, a history no one would believe.

Every vein could be seen by Ollie, every crinkle that sat uneven in the thick old pages. The front page curved into Ollie's palm perfectly, like the stone ornament on the front was made for her to hold in her delicate hands. The pages smelt of old spices, herbs and something else Ollie couldn't make out.

Cruze sat down on the bench and waved his hand in front of Ollie's face to get her attention away from the wonderful book that had spoken to Cruze long ago.

"Ollie, please talk to me."

"What do you want me to say, Cruze? Honestly, what do you expect from me because all this information is a lot to take in. One minute I'm being told I am adopted or kidnapped or whatever and the people I grew up with are actually fakes, and then the next I am being handed a book about ancient Werewolf's that has 'something to do with me'," Ollie handed the book to Cruze forcefully. "Have you read this before?"

"Yes."

"I'm not going to ask if it is a true story because I don't want to know, but what I do want to know is why did it happen? Why was I adopted out? Why?"

"Because it wasn't safe for you in our world. You would've been in danger and we couldn't have that. After two years it was shown to us that you were not safe and none of us wanted to put you in that danger," Ollie turned her complete attention to Cruze as she waited for him to tell her more.

"So you erased my mind?"

"No! Never, we just gave you to Jane and Greg. We thought that they would take care of you. Love you like their own. They were the best fit for you at the time; Greg seemed so caring and fatherly, always had been with younger children. Jane, Jane was so lovely, so kind," Ollie couldn't help the laughter the came out of her at the false description.

"They are horrible people, Cruze. Horrible people. People that deserve to die a painful death," Cruze was shocked at Ollie's description.

"I knew they weren't always there in your life, Sally and Charles made sure we knew what was going on when you and Lacy became friends, but don't you think that is a bit extreme Olyanah?"

"No. I can honestly say it is not extreme, Cruze. You live my life for a week and tell me I am overreacting," Ollie stood up and looked down at Cruze. "I never had a bed of roses or anything handed to me on a silver platter. Instead I was the girl that slept on a bed of nails and always made up food on a wooden platter. I wouldn't expect you to understand something like that Cruze. But understand that I just want them out of my life for good."

"What is your dream?"

"Excuse me?"

"What do you want to do in life? What do you want out of life?"

"I want to be happy, I want to be carefree and I want to dream everyday. I want to act, but I cannot do any of that if you people keep telling me that I am adopted or given away or that it is unsafe for me to even be alive. You hand me a book telling me about the history of Werewolf's, what does it even mean, Cruze?"

"Don't you understand, Olyanah? When you give up on your dream, you die. Don't ever give up on your dream. Promise me you will never give up on your dream and you won't die," Cruze handed the book back to Ollie and walked away, leaving her wondering what Cruze was on about.

Chapter Eleven

Learn The Rules Like A Pro, So You Can Break Them Like An Artist

OLLIE AND LACY tried to spend the rest of the week trying to avoid Cruze, Jason and their two friends Drake and Josh. They seemed like a ball of fun and the girls wanted to get to know them more but it was hard with being angry at Cruze and Jason.

Lacy was taking it the hardest that Jason had been in on it all but being, as she called 'mates', and being away from each other for a long period of time made them go a little crazy.

Ollie was feeling the same about Cruze, but because she refused to him about what happened, she sat with the book of Anubis and remembered the smells Cruze had told her about and that got her through the rest of week. And watching him surf everyday, which helped too.

Ollie and Lacy hugged everyone, despite a rough week they had made up with all their friends, Ollie and Jay were still on thin ice but they were talking, an improvement in the eyes of their friends.

"We will see each other again. One year and we will all meet at the local!" Lacy cried out as she hugged Polly.

"One year and we will all meet at the local. One year people!" Ollie cried out in agreement as tears poured from her eyes. Harry embraced Ollie's small form, lifting her up off the ground and twirling her around.

"We will all miss you two!" Liam said as he hugged Lacy. Ollie looked over the room at Jay, who stood with his arms over his chest and a small smile on his lips. Ollie didn't know if she should go over and hug Jay goodbye, or if she was still too angry with him to hug him.

"Ol," Lacy appeared at her side. "Just say goodbye and then at least you won't feel bad," Ollie understood where Lacy was coming from but her emotions were clouding her better judgment. "Do it, Ollie," Ollie nodded her head and walked over to where Jay was standing on the edge of the group.

"I really am sorry, Ollie," Jay dropped his arms from his chest, opening his stance and showing that he wasn't angry or upset.

"I know you are, but you can understand why I'm so upset can't you? You lied to me and I don't know how I'll be able to forgive that quickly. I love you, Jay, you're like a brother to me and that will never change but this won't go away so easily."

"I know it won't but I love you too and I really do hope you have a good trip," Ollie reached up and embraced Jay in a warm hug.

"I will. I'll see you in a year?"

"You can bet your life on it," Jay kissed Ollie's cheek before Lacy broke up the moment.

"How touching! Our resident flirts have made up! Now as much as I love that you two are talking again, Ollie and I need to head off and start the rest of our lives together," Lacy winked at Ollie as she gathered her suitcases. "Pun intended of course."

The airport was a buzz with activity as Ollie and Lacy walked up to the check in counter where they could get their tickets and finally start their lives. Lacy got a message from her mum as they were waiting in line and almost fell over as she read it.

"Oh my god!"

"What?"

"Oh my god!"

"Lacy, what?" Lacy handed her phone to Ollie and let her read the message Sally had sent.

Sally Larkin: Hello my dear girls! We are missing you very much and have a surprise for you! Papa C and I have arranged for you two to take a bit of a detour. Just tell the lady at the ticket desk that 'We're the two you have been waiting for'.

Ollie and Lacy looked at each other with shocked expressions. What exactly could Sally and Charles have in store for Ollie and Lacy as they waited in line. Finally they reached the front, bouncing on the balls of their feet to keep themselves from exploding with excitement.

"How can I help you?" the lady asked with a smile on her face.

"Apparently we have to say 'We're the two you have been waiting for'," Lacy said with a wide grin on her face.

"Lacy Larkin and Olyanah Kent?" the two girls nodded their heads. The lady started pressing things on the keyboard of her computer and asked for their passports. Checking everything over, the lady printed two tickets as Ollie and Lacy pushed their suitcases onto the conveyor belt. "Here you go," eager, the two girls tried to look at the destination on the ticket, but instead were greeted with '*Unknown Destination*'.

"This is so exciting," Lacy cried as they went to a café with their carry on backpacks. "Who would've thought our plans would be thrown up like this. OK, it is investigation time. Mama S and Papa C have been to Europe and America so it leaves a lot of places up for debate about where we are going."

"They would send us somewhere they've been because they know it is good there. What states and countries?" Lacy started rattling off names of countries and states as the two sat and eat before going to the gate where their mystery flight awaited them.

Phoenix, Arizona.

Ollie and Lacy were going to Phoenix, Arizona.

Home of some of arguably the best botanic gardens, museums and the chase fields.

"Never leaving. You are never leaving because the minute you leave, I lose my income and I refuse to be poor. I refuse to be like you," I hit the floor with a loud thud and soon was left in the fetal position as a steel-toed shoe hit my stomach.

"Stop now. Please," a small voice cried from somewhere in the shadows. I knew the voice and hated it whenever she called out. This was a battle that she could have fought but chose to stand on the edge and cheer for the wrong team. This was not going to be forgotten in my eyes. No way in hell. Even as I lay in pain I know for a fact that she was of course at fault here.

"Shut up! You do not get to change your mind whenever it suits you. You chose this as much as I did," I cringed as their fighting started. I had heard this way too much and had learnt to block my ears whenever they started one of their mini battles in our large war.

She wanted to help, but she had waited too long and now it was far too late to try and help what had happened to me and what was going to happen in the future.

A purple gomphrena of the amaranth group, angraecum and arbutus branch sat on the two different chairs on the plane. Ollie read the ticket and saw that they were the two seats Ollie and Lacy were to be sitting in.

"What are they? I do not want a freaking forest in my seat," Lacy looked over Ollie's shoulder as she saw the flowers.

"Lac, those purple bulb flowers symbolize immortal love. The dark green branch thing means royalty, no idea why that is there and then the branch with the dark green leaves, red bulbs and yellow buds means 'You are the only one I love'. Small feeling these are from Cruze and Jason," Lace curled her nose up at the flowers.

"I am going to write him."

"We don't live in the 50's, you can just call him," Ollie removed the flowers and put them in the pouch of the chair in front of her, taking her seat. "You don't have to say anything. I know it is easier writing things down instead of saying them," Lacy didn't fully understand what Ollie meant, but she took her word for it and pulled a note book out of her bag with a pen so she could start writing.

Ollie opened the old book she had been given by Cruze for the first time since she had gotten it. Something was still screaming at her from the book, something inside was begging for Ollie to read what was written on the pages and discover its secrets.

> Plures annos rerum confusa. Aegyptum Nilus amnis stetit, his dantem semina aquarum viventium tulit Nilus amnis in villas.
>
> Cibum et potum populus paulatim deficiebat, omnia prospiciens Denique cum copia et dolore deos eorum factum est.
>
> ANUBIS ipsum dolor observantes populus venit ad eum salva animam pro solutione.
>
> Nilus amnis mansit populi consona lupi brevi vita opus sunt lupi cum adeo ut propter cibum. Populus multus cibus necessarius. Cibum capere non poterant populum suum cibum quaerendum, quam citius posset lupis.
>
> ANUBIS ascendit cum idea trahendum duo pariter. Hominum luporum id genus est superior et alia faciendi.
>
> Omnis luna plena, per menses singulos, a pauci populus in se derivare Nilus amnis. Lupus et mutamur in forma humana se redituros mane humana forma naturali plane nudum. Qui novam venántium adducerem tergum eorum et alat occiditis totum quod villiage appositis Nilus amnis.
>
> Postquam docti homines maiores vires continere, iam non haberent in lupos converti ad auditum et visum lupum.
>
> Donec Nilus amnis erat absconditus sumpto, novum manere, ne gens illi ligula.

(Many, many years ago the world was in chaos. Egypt stood on the Nile river, giving water to those plants that gave life to those living in the villages around the river Nile.

Slowly people were running out of food and water, everything was in short supply and the Gods looked down with pain at what had happened to their people.

Anubis watched with real sorrow before the solution of saving his people came to him mind.

Wolves lived in harmony with the people on the river Nile, but soon they needed those wolves they lived so closely with as a source of food.

Food that was much needed by the people. The people were unable to catch their own food as quickly as the wolves could hunt for their food.

Anubis came up with the idea of pulling the two together. Humans and wolves, creating a species that would be superiour then all others.

Every full moon, every month, a select few people on the River Nile would shift. They would change forms from human to wolf and in the morning they would go back to human, completely in their natural form, naked. Those new form of hunters would bring their kill back and feed the whole villiage that was set on the River Nile.

Soon those selected people learnt to control their powers, and soon they wouldn't have to turn into wolves to have wolf hearing and sight.

Unfortunately the river Nile was over taken and the new tribe had to stay hidden for fear of those people around the world.)

Ollie's hands were shaking as she read the old Latin words in front of her. Every work ran true in her heart, but in her head it seemed almost impossible. It wasn't some type of bible; instead it was almost like a history book.

Ollie wasn't a religious person, but she felt she thought they way people felt when they read the bible and were enlightened. A pure sense of relief washed over Ollie, and at the same time a sense of dread. Was leaving Cruze like that such a bad idea? Did she need to go back?

"Lacy?"

"Yeah?" Ollie had to tap Lacy on the shoulder to get her attention as she had her headphones in, listening to music as she wrote her letter to Jason.

"Can I have some paper and a pen?" Lacy handed Ollie a few pieces of paper and a four pen. With that, Ollie pulled the tray table down and started writing a letter to Cruze, which she would mail the minute they landed.

Ollie began writing down her feelings in a rushed letter, along with why she was angry and how she felt when reading Anubis's book. Everything was rushed when writing it, but Ollie was already feeling a lot better about expressing her feelings and emotions.

Not long later the captain announced that they were landing in Phoenix and everyone had to set their seats in an upright position. Ollie's hands shook nervously as she felt the plane slowly descending in the air.

The two best friends sat in the taxi on the journey towards the hotel Sally and Charles had booked for them. *Waldorf Astoria* was the most beautiful five star hotel that had been booked. Ollie and Lacy got a private suite for this amazing experience.

Phoenix was already shinning in Ollie's eyes, showing her that the world had so much more to offer her then what it had already shown. So many unseen sights the world had kept hidden from her for such a long time and now it was starting to open its wings and let her see the what was underneath the surface.

"Do you want to go out for lunch? Do a little bit of exploring?" Ollie asked as they walked into the lavish suite they were being given.

"Hells yes!" Lacy jumped up and down as she danced around the suite. It wasn't too big of a suite, a room with two beds, a lounge room and a dinning table along with a small beautiful looking kitchen.

"Get changed then, because we look and smell like airport," Ollie laughed, throwing a towel at Lacy.

"Speak for yourself. It was your first time; it rubs off on you a lot more," Lacy let out a cruel cackle of a laugh as she pulled off her leggings and jumper and changed into a pair of black jeans with a white long sleeve, and a flowery scarf around her neck. It was a lot colder in Phoenix then back at home in Melbourne so the girls weren't used to dressing for the cool weather.

Ollie changed into a high neck pale blue dress that buttoned up at the front and had a flower pattern at the bottom of the dress. It sat just above the knees and had a cute collar at the top and three quarter length sleeves. Ollie added black stockings and small-heeled baby pink strapped shoes.

Looking very retro, Ollie smiled at Lacy before grabbing her bag leaving the door open for Lacy.

"Like the gentleman you are," Lacy laughed, poking out her tongue.

"Hey, Lac?"

"Yeah?"

"Did we make a mistake leaving so soon after everything?"

"I don't know. Honestly, I don't know," the two girls went down into the streets of Phoenix in silence, amazed at how in sync their thoughts were.

Ollie and Lacy walked around with arms full of shopping bags as they explored the amazing shops in Phoenix. So many different brands were lining the shopping strip, something Ollie and Lacy had never seen before in their lives.

Although Lacy had done some travelling, she had never experienced something quite so grand. It was a new experience in both their eyes; Ollie felt as though she was finally able to experience the world that had been placed in front of her, and Lacy felt as though she was finally able to see her best friend free from what had been holding her back.

Lacy didn't know what Ollie had been going through, she had a vague idea that there was something Ollie wasn't telling her, but she was never going to push her into sharing, she knew Ollie needed to just open up in her own time.

A small, hidden café stood at the end of the long strip of shops and Ollie and Lacy took a seat, ordering some food and water.

"Lacy, how long have you know about Anubis?"

"Not long. You know when I found out. The day you got your new phone," Ollie nodded her head.

"Is it true?"

"Yes. I stormed home and forced mum and dad to tell me more about it and Matt as well. I didn't know you were adopted, or kidnapped, or whatever, but I know you are something more," Ollie waited for Lacy to continue. "You are what some would consider 'Princess' or 'Royal' in the eyes of the pack. Cruze is Beta, better then second in the pack, after the Alpha or King but not better then him, whatever you want to call him."

"If I am what you call Princess, then why would you not make the connection that Jane and Greg are not my parents if they are not the Alpha's?"

"Because I put that you were Princess in my mind, I was only told you were Royal. I figured Jane and Greg were Royal somewhere down the line. After I read Anubis, I started writing a few things down the I noticed and figured it out on the plane once you started reading," Lacy pulled a notebook out of her bag and handed them to Ollie.

Watching her read over them causing Lacy's heart to speed up. Ollie's numb, weak expression was giving nothing away, showing Lacy that Ollie was now immune to the lying and that killed her inside.

"I'm sorry, Ollie."

"It's in the past," Ollie shook it off, "It's in the past. There is nothing you can change about it now," Ollie remembered sending off her letter to Cruze, hoping he would call or write back when he got it.

"You sure."

"Positive," Ollie handed the notebook back, not wanting to look at it anymore, upset for not working it out earlier herself. She was glad, though, that she had Lacy to be there for her no matter what.

* * *

Ollie sat on the edge of her bed, her phone sitting in her lap as she waited for it to start ringing with *Fun.'s* The Gambler, Cruze's personalized ring tone. Jason had called Lacy and was on the phone to her at the moment, but Lacy had kindly informed her friend that Cruze had received the letter and was desperate to call the dyed red head.

"Slow down, we've got time left to be lazy, all the kids have bloomed from babies," Ollie dived on the big green accept button, hearing the song start on her phone, and slid it across to answer it.

"Hello?" she asked, head up high, standing and walking towards the window, which overlooked a beautiful garden and courtyard that had been created at the hotel.

"Salve, quam pulchra es? (Hello, how are you beautiful?)" Cruze's deep manly voice came through the receiver. Butterflies entered Ollie's stomach as she heard his voice.

"Sum bonus, quomodo? Quomodo Sancti Ludovici et Rosewood est? (I'm good, how are you? How is Saint Louis and Rosewood?)"

"All was well here until I got a letter begging me to think about what I had done and also to tell me that I am loved," Ollie took a deep breath in. "You can't do that, Ol, not after everything. It's not fair on me and it's not fair on you when you are so far away from me. I never wanted you to leave."

"I've been planning this for three years. I wasn't going to let some guy make me stay back in the one place I had been desperate to leave for so long," the conversation was infuriating Ollie, as many conversations with Cruze usually did.

"Some guy? One minute you love me and the next minute I'm some guy?" the outrage was evident in his voice.

"Love isn't real Cruze! There is no such thing!"

"Yes there is! It's real for you and me and it is real for mates, which is what we are. Why would you want to leave your family? Why would you want to leave me?"

"I've never seen real love. I've seen Sally and Charles, that is as close as I have gotten to real love, but I've never been in a loving home and after a week of knowing you, I am not prepared to say I love you or leave everything behind for you. You dropped a bombshell on me, Cruze, you cannot expect me to just accept everything and take it on face value. It's not something that is easy to believe."

"Do you believe it now?"

"I honestly don't know, Cruze. I honestly don't know," the answer hung in the air, waiting for someone to break the killer silence that was being exchanged between the two.

"Let me know when you believe me," Ollie knew he was about to hang up on her.

"Don't you dare say that to me! If this was dropped on you, I am more then positive you would explode in a crazy volcano of anger, so don't hang up on me just because I am skeptical about what I'm being told. Don't you dare quit on me, Cruze. Ever."

"You know I won't. I wouldn't dare quit on my mate. Ever," the definity in Cruze's tone had Ollie trying to suppress a smile.

"Good."

"I love you, Olyanah. Whether you believe in love or not, I love you. Now be careful over there. You are royalty; you are special royalty. One of a kind, only one before in your family after Anubis, Anput and Kebeechet. There are Mystics all over the world, they know about you, they know you are the original and therefore they want you for your power. Be careful out there. The world is a very dangerous place," Cruze spoke softly but firmly, making sure Ollie understood the true danger that lurked out there.

"I'll be careful, you know I'm ready and able to fight."

"Yes, but werewolves out there are strong, they are in tune with their wolf, yours is suppressed. They are stronger and more agile, be aware of everything around you, Olyanah," Ollie nodded her head, knowing very well Cruze would be expecting it. "Good girl."

"I'm not a damn dog, Cruze."

"I beg to differ."

"I haven't turned into a fur ball just yet so you can beg to differ all you want but you're the dog, not me," Cruze sighed on the other end of the phone, making Ollie laugh.

"Ollie, when you come home, would you like me to teach you to turn and would you like to meet your parents?" a lump caught in her throat. "You don't have to decide now, but I thought I'd give you enough time to think about it."

"Thanks for the consideration," sarcasm dripped from her voice.

"No worries. Jane and Greg are asking about you. Making sure you got to Phoenix alright and are well."

"Arrest them, you're Beta of the pack, arrest them. I want nothing to do with them, Cruze, ever again in my life and they are a danger to society, so please never let them have children of their own, or let them find their own loves, or mates, or whatever you call it."

"What did they do to you?"

"When I'm ready, I'll talk about it, but they are a danger."

"Simon Davis is Jane's mate."

"Then lock him away too."

"I can't do anything unless you tell me what happened."

"Then keep a close eye on them. Do not let them out of your sights. They are bad people, Cruze, they want nothing but pain to me and those around me."

"I'll keep it in mind if anything ever happens," Ollie rolled her eyes at the sarcasm in Cruze's voice. "I've known them a while, Olyanah, they are good people at heart."

"You clearly don't know them very well. Trust me, Cruze. Just trust me," the line went silent. Ollie could almost hear Cruze thinking about what she had said.

"I trust you."

"Thank you. I have to go now, Cruze; Lacy and I are going out for dinner and I have to get ready. I'll talk to you soon enough OK? Trust me, Cruze. Please just trust me with this," Ollie walked inside, pulling out a pretty yellow summer dress, pairing it with pink stockings and black ballet flats.

"Of course I trust you. And, Olyanah? Let love in. Let me love you and I can promise you will never be alone again. Just open yourself up to me and I can love you the way you need me to and the way I can. Also, listen to your wolf, call for her and she will show herself,"

"I'll try. Bye, Cruze."

"Bye. I love you and have a good night," the line went dead as Ollie clicked the red 'end call' button on her phone. She changed into the clothes she had on earlier before her shower and before talking to Cruze, then pulled on a black jacket over as well to keep herself warm as she walked with Lacy down to a nice restaurant to have dinner together for the first time in a different country.

"Everything good between you two?"

"Better," Ollie replied with a large smile on her pale pink painted lips.

"How wonderful! I cannot wait until we go back and see them now!" Ollie could hear the excitement in Lacy's voice.

"Europe. I'm second guessing Europe," Lacy looked up from the mirror where she was fixing up her makeup, making sure she looked good enough to go out on the town. Ollie saw the confusion etched into Lacy's face. "Maybe we should go back now that we know everything and know that Cruze and Jason are waiting for us. I feel so alone without him," Lacy nodded her head.

"I completely agree. Stay out the rest of this week and then go home?"

"Agreed," Ollie pulled her laptop out of her bag and logged onto a flights website, ready to book the flight home for a weeks time.

After booking the flights home, Ollie and Lacy went out, excited that they were going to be surprising Cruze and Jason like that. Everything was suddenly falling into place as they walked along the busy streets. People smiled as they walked past, covering themselves with their coats to keep the cool air out and the warmth in.

"Hello, ladies," Ollie turned to see an older, man with beady, red, glowing eyes. He had stubble all around his chin and up his cheeks. It seemed almost like he wanted to look younger, like a teenager, but it wasn't working. Instead he looked older then the twenty-five years Ollie guessed he was. The man had a light Scottish accent, telling her that he hadn't been there in a while.

"Excuse me, we are in a bit of a rush. We have reservations to make," Lacy lied easily as she stepped away from the too close to her man that seemed to have no sense of personal space.

"Maybe I can show you both a better time. You look new here. First time in America?" Ollie stared at Lacy, communicating that she was quite freaked out by the guy that was now following them.

"I think we are OK," Ollie said; snubbing him as they walked faster, further away him. "Those eyes," Ollie whispered with shock.

"Either contacts or some weird science experiment gone wrong because no one have such crazy eyes like that," Lacy's eyes widened to prove her point, showing Ollie her deep blue eyes.

"I'm calling contacts," Ollie said as they reached the restaurant they were going to be eating at.

"Excuse me," Ollie and Lacy turned around again, right before they entered the restaurant. "You ladies never let me finish what I was saying. If you would follow me, I can show you the VIP experience," Ollie shuddered at his deep, demanding voice.

"Listen," she started, "I don't know who you are but we want nothing to do with you. If you try to take us somewhere again, I will scream rape as loud as I can and get you arrested," Ollie threatened with a strong voice.

"No. You listen to me you stupid girl," the guy grabbed Ollie's arm tightly, pointing something to her waist. "Walk like nothing is wrong," Lacy was about to protest but Ollie cut her off.

"Listen to him," she said, eyeing the odd stick that was hidden under the man's jacket. Lacy followed Ollie's eyes and gulped noticeably. "What do you want? And how do I even know that is a real gun?" the questions poured out of Ollie and she begged herself to stop before she got herself shot.

"I want you to stay quiet, and I can prove it," as soon as the three turned down a dark alley way, Lacy trailing, looking terrified, the red eyed man pulled the revolver style gun from his jacket and aimed it at Lacy's head and then Ollie's. "Now, enjoy your sleep," a hand wrapped itself around Ollie's face, another around Lacy's with a cloth that was suddenly causing Ollie and Lacy to feel incredibly sleepy.

"Sleep tight and don't let the bed bugs bite," a female voice cackled as the two lost consciousness.

Chapter Twelve

The Most Important Things In Life Aren't Things

SO MANY HANDS grabbed at me, trying to touch me and hold me; make me theirs. I tried to block all my senses from the alcoholic breath that was being pushed onto me. I tried not to look repulsed as I moved slyly around the stage, using the pole as a prop. Dancing around made me feel like such an object, so worthless and so bought at the same time.

Drunken men threw colour notes and coins at me. The silver and gold coins accumulated on the floor, forcing me to dodge them in my high red strappy heels. The men called out different things, but all I could see was the man I called father chatting with another man, eyes stuck on me.

It made me feel sick the fact that my own father was oogling me, watching me as though I was there to entertain him and pleasure him. I was there for him; I was there because he made me. I wasn't here for any other reason and he enjoyed it; I could see it in his eyes.

Groaning, her deep blue eyes opened, showing the blood vessels that had burst during the ordeal she had been through while sleeping. Her head throbbed as she tried to look around the room. Instead she was greeted with a pitch-black scene. Even with her advanced sight that she had slowly tapped into, everything was still completely black. No shadows, no sign of light, nothing. Just black.

"Lacy?" Ollie croaked. Her throat was completely dry, showing that she hadn't had anything to drink in a very long time. "Lacy, are you here?" all Ollie could feel was that she was slowly slipping back into a deep slumber that she didn't want to welcome. "Lacy?" she called again before closing her eyes on the world around and falling dead to whatever lay around her.

Lacy opened her eyes, hearing her name being called over and over again. The last croak had her heart breaking, but something was preventing her from speaking or making a noise all together.

Whatever was on her mouth was making her panic. Shaky hands rose to try and remove whatever was sitting on her mouth, but there was nothing, just a sad pressure that sat on top of her mouth, preventing any noise escaping her lips.

A sharp pain rose through her scalp, forcing her to open her mouth and try and scream, but nothing came out.

"I will let you go, I can let you go; if you follow my rules and listen to everything I say. I can then and only then, promise that you will leave here alive," Lacy nodded her head, looking up at a pair of bright glowing red eyes.

"Listen to him," glowing golden eyes with a light, airy female voice behind them hissed.

"If you don't; your friend will die," Lacy wanted to cry, she wanted to scream, express herself somehow, but instead she was helpless; completely helpless.

"Get her up," the lady with the golden eyes said, directing the man with the red eyes. Their glowing eyes were the only light in room, but Jason had been slowly teaching Lacy to get in touch with her wolf and she was tapping into better sight and hearing. Second by second, her eyes adjusted to the low light around. There were no windows in the concrete room she was in and something Lacy noticed quickly was she wasn't the only one there.

Ollie. Ollie's body lay slumped on the ground, her oddly glowing eyes opened showing off her deep blue eyes that were identical to Lacy's. Her mouth hung open a bit, and Lacy could here the air whistling past her teeth with each breath. It was comforting that knowing, even though she looked gone, Ollie was alive.

A few other female bodies were scattered around the room, all with their eyes open and mouth hanging on by a thread. Most looked completely gone, as though they would be rotting soon.

Lacy was lead through a small hallway, her arms pinned behind her by the man with glowing red eyes. The golden eyed lady walked ahead, leading the way through the maze of corridors that surrounded Lacy and the two accomplices.

Her heart was pounding against her chest, threatening to pop out if something else happened. Her mind, though, was focused on Ollie. Make sure she lived. Making sure she got to live.

* * *

Dizzy. Ollie could feel the room spinning around even though there was hardly anything for her to see until her eyes adjusted to the dark. After sleeping for so long, nothing felt like it was solid anymore. Her legs felt like jelly and her arms felt as though they were ready to fall off.

She could see everything around her, those eerie glowing coloured dots, that were sadly attached to people. Ollie's heart skipped a beat as she saw that they looked as though they were dead, but she could hear every breath as it whistled past their teeth.

It scared Ollie that she could see so well, but she put it down to what Cruze had been telling her, her wolf wanted to come out. Although the thought occurred to Ollie, it still scared her to death. She didn't think she was ready to have her wolf come out, not yet anyway.

Ollie lifted her head, even though a large amount of pain coursed through her body as she did so. So many thoughts entered her head as she stood up from her crouched position on the cold cement flooring. Her head span as she tried to get her balance on the balls of her feet.

There was a soft dripping noise in the background that told Ollie that this place had been abandoned once upon a time. The pluming was old and dripping on the cold floor, a sure sign that this old building had been turned onto a personal torture palace for someone, or a group of people.

Ollie leaned with her back against the cold cement wall. Her body was clad in the yellow summer dress she remembered getting changed into for dinner with Lacy, but it was dirty and her stockings and cardigan were gone. The thought scared Ollie; she didn't know if someone had touched her or if they had just removed the stockings to scare her.

She had long ago realized that Lacy was now gone from the room, she had disappeared or she had been taken, either way Ollie's mind was stuck on Lacy. Lacy and Cruze.

A door at the end of the dark long room opened with a rusty creak. An explosion of light caused Ollie to shield her eyes and prepare·herself for a fight if need be.

Two figures stood at the other end of the long room, glowing eyes showing Ollie that they could see her clearly. A woman's figure and a man's figure stood, the woman a fair bit shorter then the man, smiled ruefully; that much Ollie could see clearly.

A pair of golden glowing eyes stood out from the lady and a pair of somewhat familiar red glowing eyes stared back at Ollie from the mans face. Ollie remembered everything about what she thought was the day before. The man hassling herself and Lacy and being dragged away with a gun pressed to her side.

"Where is my friend," Ollie's voice was strong, something that surprised her.

"She's safe; for now. So long as you listen to us and obey what we say, she will remain safe," the deep booming voice of the male with red eyes echoed around the room of sleeping girls. Ollie had realized quickly that some of those girls that she thought were sleeping were actually dead.

No breath was escaping their lips and their eyes had lost all life and their mouths hanging open had no noise, no life leaving it; it was almost as though their jaws had been broken to be left in that eerie situation.

"Where is she?" the force in Ollie's voice had her almost pressed up against the wall. The force of her own voice scared her but he knew it needed to be forceful to get a reaction from the two people in front of her.

The man and woman started walking in the room towards where Ollie stood. *'Red eyes and Gold Eyes,'* Ollie thought to herself. *'They won't tell me anything about themselves, that I know, so I might as well give them a nickname.'* The thought came easily to Ollie's mind.

Gold Eyes and Red Eyes walked further into the room, leaving the door open behind them. The girls on the ground were in some sort of a spell, unable to wake up, but Ollie had fought it; it proved to be true because she was standing and able to talk to these monsters that now had her imprisoned.

Gold Eyes looked at Red Eyes once and soon he pounced on Ollie, grabbing her around the neck, pinning her arms behind her back. Ollie tried to struggle against her attacker. Red Eyes held her strong, making sure that there was no way she was able to get away from him.

The pain that was now coursing through her shoulders and arms was something she had never experienced before in her life. Although she had had pain before with her father, it had never been so forceful, so long and so restraining.

The dark hallway hurt Ollie's eyes as they tried to quickly adapt to the gloomy light that had little break. Windows were boarded up, letting the light shine through lightly, but giving no relief to Ollie's sore eyes.

"Where are we?" she asked, trying to kill the dead silence.

"Don't talk," Gold Eyes had the same accent as Red Eyes, a slight Scottish combined with American and English.

"I'm curious. If you've kidnapped me, the least you could do is at least tell me what is going on and where I am. I'm interested to know how long I've been asleep for," Ollie couldn't stop her rambling mouth. She knew she was poking a bee's nest, but something within told her it might not be such a bad thing.

"I said 'don't talk'," Gold Eyes commented again, grinding her teeth together in frustration.

"Curiosity killed the cat," was all Red Eyes said. The ruefulness in his voice had Ollie shivering with fear.

"But I'm not a cat so I think I have a little more survival then a cat," Ollie stated smugly.

"I wouldn't be so sure," Red Eyes commented.

"I would be. Now, where are we?"

"Far away from home."

"I didn't peg you as the poetic type."

"You are pushing it girl. Shut your mouth before I shut it for you," Ollie took the warning seriously, instead she watched the old abandoned hallways pass her by. Rooms that had no occupants sat on either side of her, old beds made of metal and springs had nothing inside except that. No mattress, no pillow, no blanket.

Ollie was slowly starting to accept that this was going to be her life for who knows how long. All luxuries were gone. Peeling wallpaper was slowly coming off the walls, showing the real age of the building they were in.

"You are far away from anything and everything, scream all you want; no one will hear you," Gold Eyes commented with a sinister smile on her lips.

"Eventually a car must go past."

"Scream all you want. This place is said to be haunted so even if you scream no one will stop. Humans are too scared of what they don't understand and can't be bothered comprehending it," Ollie rolled her eyes. If there were a haunted building nearby where Ollie lived she would be more then happy to investigate.

There was a building that was said to be empty; it sat on the boarder of Saint Louis and Rosewood. Ollie and Lacy had ventured there once, but there was a lot of cars and people for it to be empty, so they left it, thinking it was someone's house.

* * *

Lacy sat in the cell, hands tied behind her back, her mouth still unable to make sound. So many thoughts and smart arse comments were rushing through her mind and it was psychologically killing her that she wasn't able to voice them.

Although it was killing her, her mind was still on Ollie and making sure that she was alright. Lacy didn't know how long it had been. She was in a small room that looked like it used to be a room in a hospital. A metal bed frame and springs attached sat to one side but that was all. The room was very minimalist, very bland, something Lacy wasn't used to. She had a colourful room back at home in Rosewood, something that reflected her personality well.

"Get up and come with me," Lacy looked up and saw the man with the glowing red eyes staring impatiently at her.

Red Eyes opened the door to the room she was in and just by the look in his eyes, forced Lacy to stand and walk towards him. Her mind was telling her to stay in the corner, but her body was obeying the call of Red Eyes.

"Walk faster," he called to her, pinning her arms painfully behind her back and walking along the hallway that was being held together by a weak wooden structure. The windows were boarded up with old flimsy boards that look as though they were about to fall over.

"Where are we going," Lacy spoke, the hold on her mouth gone like a spell and a weight was lifted off her shoulders.

"Don't talk."

"If I can talk I will talk. You shouldn't have forced me to be silent for so long. I know it was you, don't pretend as though it wasn't," Lacy said slyly, a smile forming on her lips despite everything.

"I will put the spell back on you if you make me," Red Eyes threatened.

"OK, go for it," Lacy smiled, although all she wanted to do was cry out about the pain she was in from her shoulders being bent back like they were. *'Ollie would have something to say to ease the pain,'* Lacy thought to herself.

The two stopped at the end of a hallway, right when a scream was being heard. The scream echoed around the old hallway. Lacy could see a smile form on Red Eyes lips, a smile that said he was enjoying the pain that someone was in.

"Who is it?"

"You have a choice," he started, "You either stay here, or you let your friend suffer."

"That's Ollie!" Lacy screamed; her eyes widened with fear.

"That is your friend, yes."

"I'll stay."

"Is that your final answer?"

"Yes."

"Well, you are free to go. I will have someone collect you soon, to leave. You will not remember a thing. Don't take everything people say seriously, I would've thought you'd know what and who we are," and Lacy's body crumbled to the ground.

* * *

Gold Eyes stood over Ollie, pleasure in her eyes as she brought the poison-laced whip down on her bare skin. Ollie's arms were pulled above her head, held up by a long chain that was fastened to the strong roof above. Ollie's toes touched the ground below, the balls of her bare feet resting awkwardly on the cold floor where her heels could reach.

The whip cracked in the air, slapping against Ollie's skin and ripping it open in the process. Ollie's scream echoed around the room, bringing a smile to Gold Eyes' face. Her eyes twinkled with delight as each crack ripped open Ollie's skin, leaving blood trickling down her dirty skin.

Due to the room she has been put up, Ollie's skin was covered from head to toe in dirt and filth. She had been sleeping on the floor for the duration of her stay, which by the small crack in the wood against the window, Ollie guessed it had been about a day.

It was a shock when Red Eyes had opened the bolted door, letting a small amount of blinding light in. He had pulled her from the ground with force and strapped her wrists high into the chains, lifting her small petite body off the ground slightly and then left her. Ollie had been hanging for a few hours before Gold Eyes walked in and started showing her exactly what was going to happen.

After every whip, Gold Eyes laced the whip in more poison, a poison that had been proven to cause pain but not death. The pain Ollie had coursing through her open wounds; she was more then keen to agree with the random study.

Ollie's belly button ring stood on the other side of the room, blood surrounding it and a bit of skin where it had once been attached to Ollie's body. Her own belly button was still bleeding, causing her to feel dizzy from the blood loss.

Crawling over, Ollie grabbed the ring of a werewolf and studied it in the dark light. There was a small deep blue crystal in the eye of the wolf howling on its side, something that reminded her of herself, not the wolf but the eye colour. The idea of the wolf reminded Ollie of Cruze and the way she remembered him talking about 'Mystics' on the phone one night. If them being wolves was true, then Ollie had a lot of evaluating of her life to do, she had had everything planned out. She was going to act, she was going to do everything in her power to make sure no one ever ended up the way she had when she was living with her parents.

Looking at the belly ring, Ollie's mind went to Cruze, the way he smelt, the way he moved, the way he spoke and worst of all the way things had been left between the two. She had been so excited to go back home and surprise him and they had ended on such good terms. It would be so much easier if they were mad at each other then he wouldn't miss her and she wouldn't miss him, but fate had other plans for the two, fate always had other plans.

Like a well oiled machine, Red Eyes entered the room, chain in his hands as he smiled and winked at the girl huddled on the floor, hunched over with her belly button ring in her hands and blood all around her.

Ollie shoved the wolf piercing in her black crop top, not really knowing where her yellow dress had gone. Red Eyes stood over the cowering girl, grabbing her painfully and pulling her up, attaching her wrists to the chains and hoisting her up so only the balls of her feet were on the ground, letting her dangle again.

Blood rushed around Ollie's ears, making her feel dizzier then when the wolf had been torn from her body not too long ago just before Red Eyes had ripped the heirloom from her body.

"Why are you doing this?" Ollie asked with tears in her eyes.

"One day you will know and one day we won't need you any more," he stood watching Ollie dangle for a few more moments before turning to leave, "Enjoy your sleep, Princess," a bark of laughter at his own joke left his mouth before slamming the iron door closed and locking it loudly, leaving Ollie stuck to the room with no way of moving without hurting herself.

Her body hurt from the attack it had taken the day before from Gold Eyes with the poison laced whip and her mind hurt as she tried to comprehend what was happening to her and why.

Only recently had Ollie learnt of Werewolves and now she was being punished for being something she didn't understand and didn't even believe in. Or did she?

Chapter Thirteen

A Thing Is Mighty Big When Time And Distance Cannot Shrink It

LACY OPENED HER eyes, seeing nothing but light, a blinding light that had her shielding her eyes. The room looked quite familiar, but she couldn't work out why. A phone ringing hit her on the head, the vibrations causing it to fall from the overhead table that she was near.

She was lying on the floor, looking as though she had a horrible hang over. Her head was banging and she was starting to feel as though a night on the town with Ollie had actually turned her into a crazy alcoholic that slept on the floor, too drunk to even move.

Realizing that the phone was still ringing next to her, Lacy picked it up without looking at the ID and answered the phone, sounding groggy and still a little drunk. Her movements were sluggish as she sat herself up against the wall behind her.

"Hello?"

"Lacy, thank the Goddess! I was starting to freak," the familiar voice of Jason resonated through the line.

"What are you talking about?"

"You haven't answered your phone in almost two days," panic was clear in Jason's voice.

"Haven't I?" Lacy couldn't even understand what was going on right now. The last thing she remembered was going out with Ollie for dinner the night before. Some guy had annoyed them but Ollie and Lacy had gotten rid of him pretty quickly, at least that is what Lacy remembered.

"No you haven't. Lac, what happened? Put Ollie on the phone," Lacy pulled herself up off the floor by pushing herself against the wall and walking around the suite that her parents had paid for. Looking around the perfectly cleaned rooms, Lacy couldn't find Ollie and she called for her to come out but her attempts were useless.

"I have no idea where Ollie is. Try getting Cruze to call her," Lacy was so confused as to what was going on.

"He has, since yesterday when you two went missing," there was rustling on the other end of the phone before a new, but still familiar voice, came through the phone receiver.

"Lacy," Cruze said firmly, "Where is she?"

"I have no idea, the last thing I remember was booking the flights and then going out for dinner," Lacy closed her eyes, trying to remember what she had done. "Some guy was following us, but we made quick work of him."

"What did he look like? Tell me everything about him Lacy."

"Well, he wasn't American, his accent was probably from the UK. I don't know honestly, Cruze, I feel like I had one hell of a night last night, kind of hung over I think. I honestly don't know," Lacy rested her head in her hands, tears dropping from her the corners of her eyes.

"Wait, what do you mean 'booking the flights'? I thought you already had all your flights booked?" Jason asked, the phone on loudspeaker between the two guys.

"Ollie and I decided that we were going to come home early, as in at the end of the week on Sunday we were going to head back and surprise you two. After everything we just couldn't do it. Ollie couldn't do it," Lacy's heart broke as she thought about her missing friend.

"Lacy, listen to me," Jason sounded so strong and so put together, "You go to that airport and you get on a plane."

"I am not leaving Ollie behind!"

"Then we will come to you. I am sure Enakal will be more then happy to let us and a few wolves come over while we look for her. This isn't something that will go away, I'm sure of it," Jason said.

"This is the work of wolves. Another pack," pain, fear and hate pulsed through Cruze's voice, causing him to growl loudly as he spoke.

"Calm down and do not growl at my mate," Jason growled at Cruze. "Baby," he directed at Lacy, "Being apart from your mate is a hard thing to do and we have been in as much pain as you have at the separation, but I will see you soon. We are packing now and heading to the airport. I love you."

"I love you too. I am not leaving this room until you get here."

"I wouldn't expect you to," Jason hung up the phone.

Lacy sat on the floor again, letting her head fall back against the wall behind her as tears slid from her eyes, wetting her face with a salty natural water. The pain of not being with Jason was too much for her and the fact that her best friend was missing was just too hard. Everything was going wrong, right when everything was looking up.

* * *

"I knew it was a bad idea!" Cruze cried, throwing clothes into his suitcase. Jason stood next to Cruze, trying to calm down his flaring temper. It wasn't an easy thing to do; Cruze could easily fly off the rails, so Jason was just trying to stay out of his way.

"You need to calm down, she was going to be in this situation anyway. She should have been prepared better, that was Jane and Greg's job," Jason placed a soft hand on Cruze's shoulder. "Egypt, here, either way, it was going to happen, surely you know that," Cruze did know it.

"The Alpha's didn't have the right to take us all away and put Olyanah up and away from us. She deserved a hell of a lot better!" Cruze zipped up the suitcase and carried out of the room and downstairs to talk to Enakal, the Alpha.

"Alpha," Cruze didn't bother knocking as he entered. "Why didn't we stay in Egypt?" the question was out of the blue and caught Enakal off guard.

"You know why."

"No, I don't. I know what you have told me, but I also know that isn't the truth. Why did we leave Egypt?"

"Cruze."

"Don't, Enakal."

"We left because we had to. It was getting dangerous and people were starting to guess about us. Egyptians know the story of Anubis, they know what we are and they keep their mouths shut. They don't have to, but they do. Questions were being asked and we couldn't have that," Enakal stood from the chair behind the desk and walked over towards Cruze. "You know I cannot always answer these question, but you have to trust me. We are going to go back, that much I can promise."

"When?"

"Soon. When my daughter is back."

"I will find her and I will Bond with her," Enakal nodded his head as the door opened again. A shorter lady with long light hair and light eyes walked in with a soft, sorrowful smile on her face. The lady had a neat, narrow waist, which was hugged by a simple 50's style floral dress.

"Arabella," Cruze nodded his head as Enakal's stern, sad face changed into one of admiration and love.

"Go, Cruze. My daughter needs her mate to find her. She will open up to you soon. I can promise you that. She is strong," Arabella, Enakal's wife, mate and love, said, pulling Cruze in for a hug.

"She wouldn't be in this situation if we had stayed in Egypt, keeping her safe within our walls," Cruze announced, leaving the room and grabbing his suitcase, heading out to the black Ute where Jason was waiting for him. "Just drive, Jason. Just drive," he said through clenched teeth.

* * *

Pain flowed through her veins, slowly making its way up to her head, clouding her vision and making her head foggy. Every inch of her body was throbbing with a pain that she had never felt before. Her mind was stuck on what Greg had done to her years ago, the way he used to dominate her, stand over her and tell her how worthless she was to the world and those within it.

The clouding in her head was making it harder and harder to concentrate on images she remembered, instead everything seemed like a badly drawn cartoon, playing scene over scene again.

The pain wasn't going away either, instead it was getting worse, slowly turning from a throbbing to a sharp pain that echoed through her body; like a pin knife stabbing each cell on her body. Slowly the stabbing rose to her arms and shoulders, almost paralyzing her.

Ollie's body was still suspended in the air, the balls of her feet being the only thing that was keeping her shoulders from popping out of place. Her head was spinning, her head was rocking from side to side as she tried to stay awake, instead of being woken up by a whip being brought down on her skin. It had happen twice now, and Ollie had realized she had been in this place four days now, hung up by her arms suspended above her.

She wanted to start a tally on the wall, but there was no way she could do that with her arms above her head and she felt as though it were too cliché, like an old prison movie.

The door opened behind her, unable to face the door, Ollie was forced to look out into the small crack above the window that showed if it were daylight or not. She had no idea who was behind her, no idea what they had planned for her today. The day before she had been whipped with the poison laced whip that cracked through the air. The day before had been physical abuse by Red Eyes, punched in the face, kicked in the gut, Ollie felt as though that pain was more familiar to her, more bearable for her.

She was in so much pain that the only thing going through her mind was that she wanted Lacy safe and wanted to make sure she was unharmed.

"Wake up," a deep chilling male voice boomed around the room as the heavy iron door slammed closed and bolted. "I have news for you. Good news."

"And what might that be?" after everything, Ollie was starting to wonder if her smart mouth was ever going to go away, especially after everything that had happened, she still managed to have rather rude comments to her capturer's. She knew she was going to get herself into more trouble, but the temptation was too daring.

"About your friend," Red Eyes pretended that he hadn't heard Ollie speak.

"What about her?"

"Just be grateful we decided to focus on you."

"You let her go?" Ollie's eyes widened, hiding the sleep that was lurking behind them as she spoke to Red Eyes.

"We took her home, she won't remember a thing, a night on the town is all. That was a couple of days ago," the underlying Scottish in his accent told Ollie that she should be focusing on something else in the room, not just what he was saying, but how he was saying it. "A bad hang over is all she'll have. We gave her a choice of staying or going. I guess she made up her mind all to quickly."

"You're Scottish," Ollie didn't want to think about what Red Eyes had just told her so she decided to focus on more trivial things.

"Most people don't pick that up."

"Yes, well I'm not most people. So we're in Scotland?"

"What gave you that idea?"

"I'm going to say the accent on a limb, but honestly, I don't know," Ollie said, rolling her eyes.

"You are Australian, that doesn't mean I found you in Australia."

"Everyone goes home at some point. Especially psychopaths. You feel as though you are able to connect with yourself a lot better when you are at home," Ollie deduced him. "I did psychology, I know this shit, mate," Ollie winked as he rounded and Ollie looked right into his glowing red eyes.

"You are a smart girl; too smart for your own good. I think you need to remember who holds the power," Red Eyes lifted his long arms, he was very tall, a good head and a half taller then Ollie, he clicked something above his head and Ollie fell to the ground, her shoulders popping back to their normal position, her whole body feeling so much better already. "Consider this a break. I'll be back soon and you will never see day break again," Red Eyes opened the door and slammed it closed.

Ollie didn't know what to do with herself now, the chains lay disregarded to the side, Ollie too scared to go over and move them so she let them. She lay completely hunched over, her knees pulled up to her chest and her arms wrapped around her legs.

Her head was spinning, te thought of Lacy wanting to just leave her and let her suffer knowing what Ollie was going to be in for. For some reason, the way Red Eyes and Gold Eyes had already treated her, Ollie very much doubted that Lacy had a choice in what happened to her. Ollie would risk her life for Lacy and she knew her best friend would do the same for her.

Ollie sat in the corner near the bed for the rest of the next few days. No food, no water and nowhere to go to the toilet. She was left to live in her own filth with nothing to look forward too. Her whole life was now down to whatever these people planned to do to her. It revolved around their moods and if today was going to be a good day or not and she was going to be able to eat or not.

Ollie hadn't seen Gold Eyes since she came and was put in this room but Red Eyes and herself were becoming good friends, not that Ollie liked that, no, instead she wanted to get rid of him altogether. After everything she had been through, Ollie hated violence and the thought of ridding her attacker that way was completely against her morals.

She didn't know how she was going to get past what she was now going to call her life. Ollie wanted to fight but her body hurt, her mind hurt and she just didn't think she had the strength to go on fighting against Red Eyes, although her smart mouth was something she was never going to lose, this experience told her just that.

Ollie wanted to fight, she wanted to get out of there and she wanted Cruze to hold her in his arms and tell her everything was going to be OK. His deep soothing voice was something that always had the desired effect on Ollie, making her body react in ways she had never felt before.

She could still remember the way he smelt, that deep rain smell that was entrusted within him. It was although it rained and he was in the forest at Saint Louis that boarded the beach. A mesmerizing smell Ollie could still capture in her mind now even when he wasn't' here.

Lacy sat in her room, watching as Cruze, Enakal, Arabella, Jason, a wolf called Drake, Jay and another wolf, Brent talked in hushed tones. Jason told Lacy that Cruze was Beta of the pack, Drake was second, Jason was third, Jay was fourth and Brent was fifth in the top five wolves of the pack hierarchy. Enakal and Arabella were Alpha's of the pack and Ollie's biological parents.

Something that Lacy and the others hadn't factored in was that Arabella had had another daughter, Nuru, who was only two and had been brought along. Werewolves were very possessive creatures and leaving a child was a hard thing.

"So then why did you leave Ollie?" Lacy asked after she had heard everything. She had a great deal of respect for Enakal and Arabella already, but there was something unsettling about the fact that they had kept one and not the other.

It was Arabella who answered, "When I was pregnant with Olyanah a witch came along, a dark witch, not a light witch, and she cast a spell on me, a spell on my unborn baby. She told me that unimaginable pain would come if those who wanted her for the wrong reasons got their hands on her. She was going to be powerful, very powerful. The dark witch wasn't a dark witch in the beginning, instead she was a kind woman at heart and told me Olyanah wouldn't be evil, instead the opposite with a loving heart.

"We didn't have a choice but to give her to people that would take care of her when everyone found out about our daughter. It wasn't long before they found out and everyone wanted her, they wanted the power our small daughter held so we gave her to Greg and Jane and let her lead a normal life, a life where no one would know who she was and no one could hurt her," Arabella explained, sitting at the large table in the suite. Arabella had her long light hair out in simple thick waves around her face, the thick hair and long length had Lacy reminded of Ollie.

"You look like her," except the eyes, your eyes are different," Lacy stated staring at Arabella.

"Yes, she has the same eyes as you, we have been keeping an eye on her this whole time."

"I'm not related to Ollie, why do we have the same eyes?"

"But you are. Your mother, Sally, is my sister," Lacy's jaw dropped.

"So, Ol and I are cousins? And you're my aunty?" Arabella nodded her head. "Well this has been a surprising turn of events," Lacy started thinking to herself out loud, letting everyone hear how confused and surprised she was.

"Yes, I'm sorry we haven't met before and I'm sorry this has been hidden from you, but I do hope you can understand now that you know why we couldn't keep our precious Olyanah with us," Arabella stood and walked to her niece, pulling her in for a hug, a hug that Lacy embraced with all her heart.

It felt good for Lacy to have someone embrace her, especially now that she felt so alone that Ollie was gone, but so happy that she knew Ollie really was family. They really where like sisters, blood family at least now.

"She will be alright, she is strong," Enakal spoke for the first time, and Lacy replied with a snort.

"She may be strong but it's because Greg and Jane are nasty pieces of work, cruel people. They don't deserve to be apart of the pack," Lacy started but was met with a growl from Cruze.

"Why do you two keep saying that? No one is explaining what they have done, just that they are bad people!" Cruze cried. Jason stepped in front of Lacy, protecting her as his mate from the enraged Beta.

"Watch your tone, Beta, I know you're stressed but she is my mate," this was the first time Lacy had seen Cruze addressed as Beta and not Cruze. Their first fight she had witnessed between the two brother like friends.

"Calm down, Jason, I can handle this. And Cruze, you haven't lived a day in her shoes, if she hasn't told you, then it is not my place to say. It is her past, her life," Lacy stepped around Jason, ignoring the glare he shot at her as she defied him in his possessive nature. "Oh chill out you possessive fur ball," Lacy rolled her eyes and winked at Arabella when she stifled a laugh.

"You're pushing it," Jason ground out.

"Good story," Lacy rolled her eyes again. "Now can we get onto more pressing measures of finding my cousin," Arabella smiled at Lacy's use of 'cousin'. "So what can we do that will get Ollie back and safe?"

"We can't do much," Enakal spoke up, "She needs to open herself up to Cruze and open herself up to her wolf before any of us can find her," he explained. "She needs to open up, let herself fell what needs to be felt to bring open the pack ties," Lacy nodded her head.

"OK, all well and good to say that Mr. New Uncle Man, but does Ollie know that?" Lacy asked Enakal.

"I've been informed that Cruze has in fact explained that she needs to open up about how she is feeling," they all heard a whimper as Cruze pulled a photo album from Ollie's bag and saw that she had photos of him in it, a few far away photos and a photo of them at Ollie's formal. Such a stunning couple he felt as he saw the smiles on their faces when they looked into each others eyes.

"We are going to find her, Cruze," Jay spoke up. "She is a sister to me and I will not see her gone, not when I can do something about it," the force in his statement told Cruze that everyone was behind finding his mate and getting them to bond long before there was no hope of bringing her back, not just physically but mentally too. It seemed as though she had already suffered so much in her short life.

Chapter Fourteen

Heroes Are People Who Rise To The Occasion And Slip Quietly Away

THE ROOM WAS quiet; the hallway on the other side of the thick door was silent. Everything around her super hearing was silent. The silence was a lot worse then hearing noises that would make Ollie's skin crawl. It felt as though there was nothing on the other side and her stomach was cramping with a lack of food. Her mouth was so dry she couldn't swallow and her mind was so deprived that everything in the room was spinning whenever she looked at something directly and tried to focus on its features.

There was nothing to indicate that someone was on the other side of the door, but when the lock opened up and it swung open, revealing Gold Eyes and Red Eyes on the other side.

"Well, well, well," Gold Eyes started chanting. A few weeks here and Ollie was so confused about life and everything that it contained. Torture and isolation was all she had now and it was her new life that she was already getting used to.

She hadn't seen Gold Eyes since arriving and it was a little odd seeing her here. Ollie's clothes were tattered and torn, completely gone only her black bra, which was replaced by a black crop top over the top at some point in her sleep one day and underwear were left and a black singlet that had holes in it from the whip.

"You look cheery," she said with a wicked smile playing on her thin, ice-cold lips.

"I'm always happy to see you," Ollie shot back with a raspy voice. Her dry throat was starting to affect her and she hadn't spoken for a long time in her isolation.

"He's warned me about you," they never addressed each other by names, making sure Ollie never found out what their real names where. They knew what she called them, she'd called it to their faces numerous times. "About your smart mouth," Ollie just winked.

"What can I say? Variety is the spice of life and I love different spices *and* herbs," Ollie smiled stupidly at Gold Eyes.

"That's going to bite you where the sun doesn't shine," Red Eyes smiled vengefully.

"You've said that many times before, I'm starting to think they are only empty threats."

"Don't count your chickens before they hatch."

"You don't have to talk in riddles every time you see me. Who am I going to go running to?" Ollie asked, letting them think about it for a little bit. Red Eyes stared her down while Gold Eyes just rolled her golden glowing eyes. "I think you two need to control your selves, that glowing eye contacts thing is so weird," she hadn't once mentioned that she knew about werewolves, Ollie figured by the way they spoke that they had no idea she knew that she was some freaky animal that had the ability to turn furry at the drop of a hat if her heart desired.

"You are so naïve," Gold Eyes laughed ruefully.

"Please enlighten me then," Ollie begged with narrowed eyes.

"One day, but now it is time to stop the chatter," the Scottish in her accent started coming out a bit more then usual. "We are here for a reason," it was then that Ollie wished Cruze was by her side to protect her and watch over her. She wanted so bad to have his strong arms around her small waist, making sure she knew she was loved. After everything that had happened, Ollie felt her self open up to Cruze, open up to the love she wanted him to feel and the love she needed to feel to get her through what Gold Eyes and Red Eyes were about to do to her.

They closed the door finally behind themselves and pulled something shiny out from behind their backs. A sharp blade with a wooden handle sat in Red Eyes hand and a deep black iron gun that had been polished to perfection was being swung in Gold Eyes fingers.

"We wouldn't kill you. You are far too valuable, but weakening you; that is something we can do," their smiles widened at the thought of causing me more pain then Ollie was already in.

Red Eyes pulled her from her wrists and cut them so blood drizzled out. The small slits were stinging as blood poured down the Ollie's arm and along her chest, but she held her tongue so she wouldn't give Red Eyes and Gold Eyes the satisfaction of knowing they were hurting the seemingly strong girl.

It was only the one cut that Red Eyes did before wrapping those dreaded chains around the open cuts and exposing them to whatever infections were crawling around on the metal. They tied her to the roof, letting her legs dangle with only the balls of her feet on the concrete ground again. Red Eyes pulled the knife out and flatly put the blade against Ollie's exposed stomach, not letting it cut her but letting her feel the cool silver metal that was the knife's blade.

Slowly Red Eyes turned the blade, letting it slice open her stomach in a small thin blood stained line. The cut wasn't too deep but because of that it hurt far more then Ollie had expected it too.

Blood trickled down her skin, wetting what was left of her clothes and underwear she was in. The stinging pain of her broken skin was something that Ollie had never experienced before and she never wanted to again. There was something unsettling about the whole experience, something that had her arms breaking out in goose bumps.

In all her years undergoing Greg's torture it had always been hitting and physical pain, nothing like breaking her skin and causing blood to pour from the open wounds.

Lying in bed I felt so free, so liberated because I had locked my bedroom door and was away from Greg and Jane. I knew last night was something that had never happened before and I knew I never wanted to experience it again in my life. Being forced to be a tool of many different men to bring them pleasure and the parade around on a stage in barely anything at all for more men was utterly humiliating.

I had never felt so tired and dried out then last night and now I knew Greg was going to be expecting me to perform again tonight and I just didn't know if I had it in me, but then again, being slapped across the face wasn't something I fancied either.

Ollie opened her mouth as the whip laced with poison was whipped against her open cut stomach, causing the poison to go directly into her blood stream and course around as her heart tried to pump it out. A strangled scream was all that could escape her parched lips.

The whip fell down again and again on Ollie's opened skin, causing her pain that was never ending. The draining poison made its way through her blood stream, causing the room to feel dizzy around her and if she weren't tied to the room, Ollie was more then sure she would either be stumbling around like a drunk person or already on the ground due to the shear amount of pain she was in.

The whipping went on for a long time, Gold Eyes' favourite form of torture, and then the whip stopped cracking. Ollie opened her deep blue, tear soaked eyes and looked around the room to see Red Eyes and Gold Eyes smiling with something in their hands Ollie had never seen before.

"You are ours," placing the device in his hand, Red Eyes started heating it up at an almost super human pace, the iron rode turning bright red before Ollie's eyes.

"And we will make sure you never forget it," Gold Eyes took the rode from Red Eyes and smiled as she placed it on the top of Ollie's thigh and pressed down hard, almost melting he bubbling skin away.

Finally after hours of torture, Red Eyes and Gold Eyes left Ollie, tied up by the chains, to be with her own dimming thoughts.

One thought kept circling her head; Cruze. The way he would walk with her, hold her, hug her and just want to be with her, Ollie could see a picture of him in her head, see him standing right in front of her as she waited for her shoulders to give way and pain to over take her.

She was branded, a simple eye was burnt into her skin on her upper thigh, a small rounded eye, but it was noticeable and Ollie was immediately ashamed as she felt as though she had somehow betrayed Cruze.

"How strange it feels to miss you," Ollie started singing a song she had heard a very long time ago. She couldn't for the life of her remember where or when she had heard it, but it felt so right at the current time as she saw an image of Cruze standing in front of her. His mysterious smile playing on his lips and that athletic body, begging to run over to Ollie and hold her and make everything OK. "Standing right before you. Good times seem so far and few. I've begun pretending, not to see an ending. But it's all coming into view. So hold me now, hold me fast, pretend it's not going to be the last time that we love, hold me like we love forever," was all Ollie could remember of the old fashioned slow song that was circling her slowly foggy mind.

She wanted so badly for her hallucination to come running towards her, but he wouldn't move. Cruze stood rooted to the spot, unable to move towards his beloved and comfort her in her time of need.

Not long later, Red Eyes entered the room again and unchained Ollie, threw her a small bottle filled with dirty browning water and some molding bread and rotten fruit, then he slammed the door closed again, letting Ollie slowly eat the food in front of her so she didn't waste any.

It was her first meal for a very long time and she wanted it to last as long as possible, for she didn't know when her next meal would be. She tore the mold away from the bread and eat it crumb by crumb, hoping the slow eating would make her feel fill quicker, then scoffing it all down in one bite.

"I've read about people like you," Ollie started, still curled up in the corner of the room as Red Eyes entered the room. He raised an eyebrow at her and smirked, waiting for her to continue with what she was planning on saying. "Psychopaths. You either feel inferior sexually, professionally or you love someone and they don't love you back or you want acceptance from the world or to be noticed; any of the above. Take your pick," suddenly, as though an epiphany had occurred, Ollie's mouth dropped open and she stared wide eyed at Red Eyes as he stood in front of the closed door.

"And which do you think it is?"

"You love Gold Eyes!" Ollie announced with a clap. "Oh my god! How come I haven't seen it before? You love her and you want to prove that you are man enough for her to love you back," Red Eyes stalked towards Ollie, a vicious smile playing on his lips.

"I'm getting very tired of your talking. I think we are going to have to put a stop to it, and soon," he whacked her across the front of her head, banging it against the cement wall behind her. "Fear is the only way to rule. Fear will bring you back to earth and you will learn that there will be punishments when you talk out of line, or talk at all. Or make noise; got it?" he asked but Ollie's head was far to cloudy to answer him and she got another blow, knocking her out, for it. "Fear is the heart of love."

Looking up, Lacy could see Cruze was on edge, more then normal at least. He had been pacing the suite for a very long time but now he had stopped and was looking out the window, standing out on the small balcony that the two girls had been lucky enough to get.

"Cruze," Lacy walked over to him and placed a hand on his arm, which he washed off with a shrug. It was only now that Lacy was realizing that Cruze hated anyone but Ollie touching him.

"I can feel something," he admitted quietly. Cruze didn't open up often in front of people, but Lacy and Cruze were alone, with Jason in the other room watching TV. He wanted to help but there wasn't much he could do, so Jason took his mind off everything by watching mind-numbing TV.

"What?"

"I feel as though I am close, that Olyanah might be opening up to me," the breath caught in her throat. "We are in the wrong place. Olyanah isn't in America, at all. She is somewhere else," Lacy nodded her head as she stepped out onto the balcony with him.

"Where?"

"I don't know but I can feel that she is very far away, further away then all of America, somewhere over the sea," Lacy looked out over the garden that their suite over looked.

"Where do we start? Africa? Europe?"

"Africa is too far away, not the vibe I'm getting from her. Maybe we can ask the European packs if it is alright if we enter into their territory and hopefully they'll let us go and try and find my mate," Lacy nodded her head, grabbing her phone to call Arabella.

"Yo, Ara," Lacy abbreviated her name, causing Arabella to laugh slightly, "Cruze has an ID on the location of our lost number one," Lacy started with the bad military lingo. "We are thinking her location is Europe but we need permission from the top dogs over there, yes pun intended," despite everything, Cruze laughed at Lacy. He loved her sense of humour because it lighten the situation that they were in and made him feel as though there was hope, and hope was all he needed.

Enakal made it back to the suite and pulled out his phone, calling up the Alpha from England to get permission to go into their territory. Wolves were quite territorial and they always needed to be alerted if another pack was going to be entering their territory and why. It was bad manners not to alert a pack.

"Salva," Enakal spoke Latin to the English Alpha on the other end of the phone. He had put it on loud speaker so Cruze could intervene if need be. It was common for packs to start of speaking Latin, the universal language for Werewolves.

"Salva," the pack had been lucky when it had first moved to Rosewood and Saint Louis, as there were no packs in that area for a good two hundred kilometers.

"We are requesting permission to enter England," Enakal spoke.

"What is your reason?" the man on the other end sounded like a strong Alpha, but being from Egypt, there was no Alpha stronger then Enakal from the original line.

"Olyanah Atsu Amarna. I assume you know the name," Enakal said when he heard the gasp on the other line.

"The Hidden One. Yes, I know the name and I know the story. All great and smart Alpha's do."

"Well, as Alpha to my pack and as father to Olyanah I am in great pain. She has been kidnapped and her mate feels her in Europe somewhere."

"Please, by all means come and visit and explore. We will offer you our own pack house as salvation and our pack will be there to assist you if need be," everyone in the room was humbled by the Alpha's declaration.

"I thank you. I can assure you this generosity will not be forgotten and I will forever be in your debt. I thank you again my friend, Richard."

"The honour is mine. I have a pup of my own and would expect the same generosity from other packs if anything were to happen to him.

Please come as soon as possible and I will have a wolf waiting for you at the airport to bring you to the pack house."

"Again I thank you," Enakal hung up the phone and gave a sorrowful smile to Cruze.

"Don't you just love the way they talk?" Lacy suddenly announced, doing her best Phoebe impression from friends. "Ahoy, ahoy," she mimicked in a snotty accent, when no one laughed or made a comment she just sighed and threw her arms in the air. "You know, if Ollie were here she'd get it and she'd be laughing her damn arse off with me."

"I don't doubt that," Jay said, smiling sadly at Lacy.

"She isn't dead guys," Lacy broke the sudden silence.

"How do you know?" an enraged Cruze asked, standing and pacing the room.

"Because if she was then you wouldn't be able to feel her. Says so right here," Lacy took out Anubis book and waved it around, then opened it up to the page. "So. You need to have hope. She needs us to be strong and wouldn't want us being sad. I know Ollie and I know what she would want," Lacy said, giving an angry Cruze the book on the right page so he could read it.

"I agree," Jay said, nodding his head.

"Well, we best not dwell," Arabella said, holding little Nuru in her arms as she walked into the room and receiving a sour look from Cruze. "She is my daughter, Cruze, do not forget that but I agree with Lacy and we must pack a get a move on before we lose more time on saving my precious baby," Cruze wanted to say something, something about Arabella and Enakal leaving Olyanah as a child, but he held his tongue and read what Lacy had given him, desperate the make more of a connection with his mate and find her. She was never going to be let out his sight after this; ever again.

Arriving in England, Lacy looked around the airport with a smile on her face and a sparkle in her eye.

"See, this isn't so bad. This was on our list so I guess if she is here then we've been going quicker then we expected at this travel thing," Lacy commented looking around and spotting a tall gruff looking man with a sigh saying 'Australians'. "How original," Lacy pointed out, rolling her eyes.

She took a long look at this man as the group walked over to him and noticed very quickly his scruffy chin, making him look older then the twenty-five years she guessed he was. He had a strong jaw line; athletic body and odd-looking red eyes that Lacy guessed were contacts or a wolf thing. Either way, there was something about him that she didn't like and the fact that he towered over her small frame didn't help either.

"Enakal?" he asked as Enakal approached first. The man with the red eyes bowed his head slightly as a sign of respect and that he was clearly lower in the line then an Alpha. The man was smaller then Enakal, not by a lot but smaller nonetheless.

"And you are?"

"Kane, I'm a dominant in the pack but not high up. Richard has asked me to collect you," Enakal nodded his head.

"Very well, we were informed there would be someone waiting for us. We shall follow you," Kane took them to a stretch black tinted limo that was waiting in the taxi rank and held the door open for them all to pile in then went to the drivers seat and started driving. Enakal sat in the passenger seat, riding shotgun so he could follow where Kane was driving them.

"Now this is living," Lacy announced stretching out and pouring herself a glass of champagne. "How awkward if Ollie called us and was like, 'Sorry but I've been at a week long orgy, where you at?'" Lacy laughed by herself. "No? No one is going to throw me a bone here?" Jay just shook his head.

"Can you imagine Ollie at a orgy?" he asked.

"You're right."

"Anyway, how can you be so calm and so happy all the time when you best friend is missing?" Jason asked seriously.

"Because, I know Ollie, wherever she is, she's making light of the situation and that is just what we do. I don't think we go a day without sarcasm or jokes. I don't know how to deal with loss and pain without it because Ollie has always helped me deal that way," Lacy finally admitted.

"Then by all means," Cruze surprised everyone by speaking up. "Be sarcastic or joke around. I know Ollie would be doing it and it reminds me that there is hope. So please do not take me getting angry seriously because it is just frustration with myself and not directed towards you, Lacy," he said with a sad smile playing on his lips.

"No problamo, Cruzinator. Oh! I have you a new nickname!"

"How about no."

"Party popper," Lacy sulked and downed her drink in one gulp. "What?" she asked with a shrug when everyone looked at her oddly. "Drinking always sooths the soul," she shrugged again.

Jason wrapped his arm around his mate and held her close. He knew just how much she was hurting, he could feel it rolling off her in waves and it killed him that there was nothing he could do or say to make it better, other then let her be her and enjoy whatever she could of life.

Kane pulled into a long dirt road that soon revealed a beautiful white mansion with vines climbing up the walls and very old style cottage roof on top. The grounds surrounding the mansion were that of reminding Lacy of mystical movies. High trees surrounded the mansion with a manicured ground of green grass and a few ropes hung in the trees while others had tires off it as a swing; a child's heaven.

"What a place," Lacy muttered under her breath. "You live in a place like this?" Lacy asked Jason.

"Yes."

"Can I go there?"

"Yes, but we are moving soon."

"Why?"

"Our pack is originally from Egypt but we all moved soon after Olyanah was born, you know that, so when we get Ollie back we are moving to our true home," Jason explained as Kane stopped the limo and let everyone out to stretch and gather their luggage before heading into the mansion and showing them their quarters for however long they needed it.

"Enjoy your time here," no one else paid attention to Kane but Lacy and he winked slyly at her before closing the door behind himself.

"OK," Lacy grabbed Jason's arm, "Please tell me you got a bad vibe from him and I'm not the only one."

"Something is very off with him. Those red eyes . . ."

"So that isn't a wolf thing?"

"No. Nor a human thing so I think he is up to something, or is something that is very worth an investigation,"

"Yeah well he winked at me when he left and I felt so dirty and so gross," Lacy shuddered at the image that was left in her mind from Kane. "There is something oddly familiar about him. Defiantly some Scottish in his accent, but he's trying to hide it. If Ollie were here, she'd be able to guess why, she's so good with all of that," grief overtook Lacy and it was only know that she realized the gravity of the situation. Jason felt such despair looking at his fallen mate.

"Come here, baby," Jason pulled Lacy in for a warm hug. "You know Cruze will never let anything happen to her, he will find Ollie and he will bring her back. I love you and I will be here for you whatever you need," Jason tenderly kissed Lacy's forehead and smiled down at his little fire. "I love you."

"And I you."

"Good, because I don't plan on leaving you any time soon."

"Lucky because if you did I think I would have to hunt you down and attack you for leaving me so it is best just to stay here with me and save us all the trouble of a full on man hunt for your fine looking arse," Lacy took a deep breath from her ranting and watched with a small smile as Cruze and Jason both laughed at her. It felt good that she could provide such light entertainment between everyone, but there was always going to be a hole in her heart until she got Ollie back.

They were partners in crime and making such jokes without back up was almost like cheating on Ollie to Lacy, not that anyone around her would understand so she just kept up the act for as long as possible.

Chapter Fifteen

Where There Is Love, There Is Life

OLLIE THRASHED AROUND on the ground, her body in spasms as she tried to avoid the boiling water that was being thrown on her. This water was past boiling point and the minute it hit her skin, she screamed out in pain, wondering what kind of people do this to an innocent person.

No one was in this new room with her; buckets were being filled with boiling water that was stuck on the ceiling, being thrown down every time a new bucket was full. Several buckets were stuck to the ceiling on different devices so Ollie was almost sure to get hit every time.

Ollie had been brought here by Gold Eyes; Red Eyes had been a little bit absent since last week when he gave her some food and Ollie had been left on her own since then, until today when Gold Eyes forcefully grabbed Ollie and walked her to a different room. Gold Eyes wasn't a tall woman but she was taller and apparently stronger then Ollie.

Ollie tried to remember what she had been taught when she was doing all her self-defense classes but nothing was coming to her. No fight or flight, she just wanted to survive and that meant taking what came to her.

The room was quite large and full of concrete, just like every other room Ollie had seen, with other odd contraptions attached to different areas. Ollie wondered how many people had been in this room before her and what had happened to those poor souls that were probably scared due to the physical and mental pain they had to endure.

Screaming out with tears running down her cheeks, Ollie tried to find a way away from the boiling buckets but she just couldn't find one as more water hit her body, burning the hair and skin when it came into contact.

The water suddenly stopped, leaving Ollie whimpering on the floor like a toddler that had been hurt. She didn't know what to do with herself, or even if she could move, when Gold Eyes came in, a familiar dagger in her hand and a sly smirk on her thin lips. Ollie tried to move but her body hurt too much for her to get anywhere, scared of what Gold Eyes was about to do to her already injured body.

"Let's play shall we?" a hit of evil playfulness was in her scratchy voice.

"How about no?" Ollie managed to croak out.

"I see you still haven't got our message of no talking?" there was no hint of surprise in Gold Eyes voice. "I'll just have to drill it into you," black hooded figures walked into the room and held Ollie down then Gold Eyes got to work. Ollie could feel the tip of the blade enter her skin and she screamed out in pain as fire engulfed the hole that was being etched into her forearm.

Ollie's head was being held away from what Gold Eyes was doing but she knew something was being knifed into her arm, something that was causing her deadly pain to flow through her veins and around her body.

Tears flooded from Ollie's eyes as she screamed out at the pain her legs trying to thrash against the floor to relieve some of the pain by giving her a new pain to focus on instead.

Gold Eyes was crouched over Ollie's arm as she dug the knife blade deeper into Ollie's forearm. The pain almost caused Ollie to pass out as her eyes rolled back in her head as everything became too much for her body to take and soon the world was dark around her, but Gold Eyes kept working on writing in Ollie's arm.

Ollie woke to a tremendous amount of pain flowing through her body, her head was still spinning and her eyes refused to focus on anything in the familiar room she was used to.

She could feel her whole body was covered in red raw skin that had been burnt by boiling water at what Ollie thought was the day before. Her arm was stinging from what Gold Eyes had done to her, Ollie looked over to her forearm tat felt as though it was on fire and saw *Dark Witch* written in her skin by a knife. Even knowing as little as she did, Ollie knew it was a bad thing; she knew it had now marked her as something she wasn't and that mark would never leave her skin or her mind.

The thought of Cruze went through her mind and would he still want her with this mark on her skin? Ollie had noticed the marks on Cruze's skin, like a dark tattoo marking him as a dominant male in the pack, so she had read in Anubis. When you were mates with someone the markings would appear on the female and match the males like a puzzle once some sort of 'Bonding Ritual' went on. Ollie could only imagine what hers would look like, covering the whole right side of her front, arm and back like thick and thin black waves.

As new as this was to her, she wanted so badly to have Cruze's dark markings on her body, showing to the world that she was his and only his. Thinking more about Cruze, made Ollie realize how much she was missing out on, she was no longer with him, no longer able to hold him or be held by him or have any more life changing experiences with him.

'No. I am not going to give up. I will be with Cruze again and I will make sure of it, even if I die trying just to show him how much I love him. I do love him,' Ollie told herself, and it felt good to admit that she loved Cruze, no loves him, she would live to tell him that.

Lying in the room for days on end, Ollie was able to study the architecture of the place and any little nocks and crannies that may be hiding for her to stay on. It had been days since she had been burnt by the boiling water and her skin had healed to the best of its Werewolf ability and Ollie was now pacing around the room, trying to find somewhere to hide. She was willing to stay in that position for as long as she needed to, so long as she came up with a plan to leave; for good.

All thoughts were on Cruze when Ollie painfully pulled herself up onto the beam that was hanging above the metal frame of the bed. Her arms were weak from the lack of food, the burns and the cut that was still in blister form on her forearms.

Somehow Ollie managed to pull herself up into the beams and crouched low into a dark corner on the cold metal beams. Her legs were already sore from the position she was in and as much as she wanted to be with Cruze, she didn't know if her body would be able to hold out for her.

It took only twelve hours for someone to come poking around, someone Ollie hadn't seen in a while, Red Eyes. He looked in the room and his eyes slowly narrowed as he tried to find Ollie.

"Come out, come out, where ever you are," Red Eyes played, but when Ollie kept her breathing even and stayed in the one position, Red Eyes walked in and looked around nervously. "Shit."

"What?" Ollie heard Gold Eyes ask and walk into the room, looking around as well.

"That's what," Red Eyes made an extravagant motion with his arm as he let Gold Eyes look in the room.

"Where is she?"

"I have no fucking idea. You were the last one that saw her," Red Eyes snapped and Ollie tried not to laugh at how the two were bickering.

"If you hadn't of gone back then we wouldn't be in this position," Gold Eyes snapped back. "You better find her, call everyone in and find her, because He wants her injured but alive," she threatened before leaving, having Red Eyes trail behind, leaving the door to Ollie cell open.

Ollie was just about to jump down and make a run for it when someone appeared in the doorway, smiled evilly and slammed it closed without too much of a glance into the room.

All her hopes were dashed as the thought of escape had excited Ollie and got her hopes up slightly. Resulting to the fact that she was never going to leave, Ollie climbed down and sat on the floor, tired from keeping watch up in the beams, waiting for her perfect escape.

She dropped her head on the floor and closed her eyes, in need of a deep sleep and a long cry that had escaped her for a long time. While slowly falling asleep, Ollie began to wonder what Red Eyes and Gold Eyes would say when they walked in, to try and find her and see her sleeping on the cold floor, all red from the boiling water and still bleeding from the cuts that Gold Eyes had caused with the knife work.

As scared as Ollie was about what they would say, she just didn't care any more now that sleep was taking over and all her thoughts were on Cruze and trying to open up to him, trying to let him find her, where ever she was in the world. Ollie still suspected Scotland due to the accents Red Eyes and Gold Eyes had.

As Ollie slowly started to go off to sleep, she thought of Cruze, as she did many times, but this time she thought about something he had said. He wanted her to open up to him and that was exactly what she planned to do.

Lacy held Anubis in her hands, reading further and further along trying to find out anything that would be able to find Ollie. Everything she was reading, she already knew from asking around and getting Jason to tell her everything. Reading along, Lacy stumbled along something that had her eyes bulging out of her head.

Running through the hallway and outside where the men were training, Lacy burst out into their space, holding the book in her hands. The man she had seen on the first day, Kane, she remembered his name as, hadn't returned so Lacy just guessed he was a recluse, which even she found weird as a werewolf they craved attention and being around other people and touch.

"Jason!" she panted. "Enakal, Cruze!" out of breath already, Lacy knelt down and rested her hands on her knees, trying to catch her breath. "Damn it, I need to work out more," she panted. "I found something," she said when she finally caught her breath.

"What?" Cruze threw his English fighter off him and hurried over to Lacy with Jason and Enakal. Arabella was out of earshot playing with Nuru when the men rushed to Lacy.

"Ollie, she's a," instead of telling them, Lacy opened up the book and showed the guys what she had read.

Simplex incantatores,
Simplex autem rithimi repercussio,
Et invocate nomen unum verbum vocas
Pueri cito obliviscuntur eius et derelinques animam tuam.
Hic filius est absconditum.
Et ieiunium iam invenerit inveniet.
Invenire talentum, et te, non dirigetur,
Temporibus ostendet se in occultum opus exigit,
Unus erit tantum, et non rebus.

(A simple spell,
A simple rhyme,
You call one word and cry out the name
The child will soon forget and leave your life.
A hidden child is in this life.
Find them now and find them fast.
Find their talent and you will succeed,
A Hidden will reveal themselves when the times calls for their needs,
And there will only be one in existence.)

"Ollie was teaching me Latin so I've worked most of it out, but I don't know what it all says," Lacy explained. She had managed to catch up on the things written about 'Hidden's' and the simple words, but other then that, Lacy didn't know what it said, until Jason read it out for her.

"Basically, what it is stating is that there is such thing as a Hidden and that means that they have been hidden from the Werewolf world, but not in the way you have been, it's quite different," Jason started explaining. "Your parents just made sure that you didn't know about your life because we left Egypt. Ollie's mind was actually wiped. Before she left to go with Jane and Greg at three, Aviva performed a spell on her. I have no idea how Anubis knew this was going to happen, but he did and we trust in our maker," Enakal nodded at Jason's statement.

"So, Ollie didn't leave when she was born like you told me when you met me in America?" Lacy stared at Enakal with evil eyes.

"No, we wanted to make sure she was in fact going to be hunted and she was, we moved not long after she turned one and let her go live with Jane and Greg once she was two," Enakal sat down, resting his head in his hands as he explained, despair and pain written in his body language.

"OK, and who is Aviva?"

"The High Fae," Lacy's mouth dropped as she heard the word 'Fae' and looked over at Arabella and Enakal in surprise, and then at Jason, begging him to explain what that meant.

"Lacy, if you know Werewolfves are real then you cannot believe that we are the only ones," Jason explained, taking both her hands in his.

"OK, what other 'creatures' are there?"

"I think we take that one step by step so we don't overwhelm you and we are called Mystics," Lacy nodded her head in agreement, her mouth hanging open a little as she tried to take in the information.

"Good call, Sherlock," turning her attention back to Cruze, Lacy stared at him, an idea forming in her mind. "So, Aviva is a Fae. I can live with that and my minimal understanding of that, but I have a question for you," Cruze pointed to his chest and mouth 'me?' "Yes you, Sir Beta of Werewolves."

"Not all Werewolves," Cruze interrupted, "Just the Egyptian pack," Lacy held up her hand waving it around, indicating that she didn't care about the small details.

"If you can get Aviva here or something like that, can she act like a little tracker dog or something and make a blinker to find our thinker?" Lacy asked.

"This is why I wanted to inform Lacy and Olyanah about us a lot earlier," Cruze said, closed fists clenching by his sides, to Enakal.

"What did I say?" Lacy asked, looking around the room, trying to kill the tension between Cruze and Enakal.

"You gave us an idea we hadn't thought about yet," Jason whispered in Lacy's ear.

"Not just a pretty face," she winked back.

Cruze held a priceless looking diamond in his hands as he sat in the garden of the house the UK Alpha was allowing them to stay at. His eyes were closed, focusing on the nature around him as he tried to get a feel for Aviva, finding a Fae was a hard thing to do and finding The High Fae was going to be trouble.

Lacy walked out with Nuru and went to sit next to Cruze, trying to feel the purity of nature around her. Lacy needed Ollie, far more then she cared to admit out loud, although everyone knew just how close the duo was.

Nuru was all Lacy had of Ollie and she looked nothing like her best friend and recently found out cousin. Nuru, being only two and never having met Ollie, was somewhat similar to her in personality, very funny, very light hearted, always looking for a good laugh to ease the tension that she didn't understand just yet.

"I don't feel anything," Cruze broke the silence and opened his eyes, playing with the diamond in his hands.

"I remember the first time I met Ollie. She was sitting on the playground at the end of my road, a SpongeBob Squarepants and Patrick Star suitcase at the bottom of the ladder and Ollie sitting at the top on the platform. She had mousy brown, almost blonde hair at the time and a scared look on her face. /

"Ollie was holding onto the pole next to her, like she thought I was going to hurt her. At that stage, people skills were not in her 'know how' book. I wanted to know what she was doing there," this was the first time Lacy had *really* told people how Ollie and her met; usually it was a much shorter and funnier story.

"I asked her what her name was but she refused to talk, refused to move, aside from the shaking that her whole body was doing, it was like she couldn't help being cold in summer," Lacy spoke softly, trying not to disturb the calm nature that surrounded the two.

"I climbed up to show Ollie I wasn't going to hurt her, told her my name and what I was doing there. I told her I was twelve and going to high school next year at Ashton High, this put a smile on her face and she started talking. She told me her name was Olyanah but she preferred Ollie. She told me a lot that night. How her parents always fought, how her parents were always cheating and just like that," Lacy clicked her fingers, "We became best friends that trusted each other to the moon and back.

"But I always got a feeling that she was holding back, and even when she talks to me now, I still have the same feeling, the same . . . mysterious feeling that she is hiding something, not in a bad just a way that she doesn't know how to express what she wants to say and how she is feeling."

"What do you think it is?" Cruze asked, curious to know what Lacy knew that he didn't.

"I followed her not long before we left. Two weeks before exams started. Greg held her tightly by the arm while she was dressed in such skimpy clothes, like a stripper. There was pain clear on her face but before I could go over, they entered an underground looking club and I fell asleep in my car. By the time it was morning, Ollie had emerged and went to school that day like everything was peachy, like she hadn't missed a night of sleep. Greg and Jane aren't nice people. The sooner you learn that, the better," Lacy wrapped Nuru up in her arms and stood up. "Just because people are nice to your face, doesn't make them nice all around."

Lacy left Cruze to his thoughts, making him feel angry that he hadn't been there to protect his mate and that she was in danger and there was nothing that he could do about it, nothing until Aviva decided to come and help.

"Why are you so damn fucking selfish!" Cruze cried out, standing and holding the diamond in his clutch, right next to his heart. "She is out there and she needs our help! Show yourself or so help me I will tear the world apart trying to find her and it will be blood on *your* hands," Cruze held the stone closer and tighter to himself as a single tear dropped from the corner of his eye and landed on the diamond.

A wash of wind over took nature as a figure, dressed from head to toe in a Greek Goddess white one shouldered dress with a golden wreath woven into her light purple hair. Silver eyes filled with knowledge and understanding stared down at Cruze, her bare clean and pale feet didn't touch the ground but hovered about ten inches off.

"Of course it's a damn tear that brings you here," Cruze cried out, causing Aviva to laugh slightly and reveal beautiful perfect white pearly teeth.

"You are much different from what I remember, Chike," Aviva started but Cruze cut her off.

"I had to adapt because people wouldn't have her in Egypt, so excuse me if the Australian culture has changed me. My name is now Cruze," he stated bluntly, completely ignoring the formality of the situation, being in the presence of the High Fae.

"As you wish it, so it shall be. You are a child of Anubis, why do you feel such sorrow?" Aviva asked, her voice like a beautiful musical charm being sung across the garden.

"Because you put The Hidden spell on my mate . . ."

"So The Hidden One is your mate?"

"Yes, and now she has been kidnapped by god knows who and taken god knows where to have god knows what done to her. You can find her Aviva; I know you can. She has been through more then she deserves an I'm asking you this, not as Cruze, but as Olyanah. She needs you, she needs me and I need her. I will do anything. Anything at all to get My

Angel back in my arms," Cruze wasn't crying but it felt to him as though he were exposing himself much more then if he were crying and showing deep emotions.

"How do you suggest I do this?"

"You're a Fae. You're the High Fae. I'm pretty sure you have a bag of tricks you can open."

"You have changed, Cruze," Aviva spoke, lowering herself, so her silver eyes were even with his blue ones. "You are so much more, imaginative. This is the doing of your mate?'

"Partly and spending so much time with her best friend, and surprise, surprise, long lost cousin. They are very funny," just as Cruze finished speaking, Lacy came outside only to be stunned into a quick silence.

"Shut up!" Lacy cried, followed by Jason, Enakal, Arabella, Jay, Drake, Josh and a slow walking Nuru. "That is too cool. Can you become invisible? Fly really high? Shoot webs from your fingers?" Lacy rattled off the questions quickly. The way she spoke reminded Cruze of Ollie, how only she would be able to understand the energized Lacy.

"I am not Spiderman," Aviva answered Lacy with a soft smile on her lightly purple lips.

"Your hair is so cool. Ollie would die to have hair like that. I think she's getting bored of the red a bit now; she's had it for like six years. OH! Maybe because she's all magical she can dye her hair like yours without too much hassle?" Lacy started again.

"I see what you mean," Aviva said to Cruze.

"Yes, well, it's quite good at points. So, can you help us?" Cruze asked, but begged with his eyes.

"I can. You will need to gather a few things for me though," Aviva started but Lacy interrupted her with another 'Oh' outburst.

"We're going on a treasure hunt!" she started singing to the tune of 'We're going on a bear hunt' and grabbing Nuru to dance with her in a circle. "We're going to catch some items to save the Princess from the evil man who has kidnapped her and we're going to kill him," Lacy sang quickly, with an eerie smile playing on her lips.

"Sadistic," Jason shrugged his shoulders. "My mate is sadistic."

"Yeah, well we all knew that," Cruze replied. "OK, Aviva, what do you want us to get?"

"A photo of her. Something that smells like her so I can track her scent," Cruze tensed his muscles at the thought. Smell was something sacred to wolves and something between mates, something he didn't want to share, "I know it is hard, Cruze, but it must be done, it is the only way to find her. I will also need the crystal, a candle, a bunch of Bittersweet's, pink Camellia's, striped Carnations, Primrose, a pure fire and some crystallized water," Cruze nodded his head and left straight away, going to get everything on the list that was now imprinted on his mind.

"So can you fly?" Lacy started again.

"No my child. Can you?" Aviva asked. Lacy pointed to herself and blinked a few times.

"I'm a wolf that doesn't turn furry, I don't think so," Lacy flatly said.

"Your mate has not been fully truthful with you," Lacy spun on the heels of her feet and glared daggers at Jason.

"Please explain."

"Well, Werewolves are more then just people that turn into wolves. Because of our need to survive, we have developed 'help'," Jason was slowly backing away from Lacy as he spoke.

"And what might this 'help' be?"

"Depends on the wolf."

"What's yours?"

"All wolves have super heightened sense, such as hearing, sight, taste and touch."

"I'm not asking about all damn Werewolves. I'm asking about you and I'm asking about me. What are our powers?" Lacy demanded stepping closer to her stumbling mate. It wasn't often a male was so scared of his mate, but Lacy had an aura about her at the moment, causing Jason to falter.

"I'm able to breath under water and you are able to heal quickly and heal those around you quickly," Lacy stopped and tapper her index finger against her chin, trying to understand what Jason had just said.

"What is Ollie's?"

"She has everything, that is why she is all powerful."

"Cruze's?"

"Super strength."

"That one makes sense. I mean breathing under water, you're a damn Werewolf, why would you go near water?" Lacy laughed and Jason playfully tackled her into the well-watered green grass. "What is Arabella's? Enakal's? Jay's? Nuru's?" Lacy asked, her blonde hair spread around her face, framing it.

"Arabella can shape shift, not for long periods of time but into other things then a wolf, Enakal is enhanced in combat to a degree no matter of practice can achieve. It is very amazing to watch him in hand-to-hand combat. Jay is a little different. Although a flirter, he is very much a nature person, he can control or manipulate water, that is why we are friends because sometimes, when the time calls for it, he has to drown me, which is impossible," Lacy nodded her head.

"And Nuru?"

"You develop your power at about the age of thirteen in your human teen years."

"Right, so you're telling me I'm all about the healing?"

"Yes."

"Cool."

"Not what I thought you'd say, but I can deal," Jason leaned down and kissed Lacy's soft warm lips. "I love you my Lacy."

"I love you too, Mr. Furry," the two lay on the ground in silence for a while until Lacy asked, "Can you teach me to change into a wolf?" As the two were talking, everyone else slowly walked away, making sure not to disturb the unmated couple.

"Of course. Although we aren't shifters, we still call if shifting when we change into our animal state."

"OK, I'm going to over look the 'although we aren't shifters' comment and say, when can we start?" Lacy rubbed her hands together, ready to turn furry for the first time. "Also, when will I be able to use my power?"

"When you need it, you call upon it and it comes naturally, but let's focus on one thing at a time," Lacy nodded her head in agreement.

"Perfect," she pressed her soft lips against his; letting the small whiskers that were forming on his cheeks, from not being able to shave, and chin tickle her soft skin.

I closed my eyes and buried my head under the blanket, trying to block out what was happening out in the lounge room. The yelling, the screaming, the loud noises had my skin crawling and my body shaking with fear.

I knew what he was doing and I knew what she was doing. I knew exactly what was going on and I was scared, scared to death that they would once again decide to turn their anger onto me. It had happened once before and I had ended up with a broken arm, something he managed to explain away.

I grabbed my SpongeBob Squarepants and Patrick Star suitcase and started packing. I packed a few clothes and what food I had hidden in my room and left. I didn't want to look back, I might only be twelve but damn I had had to grow up a lot faster then most twelve year-olds. Dysfunctional abusive parents usually did that to a person, no matter their age.

I walked for ten minutes to a playground on the end of a street. The beautiful houses along the street reminded me that appearances meant nothing, there were always secrets hiding behind walls, it's just a matter of how well people can hide them.

The playground sat so tall, so shiny in the full moon, almost like a sanctuary from my normal life. I had hid out in my room all day because I knew the full moon was tonight and I was terrified of people looking at my eyes, even though they only glowed at night.

I left my suitcase at the bottom of the colourful ladder and climbed up so I could see the moon, so beautiful, so out of this world.

There were footsteps around me and I looked down from the platform I was on and saw a young blonde girl standing at the ladder, looking up at me in curiosity. I didn't know what to say so I kept my eyes covered from her, avoiding eye contact.

"I'm Lacy, what's your name?" she asked, I could almost see the energy about to jump out of her. Slowly the girl moved towards me and climbed the ladder to get closer to me. I must've looked scared because she did everything in her power to make sure I wasn't afraid.

"I'm going to Ashton High next year, what about you?" Lacy asked.

"Same," I replied, softly and quietly developing a little more confidence.

"I'm twelve."

"Same."

"I'm Lacy."

"You already said that."

"Yeah, but when someone tells you their name, you tell them yours."

"Ollie. Olyanah but I prefer Ollie."

"Well, Ollie, I'll see you next year, or tomorrow if you want to come and play with me," Lacy suggested.

"I'd like that."

"Hello my dear," Ollie opened her heavy eyelids and looked up in a kind looking girls face. She had simple blonde hair that was tied up into a tight braid, keeping it out of her face. Ollie didn't trust herself to talk at the moment so she let the strange girl enter and close the door behind her, a caring smile playing on her lips.

"My name is Ally," Ollie nodded her head, still keeping her mouth shut. Red Eyes was really getting to her with the whole 'no noise' phase he was going through at the moment. "I'm going to help you," Ollie rolled her eyes at Ally's sweet tone. There was no one sweet here, no one.

"Go away," Ollie said, no longer scared of speaking. She knew that if Gold Eyes or Red Eyes wanted to hurt her, or even Ally, then she would deal with it because nothing could be worse then what had already happened.

"I'm here to help you."

"Bull shit," this made Ally change her tune, forcing the sweet smile on her lips to turn into a snarl.

"Excuse me?"

"You heard me. Bull. Shit," Ollie spat at the young blonde girl. Before Ollie could react, Ally had her hand wrapped around Ollie's throat and her body push up against the wall, Ollie's feet dangling off the floor a bit.

"You do not want me on my wrong side. You do not want me as an enemy. Remember that," letting Ollie go, she grasped for air.

"Where's Gold Eyes and Red Eyes?"

"Who?"

"The people usually attacking me and making what left of a life I had a literal living hell," Ollie explained, getting an evil smile from Ally, like she enjoyed the description of pain Ollie was currently experiencing.

"They'll be back. They have other business to attend to," with that Ally started walking out of the room.

"Wait!" Ollie called her back.

"Yes?"

"When will they be back?"

"Whenever they feel as though you need food, so a week or two," Ally stepped out of the cell and slammed the door closed, letting Ollie deal with the new information that she had been given.

Her head was spinning as she tried to deal with everything that had happened in the last few minutes with this new Ally girl coming into the picture. Everything was too much for her under sustained body and Ollie wished that she could just heal herself and maybe find some cool, crazy, 'James Bond' way of getting out of this place.

Sighing, Ollie thought of the stories she would be able to tell Lacy and Cruze about her getting out in the most spy way possible.

Laughing to herself, Ollie placed a hand on her red, burnt skin, wishing it were healed and wishing that it didn't hurt like it did. The fiery pain was more then unbearable now and Ollie was starting to question herself and how long she would be able to live like this before the pain over took her.

Slowly, a large circle around where her hand was, started to feel better and it slowly migrated down around her whole body, relieving the burns that adorned her skin. It was like being dropped into a bath filled with ice, letting her skin start to heal.

The miracle happening right in front of her, had Ollie with wide eyes. She was magically healing herself with only her bare hand on her stomach. This was something Ollie never thought she would ever see in her life, only something she had read about in fiction books, things might be turning around for her.

The silence was killing Ollie and the only thing she could think to do was to work out ways to entertain herself. She had discovered the supernatural power of healing herself not long ago and she wanted to know if there was anything else that she could do.

Just to test out her fun new ability, Ollie looked at the metal outline of a bed on the opposite side of the room and focused on the frame, begging it to move forward or do something that told her she wasn't going crazy and imagining that she had healed her whole body with just the use of her mind and hand.

Focusing on the old bed frame, Ollie saw that there was some cream paint pealing from the frame. Keeping her undivided attention on a fraction of the pealing paint, she imagined it falling off the frame, and just like she imagined it, the paint fell to the floor, floating in the air on its way down.

Wide eyes, Ollie decided to go with something bigger like a spring in the middle of the frame where a mattress would've been supported. She used all her 'powers' and paying careful attention, begged it to shake a little. She didn't want to start out too big so she stuck with small movements.

The middle spring her eyes had been on started to move slightly, shaking other springs around it as the tight metal tried to obey Ollie's mind.

"What an interesting development," she said out loud to herself, the first time she had smiled in weeks was now and due to a good reason.

Chapter Sixteen

Your time is limited, so don't waste it

LACY CLOSED HER eyes and kissed Jason's neck, letting him growl in desire for his mate and her touch. Lacy wanted to show him exactly what he meant to her and how much she needed him right now. Jason was her world and he was trying hard to make everything OK, but even though he couldn't make everything OK, he was trying hard and that meant everything to Lacy.

Doing everything in his power, Lacy was so grateful for Jason sticking by her side through everything. She had been spending a lot of time with Cruze, trying to give him hope and telling him more about his mate and what she was like from the hidden side he hadn't seen yet, but Jason was her mate and that's all that mattered to her.

"I love you, Jason," Lacy whispered against his ear before sensually biting the lobe, holding it lightly between her teeth.

"Don't tempt me, baby," he whispered back, sounding incredibly out of breath.

"Is there an unwritten rule that no sex before marriage with wolves?" Lacy asked, moving away and laughing.

"Something like that," Jason nervously scratched the back of his neck.

"Spill it now, wolf, or I'll neuter you," Lacy threatened, moving away from Jason so she could sit on the couch in their room and motioned for Jason to come and sit next to her so she could hear the full story.

"Have you ever read Werewolf books?" Lacy shook her head.

"Ollie was always the reader, like a hidden world for her, so she knows all about Werewolves and tells me but I haven't read them."

"Do you know about a thing called a Bonding Ceremony?"

"I've heard of it," Lacy eyed Jason off sideways.

"Well it is more sacred then a marriage. It binds the souls of two mates together because one cannot live without the other. The Bonding Ceremony, part of the Egyptian culture where we come from, will bind our souls together and consummating at the end of the ceremony is the final stage."

"How many stages are there?"

"The first stage is what happens before the ceremony. The female gets her hands and feet bleached with mosaic designs in henna. This will show your background and that you respect, not only Werewolves, but also the humans in which accepted us from the beginning.

"The second stage is what we wear. Traditionally the groom and bride wear linen outfits with gold and silver on them to symbolize that we will provide for each other and give each other everything we can.

"The next step is the *Kosha*. The Kosha is a decorated chair that is on a raised platform for everyone to see, it is where we will sit for the duration of the Bonding. *Sharpat* is served to us, which is a rosewater drink. We take a sip from the gold glass we are given and then swap; next we pour the pure rosewater that we both have touched into a silver rounded platter. Next we take a decorative plate each that has dirt on it. The dirt is from our native land, showing that we are in fact what we say we are, a Werewolf. We toss that into the silver rounded platter.

"The next element is wind. We place our hands in the rosewater and earth combination, holding each others hands under the water, uniting us as one while our Alpha, Enakal, reads out our vows that we repeat while he sets the water on fire. Placing our hands in the water creates ripples that symbolize water; an element of nature and the fire is the last element.

"You mustn't worry because the fire will not touch us and will only consist of a blue flame to show the supernatural nature of our world and that we can manipulate nature, not for bad but for good to bring people together.

"After all of this has happened and the vows are read out, I, as the male and provider, present you with an offering. An offering that you can choose to accept or reject, it is rare to reject as it shows that you want to in a way, reject your mate in some aspects.

"Because we are anticipating a Bonding, we will get rings, rings that we will hold on our right third finger, and after the vows and offering, we change it to the left ring finger. We then party. There are musicians called *Zaffa* and belly dancers, flamethrowers, flaming swords men and singers. This is the time where our food is served and we can mingle.

"The ceremony is very intimate, only our close family and friends will be there, but once the Zaffa's and entertainers come out, the pack come out to celebrate and congratulate us," Jason finally finished explaining everything, using a large range of hand gestures.

"So where does the whole no sex before Bonding come into it?" Lacy asked.

"It is said that if you sleep together before Bonding then your souls will not connect to the same extent. It doesn't have to be straight after but it is preferred to be after the Bonding at whatever pace is best for the mates," Lacy nodded her head.

"For once, I think I understand something," Jason laughed at his adorable mate.

"You need to give yourself more credit, my darling," Jason slowly and passionately kissed Lacy's soft lips. "I want to find Ollie before we Bond. I want her to be there for it; for you," Lacy smiled at the beautiful words spoken by Jason.

"Thank you," before she could say anything else, Jason pulled out a dark velvet box.

"Be mine, Lacy," he opened it, revealing two beautiful silver rings that had leaf designs all over them.

"Always," and she put the ring on her right hand. "See, I listen," she winked.

Cruze paced, he paced with his hands clenched in fists and he paced with his hands in his hair, ready to rip it out. He needed to find his

Olyanah; he needed to find his mate, not only for his wolf but for the man in him as well. Olyanah completed him, she was his other half, the only other person that could complete him and give him peace within himself.

A knock on the door pulled Cruze from his thoughts and made him calm himself down before answering. If it was another wolf, then he could provoke them by being mad and start a challenge or fight for dominance, something Cruze knew he'd win at, but still he wanted to avoid a confrontation in another Alpha's house and territory.

He opened the door, only to be greeted by Kane, the wolf who had collected them from the airport and taken them to the UK pack mansion. The Egyptian/Rosewood and Saint Louis pack had been here a whole week and a half now, without so much of a sign on the mysterious red eyed stranger.

There was something about the man that irked Cruze, something unsettling that had his skin crawling and yet something smelt familiar on him, but Cruze couldn't pick it just yet. Kane stood with a sly smile that slowly turned into something more welcoming and more inviting towards the Beta that stood in front of him with his arms crossed over his well toned chest.

"I have come to extend my hand in order for you to help find your mate," Kane address Cruze formally, so he should, Cruze was a Beta and as far as he could see, Kane was fighting to be more dominant then he really was, a poor choice in Cruze's eyes.

"Thank you, I do appreciate it," Cruze opened the door for the room he was sharing with Arabella, Enakal and Nuru, to allow Kane in. He wanted to find out more about this puzzling wolf that had been strangely absent since their arrival.

"You are Beta of the pack am I not mistaken?" Kane asked, taking a seat on the couch that was in the large suite like room. Cruze sat on the couch opposite him, trying to get a feel of Kane. Cruze was usually a very good judge of character, but with this man, this wolf, he couldn't decide.

"I am."

"You are the Egyptian pack?"

"We used to be," Cruze thought the story of the pack was well known around other packs. "Due to circumstances . . ."

Kane cut him off, "The child. Olyanah. The child of your Alpha's?"

"Yes, Olyanah. She was far too powerful and people wanted to so we took measures to keep her safe, but they all seem to be in vain as she is now taken from our protection," Cruze grimly told Kane as he rested the heels of his white sock covered feet on the old looking coffee table between the two couches.

"My condolences. I must ask though, why were measures needed to keep her safe? She is an Alpha's child, a strong child."

"She is also a very powerful child. You know we all have powers, abilities that are extended to us by the Moon Goddess to help us survive over the ages? Olyanah was given all the powers known to man and wolf, she is known as a White Witch but because she is a wolf, it is unheard of. That makes her a target because others will want to mate with her and want her for her powers to drain them and make her a shell of a person," with every word Cruze spoke, a picture of Olyanah formed in his mind, he hated the idea of his poor mate being in such a horrible situation that he couldn't stop.

"But can you not do that to other White Witches?"

"No. Because she is a wolf, an unmated female wolf, she is more vulnerable," Cruze hated talking about this, but something told him to be open to get Kane's trust so he could figure the odd wolf out.

"Once again, I am sorry for your loss," Kane stood with formality, lowering his head and showing his neck as a sign of submission to a more dominant wolf. "I shall see you around," he finished before leaving with a smile that had Cruze on edge, his eyes glowing as he left the room.

Lacy sat in the garden with Jason standing over her like a schoolteacher talking to a naughty child. He wanted to teach her how to shift into a wolf and let her wolf out so when they Bonded it would be a Bonding of not just Jason and his wolf to Lacy but to Lacy and her wolf as well.

"You talk about your 'wolf' like a third person, what's the deal with that buddy?" Lacy asked; confusion clearly etched onto her face.

"The man, or woman, and wolf are one, but the wolf is like a conscious type of voice in your head. She is the one that is telling you I am your mate, she is the one that is, not in control of your heightened senses, but being a wolf shows you what you are and how to use your ability and senses. Make sense?"

"Not really but I'm sure I'll understand when I'm all furry and running around on all fours through the open forest," Lacy shrugged her shoulders, eager to get ready for the first shift of her life.

"OK, so you need to focus on your wolf. Focus on what it would be like to be in wolf form. Running in the forest, running on the beach. The wind through your fur," as Jason spoke; Lacy closed her eyes and though of what Jason was telling her. She thought of having light fur flowing in the wind as she ran on all four legs.

Opening her deep blue eyes Lacy looked up into Jason's brown eyes, he looked taller to her then before, a lot taller. Tilting her head to the side, Lacy went to talk but instead a bark left her mouth and she heard teeth snapping together.

Stepping back a bit with fear, Lacy witnessed something she had once thought was just made up in books. Jason, right in front of her, crouched down, turning into a wolf, almost like a hologram as he crouched, bones moving into another position to create his other form. Jason had dark fur and glowing light brown eyes that were staring back at Lacy with almost a smile in them as they looked at her, happy to have this new experience with Lacy.

'Welcome to being a werewolf,' Lacy heard Jason's voice in her head and jumped back again with a whine coming out of her jaw. *'As wolves we can talk through telepathic communication. You can only do this when you are in wolf form, to communicate from wolf to human or human to wolf you use images,'* Lacy nodded her wolf head, still incredibly shocked and scared as to what was happening to her right now.

'This is some real crazy shit right here,' Lacy said, fear and excitement in her voice, or mind. *'So that means that it is like a 'Pack Link' or something? And how do I go back to human?'*

'Yes and the same as you turned into a wolf. You call on your human. It will soon be second nature for you but for now you will need to imagine yourself in your mind to shift back into a human, I must warn you, you will be naked when you turn back into a human. That is something you will get used to but being your mate, I refuse to let other males see you in your most natural state, that is only a privilege I can have as your mate,' Jason left no room for argument in his voice.

'Sure thing ding-a-ling,' Lacy sang as she closed her glowing eyes and pictured her human self again in her mind, ready to be human and normal again.

Opening her eyes, Lacy saw a very naked Jason in front of her and looked down to see she as pure and fresh as Eve. Jason smiled, winked and handed her the clothes Lacy was originally wearing. Jason changed into his pants but left his torso shirtless.

"You are making it hard to wait until we find Ollie to Bond," Lacy sensually said as she walked towards Jason in a stalking motion.

"I am not your prey, I am your predator dear mate," Jason grabbed Lacy by the waist and pulled her in for a heated, passionate kiss. "I love you my cute little Werewolf," Jason kissed Lacy again, down her chin, her neck and finally onto her collarbone, tracing the outline of her bone.

"What colour am I? You're a very dark wolf, but you have the same eyes. What colour am I?"

"Your eyes glow their natural colour when you are in wolf form. You're light, just like your beautiful hair," Jason pulled Lacy's wavy blonde hair into his hands and smelt it. "You smell like fresh cooked banana and raspberry bread to me," Jason whispered in Lacy's ear.

"And you, Sir, smell like muffins that were just pulled out of the oven," Lacy kissed Jason softly. "And now I'm hungry," she winked; leaving Jason in the dirt as she ran off at a much faster pace then she had ever ran before.

Ollie tried to remember everything Cruze had told her. She was trying to open herself up to him so he could find her; she was also trying to open herself up to her wolf so that she could change or phase or whatever it was called. Ollie wanted to be with Cruze again. She had gone far too long without him and was far too depressed to go on any longer. No matter what they did to her, she didn't think she was going to be able to handle it because Cruze was no longer with her.

Everything was spinning in her mind as she tried to focus on only one thing. She couldn't remember exactly what Cruze had told her to do, something like open her mind to him, to their love and what they had as mates.

She tried to open her mind to everything Cruze; everything about him like his smell, his body, and his face, his everything. She had seen some amazing tattoos on his body, something she admired from a distance for a very long time. One day she hoped to get something like them.

She had moved along with her telekinesis, being able to move the bed a few inches to each side, but it took a lot of force on her end and she usually ended up with a bad headache and the room spinning a lot more then usual.

Along with the telekinesis, Ollie had been trying to remember what Cruze had told her and what she had read in Anubis about other Mystical creatures and what forms they were in.

Vampires, Elves and Fae, they seemed like normal and reasonable creatures to think about, if Werewolves were real then why couldn't those creatures be real? Ollie racked her brain to think of other creatures she had read about in history.

"Witches," Ollie started saying out loud, not scared to talk while she was alone in her cell. "Mermaids, Banshee's although I think that is a little far fetched. Lilitu's are in religion so who knows if they are real, Hamadryad's are a type of nymph, that much I know, other then that I am bloody confused about what other creatures might be lurking in the dark when the lights are out."

Ollie stood up from her hunched over position, grabbing the Werewolf belly button ring from her black crop top and studying it in the dark light that was barely there. Calling on her new sense, Ollie looked at the piercing and focused with all her might, trying to gather if there was a hidden message in it somehow.

Maybe, like most thing, Greg and Jane had lied and her grandfather hadn't really given it to her, maybe, like everything else, there was a hidden meaning behind it that could help Ollie, or bring her closer to those she loved dearly.

Ollie could hear the iron locks on the other side be opened, so she shoved the piercing back into her crop top, fell onto the ground and looked up like she had been sleeping. Wanting to act all her life, she was able to easily get away with the act.

"Get up," Ollie heard the sweet voice of Ally say, interrupting the silence in the room.

"No," Ollie was over playing the victim and wanted to take a stand for herself.

"Excuse me."

"You're excused, you can leave," Ollie waved Ally off like she was nothing but a lower class girl looking down at an upper class girl.

"Get. Up."

"No."

"Don't make me get the others," Ally's upper lip was turned up in a snarl as she spoke.

"Whatever," Ollie wanted to asked more, she wanted to know what creature Ally was because she sure wasn't a Werewolf, Ollie could just sense that and she could also sense the power around Ally but she just didn't know how she got it.

As far as Ollie knew, these people didn't know that she knew about Mystics and she wasn't about to give it up so easily in a stupid question.

"Don't forget, you asked for this," Ally left the room, slamming the door behind her making Ollie jump.

Not too long later, Ally returned, opening the iron lock and then the iron door with Red Eyes and Gold Eyes standing behind her. Their glowing eyes seemed so much more luminescence then normal, bringing visible goose bumps to Ollie's arm.

"You refuse us? You defy us?" Gold Eyes asked, stepping forward with a soft smile on her lips.

"That is a big mistake," Red Eyes took his placed next to Gold Eyes, standing tall and strong, puffing out his chest to make himself look meaner. Ollie shook her head, now realizing what she had just done to herself and exactly what she was now in for.

After missing Cruze for so long and not being able to be near him, she didn't know how she could go on, and now by provoking those who had taken her, she saw how not smart her smart arse comments had been. This was going to be the literal death of her, it was almost painfully obvious to her.

"We have a new friend for you to meet," Red Eyes grabbed Ollie, pulling her up by her hair and wrapping her burnt arms around her back and pinning them there while he wrapped them up with rope.

"I like meeting new people, will I like her?" Ollie asked with fake enthusiasm.

"Only time will tell," Gold Eyes laughed. Ally walked in front of Ollie with Red Eyes still holding her arms behind her back and Gold Eyes bringing up the rear, making loud foot steps as her steel toed shoes tapped along the ground.

It wasn't long before they stood outside another room with a dead bolted iron lock and steel handle. Ally opened the steel handle and pulled out a key, placing it in the lock and turning it.

There was a loud noise when Ally turned the key, opening the door to reveal a room exactly like Ollie's. A very scared girl sat huddled in the corner of the room, shaking back and forth as she tried to control her racing mind.

"Enjoy your time together," Red Eyes pushed Ollie into the room. Ollie fell face first into the cold, hard flooring. The door was slammed closed behind Ollie, leaving the two in pitch black. This room didn't have any cracks in the boarding on the window and no light in the ceiling.

Ollie didn't say a word as she wormed her way to sitting up and resting her tied up arms and back against the cool wall that Ollie accepted as homely now. The young light haired girl stared at Ollie, some how creating her own form of light like an aura around her body. It was a very light colour around her body, making Ollie feel at ease straight away for some strange reason she didn't understand.

"You're new here," it wasn't a question but a statement on Ollie's part. "How long have you been here?"

"I don't know," she had an airy voice, almost like an angel.

"Not long though?"

"No, not long."

"I'm Ollie," the airy girl's eyes widened, almost as though Ollie was a special name and said something about her.

"Ollie as in Olyanah?"

"Yes?"

"I'm Rebecca, but everyone calls me Becca. I know all about your story."

"Please enlighten me then because I know jack-shit about my own life but apparently everyone knows," Becca's posture and position changed almost straight away and she relaxed visibly.

"You are the product of the most powerful Alpha's in the Mystics world and a spell put on your unborn body while you were still in your mothers stomach. Although a Dark Witch, she was light at heart and struggling against the forces that had been cast upon her. Being the product of those two, you have been given all powers," Becca got up and walked over to Ollie to untie her wrists.

"Powers?"

"Or abilities, whatever you want to call them."

"I'm still lost. I have powers?"

"All Werewolves do, it is to help with the evolution of your kind. Every Werewolf only has one ability, because of what has happened to you, you have been given all abilities, you can do everything," Ollie looked at Becca with wide eyes.

"So the healing myself and moving the bed, not just in my mind?"

"No, not just in your mind. Why do you not know this?"

"I was taken away when I was two to 'keep me safe' but I feel as though it was the opposite and now I am here all because of what they did. I honestly don't know how to feel about life any more. I don't know whether or not to believe you because I feel as though if I do believe you then I'm confirming that I am in fact in my own mind and sitting in an insane asylum. But if I don't believe you then everything I know and have learnt doesn't make sense," Ollie's hands started shaking the more she spoke to Becca about her fears.

"You have found your mate," it wasn't a question but a statement.

"Yes, what are you? A mind reader?"

"No, a Fae, my mother is the High Fae, Aviva and my father is the High Elf, Winslow. Together they are King and Queen of Elves and Fae and I am the Princess."

"OK, that is a hell of a lot to take in at once, but just let me breathe and then continue," Ollie shook her hands out and ran them through her hair.

"Fae and Elves are two different species, but Fae are only female and Elves are only male, that means to continue living we must mate with one another. It is pretty odd, I mean for someone that has never understood what is going on, but normal for someone like me."

"I don't think 'someone' is the right word. I think 'some Fae' suits better," Ollie got up from her spot on the floor and started pacing.

"I might be a Fae but I haven't reached twenty-one yet which means I don't have all my powers, do you mind healing me a little bit?" Rebecca had a long dress on her body and lifted up the long sleeves, showing a few bruises. "They aren't nice people, been set upon twice now," Ollie just chuckled.

"You've gotten off easy, I wish that was all that had happened to me."

"You do know why they are doing this right?"

"For their idea of fun?"

"Because if they can exhaust you enough and make you scared enough then they can drain you of all your powers and become the most powerful creatures in the world."

"Oh, my, god," and Ollie dropped to the floor.

Ollie woke with a start, her mind racing as to what she had just been told by her new friend. She didn't know how to process all the information so she just let it consume her.

"Ollie," she looked up and saw Becca's beautiful, puppy dog like brown eyes.

"I'm not giving up. I am not going to let them get this power."

"Neither am I."

"Promise me you won't give up," Ollie held her pinky finger up for Becca to shake it with a promise.

"I will never give up."

"Good."

Lacy ran through the woods, letting the wind fly across her fur, ruffling it slowly as she hit a falling branch. She could hear Jason behind her, slowly catching up but keeping his distance, letting her discover where he was by using her senses to the best of her ability.

'You need to be careful, lay low and use your senses to guide you. You have to be silent as a predator,' Jason guided Lacy as she ran.

'Easy for you to say, you've had a whole lifetime to learn this. It was just thrown on me one day,' Lacy shot back, annoyed at how hard it was for her to get this. It was like her bubbly personality was working against her for once, making it hard to be out of the limelight and lay low without making a noise.

Lacy stopped in the middle of the forest, keeping her panting breath even and quiet, she waited until she could hear Jason coming up behind to her right. She could see a flash of dark hair before knowing that he had passed her. Perfect. Now she could show him exactly what she had learnt.

Slowly and quietly, Lacy picked up pace again, making sure her feet barely touched the ground before taking the next step. She ran on all fours, spotting a running dark Jason in wolf form a few hundred metres in front of her. For once, Lacy was thankful for these heightened senses that had been bugging her since she first shifted into a wolf.

Having super sight was a good thing when she was going to jump up and scare the crap out of her mate. Oh how Ollie would love this, Lacy thought as she crept up on Jason who had stopped and was looking around for Lacy in front of him.

Before he could make a move, Lacy bounded out of the trees and jumped on top of Jason, scaring him and causing him to fall with Lacy on top of him.

'Can't master the skills my arse,' Lacy laughed in his mind, winked in her wolf form and then was off, bounding through the trees as she ran away from her mate, making a chase out of it.

Jason had no idea what had just happened. The only people that could get the jump on him were Enakal and Cruze and that was because they were older and more dominant, therefore able to hide so much easier. Lacy was surprising him and herself everyday with her improvements in her wolf form.

Tomorrow he planned on teaching her to fight in this form so that she was prepared, then came human fighting, something Enakal would teach her without Jason watching so he wouldn't growl at his Alpha fighting with his mate and potentially hurting her.

That was the part that was going to kill Jason, not being there when Lacy started fighting because he was her mate and he was meant to keep her safe; no matter what happened and he had already failed once, that would not happen again, he had promised himself and Lacy that.

Lacy pulled on some clothes after have a long warm bath and walked down the UK pack mansion into the empty smaller of the three lounge rooms. Kane sat there with a book in his hands and a few bags at his feet like he was ready to go on a trip.

Lacy just shook off the feeling of being around Kane and pulled out her book. It was Ollie's favourite, Lady Chatterley's Lover. She could remember the day they were packing, she was in a rush and Ollie was sitting back reading the tattered old book. Lacy found it in Ollie's stuff that was left at the hotel suite in Phoenix when she woke up and Jason and Cruze came.

Just opening the book, Lacy could smell Ollie's scent on the book and for once thanked her amazing new senses for the ability to be with Ollie once again.

"Light reading?" Lacy looked up at the man with glowing eyes and visibly shivered.

"Some might say," Lacy didn't want to talk right now. She wanted to read the words Ollie had read many times before, finally seeing what she saw in the written word. It wasn't the words themselves; it was the story behind them, being in the readers mind, being in the writers mind, being in the characters mind.

"Lovely book. I'm more a fan of the cinematic version myself," Lacy didn't want to imagine what Kane did in his spare time.

"Charming, I must say," Lacy rolled her eyes and spoke flatly.

Chapter Seventeen

You Must Be The Change You Wish To See In The World. Don't Make Me Walk When I Want To Fly

OLLIE SPOKE EASILY with Becca while still trying to keep her energy levels down because they hadn't been fed or had anything to drink in a long time. Becca was teaching Ollie all about other Mystics in the world and what forms they took and their powers, along with the way they lived on the land.

"OK, start me off with something easy today, my mind is shot at the moment," Ollie lay on her back on the cold floor, looking up at the graphitized ceiling that teenagers had attacked long before it had been taken as a torture chamber. Becca sat on the metal frame of the bed with the springs moving underneath her form.

"Vampires?"

"Go for it," Ollie had her arms folded behind her head as she started listening to what Rebecca had to say.

"Vampires are like what you hear about. Pale skin, fast, energetic at night, tired during the day, able to handle poisons, alcohol and all that very well. They look very young for their age, very good sense, the problem with

Vampires evolving through the ages is that killing humans is a lot more noticed now and they have had to turn to other 'resources'," Becca got up ad started pacing around the room as she explained everything to Ollie.

"And that changes them?"

"Yes, they are a lot, to put it nicely, sillier. It is almost as though human blood fed their intelligence and now that they have started hunting animals. You know those unsolved murders?"

"Yeah," Ollie sounded skeptical.

"Vampires gone rouge, The Council is then forced to find them and get them."

"Council?"

"Yes, of all Mystics."

"That sounds so far fetched and yet so believable I almost want to cry," Becca let out a bark of laughter. "I thought you said you were a Fae not a Werewolf because you have me pretty fooled."

"You're going to pay for that comment," Becca lay on the floor next to Ollie and the two new friends started laughing. "The Council of Mystics is basically made up of all the Alpha's King's, Queen's, Captains and whatever else they are called, of the different Mystics. It is hard to keep order but they manage to all follow the laws that have been set out by the Goddess," Becca explained to Ollie, trying to make this all as easy as possible for her. There was a silence in the room after the explanation, letting the two girls hear every noise outside the room, the water dripping and the footsteps walking away from their cell.

"Are we ever going to get out of here?"

"If I have it my way, then hell yes."

"Glad I can count on you. You'd love Lacy; she's like a sister to me. We can be the Three Amigo's when we get out and you can find your mate and we can all live happily ever after," Becca sighed and closed her eyes, admiring Ollie's optimism after everything she had been through. "Why do you think they put us together? It would have to be a part of their plan."

"I don't know, maybe so you would know all of this and they could use it against you."

"Because they weren't doing that already," Ollie rolled her eyes. The two fell into a comfortable silence and their breathing evened, showing that they were falling into a much needed sleep.

The two had been awake for a long time, not knowing what time it was, and were tired from all the learning and expressing of information. For the first time since being here, Ollie was actually happy; happy that she had met Becca and happy that she had learnt all of this new information about herself, her species and those that she would soon be living among.

Ollie promised herself that she was going to learn from this experience and that she was going to come out of it alive and be a better person. No matter what happened in Ollie's life, she was going to leave this place at some point and she was going to experience the world she had at one point been so desperate to see.

Being with Becca felt like a dream, this didn't feel right as she was being left with someone that could possible give her all the answers she needed.

Ollie sat up in the middle of her sleep, trying to rub her eyes from the light that was shinning into them, giving her an unforgiving headache. Blinking, Ollie remembered that the room she had last been in had no light in it at all.

"Where am I?" she asked herself, or at least she though herself.

"Where you belong," Ollie tried again to rub her eyes but something was restricting them, chains moved around the room and a weakened feeling Ollie stumbled around on the balls of her feet.

"You have been warned about talking, and since you won't listen to us, we think you might listen to her," Gold Eyes stood with a wicked smile on her lips, her eyes showing just how much she was enjoying the pain that Ollie was in.

"Ollie," Ollie looked up and saw the blade of a knife reflect the protruding light into her eyes, the knife was leaning against the fresh flesh of an almost glowing girl with tears running out of her eyes.

"Becca."

"You have a choice. Listen to us and she lives or defy us and she will die," Red Eyes was holding Rebecca, not letting her move an inch in his grasp.

"Don't listen to them!" as Becca spoke, the rusty blade was pressed against her neck and a small trickle of blood started streaming down.

"I'll do whatever you want," they nodded.

"Smart girl," Red Eyes pulled the knife away and used the handle to hit Becca's temple, letting her crumple to the floor. "Now that we have your attention, we are going to take you to a place where we can get to know each other a little bit better," Ollie's eyes widened as Red Eyes walked over and hit Ollie in the same place with the handle of the knife, letting her head drop to one side.

"This is going to be a lot more fun then I thought," Gold Eyes cackled, walking ahead as Red Eyes guided Ollie away from her new friend.

A pain resonated around Ollie's wrists as the tried to pull her hands to her face to rub the sleep from her eyes and clear them but something was burning her wrists and not allowing her to move.

Opening her eyes, Ollie saw herself in a very familiar scene with her wrists tied to the roof with poison laced chains that were attached to the roof and her feet almost dangling from the floor. Her body and mind were overtaken by panic at being out in this situation, everything from her memory becoming a blur as she realized what had happened to her.

The room she was in looked different from the room she was used to. It was smaller with no furniture and bars at the front of the cell. Ollie felt as though she was in a jail cell and like she was being hanged for murder in 1892.

Everything was a blur to her, the last thing she could remember was Ally stepping in the room and telling her that she was basically going to suffer, telling her that everything she had been through so far was just a test, a test that was about to get serious and cause her pain she had never experienced before.

Everything Ollie could remember from her 'dream' was all about those Mystics, those creatures that Ollie was learning about from Becca, if she was even a real person. Nothing was making sense to Ollie anymore and the fog in her mind was starting to make it very hard for her to concentrate on one thing, she couldn't work out if her new friend was just a figment of her imagination while she was asleep or if it had actually happened, the poison was flowing too fast through her veins, weakening her and making her feel dizzy, not letting her know the difference between realist and imagination.

"You're powerful. Very powerful, something you don't know yet," Ollie was able to spin on the balls of her feet and moved around so she could face a very unfamiliar look man.

"How so?"

"Did I say you could talk? I do believe we have made this clear to you that you are unable to talk or make a noise. Ever," the man had a very steady, caring voice even though there were some very malicious things coming out of it.

Ollie bit her lip, remembering the boiling water on her skin and the pain of the blisters and the pain of the sting when they popped, causing her to scream and cry out, begging for release of the pain she was in. It was a very unpleasant experience that Ollie didn't want to call on again.

"Good, that's better. Like I said, you are powerful. Very powerful, and it is our job to drain you of life and to drain you of your power, something that is proving to be harder then we first thought, so we are changing our method. Welcome to the hospital," he didn't smile, he didn't laugh and he didn't show any form of emotion on his face or in his voice.

He pulled out a key from his pocket and looked up with a smile, his eyes suddenly glowing a dark colour, not black but close to it, there was no real difference between the pupils of his eyes and the colour other then a hint of a honey colour.

The sinister look in his dark brown, almost black eyes had Ollie wanting to step back from the man and protect herself, but the poison in the chains were weakening her, she could feel her muscles relax, not giving her a chance to fight back at all.

"You have beautiful eyes," he stepped in and moved towards Ollie, letting a hand trail from her hair down to her chin, lifting her head up to his eyes. Ollie's short frame, even when almost completely suspended in the air, was still shorter then the man in front of her. "Such beautiful eyes," a snarl escaped his lips and a tear left the corner of Ollie's eye. She knew it wasn't malicious but lustful and Cruze had made the noise many times before when he had Ollie in a warm protecting hug.

He didn't touch her any further, instead choosing to break the chains about her head and pin her arms behind her back, getting her hair tangled in there too and pulling Ollie's head back painfully.

As the two walked, it was like all the good in the world was being sucked with each step. Dark Eyes, as Ollie named him in her head, walked with a purpose down the hallway that was littered with barred cells that Ollie couldn't see into because her eyes didn't have enough time to adjust to the darkness that was surrounding them.

Ollie didn't know where she was being led, but by the sounds of the dripping water and their echoing footsteps, it wasn't going to be a good place. She could hear rats scurrying along the floor and moans from other cells, but her eyes still wouldn't adjust to the new light around them the two moving far too fast to give her any time to adjust to the light.

All that was going through Ollie's mind was Cruze. His sandy hair, his muscles, and the way he looked when he surfed and how at peace he seemed with the world. Her emotions grew stronger and stronger being away from him everyday, but that didn't help heal the hole in her heart that was growing everyday at his absence, she just needed his touch, just once, to keep her going and then she could handle anything they threw at her.

The things she had learnt in her dream, Ollie couldn't work out if they were real and her mind was just uncovering them, or if she had made them up in her drug induced sleep. It felt like it had been a dream, how stupid would they be if they had left her in a room with a Fae to tell her everything about her life and other Mystics?

"Welcome to Hades," Dark Eyes stopped and opened a door for Ollie that opened onto a very dark looking room with only a single light hanging above a cold, stone looking 'experiment' table.

"Long time, no see," Ally stepped out of the shadows like a movie figure, her hair perfectly in a French Twist and her makeup down without a blemish. She was wearing a pair of high waisted leather pants and a white tucked in sweater and necktie tied to one side.

Ollie didn't say a thing, taking the threat from Dark Eyes seriously. Red Eyes and Gold Eyes were in the room too, both wearing the usual simple black clothing like they were ready to go in and fight.

"Come here," Gold Eyes instructed Ollie. Dark Eyes let Ollie go and she walked slowly towards Red Eyes. Her feet shuffled along the floor, knocking rocks with each barefooted step.

"So," Gold Eyes stopped talking as she paced around Ollie as she stood nervously with her hands clasping each other in front of her. "So clean, so strong. Something I would love to change," Gold Eyes spoke with an alluring voice, licking her lips as she walked around Ollie.

"Come now, we must get down to business before we start our pleasure," Red Eyes said with a smile, gently bringing Gold Eyes back from Ollie, holding the top of her arm almost seductively.

This was one odd romantic triangle or square or pentagon that Ollie didn't want to get involved in. Watching the Three Psychopath's and their new dark-eyed friend chat silently in the room had Ollie shaking. She was terrified of what they might do to her, some 'experiments' were their words and she did not know what that might mean for her.

Her screams could be heard all around the old unused building. She tried to kick against the stone table she was tied to with those draining chains, her kicks echoing around the hallways that were adjacent to the Torture Chamber, or Hades as they had referred to it as.

Every time the hot pliers were placed around Ollie's chewed nails and pulled, she screamed. The nails ripping from the skin made a terrible noise, making it even harder to ignore the pain radiating around the fingernails and through her body and felt to an extent she didn't know she could feel. Her body wanted to give up, it wanted to just give in to what they were doing, but her mind refused as she hung onto the 'dream' she had had and begged for it to be real.

She had promised Becca, not that she knew if she was real or not, but it was a promise she wasn't going to break. Ollie never broke promises and she wasn't about to start now.

How anyone could heat pliers to the red hot stage, place them on and around fingernails and pull them off their victim while they were lying, screaming right in front of the attacker, was something Ollie would never be able to understand. Ever. It seemed so old; so barbaric to her, like some form of torture they would've used in the Spanish Inquisition.

"That is life," Gold Eyes whispered in Ollie's ear before ripping another nail off her finger, letting Ollie feel her hot breath against her cheek, trying to pull away from the Gold Eyed woman that was trying, and succeeding, to sow fear in Ollie's mind and heart.

"That is enough now," Ally called. Ollie had stopped counting due to the pain but she guessed a few nails off each hand were taken and a few toe nails too. Ollie couldn't believe the pain she was in due to the nails being pulled out, the hot pliers and the exposed skin in the stale, old, chemical air.

"Here," tears blurred Ollie's vision as she tried to look around and see what was going on with the four that were trying to cause her as much pain as possible.

All Ollie could hear were murmurs from their direction, but nothing other then that as her tears clouded her sight far too much and the sounds of her sniffles blocked her hearing.

Instead Ollie closed her eyes, trying to transport herself to a much nicer place, a place where she was sitting on the beach in Cruze's arms, Lacy and Jason sitting next to them as they watched the sun set over the waves that were flowing in Saint Louis. The scene was so beautiful; Ollie was determined to make that image in her mind real one day.

She wanted to be in the water that she was picturing in front of her, stopping the pain that she was feeling in her body, Cruze's body stopping it and the warm salt water helping with the infection that was no doubt about to come and riddle her body.

She wanted to be working at the diner with Lacy and have a joke with her old friends as they all sat around with smoothies and chips. There were so many things that Ollie missed but the ones most prominent in her mind were of Cruze and Lacy.

Her legs trashed against the stone, scratches and scrapes appearing and bleeding with each kick of her legs and each thrash of her arms. She could feel the warm liquid over her skin and couldn't help as more tears formed in her eyes, not really clouding much as the only light in the room was turn out and Ollie's sight was quite bad at the moment, only seeing the same room and the same artificial light for god knows how long.

Ollie was longing for her old cell back where she was tied up to the ceiling and only being whipped. Everything was a big mess but now it was even worse because she didn't know how long she had been gone, but she knew it was a very long time, guessing that they came once a day, maybe once every two days, then she had been here a good few months.

Almost every torture technique had been used on Ollie, and new techniques she had no idea about. She had been branded like a cow on a number of occasions, different shapes marred into her skin that would never go away. She felt like an object of their enjoyment as they used new devices on her body, forcing her to feel the pain even when she tried to hide from it.

A taser had been placed on her upper thigh by Gold Eyes and pressed to a degree that Ollie smelt burning flesh and knew by the smell in the room right now that there was some infection crawling through her skin, underneath her skin attacking her body and making her weaker then the chains that were holding her to the table.

It was like her whole insides were on fire, burning away and causing sweats and the shakes every few minutes. It was uncomfortable being tied and shaking uncontrollably and she was getting bad scratches along the exposed skin of her heels and the back of her hands.

All that she was left wearing was a simple black crop top and black undies that she was scared Gold Eyes would soon destroy, the same uniform as before, her body would be covered in sweats one minute and then goose bumps the next.

She could see the indent of the wolf piercing in the crop top, but those touching her hadn't touched it yet, the only thing she was grateful for. If they had touched it, Ollie didn't know what she would do. It felt as though the piercing was a part of her now, like there as something deeper then just silver and a diamond in it, something sentimental she had yet to uncover.

Ollie had been violated before, by men, but never in such a way that she didn't have some form of control over the situation. She was usually able to push people off he when they got too out of control, but this situation was so different, so much scarier for Ollie; making everything that was happening to her so much real, Gold Eyes was her main concern and whenever she got too close Ollie would retreat into her old dream world and think about the Mystics the Fae, Becca, had told her about.

Every now and then she would have snippets of her 'dream', but never again had she had the same dream. She wanted so bad to have that world back, have Rebecca by her side, if she was even real and to learn about other 'Mystics'. That life Ollie longed for was something she felt was slipping further and further away from her, not only physically but mentally as well.

Slowly her mind was leaving her and she was forgetting details she felt as though she should know back to front.

Ollie amazed herself by the fact that she was at least able to remember Cruze's name and Lacy's name along with her own. It had been so long since she had been addressed by her name that it was almost gone from the memory bank.

Chapter Eighteen

Dreams Are The Essence of Learning

LACY SAT ON the balcony that over looked the beautiful sandy landscape of Kharga, her home in Egypt for the past few weeks. It was tough for her to adjust to this lifestyle, a lifestyle she never thought she would have.

Living in Egypt, getting used to a mansion with unfamiliar male and female Werewolves in it along with an Alpha Female and Alpha Male, her brother finding his mate and her parents being so happy to uproot their family and come to their 'home' as they liked to call it. This was a life Lacy wouldn't mind; if Ollie were here to share it with her.

In two months it would be a year since she went missing.

Three months ago was when they gave up all chances of finding her.

Four months since Cruze withdrew so far into himself, he barely left his room unless it was to blow off some steam and go for a high speed run through the sand and trees that scattered their land.

There was a beautiful forest near by and it was a favourite place for all wolves to go for a run in. The forest was quite large but Lacy hadn't gone exploring yet, too scared to be in her wolf form since arriving here.

All of those count downs for Ollie were far too long for Lacy's liking and she knew she had to get back into her daily life soon or else she would withdraw like Cruze had done not too long ago.

Soon, Jason and herself would Bond, this was a dream for Lacy, to Bond with the man she loved in a place that felt like home for the first time in her life, even if her best friend wasn't there.

"Lacy, my love. Please. I know that you are upset but we have done everything we can do and you need to start living again. Come out tonight, Cruze, Jay, Harry, Liam, Polly, Sarah and Martha are all going out, join us," Lacy knew Jason was right and having his arms around her had her heart pumping.

"OK. For you."

"No, I want it to be for you."

"Then for both of us," Jason leaned down and kissed his beautiful mate. Her lips were so soft to him, so lovable and so familiar. Every time he kissed them it was like a new experience of emotions running through his veins.

"I love you."

"I love you too. Come on, I have to have a shower and get changed."

Lacy sat in a booth with Jason's arm around her while Cruze stood dancing with a few girls and the other six were off taking shots at the bar. It was the first time Lacy had seen Cruze happy since Ollie disappeared and it warmed her heart. She might not be here but that didn't mean they were going to forget her; never.

"Yeah, Cruze!" Lacy called over the loud music and fist pumped when he looked over. "I guess you were right about going out," Lacy conceded when she looked at Jason. "I still find it weird that they know we are Werewolves. Is it only Kharga that know about us?"

"Sworn to secrecy by Enakal," Lacy nodded her head as a man brought over two more drinks for them.

"This place is so cool," Lacy looked up from her cocktail and saw Cruze had picked a blonde girl to sway in his arms. Her heart twanged at the betrayal Ollie would feel if she were here, but Lacy knew she wasn't and he needed to move on with his life, like everyone did.

"Our secret baby girl," Jason's exploring lips found Lacy's neck and gently kissed her where her shoulder met her neck, causing her to move to that he could have better access. It was a feeling Lacy had never experienced and she suddenly wanted them to be Bonded so she could throw everything out the window and let him take her.

"I want to be yours, completely yours," Lacy moaned as Jason's lips got to work on her neck.

"Then so you shall be," he whispered against her sensitive skin. The loud music drowned out Lacy's moans as Jason worked his way to her lips and captured them like a prisoner.

"I hate Werewolf law and Bonding rules," Lacy breathlessly said as she pulled away from Jason's mesmerizing lips.

"For the first time in my long life, so do I," Lacy spun around again so that her back was leaning against Jason's front and let his hands play with her long blonde hair, twisting it around his index finger and letting the fake curls fall around Lacy's face.

"How old are we talking here?"

"We age one year to every five human years. I'm twenty converting it to human years and one hundred in our years."

"Oh," the two were silent for a little bit. "Where do you see us in five years? How do you see us?" the music wasn't too loud around their booth, but Lacy still had to raise her voice so Jason could hear her.

"A child," he whispered closely in Lacy's ear, "A beautiful blonde haired baby girl with big blue eyes and a mesmerizing smile that has all the other wolves on their knees. She is young but knowing and understands that life is meant to be lived, not watched," the imaged appeared in Lacy's mind as he spoke, a picture of the three in a park, their daughter playing on a swing while Jason pushed her and Lacy stood with a camera, trying to capture the perfect family moment.

"Sounds perfect to me," Lacy sighed to herself. Throughout the image she couldn't help but see little bits of Ollie in her daughter. A smart mouth, a sarcastic vibe and a want to see a world that had more install for her then anyone could have ever thought.

"I will make our future whatever you want, you are my world and you are the reason I live. This is our future and our land," in Lacy's eyes, Jason couldn't put a foot wrong.

"Want to dance with me?" Lacy asked, getting up and taking his hand, pulling Jason up off the booth.

"Always and forever."

"How cliché, Romeo," Lacy rolled her eyes.

"A rose by any other name would smell just as sweet," Jason winked and Lacy hit his shoulder as they started dancing together in the crowd. The two moved closer to Cruze and his anonymous blonde, Lacy and Jason winked at Cruze while he danced with a sly grin playing on his lips. He had plans for later on and Lacy couldn't help but smile to see her friend back on his feet, even if it wasn't with Ollie.

Enakal rose from his chair and walked around his desk, warmly eyeing the small girl in front of him who stood nervously playing with her long hair. He moved around and leaned against the front of the desk, smiling at her.

"You are asking for something that is only for mates."

"Yes."

"And you are sure this is what you want with your life."

"Yes."

"You know what happens?"

"He has explained it to me and I could think of nothing more fitting. Do you ask everyone these questions?"

"No, but you are like a daughter to me and I want you to be sure of your choice, Lacy," Lacy nodded her head, understanding her Alpha and her Uncle. "Jason is a good wolf, very noble and loyal, you are good together and you are true mates, I can see it when you are together," it meant a lot to Lacy to hear Enakal say that to her.

"Thank you. We want to do it as soon as possible."

"Tomorrow. Your mother and Arabella can go shopping with you today and you can be Bonded tomorrow with your close family and friends."

"OK, faster then I thought but I'm happy to jump him with your permission," Enakal let out a booming laugh. "Yes, Ollie was just like me, in fact, she was a lot worse so consider me her replacement," Enakal nodded his head.

"As you wish it," he dismissed Lacy.

Once Lacy was out of the room, Enakal went back to the other side of the room, behind his oak desk and picked up his phone. Dialing a number that was familiar to him, Arabella walked in and locked the double doors behind her.

"Any news?" Enakal asked into the phone. There was a short silence before Enakal spoke again, "Keep looking. I refuse to give up."

"No news?" Enakal slammed the phone down and ran his hands through his hair, shaking his head at his beautiful mate. "We will not give up and so long as we don't; there is always hope. I will never give up until I see a body," she rounded the desk and rested her chin on Enakal's head.

"I love you, you have been so strong."

"We have another daughter to think about as well, not only one we can't see. Nuru needs us as much as Olyanah does and I refuse to focus on what isn't there. We have a pack to worry about and a family to think about," Enakal felt Arabella's words right down to his heart.

"You are forever the wise within my world," he kissed the top of her hand, never once losing this love he felt for his mate. He felt the same way about her now as he had when they first meet many years ago.

"You better remember that too. Now I have some shopping to do," Arabella kissed Enakal's hand before leaving the room with a sway of her hips.

"You are a cruel woman."

"And don't you forget it," she winked before closing the two doors and heading out to see Lacy and Sally.

"Lacy is rubbing off on you," Enakal moaned.

"All the better to annoy you with."

Lacy looked through the racks of dresses in the small mall that was in Kharga, many linen outfits lined the walls, silver and gold were the main ones, keeping with tradition. So many different choices were throwing themselves at Lacy and she had no idea what to pick.

"Try these ones on," Lacy turned to see Arabella and Sally standing with their arms full of clothes.

"Egyptian Werewolf Princess?" Lacy asked rolling her eyes.

"Come, my lady," Sally started, putting the clothes in a dressing room. "Here, try these on and come out and show us once you are in a dress," Lacy nodded her head as her mother and aunty sat down on the 'dad chairs' near the dressing room and waited for Lacy to come out dressed from head to toe in a beautiful linen dress they had picked out for her.

Lacy slipped on an airy linen dress that flowed under her bust with a gold and silver linen belt. It came to a v-neck and straps went over her shoulders and connected to a low back at her waist, the v-neck reminded Lacy of the dress Ollie had worn to their school formal not long before she disappeared.

Stepping out, Lacy felt so beautiful in the dress if she had her hair curled and softly laying around the front and the back of the dress. Soon she would have Jason's marks on her body, adding the exotic look the dress was giving her.

"Oh my Goddess!" Sally put her hand over her mouth as she saw Lacy step out. Her eyes filled with tears as she looked over her beautiful daughter. "You look beautiful," she sobbed into her hand.

"Such a sob story, mum, stop now OK," Lacy rolled her eyes but couldn't help feeling a little thud in her heart that her mother was so excited and tearful at her appearance and that she was going to be Bonding with her mate. It felt so surreal to Lacy, even after everything she had learnt and everything that had happened to them recently, she was so excited to see Jason tomorrow and Bond with him.

"I'm just so proud of you. Everything that has happened and you can still hold your head high and live each day," Sally stood up and gave Lacy a hug. "Do you want the dress?"

"Yes, am I allowed to get it?"

"Of course," Sally sat back down and ushered Lacy into the dressing room to get changed into her leggings and top again.

"She looks amazing," Arabella agreed with Sally.

"She really does, doesn't she?"

Lacy saw Jason standing outside the smaller mansion, watching the wind flow through the leaves of the trees that surrounded the Pack house. The pack members walked around outside, interacting with one another or walking by themselves; being the largest pack in the Mystics world, there were about twenty-five members of the pack.

"Jason," he turned around with a smile on his lips.

"You will be mine tomorrow, mine and only mine, my love," Jason pulled Lacy in for a hug and kissed her on the cheek.

"I never thought I would be this excited to be married at such a young age."

"We aren't getting married."

"I know, but I'm bringing it back to the human life I used to know and left behind to make it all feel a little more real, you've got to give me that one at least, right?" Lacy swayed around in Jason's arms, moving with the wind that was dancing with the leaves and moving around their quiet secrets. "I cannot believe we are going to be one tomorrow, no longer two more souls, just one."

"You will be forever mine."

"Who is going to be there?"

"What do you mean? In our soul?"

"No silly. At the ceremony?"

"Your mother, father, brother, his mate, the Alpha's and a few close friends," Lacy couldn't help but think of the one friend that would be missing from that circle of friends that should be there on a girls biggest day.

"Can we go back; to Rosewood in two months? On our last day in Surfers, we all agreed that we would meet back at The Local in a year and I still have hope, even if no one else does," Jason didn't let Lacy go as he held her, she was trying to keep hope not just for herself but also for Cruze and the Alpha's.

"Do you think she is safe?"

"I don't know, but I'm willing to risk it," Jason knew what this meant to Lacy, so he needed his head as a promise to make and keep her happy.

Lacy had always had hope that Ollie was safe and that she was going to be coming back into their lives soon enough, but she just didn't know when.

As much as she wanted to move on, Lacy didn't want to forget about Ollie, she was determined if she had a child before Ollie came back that she would name her child after Ollie, keep her memory alive for as long as possible.

Their room was scattered with photos of Ollie and Lacy, Lacy and Jason, Cruze and Ollie and the eight friends and their time in Rosewood and on schoolies and their whole friendship.

Cruze didn't go into their room, only because of the photos that were scattered around of him and Ollie, the only way he was going to be able to move on was if he forgot and that was something Lacy hated but knew he needed to move on and live his life somehow.

Lacy closed her eyes while in Jason's arms, enjoying the warmth of his arms around her body and the feeling of his love soaking into her skin, soaking into her body.

"Soon we will be one and I will never let you out of my sight," Jason kissed Lacy's temple.

Chapter Nineteen

The Marks That Are Left Are Too Often Scars

It had been a long time, a very long time and she didn't know where she was any more and she didn't know who or what she was. Everything in her mind was spinning but there was always one thing that she remembered.

She had promised never to give up, she had pinky promised never to give up and she was going to keep her promise until the day she died, or the day they killed her in some creatively painful way.

Becca stood in her room, trying to focus her eyes, trying to focus on something in the dim, harsh, unforgiving light that surrounded her. Everything was so confusing, she didn't know what to do and she didn't know how to act, pacing around the room as her mind worked to fit the puzzle together. Half the time she couldn't work out which way was up and which was down because everything was so dark in the room. When she lay down on the floor it felt as though the room was spinning with her going the opposite way.

The door opened to her room and Red Eyes stepped in, Becca could remember a light red headed girl calling him that and it had been a very long time since Becca had seen him. His stubble around his chin hadn't change, still giving him that aura of wanting to look older and meaner then he really was.

There was a soft yet harsh light flowing in from behind Red Eyes that had Rebecca shielding her eyes as she backed away into the wall behind her so he couldn't touch her. She fell down, hugging her knees to her chest as

"You're time has come," he cryptically said, leaving the door wide open. Becca didn't respond. "Get up. Now," there was no room for argument in his voice so Becca got up and walked towards the door, stopping just before she was able to step out for the room.

"More," a familiar female voice echoed around the room and Becca obeyed, stepping out of the room into the hallway to see Ally standing with her hands on her hips. She had that kind look about her, that sweet voice and those immaculate clothes covering her body, everything seemed so perfect when it came to Ally, never judging a book by its cover had never matter more then when it came to this secretly evil young girl.

"Welcome home," Red Eyes grabbed her by the upper arm and pulled Becca along the hallway, down towards a large open space with a stage at one end. Curtains and drapes were falling down on the windows and torn through the middle, leaving Becca's eyes sore as they adjusted to the new bright light, it wasn't an artificial light, rather natural, something Rebecca wasn't used to.

"Enjoy the view," Red Eyes let Becca's arm go and stepped back into the frame of the double doors that led into the grand room with the stage. The doors slammed closed in front of him, leaving Rebecca in the room alone with only the new light and her thoughts to float around with.

She could hear the dead bolts on the other side of the doors close, locking her in the room that was letting off too much light for her liking.

For the first time since being here, Becca felt free and light and like herself again even if she couldn't fully remember who she was. She could feel the power she once had but that had been sucked away when she had been taken.

'I am Rebecca. I am daughter to Aviva and Winslow. I am a Fae. I am going to survive and I am going to fight. I promised her,' Becca chanted to herself as she called on her Fae powers, something she hadn't felt in a long time, the feeling of being in control of herself again.

A weight lifted off her shoulders, giving her the feeling that she was floating in thin air, just letting the world pass her by slowly. Looking down, Becca saw that she did in fact have her hover back, her feet not touching the ground by a few inches as her light returned to her.

Her hover was the thing that made her feel like a Fae, made her feel light and free. She hovered a few inches off the ground, letting the air keep her light frame up off the dirty ground that had almost blackened her bare feet.

"It's good to be back," Becca floated around the room, speaking to herself as she started exploring it as she moved. The windows were bolted up and her mind went to those that had taken her; did they want her to escape and get help, or did they think they had broken her enough to think she wouldn't escape. If they thought she wouldn't escape, they were sadly mistaken.

She had made a promise long ago and something Becca was, was a Fae, and they never broke their promises, not when it was a life and death situation. She remembered the red haired girl, the colour of her dyed hair fading along with her as they attacked her and beat her and god knows what else after they had taken her away to a different part of the building they were locked in.

Becca remembered a sweet girl only wanting to help those that had been cast aside, when she was the one that needed help but refused it. Ollie was so strong in her eyes and yet she just refused the help that she was given because she had never had it offered to her before and didn't know how to accept it.

Pain echoed in her heart as she pressed a hand against the glass, the other side of the glass showed her that outside was cold, very cold, freezing the exterior side of the glass. Becca removed where her hand was, showing that there was an outline of her small hand.

"Thank the Goddess for the wonderful power of heat and destruction," Becca murmured under her breath as she picked up a discarded chair and threw it at the window, covering her ears as the shattering glass made a tremendous noise.

Ollie looked around the room, her eyes overlooking the stone benches and medieval instruments that had been tossed aside, instead focusing on things she couldn't see, like how the air felt in the room and the way she saw the light bulb above her create shadows in the cave like room. She had been here far too long in her mind and she couldn't even remember her own name.

The one thing that stuck in her mind was rain. She couldn't remember the texture of rain on her skin, but she could remember the smell of fresh rain and the smell of a wonderfully clean beach near by, wet trees and earth.

It wasn't a picture that formed in her mind but a smell that formed in her noise, not of earth but of a person she could no longer see in her mind. Everything she remembered was gone, everything she had once loved was gone. Light hair, two sets of heads with light hair, one long and one short, that she remembered and the smell, that was all.

Ollie knew what freedom felt like; in her mind, but not in her heart, she didn't have freedom any more, the concept was something she could only dream of, imagine in her mind and body as she lay attached to a stone bench, her body trying to heal as fast as it could from her injuries but the infection that was riddling through was refusing the fast healing she had been blessed with somehow.

Torn nails, burnt skin, tagged and branded skin, opened wounds, infected blood, everything she had now accepted as her life and her broken body. A growling stomach caused a pain Ollie knew well, her parched lips stuck together as her tongue moved around in her dry mouth.

"You look sad," Ollie opened her eyes and saw glowing golden eyes in the distance. "Why are you sad?" Ollie just closed her eyes and wished Gold Eyes to be gone from the room and her life. "You are a stubborn girl, you have taken the longest of all to break. Like an obstinate horse, you think you are right," she rounded the table and leaned down, taking in a long breath of Ollie's scent, Ollie wanted to move away and recoil as she felt Gold Eyes so close to her.

"Just like you should, fear us and fear what we will do to you," Gold Eyes stepped away a little, Ollie just kept her eyes closed and tried to calm her beating heart. "You are strong. Do you know why we are doing this?"

'Yes.'

"Because you deserve it."

'Wrong.'

"You need to be taught a lesson and a lesson only we can teach. You will be let go soon, but you still have a little further to go before we deem you 'fit' enough."

'You mean drained enough.' Ollie commentated in her head, taking the information from the dream she still remembered in detail with the light haired girl.

"Feel lucky that we have taken you first, there are other out there that want you more then we do but we put in the hard yards for eighteen years and are reaping the rewards for our hard work and planning," Ollie opened her eyes and saw that Gold Eyes was pacing, pacing around the table Ollie was attached to and pacing around the room she was in.

'I will get out of here because I have promised I will never give up and I will not let you have me,' Ollie told herself and wanted to say out loud to Gold Eyes but she knew she didn't have the courage or the energy to open her eyes or mouth and tell Gold Eyes what she really thought.

Without another word, Gold Eyes left the room, slamming the door hard behind her. Ollie lay with her eyes closed tight, trying to think of ways out of here, racking her brain and her memory to unlock something that might let her escape before it was too late and they got her weak enough to drain her and ruin the Mystic world and then the human world.

A cell.

An old hospital room.

Laying on the floor.

Different images flashed in Ollie's mind of her first few days or weeks here and her laying her a different dark room with a crack of the boards on the windows, her last experience with real light.

A spring moving.

A bed moving.

Paint moving.

Everything of her time here came flooding back in short scenes like a black and white silent movie. She could see herself focusing on different things in the room and getting them to move, not a lot but they had moved and that single thought gave Ollie hope that she might still be able to change what was happening to her and how it was happening to her.

Opening her deep blue, pure eyes, Ollie looked down at the chains that were holding her in place around her wrists and ankles. She tried to see where they were attached to and if she would be able to move them. They were held to the wall by a lock that she hoped she would be able to unlocked with her mind. If she had nothing, she at least had hope and that was something she wasn't going to give up easily.

Lifting her head, Ollie could see just how skinny her frame had gotten she was able to see her robs lift us as he head brought her skin closer to her insides, every breath had her ribs being exposed, the thin bones clear to her deep blue eyes.

Shaking her head from the sickening sight, Ollie looked at the back wall as she tried to zone in on her wolf sight and saw that the chains were locked to the back wall, connecting at some point. If Ollie could focus on the lock, she'd be able to unlock it, lift the chains and move for the first time in god knows how long.

She knew it would take a lot of practice to get to the level of moving the lock, but Ollie was very prepared to use her energy on practice so she could escape and then maybe get some food and water into herself.

She moved quietly, hovering above the over grown weeds as they swayed in the wind. Her stomach growled and cramped as she used a lot more energy then she had in a very long time, at least longer then she cared to remember.

Stopping near by an empty road, Becca sat down on the ground, hovering a few inches so she didn't get dirty, she looked behind her and saw that the building was just a dot in the distance now but she know she wasn't out of the dark yet. She needed to be in a different county for her to be out of the dark.

"Terra, in vento et igni
Nuntium ferre mea
Sentio desiderium meum
Sunt quidam qui invocant
Qui genuit me vocaret puerum
Liber sum
Ego viverem
Ego, vivit mendacium.
Opus salvationis
EGO postulo ut reperio meus

Obsecro autem eos, qui mihi non perdidi nunc.

(Earth, water, wind and fire
Carry my message
Feel my desire
Call on those who are my kind
Call on those who bore me as a child
I am free
I am alive
I am here, living a lie.
I need salvation
I need to find mine
I call upon those who have lost me, now.)" Becca called of the Moon Goddess that had created Mystics and called upon Fae, Elves and her parents, asking them to respond and come and help her and save her and bring her home.

She didn't have a plan other then to try and find somewhere to stay, she would have to pull in her Fae so she wouldn't make those humans around suspicious that they weren't alone in the world.

It seemed farfetched and a very scary thought, but Becca knew she had no choice, although it did bring a smile to her lips when she was able to perform magic and see the spell and message go up into the air and find its recipient.

Becca kept her magic showing as she made her way down the highway looking road that lay out to her right, determined to make good time on her way to where ever she was headed, her fingers were crossed that there was a town close by so she could get some food and water into her dizzy mind.

The sun was slowly setting over the mountains and once it had set it didn't take Rebecca long to see a glow of lights in the distance, telling her that humanity was near by.

Becca turned her magic off, pulling it in and dropping to the ground, her dark barely-there clothing jumped up around on her body. The black crop top and bike shorts was not Becca's style, she was more into the white chiffon, lose fitting dress that her mother had her wear due to her background. It fit loosely around her body and let her magic flow freely around her, creating a small magical wind that moved the dress in a beautiful way.

She could feel her whole body become excited as she moved further alone the road and rounded a corner, seeing the town brighten up even more then when she had see it before. This was going to be her way to get back to her old life and never give up on the girl she had met in that hellhole.

Walking to the town, Becca felt the wind around her pick up and a feeling of magic drift through the wind. A message was coming her way, a message from her mother.

"Terra, in vento et igni
Nuntium ferre mea
Sentio desiderium meum
Filia vivit amans
Ejus corpus vaganti orbem mentimur, et sustine
Satin salue?
Tutus es?
Veniat ad me, mea infantem
Ubi tu errare?
Ubi sustinetis?
Ubi fuisti tam diu?
(Earth, water, wind and fire
Carry my message
Feel my desire
My loving daughter is alive and well
Her body roaming the world as we lie and wait
Are you well?
Are you safe?
Come home to me my baby
Where do you roam?
Where do you stay?
Where have you been for so long?)" Becca received the message and couldn't help the tear that left the corner of her eye. She felt so loved and so wanted, so at peace with herself and the world around her now for the first time in a very long time.

Becca didn't have time to return the call from her mother, she wanted to get to the town and ask to use a phone. They might use magic to communication, but that is only when new forms are unavailable, Rebecca would be able to call her mother when she got to a place with a phone and get them to come and get her.

It didn't take Becca long to get to the town, a pub was in full swing in the centre and Rebecca, completely terrified what people might say or do with her dressed so horribly, stepped in and made her way to the bar.

"Can I please use your phone?" she asked the light haired man behind the bar. He looked her up and down and nodded his head, jerking it in a way that told Becca to follow him around the bar and out the back.

"Here," he had a thick Scottish accent and handed Becca the landline. "Don't be too long if it is a long distance call, or you're paying," Becca nodded her head and typed in the number she knew so well.

"Hello," the light airy voice on the other end of the line answered after a few rings.

"Mother?" Becca asked, she hadn't heard the voice in so long she couldn't be sure that it really was her mother.

"Becca? Is that you?" the tone was frantic, excited, happy, fearful and teary all in one. Becca could tell that she had been crying and the water works had started again, only harder this time.

"I miss the sound of your voice so much. I am in Scotland, I don't know where but there is a whole building filled with girls that have been taken, I got away though. I got away," now Becca was the one who was crying. "I have to go back and keep my promise, can you please come and help me fulfill my promise?" Becca was sobbing into the phone, rambling as she spoke.

"Where in Scotland, never mind, we will track you now; I have missed you so much, we were almost losing hope. I am so sorry this happened to you, I am sorry we didn't keep you safe like we promised you. We thought keeping the Elves away would keep the pain away until you were twenty-one and able to find your mate."

"You don't have to find your mate at twenty-one, this happened because I wasn't allowed to experience the world. I don't want to fight with you mother, please just come and get me. I miss you and I love you.

Is father there?" Becca only wanted a hug from her mother and father, not a fight after not seeing them for however long she had been locked up for.

"Yes, I will get him now. I love you too."

"How long have I been gone?"

"6 Months, we thought your case could be related to Olyanah's but you haven't been gone as long and you have escaped, clearly."

"That was her name. Olyanah. I promised her never to give up and I will find her. I have to mother. I just have to. She is in a lot of pain, they want to weaken her, and they want her power to drain. We have to help her, mother," tears were starting to fall from Becca's eyes, faster and thicker then before.

"We will be there soon," there was a noise on the other line before another voice was introduced into the conversation.

"My darling child, I am so sorry. I love you. I love you so much," Winslow, Becca's father chanted over and over again.

"You have nothing to be sorry about, please just come to me," she begged on the phone.

"We will be there soon, your mother now has your location. Stay there," Becca hung up the phone and waited, drumming her fingers against the wall as she leaned her back against it.

Seconds later, a flash occurred in the corridor, causing Becca to shield her eyes before two sets of arms wrapped themselves around Becca and hugged her tightly. Becca felt the warmth and felt the love flowing from them as they embraced their lost daughter.

"Oh Becca, we have missed you so much," Becca opened her eyes and saw the light purple hair of her mother, Aviva. Her light aura was gone, the only way Fae could see that they were with their own kind, not wanting the humans around to think that something was going on.

Becca could see her father standing there, his light hair messed up and his normally pointed ears were rounded at the end, both of her parents had their crowns gone from their foreheads, not wanted to alert the humans to anything.

Mystics had to be so careful around humans to make sure they didn't give themselves away. They knew that humans were curious and would want to know what made them Mystics and therefore they would experiment on them to try and find their answers.

"I missed you too."

"Come, we must go home."

"No, I have to help Ollie. I promised her, I pinky promised that I would never give up and I promise I will find her again and help her," Becca held her head high, showing just how strong she was and how much she had learnt about being away and being locked up, getting a perspective on life and being Princess and Queen to her people. She needed to be strong and that was something she was prepared to show her parents that she had learnt.

"As you wish it. We will go home first and alert those who are close to her," Winslow, Becca's father, spoke deeply but with a caring tone to his daughter.

"I know where the place is. Let me show you first so we can Flash to it straight away and know where it is," Aviva and Winslow nodded their heads, letting their daughter lead them out of the pub and onto the road.

"You are so thin and so frail," Aviva commented, tears pricking in her eyes again.

"Do you have any dust?" Becca asked. Aviva pulled a small velvet bag out of thin air with drawstring to open it and handed it to her daughter. Inside were little bits of dust, Rebecca breathed in the dust and felt it energise her. The dust was a form of energy, food and water all in one for a Fae or Elf on a long journey that couldn't carry a lot about of supplies with them.

"How long has it been since you have eaten or had something to drink?"

"I don't know, I can't remember; I can't remember anything," her head was starting to spin as she tried to remember what had happened to her. "They weren't nice people, they hurt me and they hurt Ollie to control us. There were other girls there but they weren't kept for as long as us. They put me in a big room with light and I smashed a window and escaped. I don't think they wanted me to, but I don't know anything any more," Becca still kept her head high, not letting her parents see her pain.

"You are strong, Becca," Winslow quickened his walk to keep in pace with his determined daughter. "You have been so strong during this for such a young child. We're sorry, we're so sorry," Becca nodded her head, understand just how much her father needed her to understand what he meant and how he felt.

They arrived at the beginning of the field, all three letting their magic out now that they were away from humans, the two Fae's hovering a few inches off the ground naturally, while Winslow's ears were pointed again and his crown appeared in waves on his forehead, like it had always been there and would never be able to leave his skin.

Becca felt more at home seeing her parents in their real form, seeing them natural and how they had lived for so long. Winslow, an Elf, wasn't able to hover, but was still taller then both his wife and daughter as they hovered, their form of walking when they let their power flow around them.

It was a common mistake that humans had created in their minds and in stories that Elves were short, in fact they were rather tall creatures and Fae were also a normal height, although still small compared to the height of Elves.

"You lived here for six months?" Aviva asked as they saw an old building come into view.

"I wouldn't say 'lived' but yes, this is where I have been for six months," Becca saw the smashed glass on the ground, reflecting the moons light around the field they were in.

"Why don't the humans come?" Winslow's eyebrows furrowed as he looked behind him where they had left the town behind.

"They think it is haunted and refuse to come near it. They think Ghost's are here and living waiting to scare them," Becca snorted. "Such silly creatures, Ghost's have better things to do with their lives then to scare humans," she shook her head, confused at how they lived their lives, scared of the unknown and what they didn't fully understand. If only humans were more prepared to look around then they would be able to freely without having Mystics hiding from them.

It was something Becca had dreamed about, living in peace and harmony with the humans, not having to hide herself and having them accept who she was and who her people were. If they all lived in peace then it would be easier to find mates that were in other packs, something she knew other Mystics longed for.

When mates weren't in the same pack it was unlikely that they would ever find each other because packs didn't often mingle, too stuck in their own way of territory to let other packs come onto their land unless something big had happened and they wanted to extend a hand and prevent a war from breaking out.

"They live how we want them to live. Naïve to us," Aviva placed an arm around Becca's shoulder. "Understand that because it is the heart of our existence."

Chapter Twenty

If Life Gets Too Hard To Stand, Kneel

THE CHAINS RATTLING around the room, giving Ollie a deep headache that she knew she had to push past if she wanted this to work. They kept rattling as they started moving and the lock started to twist on the inside, the mechanics unwinding and opening up.

The quiet sound of different things moving on the inside of the lock had Ollie's heart racing, a smile playing on her lips as she thought about freedom and what could be waiting on the other side of this building. She couldn't remember what it felt like to have the wind playing on her skin, the sun beating down and the moons light reflecting off ocean or the rain falling on her skin, dampening it with every drop.

A snap grabbed Ollie's full attention and she saw the lock was hanging on an angle, the metal circle disconnected to the bronze contraption. Her deep blue eyes widened and a smile appeared on her plump, dry lips as she realised what had just happened right in front of her eyes.

Her energy levels were down, her mind was hurting but Ollie knew she had to stay focused; she was so close to getting out, so close to being free from this place, so close from leaving the Hades she had grown to know so well.

Keeping her mind on the chains, Ollie thought about the lock lifting off the chains and loop that was on the wall, setting her free from this hellhole that she had been kept in. This was finally her escape and it was happening right before her eyes.

The lock lifted and dropped to the ground, letting the chains drop too. Ollie dropped her head back to the stone table and felt utter relief as her neck strained from all the work she had been doing to free herself from Hades.

Ollie knew she still had to move but her body and mind were so tired, so worn out, but she had to keep fighting, not only for herself but also for the girl she had promised. Ollie wasn't going to let simple starvation, dehydration and exhaustion stop her from achieving her goal of being free.

Lifting her legs for the first time in god knows how long, Ollie felt so stiff, so broken not only psychologically but also physically. She had been stuck on the experimental table for a long time, longer then she thought she should or could have survived.

'I've come this far surprising myself, may as well keep going,' Ollie told herself as she slowly lifted her legs, moving herself up so she could unwrap the chains that were around her wrists. Moving her legs off the chains loosened the ones on her wrists, making it easy for Ollie to disconnect herself.

An extreme amount of dizziness overtook Ollie as she sat up on the table, her legs dangling from the floor and her body swaying from side to side and front to back, almost in a circle. It took a few minutes for Ollie to get over the dizzy feeling and she decided to search the room she was in to see if there was any food or water.

Tables littered the dark corners of the room and Ollie was able to see where they got their instruments of torture and pain from. Draws filled top to bottom and tabletops had everyday items and specialized items that you wouldn't be able to buy in a normal shop. It scared her that they were so prepared for this, for hurting people and seeing the pleasurable side of things.

A cabinet at the end of the room had a lock on it, hiding what was inside from Ollie. Using her newly polished skills, Ollie unlocked the cabinet with her new powers, coming easier then the first few times she had tried to use them, and opened it; a few pieces of molding bread sat inside and a half full bottle of water was also in cabinet, giving Ollie some hope in the pit of her stomach.

Eyes wide, Ollie grabbed the bread and started eating, loving the taste of the mold and stale bread in her mouth, she had missed something solid, and the water sliding down her throat, wetting the dryness that had taken over from her. Already the food was clearing her mind, letting her see everything in focus without the room spinning and giving her strength she didn't think she had anymore.

'Escape,' Ollie concentrated her mind on that thought and looked around the room at somewhere to hide, somewhere to conceal herself so that when they came in she would be able to slip away and out the door, she just hoped they were stupid enough to fall for it.

Something Ollie had noticed was when they came to talk to her, laugh at her, attack her or torture her, they left the door open; not afraid that she would escape and as a warning to the other girls Ollie guessed they had kept in other rooms down the corridor and littered in the building in other cells.

It was a sick game that they played with lives, minds and bodies, but they were sick people, people that needed help to straighten themselves out and Ollie was more then happy to let someone else do it for her. She wasn't a violent person, although she couldn't remember much about her life, she knew that violence had been a constant, something she lived with for a very long time even before coming here and after this she didn't want to relive it or turn into the people that had done this to her.

Ollie watched from the shadows of the corner closest to the door but that was still hidden from all light. There was no way they would be able to see her in the place she was crouched down in.

The door swung open and Ollie jumped, seeing those three sets of eyes that had caused her so much pain for so long. The temptation was there to go over and attack them but she knew she wasn't strong enough and wouldn't be able to handle it so instead Ollie decided to stick with her original plan.

"What the . . ."

"Fuck," Red Eyes looked around the room, eyes wide as he stared at the empty table that usually held a frightened girl on it, tied down with poisoned chains that were sure to make the weakening process go faster.

"How . . ." Gold Eyes stumbled over her own words as she stepped over to the stone table and placed a hand where Ollie had once been. "It's cold," she spun around with wide eyes as she looked at Red Eyes and Dark Eyes, both standing stunned at what had greeted them when they entered for some fun.

"But how?" Dark Eyes asked, his mouth opening and closing like a fish trying to breathe.

"How can this happen?" Gold Eyes asked as Red Eyes and Dark Eyes stepped forward both put a hand on the stone table, feeling the cool natural material underneath their hands.

"We have a shield, no one can use magic, especially someone that doesn't even know what she is," Red Eyes stood shaking his head, staring at the other two for answers they didn't have. "How can she have done this?" he asked over and over again, mumbling it under his breath.

Ollie watched the scene unfold in front of her, interested at the interactions that were going on in front of her. Normally they were so sure, so confident; it was fascinating to Ollie that they were in such disarray at the disappearance of their main project, the thing that had kept them entertained for so long.

Turning her attention to the open door and the fact that the three were now arguing with their backs to the door, Ollie took it as her chance. They wouldn't be able to hear her small footsteps as she moved along the cool ground towards the door, out of the shadows, they were fighting too much with each other, raising their voices in anger as they tried to work out what had happened and what was going on.

If they did catch her, at least they were confused and angry at each other over Ollie, something she wasn't used to; it brought a smile to her lips that she had caused this chaos for them.

Not once did the three look back at the door or check for any noises as Ollie reached the door and stepped out. There was light out in the corridor, the same luminescent light as in the hellhole but there was more of it, not just concentrated over her sensitive eyes.

Deciding that she needed more time to get away, Ollie grabbed the handle of the heavy door and slammed it closed, the noise echoing down the corridor and shaking her from head to toe. She could hear the yelling and anger coming from inside, but her mind was now on escape as she locked the door and started walking to her right. Ollie didn't have any reason to go to her right or left, but going right just seemed like the safest option at the moment for some reason; it just felt right to her.

In front of her, further down the corridor, sat a stairwell that spiraled around to one side and off into the distance. Instinct took over from fear and Ollie's tired body started climbing the stairs, following them to what she prayed was her freedom.

The spiral stairs, all stone, exited into a hallway, a hallway that was lit by natural light that seemed to call Ollie to it and at the same time make her want to turn away. The feeling of natural light burnt her eyes and caused her to lift her tired arm to shield herself from the intrusion to her senses.

On the other side of the windows sat a line of doors that were similar to the one Ollie had slammed closed not too long ago. Whines and cries could be heard from Ollie's side and she started walking along the corridor, peeping into the rooms.

Girls lay crouching on the floor on huddled up in a corner, heads down and sobbing into their arms. They were all wearing the same thing; a black crop top and black bike shorts.

None of the girls look roughed up yet, just scared for what might happen to them and the fact that they had been taken in the first place. They had probably been shown someone that had been attacked and were begging for it not to happen to them.

Even though Ollie was walking freely now, she felt envious of them; they hadn't experienced any pain in their time here yet and she knew they would be released soon, Red Eyes had once told her about how the longest they kept girls was two weeks and they let them go with no memory; It was sick game the four enjoyed together, torturing young girls and then letting them go with no memory of their violation.

Ollie wanted to let the girls go, wanted to help them, but she didn't have time and she wasn't strong enough. The girls wouldn't trust her and she didn't trust them, there was no way to trust anyone in here; everyone had another motive and Ollie didn't want to find theirs.

'One day I'll back and one day you'll all be free,' Ollie chanted in her mind as she continued moving along the hallway to another door that she

pushed open. The doors were so heavy and old; making it harder for Ollie to move along the building she didn't know, her muscles were almost gone, not strength left in them from being tied down for so long. Every step she took looked like she was drunk or high, weaving and leaning on walls to keep herself steady.

The next room was opened up by natural light again; silk and chiffon curtains were flowing in the wind from outside, opening the room up. There was a stage at one end, covered in old worn out curtains that they didn't have a use for, aged chairs were tossed over on the floor and broken in every direction.

The room felt as though so many plays were heard and watched here, so many memories had been had but were now faded, only remembered by those who had witnessed them and were now lost. All laughter and happiness had been soaked up into the walls remained there, desperate to come out and surround the room with light again.

Ollie shivered and goose bumps rose on her arms, leaving no surface uncovered with hairs that were standing on their ends. Turning, Ollie could see why the curtains were flowing around the room, lifting and dropping like they had minds of their own. A window had been smashed open and a chair lay to the side of the room. It was the first time in a long time Ollie had felt the wind on her skin and closed her eyes, letting the feeling consumer her as the sun shifted and beat down on her pale, destroyed skin.

The sensation brought a smile to Ollie's lips before she walked over to the window, jumped out and started running with what little energy she had lift. She could hear a noise she hadn't heard in a long time and soon came face to face with a long black road with white lines down the middle.

'Left or right' Ollie asked herself, weighing up the options. *'I haven't taken left in a while, may as well mix it up a little,'* forgetting that she was free, Ollie was determined to get herself as far away from that place as possible and started running to her left of the road, praying that something lay near-by. Maybe a town, or villiage or airport; her mind was racing with different ideas that she could come face to face with.

While running, Ollie pulled the piercing out of her crop top and held it tight in her hands, wishing that it would tell her the way to go, tell her something about what she had been doing and what had been going on.

She could still remember a simple conversation about other Mystics and Ollie knew if she found some they could help her recover, they could help her live again and find those who had raised her and who Ollie had loved a long time ago but had now forgotten who they were.

"We can't just leave her!" Becca paced the lounge room of their small cottage house. "She needs us and so do many other girls," the white chiffon dress that flowed neatly around her petite body flew around with each new hand movement from Becca. The dress came in at the waist and came out with a very Fae feeling about it, that was one thing humans got right about the species, what they wore and how breezy it was.

"Becca, please," Aviva stood next to her husband, her hands rubbing her temples as her daughter paced the room.

"No, mother! You looked when it was me and now I will look because it's Ollie," Becca gave her father a begging look, asking him to back her up in what she was saying. "Can we not get some Fae and Elves together and get her back? I know we have an army, even if you refuse to tell me about anything that happens to the people I am meant to lead one day," Becca stopped pacing and stood in front of her parents. "I am asking you to do this for me, do this for the fate of our world and do this for Ollie. I'll meet the Elves and Fae the tell them what we are planning to do," Aviva and Winslow nodded their heads, trying to understand where Becca was coming from.

"Winslow," Aviva turned to her husband. "Call the Elves here. I'll call my Fae," Becca smiled softly, happy that her parents were listening but not pleased at the fact that this had to be done in the first place.

"I'll call the wolves," Becca started.

"No. Not yet. We will study the place and scope out what is going on, then we will decide the best way in, that is what we do best," Winslow said. "We are Elves, we are shady by nature, it is the Fae that brings our calm and truthful nature forward as they are our other half," hearing her fathers words made Becca want to find her mate as soon as possible, she wanted that love that she saw between her parents.

"OK," she conceded to their instructions.

Becca sat in her small room, the English style cottage they lived in, in a forest in a hidden place in England. Becca had a simple English accent, her voice very elegant and airy, while her mother and father had royal sounding accents that made them feel higher in their clan of Fae and Elves.

Due to the two species being brought together, they had to address the group as Seelie, meaning Fae and Elves together as a collective group.

Becca was nervous about the speech she was about to give to the Seelie, she hadn't had any contact with Elves before, aside from her father, but she wouldn't consider that male attention; he was her father after all.

Aviva poked her head into her daughters room, "Are you ready?"

"I don't know, I think so," Becca was playing with the chiffon of her dress, pulling it around her like she was spinning around and the wind was lifting the skirt. "I'm just nervous because I don't know the Elves and I don't know how they'll react to me," Becca walked from one end of the room to the other.

"You will do magically."

"Pun intended?"

"I have no idea what you are talking about," a quick wink from her mother helped her nervous before she started talking formally again, "Now come on, the Seelie are ready to hear what you have to say," Becca followed her mother out the door and downstairs into the living room where she peaked out the window and saw her father talking to a group of males and females standing in the garden. Her father was standing tall on a log, looking down at them with a caring and fatherly look.

"I can do this," Becca chanted to herself as she stepped outside and Winslow stopped talking and stepped down. "I can do this," the door opened and Becca stepped out, using her power to hover over to the log Winslow was, Becca pulled her powers out more and she rose higher up into the air so she could see everyone that was below her.

"Nice and easy," Winslow mouthed to his daughter.

"Our world and our way of life is in danger," Becca started. "I have been gone for six months against my will and I saw Olyanah," a few gasps echoed around the forest as Becca mentioned Ollie's name, "I have been attacked and abused, but worse has been done to that powerfully amazing girl, she has been tortured to weaken her so they can drain her power and use it for themselves," Becca explained. "We have to stop this, if we don't then we are in danger of being wiped off the face of the earth. I am asking that we all form together," Becca looked out at the Seelie group of about two hundred. "And go seeking the one who will save us all," a round of a applause greeted Becca.

"When?" a girl with a light pixie hair cut called out, her hair was a light pink colour.

"As soon as possible. The building is in Scotland and we have flashed there, but it will be hard to find," Becca lowered herself from the height she was currently at, trying to make sure she was personable to those she was talking to.

"We have trained you all well," Winslow started, "My Elves, you can do well in combat and I know you Fae are very talented, we can do this," a cheer erupted throughout the large group.

Becca looked over the crowd and smiled, letting everyone know exactly what was happening and that she was going to be there for them. There were a lot of Elves out there that Becca had never seen before and Fae that she had only met briefly before.

She knew the names of a lot of Fae but her parents had kept her hidden from the Elves for a reason she didn't know, but she felt as though they weren't ready to let her find her mate, again she didn't know why but it was something Becca had grown used to and this being her first address with the Elves, it was quite frightening but also rather interesting to see so many handsome faces out there.

Becca jumped down and walked back inside the cottage, her heart beating faster as she tried to get over what had just happened. She had given her first speech and she had done well, getting all the Elves and Fae ready to fight and all wanting to fight for someone that could possibly save their lives.

Olyanah was so much stronger then they all thought, she had sustained a lot of beatings and torture and yet she was still going strong, still fighting, trying to stay alive for those that needed her.

"You did so well, my dear," Aviva walked in and hugged her daughter.

"We are so proud of you," Winslow wrapped Aviva and Becca in his arms, letting them feel his love as a mate and a father.

"I can't believe I just did that," Becca's heart was beating faster in her chest as her parents let her go and let her breathe for the first time since stopping her hover and coming inside to her small cottage house. "So when can we go and rescue our beloved Princess?"

"We still have to train the Fae and Elves to the degree that will be needed so in a week or two and then we will depart," Winslow sat on the couch and smiled at his daughter as she stood, hovering a few inches off the ground just like her mother was.

"OK, but we will go, won't we?"

"Of course, why would you ask that?"

"Because I know you are going to want to make me stay back and I am going, I will go. No matter what and no matter what you say. If we go in then I know my way around," Becca stood standing strong with her arms over her chest.

"If something happens."

"No, not if something happens."

"If something happens."

"I hope you know I am going whether you like it or not. She is my friend and I told her about Mystics. I am not going to leave her. I promised her I wouldn't give up and I'm not. I will be there if we can get in and if we can get here," Becca wasn't leaving any room for discussion as she left the room, storming upstairs.

Chapter Twenty-One

Love Is The Beauty Of The Soul

LACY LAY IN bed by herself, her hands in the air as she studied the mosaic designs that had bleached her hands in henna. The designs fascinated Lacy as she followed the swirls and designs that reminded Lacy of a vine on a tree with little flower blooms coming off the sides.

She could see the simple leaf like ring Jason had given her on her right hand; she spun it around with her fingers, feeling the warm sterling silver and designs that had been etched into it. She couldn't believe the day was here; today Lacy was going to be Bonded to her mate.

Her mind was on the all important linen gold and silver dress that she had picked out only the day before. Lacy hadn't had too much time to decide on what dress she wanted, but when she tried to dress on yesterday, it just felt right when she had slipped it on.

"Lacy," there was a knock on the door and Lacy recognised the voice on the voice on the other side of the door.

"Yeah mum?"

"You need to get up so I can get your makeup and hair done," Lacy got up from her bed and went to unlock her bedroom door so that her mother could enter and help her get ready for the afternoon ceremony.

"Morning," Lacy rubbed her eyes as she opened the door.

"Are you nervous?" Sally closed the door behind her and Lacy stepped back and fell back onto her bed.

"That would be the understatement of the century," Lacy lifted her head and smiled at her mother, "But I'm bloody excited at the same time. This is my future and it's something I've been looking forward to for a long time," Sally sat down next to her daughter, a tear in her eye.

"I just want you to know that I'm so proud of you. So proud of how you have handled everything and how you have moved on and let Jason help you. Everything has made you into such an amazing person and I'm pleased to call you my daughter," Lacy didn't know what to say to her mother, she just felt to happy that she thought of her like that.

"Thanks, Mama," Lacy sat up to hug her mother, letting her know just how much that meant to her. "Stop those tears and let's get this dress up party going," Lacy walked over to the speakers in the room and connected her phone so she could blast out some good music to pump up the vibe in the room.

"OK, what do you want to do first?"

"Hair," Lacy sat down in front of a simple desk with a mirror on it and makeup left all over the white painted wooden table. A straightener, curler and drier, along with brushed, combs and clips were scattered around too.

"Go have a shower and wash your rats nest and then we'll get started."

Lacy didn't take long in the shower and came out with a towel wrapped around her hair and a simple pink silk dressing gown around her body. Arabella was in the room now too, talking to Sally about something serious.

"Blushing bride ready to be made over, this conversation can wait until I am all prettied up," she placed her hands on her hips, interrupting the conversation between the sisters.

"Yes, of course," Arabella got up and unwrapped the towel from Lacy's head. "Do you mind if I stay and help?"

"No way; stay and help. Mum will need all the help she can get," Lacy winked and Sally got up and playfully whacked her daughter's bum.

"No bad mouthing the me while I have the power to turn you into a zombie."

"You wouldn't dare."

"Don't test me," Lacy and Sally stared off before Arabella cut the laughable tension with a giggle.

"I wish I had been able to know Olyanah like you two know each other. I am sure she is really lovely but I can't help think about those lost years," Arabella pulled Lacy into her seat and started playing with the wet hair.

"Ollie would've loved you."

"She prefers Ollie?"

"Yeah, like I said, Jane and Greg weren't entirely perfect to her so she always saw Olyanah as a bad thing because they only called her that when they were angry. Until Cruze came along and changed the meaning to her," Sally stood behind Lacy and brushed her hair before turning the blow dryer on and brushing the hot air through.

"I wish I could tell her how sorry we're for leaving her in that place, we did not know how bad they would be to her."

"I'm sure you would have but you said you were watching her, would you not see?" Lacy asked.

"Lacy," Sally interrupted her daughter.

"What mum? She said they were watching her but didn't know the situation, I'm just enquiring about why they didn't see it," Lacy reasoned, turning around in her chair, "I don't mean to be disrespectful or anything but finding out you were watching, I don't know," Arabella nodded her head in complete understanding.

"We are family and no matter what, you can't offend me. We could only have a certain amount of visual on Ollie as she was often inside or with other people and in crowded places we lost track of her," Lacy turned back around and let her mother get back to drying her hair straight.

"She would love you, just so you know," Lacy watched Arabella in the mirror.

Jason stood, shifting around on the balls of his feet like he was ready to go for a long run. Cruze stood behind his friend, resting an open hand on Jason's shoulder as support.

"You're nervous," Cruze stated, not really covering his rough deep voice, the pain of losing Ollie still very raw in his tone, he thought he would be in this situation a lot quicker then his commitment freak friend.

Jason was a great guy in Cruze's eyes, but he was very much still Cruze's best friend.

"Yeah," Jason knew Cruze's resentment but also knew he was starting to move along with his life, slowly but surly.

"You're doing what your heart wants, let it go as it is meant to," Jason nodded his head at his friends words. He stood in a simple linen white shirt and white linen shorts with gold and silver embroidery on the hems of the shirt and shorts.

"I know, my heart can't wait, but I have never lasted this long in a relationship before, my excuse always being that I was waiting for my mate, but now she is here and I want to get down there as fast as possible and run in the opposite direction at the same time. You've always been so sure about these things, Cruze, so convinced and I envy you deeply for it."

"You have your mate, I'm the one who envy's you," Cruze stepped back, letting his hand drop, "I did not mean it like that."

"I know buddy, I know," Jason understood Cruze's pain and let a lot of things slide with him as he didn't want Cruze anymore upset or in pain.

Lacy spun in her chair, seeing her light blonde hair beautifully done. A few pieces at the front had been pulled back and letting the light waves and curls her mother had created fall down her shoulders and stopping just under her breasts.

"Nice work, Mama," Lacy got up and looked at herself closer in the mirror.

"This is why you need to have more faith in me," Sally rolled her eyes at her daughter. "Now I'm letting Arabella take over with the makeup, she always was better at that side then I was."

"Yeah, same with Ollie and I. I can do makeup and she rocks the hair," Lacy turned around in her chair again, getting odd looks from the two sisters. "What? I don't want to see myself until the makeup is done," Arabella got straight to work, finding the right concealer and foundation for Lacy's skin colour.

"The finished product's always the best," Arabella agreed while Sally stood back and watched her sister work on her daughters face, making her look like the Princess she was for her Bonding day.

"This is so weird," Lacy started talking as Arabella commanded her to close her eyes, "It feels so weird to me. Every girl looks forward to planning her wedding day and here I am, growing up thinking I was going to get married and decided I was going to Bond with my mate only yesterday. The things Ollie would say."

"What would she say?" Arabella looked at the eye shadows and decided on simple silver.

"She'd start laughing and say something like, 'What do you expect, you find a fella at the beach and jump on him the second you see him, of course your mind is clouded when the Sex God walks into the room,'" Arabella turned away as she let out a bark of laughter. "Always the comedian, never the audience with that girl," Lacy rolled her eyes under her eyelids.

"And now she is the bridesmaid and not the bride," Arabella added, gathering her composure.

"So you're where she gets her humour!" Lacy cried out with her usual loud voice.

Once Lacy's makeup was completed, she left the room and went into the adjoining bathroom to change into her long white linen dress with the silver and gold embellished belt around her waist. The thick rope sleeves on the dress had gold and silver threads flowing through them too.

She changed into the dress and twirled around in the full-length mirror in the bathroom. She felt like the perfect blushing bride with her hair in waves and pinned back and her dress flowing around her petite body.

Stepping out, Lacy saw her mother sitting with Arabella, they looked up and both had tears in their eyes. Arabella was already turning into a second mother to Lacy and it felt right that they were both there to see her all dressed up for her special day, the emotions were flooding around in Lacy and she was trying not to smudge her makeup by crying.

"Don't, you'll make me cry," Lacy waved her hands in front of her eyes to stop the tears.

"We can fix the up the makeup, you look so beautiful," Sally gushed; she pulled her daughter in for a warm hug.

"I can't believe you are Bonding with your mate, it feels like yesterday we met and you just found out about all of this," Sally passed Lacy on to Arabella so she could hug her newly found niece.

"Life is one crazy ride now," Lacy giggled nervously.

"Come on, let's fix up that makeup and get you down to Jason before he comes up here himself and tries to Bond with you now," Arabella sat Lacy down, fixed up her makeup and gave her a smile. "You are ready, time to go," Lacy got up and left the room, her mother and aunty following close behind, showing her where to go so she could finally be with the man she loved in every way possible in their Werewolf life.

The large lounge room Lacy remembered had been transformed into something she didn't recognise. Colourful candles lit the room creating the feeling of romance, along with the coloured crystal decorations and chiffon fabric hanging from the roof like a big top circus.

Lacy felt like she had just walked into Aladdin as her eyes widened at the scene in front of her. Jason sat on a decorated chair that was on a make shift stage at the front of the room, although the stage hadn't always been there, it looked like it had been made perfectly for the room.

The decorated chair, Lacy remembered was called a Kosha, had wooden legs with wooden arms and a velvet red seat and back.

Jason stood and stepped down, the biggest smile spread onto his lips as his eyes caught Lacy's and she smiled back. He couldn't believe how wonderful she looked, her hair looked amazing, her body utterly beautiful in the dress she was wearing and she was his, all his.

"You look beautiful," he kissed her cheek before helping her onto the stage and letting her sit on the Kosha, looking out at their friends and family. Sally, Charles, Matt, Ain who turned out to be Matt's mate, Sarah, Harry, Liam, Jay, Arabella and Enakal were all in the room. Martha and Polly weren't allowed to be in for the ceremony as they were Fae, but they were going to come in for the celebrations at the end.

Enakal stood on the stage with Lacy and Jason, acting as the one to Bond them as he was Alpha of the pack and did this for every Bonding mates when it came time to perform the ceremony.

"I welcome those who have been asked to sit in watch of this wonderful ceremony as these two true mates Bond and become one for the rest of their lives," Enakal walked over to Lacy and Jason and handed them each a gold glass filled with a liquid. "Sharpat, to cleanse the soul and present you two with the love of your pack," Lacy and Jason took a sip from their glasses and then swapped them so they drank from both glasses. Enakal produced a sterling silver platter in front of the two with a dip in the centre.

"Place your Sharpat in the platter to combine the two you have drunk from," Enakal placed the platter on a stand and let Lacy and Jason pour the Sharpat, or rosewater, into the platter. "The Sharpat represents water," Enakal grabbed two silver decorative plates from either side and let Lacy and Jason take a handful from their own plates. "The dirt represents our native land and what we are," Lacy and Jason threw the dirt into the Sharpat and first silver platter, feeling the supernatural effects take hold of them.

"Place your hands in the Sharpat and earth," Lacy and Jason placed their hands in the silver platter and moved them around, creating rippled on the top, "This is the wind our created has blessed us with," Lacy could feel her soul reach out and try to find her other half, like an out of body experience.

"Do you Lacy Mandisa Larkin, accept Jason Bomani Miles as your mate, to be one with him and live together as one in our world and live together, raising a family and raising our pack together?" Lacy stared into Jason's light brown, honey eyes. "Do you take your mate to live together forever in peace and in love, to let him protect you when the time calls for it and let him be the wolf he was meant to be by fulfilling his life?" Enakal's words spoke true right down to the very heart of Lacy.

"I promise to love and live in peace with Jason, to care for him and let him be the wolf he needs to be, be the man he needs to be and be the man I love," Lacy answered Enakal, not once letting her eyes waver from Jason's, feeling the love pouring off him into her soul as she spoke.

"Do you, Jason Bomani Miles, accept Lacy Mandisa Larkin as your mate, to be one with her and live together as one in our world and live together, raising a family and raising our pack together as a dominant?" Jason stared at Lacy's deep blue eyes, giving his soul to her. "Do you take your mate to live together forever in peace and in love, to let her be there for you in times of darkness and in times of light, to share laughter and to share tears. Do you accept her to as the wolf she is and let her fulfill her life with you?" Enakal asked Jason, watching him stare into his mate's eyes.

"I promise to love and live in peace with Lacy, to care for her and let her be the wolf she needs to be and let her grow and be the light in my life.

I agree to let her be the love of my life and share everything with her as my mate and let her be the woman I love," Jason answered Enakal, looking at his mate sitting next to him, facing her.

Leaving their hands in the silver platter, the water rippling as they let their fingers move around. Lacy knew the meaning behind this, it being a symbol of water and nature, something Werewolves were a lot more in tune with then most people thought.

"I will place fire over the water," Enakal waved his hand over, letting his Alpha powers create fire over the water, not once did it touch their skin. The flames were blue, showing the supernatural nature of the world they lived in, letting nature be around them but not to manipulate, instead to show that they were one with nature and lived in peace.

Enakal nodded to Jason and Lacy, letting them take their hands out of their water that was in the silver platter. Jason leaned over to the opposite side of the Kosha and pulled something in a simple white box out. He opened the box and showed Lacy a crystal that was attached to a woven rope out of a vine, connecting it to nature.

"I offer you this gift as a healer, the only healer in our pack. The crystal is a symbol of a healer and the rope is to show that you are one with nature and that you will protect this pack as our healer," Jason had explained to Lacy that every pack could only have one healer at a time and she was the healer of their pack, a lot of responsibility on her shoulder, a burden he would help her carry as her mate.

"You two are now one, one as mates, one soul," Jason pulled Lacy into his arms, hearing Enakal's words and kissed her lips, slowly and passionately.

"Welcome to Bonded life," Jason whispered against Lacy's lips.

"Enjoy being mine, my love," she whispered back, pulling away and winking at Jason.

"Let the party begin!" as Enakal spoke, a group of people, all dressed up from head to toe in their culture walked, the Zaffa's walked in with musical instruments, making a loud noise. Belly dancers from the pack came in, their skirts and tops making noise as they danced around.

"This is what I'm talking about!" Lacy jumped up, Jason's hand clasped in hers, as she hugged her friends and family and got into the grove of things, shaking her hips to the beat of the music.

Everyone jumped to their feet, joining in the dancing and laughter and love that was surrounding the room. Lacy had never felt so in love before, she was Bonded to her mate and that was never going to change; not now, not ever.

"What am I going to say? I can't just call up and tell them everything straight away, Becca. You have to ease into something like that," Becca stood behind the couch and rested her hands on the back of the couch while her parents stood in front of the roaring brick fire place.

"Just let us do a little bit of an investigation first, then we can get in contact with them. We don't want them to worry if we can get in and find Olyanah," Aviva was cut off by her daughter.

"Ollie, she preferred Ollie over Olyanah," Becca cut in with a firm face.

"Well we don't want them to worry in case we are able to find Ollie and get her back without so much as blinking an eye," Becca had no choice but to listen to her parents, there was no way they would let her leave their sight knowing that she wanted to go and they were not going to let their daughter be in danger again. Not if they could help it and Becca knew it too.

"Fine, but I hope you know that I am going with you when you go," Winslow's face hardened as Becca spoke.

"That is not going to happen. I am not going to be putting you in harms way again."

"I've been there before, father, I am not letting Ollie stay there without seeing my face to know that I am keeping our promise and to know that there are people trying to look for her."

"Becca."

"No, father, I am going. You can give me the 'I am your father and I must look after you' speech all you want but that won't stop me from back there because I have already been to hell and back more times then you can count at the place and I will be there for her," Becca's tone told her mother and father that was no room for argument and she was going to go back for her friend, no matter what.

"Fine, but you can't leave our sides," Aviva stared at her daughter, not happy about what was going on. "No matter what. Got it?"

"Aye, aye Captain," Becca rolled her eyes, reminded herself of Ollie and the way she spoke. "So the investigation will be soon? We're going to flash there soon enough, yeah?" Elves weren't able to flash but they could if they were connected physically to a Fae at some point, they could hold hands or any physical contact so long as they were touching a Fae.

"A week. We're getting closer with the Elves to their warrior statues. We haven't had to fight for a long time so we need to train again but Fae are able to shrink so they don't need to be too quiet. The communication is a big thing that we are working on, letting the wind carry our words so we can still talk but no one else but Elves and Fae can hear us."

"OK, anything I can help with?" Becca asked her father, knowing as the man he was going to be in charge of the training and the warriors.

"I don't think so, I promise I will let you know if there I," Becca nodded her head and stood, ready to go upstairs and do something to take her mind off everything. She was quite fond of history and usually took some of the history books from her father's office and would go through them, learning about other Mystics and the world she lived in. Before her speech, she had only ever seen Elves in her history books, not that her father knew she would go through and read them.

Becca looked at her father, so tall, brave and strong, talking to the Elves, preparing them for what was to come. The Fae were being spoken to by Aviva who was also preparing them for what they might see, what might be happening in that place.

Becca had spent a lot of her time in her room reading so she could take her mind off what was happening and if she wasn't doing that then her mother was teaching her to talk through the wind and to other Fae and Elves.

She had been shrinking and walking around and changing her form, extending the time she could change her form for. The longest recorded time for a Fae to be in a different form was about ten minutes, which made it easier for them to shrink when they wanted to sneak around, it also gave humans something to believe.

"Becca," she looked up from her book as she sat on the couch, enjoy the fire as it was burning the wood in front of her.

"Yes, mother?"

"It's time," she nodded her head, closing the book and leaving in on the couch as she stood, her white chiffon dress flowing around her as she walked. The hover and aura around her had a silent soft wind, moving the dress a little.

Becca walked outside and smiled at a warrior her father introduced her to, she could tell that he was a submissive Elf, a tactic by her father so he couldn't be her mate because she needed to have a dominant Elf as her mate.

She nodded to the Elf and took his hand, flashing them both to the outskirts of building that she had been kept in for so long. The building was so far away that it looked like a dot in the distance, it gave the Seelie, the group of Fae and Elves, a chance to get themselves ready to shrink and pull their magic in to start creeping their way towards the building.

The Elves got down on their stomachs and army crawled their way towards to the building while the Fae shrunk themselves and started walking along.

"Becca?" her mothers voice carried through the wind to her ears, a question being asked, "Are you OK?"

"I'll be fine, let's get going," the building was slowly starting to creep up on them, the wind moving around the Seelie as they quietly crept along the ground, every now and then Becca or Aviva would grow a little to see just how far away they were from the building and how quiet they needed to be.

"Just stay quiet and low," Aviva mouthed to Becca, letting the words flow through the wind and land on Becca's ears.

"We are almost there," the small voice of Becca carried through the wind to those who were around in the tall grass. Shrinking again, Becca quickened her pace through the grass before hearing panicked voices.

"Where the fucking hell is she?" a loud booming voice, Becca recognised, shook the floor in which they ran along.

"Stop," her voice travelled through the wind, stopping only at the ears of Fae and Elves. "Something is wrong, something has happened," growing slowly to see over the grass and into the window, Becca saw the tall man with red eyes, barking orders at people as they hurried around.

The window she had broken still wasn't fixed and she could see inside as Red Eyes stood, Gold Eyes on one side and another man with darker eyes on the other. Becca could only imagine Ollie already had a nickname for the man with darker eyes.

"She couldn't have just got up and run away, she was chained to the damn table; those chains had poison on them that were unbreakable!" Red Eyes was fuming; smoke almost erupting from his ears.

"She's gone," Becca pulled back, heading in the opposite direction of building.

"I want her back!" a shrill voice called through the broken window. "I want her back now!" Becca again recognised the voice; Ally. "Where is she? She is gone because you are incompetent and unable to do your damn job!"

The comment confused Becca, she thought Gold Eyes was in control of the situation and Red Eyes was her right hand man, but by the sounds of things, the sound of her yelling, Ally was in charge. Ally was playing the game, keeping her statues close to her chest so she couldn't give any of her cards away.

The realization had Becca going back, going against the Seelie to see what Ally was saying and to see what was really going on and who was really in charge. The more information she could find out the better.

"Tell me again what happened," Ally walked up to the three that stood on the stage at the front of what would have been a ballroom a long time ago.

"We went into the chamber and she was gone, her chains were lying limp on the ground and the lock was undone. The cupboard was opened and inside, the things we had in there were gone, all gone. We went in, trying to find her and she was gone. The one we needed was gone, her powers gone with her and then the door slammed closed and we were locked in there until you came and got us out," the man with dark eyes repeated to Ally, probably not for the first time.

"How could you all go in there?" slaps resounded through the room and Becca cringed, knowing the noise all too well.

"Becca," Winslow appeared at her side. "You called us to go back to where we started and yet you yourself stay here to hear what they have to say," her father was mad at her, mad at her giving orders and made at her for leaving his side and possibly getting herself in trouble.

"All knowledge can help. Now shush so we can hear them," Becca commanded of her father and he obeys for the first time in their father-daughter relationship, Becca was usually the one having the listen to everything he told her, it felt good to be the one giving the orders. Winslow brought his body up so he could see what was happening in the room. "See that window?" her father nodded, "That was how I got out."

"This is the second time you have screwed up!" Gold Eyes cried out, not only at Red Eyes but at Ally and Dark Eyes too. "First the Fae and now the Wolf! You need to get your act together. We were told of their coming! We have been watching them, had someone on the inside, for eighteen years and you all fuck it up!" Becca knew they had outstayed their welcome, if someone stormed out then their cover would be blown.

"Time to go," Becca and her father said at the same time, hurrying back to where the rest of the Seelie were waiting.

Aviva was waiting until Becca was back to her normal size and Winslow was standing, guiding her towards the Elf that Becca had flashed with. She nodded at the Elf, asking if he was ready to flash, when he nodded she flashed and soon they were back in the forest in England they all knew so well.

Chapter Twenty-Two

He Who Fears Of Being Conquered Is Sure Of Defeat

LACY STEPPED INTO the bedroom, dragging Jason behind her and closing the door of their now shared bedroom. The room was quite large and reminded Lacy of a royal bedroom with a white marble ensuite and walk in wardrobe that had all their clothes folded and hung in it already.

"Come here, my mate, my soul, my love," Lacy pulled Jason in, letting her arms wrap around his neck and pulling his lips down to hers.

"You are mine and mine alone forever," Jason whispered against his mates lips, pulling her back and letting the singlet, rope sleeves fall down her shoulders so he could feel the soft skin of his mate under his fingers.

Letting the tips of his fingers play across her slightly tanned skin, letting the unblemished skin tickle his fingers. Lacy locked her fingers together around Jason's neck and stepped forward as she let her fingers wonder down the back of his shirt and around the front as Lacy started unbuttoning the shirt, letting it fall onto the floor below them. Lacy had wanted for so long to feel her mate under her, feel his toned skin hold her up.

Jason turned the pair around and let Lacy fall onto the bed, standing over her like the dominant animal her was. He looked down as Lacy started slipping the dress down her body.

"You are so beautiful, so beautiful," Jason fell down onto the bed, knees on either side of Lacy's body as he placed a hand on either side of her face before letting his lips lean down and kiss her lips again with passion. There was so much longing behind the kiss, so much need as Jason let Lacy slip his shorts off and kiss his jaw line, down his neck and along his collarbone.

"I love you," she whispered against his skin, letting her breath tickle Jason's skin. "I love you so much," Lacy let her hands explore Jason's body, slowly feeling her way around what she had left to the imagination for so long. Everything was so much better then she had ever thought it would be. Everything was perfect, so perfect right now that nothing could ruin her moment with her mate; nothing.

Enakal sat in his office, sitting on the double couch with Arabella under his arm, playing with her long almost white hair. Arabella's long white hair had been braided at the back, only a small section had been braided and Enakal was twirling the piece around his finger.

After the days celebrations, the two mates wanted to wind down into the late hours of the evening, embracing each other as they had seen the two new loves together today.

Interrupting the simple embrace of the mates was the ring of the phone. Enakal cringed at the sound but knew he had to answer the phone. It confused him as to who would be calling at this time of night, almost midnight in Egypt, but he figured it might be another pack or species calling upon him and his powers.

"I have to," he explained to Arabella but she stood up and let him get the phone. "Salve," he answered the phone.

"Salve, Enakal. It's Winslow," Enakal recognised the voice straight away.

"Winslow, it is wonderful to hear your voice again, old friend," Enakal and Winslow had known each other a long time, but since moving, Enakal and the Elf had lost contact.

"As yours. I am calling in regards to Olyanah," Enakal placed the phone down and put it on speaker so Arabella could hear what the Elf was about to say. "My daughter, Becca was taken long ago, as you were informed, she had been returned to us. She saw your daughter there; she was there with her. My daughter escaped and we went to investigate today, she has escaped. Your daughter is free but we have to inform you that she is free, she is out of that hell hole and she is never going to give up," tears started escaping from Enakal and Arabella's eyes. Tears of joy soaked their skin as they thought of seeing their daughter again; it might be able to come true.

"Thank you, thank you, Winslow," Arabella sobbed into Enakal's shoulder as she spoke to the phone.

"We are here to support you in finding your daughter. If you need any of us, Fae or Elves, then we are at your service. Becca is very excited to help, she said she was quite good friends with Ollie when they met for a while and she told her all about Mystics. She is very keen to meet Ollie's friend Lacy, whom Ollie spoke fondly of according to our daughter," Enakal listened to his old friend and held his wife.

"How will we ever thank you and find our Ollie?"

"We'll help in anyway possible. We'll take you to where the building was and we can go from there to find her."

"You have seen these bastards who have done this to our daughter?"

"We have."

"We'll meet you at the Seelie forest when we can get on the next flight. I refuse to tell my whole pack until we know everything. I'll inform only those that need to be informed and out my Third wolf in charge and then we will head over. I will also inform Richard, the UK Alpha of what has happened and that we will be entering his territory again, I am sure he will help us," Enakal sat down and started writing things down as he spoke.

"Who will you bring?"

"My mate, Arabella, my Beta, Cruze, my Second, Drake, my Fifth, Brent along with Charles and Sally. I want this kept under wraps until we find her and if it takes longer then a month or two then we will inform the rest of the pack and get more out there trying to find her."

"As you wish it," Winslow replied and the line disconnected.

"Lacy will look after Nuru because I refuse to let our three year old daughter come in case she gets taken from us too," Arabella stated. "We were be here to celebrate her third birthday and now we must find our other daughter to celebrate her nineteenth birthday and all the others we have missed," Enakal kept scribbling down notes before picking up the phone and dialing a number.

"I will inform Jason that he is to keep Nuru and I will inform him not to tell Lacy of our intentions on leaving, she will be too emotional and is planning to go back to Rosewood soon in case Ollie goes back, she needs to do that," Enakal had the phone to his ear as he spoke to his mate. "Salve, Richard," Enakal said when there was an answer on the other end. "We have news on Ollie."

Arabella left the room, ready to go and inform Jason of what was to be happening. She knew she would be interrupting something, it was their Bonding night after all and Lacy would be in a little pain after their adventures as her marks started showing on her skin.

Arabella, Enakal and Jason had neglected to inform Lacy that when the female got matching marks to her mate, she would be in a little pain as the black lines appeared on her body.

Walking up to the door, Arabella could hear Lacy's pain, telling her that the process was starting and soon Lacy would be forever marked by Jason on her body, tattoo like marks from her right arm along her shoulder blade and right breast.

"Excuse me," Arabella knocked quietly on the door, she could hear movement and Jason opened the door only a little so he could poke his head out. "I must speak with you."

"Can it wait? Lacy is in need of me," Jason looked back as a small whimper was hear from inside the room.

"Once she is fine, we must speak with you immediately," Jason nodded and closed the door to comfort his mate as she lay in a degree of pain. Arabella left the door and walked back to Enakal's office where he sat writing away, the phone off his ear again.

"Lacy is marking so he is busy, but I informed him we must speak with him."

"I have booked flights for us for tomorrow and flights for Lacy, Jason and the others for a week away. It is a month until Ollie disappeared, I have extended their stay for a good month or two, depending on what happens while they are there," Enakal explained to his mate, not looking up once.

"Darling," Arabella tried to entice her mate to look up and when he didn't, she walked over and wrapped his head up in her arms. "Please, look at me," he looked up through her hair and smiled softly. "Just breathe and stay calm, you are an amazing man, Alpha and mate, you need to stay calm and I want you to just think things through before you start making plans," Arabella tried to calm her mate, letting his listen to the steady beat of her heart in her chest.

Enakal and Arabella walked out of the pack house, giving their wonderful daughter a kiss on the cheek before walking out the door, it was a seven and a half hour trip from Kharga to Cairo and their flight was leaving in twelve hours so they had to get a move on if they wanted to make it to England in time.

Drake, Brent, Sally, Charles and Cruze were already waiting in the car, ready to hear why they were leaving, Arabella and Enakal had kept everything under wraps, only informing Jason of his role in their plan to get their daughter back.

"Be a good girl for Lacy and Jason," Arabella called out to Nuru before closing the door and getting into one of the large hummer like cars they had for the pack.

"What is going on Alpha's?" Brent asked from the back. Charles was driving with Enakal in the front, Arabella and Sally in the back with Cruze and Brent and Drake in the very back-back of the car.

"We got a call from Winslow, King of the Seelie and he informed us that his daughter had been kidnapped by the same people that took Ollie. We are going to England to talk to them and see if we can find her. They have been back to the building they were kept in and have heard that Ollie has escaped so it is our turn to put in some effort," the car could feel the tension and fear rolling off Cruze in waves at hearing his mates name.

"And you are only telling us now!" he cried out.

"Yes, we heard last night and couldn't have Lacy knowing or her plans to go back to Rosewood in a week would change. What if Ollie goes there and we don't know?" Arabella asked.

"That's why we left Jay behind?"

"Yes. Once they go, Donkor will be in charge. He is very strong and there will be no other dominants aside from himself there while he is in charge, he will be fine," Enakal answered Cruze.

"I thank you, Alpha's, for allowing me to come along," Cruze spoke formally, trying to show just how grateful he was with his Alpha's allowing him to come along.

"You are her mate and we know how this has affected you, we want you to feel comfortable and as our future Alpha and son-in-law, it is our duty to make sure you are apart of the family," Arabella was sitting in the middle and took Cruze's hand as she spoke. "You are like a son to us as you lost your parents so young."

"Thank you, Arabella," Cruze tapped on Arabella's hand, letting him know just what those words meant to him.

"You're our son, and will soon be by blood when you Bond with our daughter, I have no doubt that we will find her and with your assistance," Enakal looked over the seat and smiled at Cruze.

"You're a strong and thoughtful, Alpha. I'm lucky to have been born into this pack," Cruze answered and the car fell into a very comfortable silence as they watched the scenery fly by, soon they would be on the road next to Nile and watch the other cities and towns that had no idea of the people living on the same land as them.

Lacy sat Nuru down and held out a doll for her to hold like she was a mother holding her new born child in her arms. Lacy couldn't help the smile that spread onto her lips, soon they would be going back to what she thought was her birthplace and Ollie might be there too, she still had hopes that Ollie would be sitting at The Local, tapping her fingers on the table like she had been there a long time waiting for the others.

"What's her name?" Lacy asked Nuru as she tried to brush the red hair of the doll she was holding.

"Ollie," Lacy had to hold back tears at the answer.

"Why?"

"I have a sister. Her name is Ollie and this is her until she comes back and I get to meet her. Mama and Papa showed me a picture and she has the same hair," Nuru sat with her legs crossed; the two were sitting outside on the grass watching the wind flow through the trees and rustle the leaves.

"I was good friends with Ollie, we were like sisters," Lacy held Nuru close and hugged her, letting her play with her doll. The outside of the pack house was surrounded by grass and forest and woods, segregated from the rest of the city they lived in by a few hundred kilometers.

"Was she nice?"

"She was very nice and funny and pretty."

"Do I look like her?"

"No, but that isn't a bad thing. Don't you think it is better to be you then to be like someone else? I think Ollie will love you when she comes back and she will love how different you are. She would hate it if you were just like her; her motto always was there had to be a spice to life, change it up," Nuru listened to every word Lacy said as she watched other wolves walk around the large yard and emerge from the forest after a long run or hunt.

"Do you know them? I forget names?" Nuru pointed to the wolves emerging from the forest in human form.

"That one," Lacy pointed to her brother, "That is Matt and his mate Ain. He is fifteen and she is sixteen. They aren't allowed to be Bonded until they are at least seventeen, so as not to arise suspicion with the humans. Those two," Lacy moved on from her brother and his mate who were entering the forest until a thought formed in her mind. "Matt!" she called out getting his attention.

"Hey, Lac."

"You are still fifteen so mate or no mate, you are to remain as pure as possible. Got it?"

"Always, Your Highness," Matt bowed before taking Ain's hand and running into the forest.

"Your brother?" Nuru asked.

"Yup. Younger brother. OK, now that is Donkor, he is one hundred and twenty-five. Next to him is Sarah, she is ninety-five, then Harry, one hundred, Liam, one hundred and Eshe, she's one hundred and fifty-five," Lacy rattled off the names of people she had met and people she already knew.

"Do you like it here?"

"I love it here. It is home here."

"Home," Nuru repeated, enjoying the way her dolls hair felt now that it was all untangled. "Will she be home soon?"

"Who?"

"Ollie?"

"I hope so. I miss her," Lacy didn't want Nuru see her cry, she was meant to be strong, she was meant to be her aunty and yet she wanted to break down now and hold Nuru as she cried.

Almost like he sensed her emotions, which Lacy guessed he had, Jason emerged from the house and sat down on the grass, asking if he could see Nuru's doll, plaiting the long hair of the doll.

"You are a lucky girl, Nuru," he tied the end of the plait with a hair tie Lacy gave him and gave the doll back to Nuru. It was dressed in a summer dress, ready to go to a tea party with the Queen if she called asking for an invitation.

"Why?" Nuru spun off Lacy's lap and the three sat in a triangle, letting the sun beat down on their skin.

"You have wonderful parents and a pack that loves you and a sister that will be home soon to meet you, to me that adds up to a very lucky girl," Jason smiled. "Plus you have Lacy and I in your life, we are pretty amazing to have as an aunty and uncle," Jason winked at Nuru and stood up. "Want to go play on the playground?" there was a playground to the side of the house with a swing, slide, monkey bars, steps, rock climbing wall and many other fun things for kids to do so they don't get bored.

The were lucky that there were eight swings because Jason started pushing Nuru on the swing and Lacy got to swinging next to Nuru. The playground had a wooden support structure that looked as though it had aged well, just like Werewolves.

Chapter Twenty-Three

Remember The Reasons You Are Running

OLLIE HUNCHED OVER, panting as she tried to draw more air into her lungs so she could get running all over again. Last she had checked she had been on the move for a long time, probably hours, if not days. She had stopped watching the sun and the moon, only seeing what was in front of her, which proved not to be a lot.

Ollie's heightened senses were working in her favour to keep her focused when it got a bit dark, letting her keep running like she was now. The sun was down and the moon was up, lighting her path to freedom. No one had come after her that she had seen but the molding bread and little bit of water had worn off a long time ago and now she was running off adrenaline.

The path in front of her seemed to look like a forest, a well kept, manicured forest that had a path leading down the centre and benches along the sides of the sidewalk.

Trees stood tall above the path, disrupting the picture of the moon that stood above, watching Ollie as she had moved around the unfamiliar area. The path wound around the trees and split off in different ways, letting Ollie explore the forest she was in a little more. Benches were everywhere on the paths, scattered along to bring relief for those who got too tired when walking through the nature that stood so tall in front of Ollie, so beautiful and so magic to her.

Ollie looked at the benches and thought how lovely it would be to lay down and have a sleep but her mind was too scared that someone was following her and waiting until she stopped and slept, ready to take her again.

Her eyelids started to fall, telling her that no matter what her mind was saying, she was tired and she wasn't going to be able to stay up any longer.

Ollie walked over to one of the benches and stretched out, letting herself get comfortable on the wooden seat, looking up at the stars that were twinkling in the sky, Ollie felt as though they were looking down at her, watching and making sure that she was safe for her journey home, where ever that was.

Lying on the bench, Ollie realised just how much she had forgotten about her life. She wasn't even sure she could remember her own name. Her name was starting to become a shadow in her memory, along with other names that seemed to evade her. She could remember smells, and a few details of faces but other then that she couldn't remember too much that had happened in her past other then recently.

Her life was unraveling in front of her eyes and yet there was nothing she could do to stop it because there was nothing to remember in her memory, everything that had happened had caused Ollie to suppress everything that had been in her former life.

There had been someone close to her and a recent person that had consumed her mind, but she couldn't picture faces, only smells and that hurt her deeply in her heart as she so desperately wanted to know those who had been so dear in her life and so close to her.

The pain of forgetting was taking its toll on Ollie, she felt like a horrible person at the thought of not knowing those that had clearly meant so much to her in her life at one point or another.

The stars twinkled up in the sky, still watching Ollie as she lay on the wooden bench seat. Ollie could feel the sleep she had been resisting for so long starting to creep up on her, starting to show itself that no matter how much Ollie tried, she wasn't going to evade it for much longer, sleep had its claws in her skin and it wasn't going to be letting go any time soon.

Her dreams were filled with what had possessed her in that building that stood so far away, the girl she had promised and what that girl had told her. Ollie's eyes had been opened for those days; letting her see what world she really lived in. If she believed the girl, she wasn't sure, but the images she had created seemed to float around in her mind, letting her see wolves running together, slowly turning in humans as their run slowed and their breathes died down.

Ollie could see feathered wings flapping around, four wings on each creature, each a different light colour as light reflected off their feathers, off their means of transport and off their magic as they lived.

The birds chirping were a pleasant and confusing wakeup for Ollie, something that had her mind confused as she opened her eyes and saw the sun shining down on her. The light was blinding but not in the same way as she was used to, she was used to a fluorescent light that sat directly over her eyes but this light was coming from a different direction and was much more natural.

Opening her eyes, using her arm to shield her from the light, she sat up in the bench seat. There were so many noises around her, so much laughter and talking and chirping from birds, along with barking dogs and the sounds of people running along the pavement not too far away.

Wherever Ollie was, it looked like a peaceful place, a place that people would come to think, a place where people would come to experience nature and be one with nature.

A school group was near by and Ollie could see that the group was only filled with girls that sat with books in their hands, sketching what was around them, bringing nature back to their art.

"Miss!" a young, female, Scottish voice called out, overtaking the loud noises that were all around. Ollie looked around, trying to find the source of the girl's voice.

"Yes, Aggie?" another Scottish voice was heard, but this time it was older.

"Come here," the younger voice, Aggie, cried, calling the older lady over, Ollie could hear the footsteps and soon she could see a girl, about fifteen, maybe sixteen, in a school uniform of a black skirt, white blouse and black blazer with green around the edgings of all. The older lady had a simple long skirt on and a buttoned up cardigan over the top. Ollie couldn't imagine being rugged up with this sun beating down on her bare skin, letting her feel a warmth she hadn't felt in such a long time.

"Aggie, what is it?" the lady stopped when she saw Ollie sitting there, look utterly stunned at what was going on around her, her whole body covered in bruises and scars and her face looking terrified.

"See, Miss? We saw her before and she didn't more so we thought she was dead. We wanted to make sure and you're a nurse so we thought you could talk to her. She looks hurt," Aggie said to the teacher.

"Excuse me, Miss?" the teacher walked over to her, trying not to look as though she was going to hurt her. "Miss, are you OK?" Ollie just stared at the lady, rather scared of what might happen. She didn't know these people and she didn't know if they were in connection to those who had kidnapped her a long time ago, longer then she cared to remember.

"Is she OK?" the one called Aggie, asked.

"I think she is scared. Miss, we are not going to hurt you, we just want to help. What happened to you? Are you OK?" the questions were thrown at her and she took a few steps back, not knowing what else to do. The questions were too much for her and the light was blinding her sensitive sight that she had been developing in her running.

"Would you like to come with us?" Aggie asked.

"We will let you use our shower? Make a bed for you to sleep in?" the teacher looked at the poor torn girl in front of her and slowly stepped forward, leaving Aggie behind, trying to gain her trust. "Please let us help you."

Her mind started racing as she thought about what the lady was saying. What would be worse? Wondering around or going with these women and either ending up with those who had originally taken her or actually being treated well.

Deciding, she stepped forward, folding her arms over her chest and looking utterly terrified as she let the lady touch her around the shoulder, trying to embrace her and let her know they weren't going to hurt her, but instead she recoiled, not meaning to as she was still scared of someone else's touch.

"Please, we want to help. How did you get here? What happened?" the lady asked. "My name is Nora, I am the English teacher at The Girls

Boarding School of Dingwall in Scotland," she had a strong Scottish accent but the poor, broken girl was able to easily understand her. "What happened to you?"

She didn't respond, just walked with Nora to when a large group of school girls a few other teachers stood, she stopped in her tracks, her heart beating faster as she was over whelmed by so many people.

"Please don't worry," Nora tried to calm her down. "These are the students and some of the other teachers, please don't feel alarmed, they are wonderful people," Nora calmed her down enough to let her walk a little forward and be accepted by the group.

"OK," one of the teachers, they all seemed to be female from what Ollie could see, called attention to the group. "This girl needs our full support, as you can see she has been through a lot and I want you all to be careful with her," Nora leaned over to smile at Ollie.

"That's Donalda, she is a humanities teacher at the boarding school," she nodded her head, trying to wrap her mind around what was really happening to her. It felt so surreal to her that she had escaped, but at the same time she was worried that they might come after her or these people might be working with those who had kidnapped her in the first place.

"What's your name?" Donalda came over and smiled kindly at her. She refused to talk, shaking her head in fear of her life still, she wasn't even sure she remembered how to talk, it had been so long since she had opened her mouth to talk.

"Do you want something to eat? Some water?" she nodded her head, accepting a bottle of water and drinking it in a few seconds, enjoying the feeling of hydration in her body. Her throat started not feeling as dry and she was able to open her dry lips.

"Food?" Donalda asked, getting a nod from her and she handed her a sandwich and watched as the under fed girl gobbled down the sandwich, the feeling of fullness erupting in her stomach.

Her form of thank you was a simple smile, showing the first bit of emotion in her expression and her eyes. The ladies took her to the bus and let her lay down so she could sleep more and went back to the school group.

"What'd you think happened to her?" Nora asked Donalda as she walked back to the rest of the group.

"I don't know, but whatever happened clearly hurt her mentally and physically, did you see the scars all along her back, legs and stomach?" Nora nodded, "We should do something to help her? Maybe you could try and get her to talk? You minored in psychology didn't you? You could help her open up?" Donalda sat down on a bench and spoke easily to her colleague and friend.

"I did, but I don't think a minor in psychology would be able to deduce what happened to that girl."

"You can try, that is all you can do."

"I'll try, when we get back, and I'll talk to Mabel about getting her a room on her own and then we can try to get her to talk, I am not leaving such a young girl that has been hurt on her own until we know she is OK and she might be rather smart and be able to teach as well," Nora nodded her head.

"Maybe she speaks another language?"

"She understood when we spoke English to her."

"Maybe she speaks other languages too? Doesn't Aggie know a little sign language? She might be able to talk to her?"

She woke with the rattling of metal and plastic together and her body bumping around in a way that didn't feel familiar to her.

Opening her eyes, she saw windows surrounded her and lots of schoolgirl laughter and conversations. She didn't recognise where she was or where she was going.

Sitting up, she looked out the window, trying to follow the landscape that flew past her large open window. Looking around there were a few familiar faces around, but other then that she didn't really understand what was going on.

"Good morning sleepy head," she looked up and saw Nora sitting in a pair of seats opposite her.

"You've been asleep for a good four hours," in front of her sat Donalda and another older lady.

"We're on the way back to Dingwall. We've called up Mabel, the Principal, and she has agreed to get a room ready for you so you can shower and make your self at home, the girls are also offering a few clothes for you too so you can get out of the ones you are wearing," Nora smiled kindly.

She held out an open had and touched her fingers to her chin like a reflexes she didn't know she had, she moved the hand away from her chin in a small arch motion.

"Do you know sign language?" she pulled her fingers into a fist and using her wrist, she moved the fist up and down like it was a head nodding. Nora looked over at Donalda, speaking in only a simple look before letting Ollie close her eyes and rest her head against the window so she could sleep some more.

The thought of being able to have a home again, even if she still didn't trust these people, it was going to be more of a home then she could remember.

The sign language to she felt as though it was second nature to her, like she might have learnt it at a young age and it had stuck in her mind through everything, letting her communicate with others.

The scenery around the bus she was in flashed past as she opened her eyes, seeing the sun shinning into her deep blue orbs. She could see birds flying together, free from pain the humans endured everyday, able to fly away at their own will whenever things got too bad.

The trees that moved with every slight wind that passed through their branches, letting the leaves dance and letting them pass their secrets around as they danced together as one.

The made road left little bumps as the bus passed over it, every now and then Ollie lost her guts, the feeling of being in a bus unfamiliar, being so enclosed with so many people around her, having such a comfortable place to sit, having such a comfortable place to sleep. Everything was so foreign to her, so strange as she lived a life she couldn't remember as a person she didn't even know.

Was she a happy person? Funny? Calm? Charming? Beautiful? Did she have a lot of friends? All the questions ran through her mind as she sat in the bus, watching live pass her by out the window, not even looking twice at the poor girl who had suffered for so long.

"Do we have a room ready?" Nora asked Donalda.

"I think so," Donalda pulled out her phone and dialed a number, moving to the very back of the bus so she could talk to whoever was on the other end of the phone.

"We'll take care of you, I'm sure we'll find a place for you and you can stay with us for as long as you need," she nodded her head in thanks, so humbled by the generosity that these people were showing her.

"We have a room ready," Donalda smiled. "It's private, we imagined it'd please you considering we're all strangers," she noticed that the ladies spoke very formally to each other and to her, trying to gain trust but keep a professional relationship about themselves.

"Thank you for helping, Donalda, it means a lot to me and I'm sure to her too," Nora thanked her friend as the two watched her lean back against the window and close her eyes, trying to get back to sleep so she could escape what was going on, she still didn't know just how much she trusted the people around her but it was better then before as far as she could see.

Chapter Twenty-Four

Memories Warm You Up From The Inside, But They Also Tear You Apart

SHE LOOKED DOWN on a tub filled with warm water, bubbles moving around the top, popping as they combined and rose higher in the tub. The sight was a new sight, a sight she couldn't remember seeing before in her life, such luxury lay before her, calling her to step in and clean herself of what had happened to her so she could start again and forget what had happened to her, what she had been through and what she had lived through and escaped from.

Slowly dropping her clothes and seeing the wolf piercing, which she placed on the bench top, she pulled her black crop top and bike shorts off and lowered her tired, battered and sore body into the bathtub, ready to clean herself.

The warm water surrounded her skin, replenishing it as her malnourished skin soaked it up. The water soon turned a dark colour, showing just what Ollie's skin had picked up as she lay on the stone bench.

Using a small square towel, she started scrubbing her skin, pulling her legs up to her chest so she could wash her legs, feet and toes. She didn't emerge from the bathtub until her skin was clean and her hair was washed. Emerging from the bath, Ollie dried her body and pulled on some underwear and clothes that had been left for her kindly by the school.

"Hello," someone knocked on the door of the bathroom, trying to get her attention, but her mind was somewhere else as she grabbed a brush and started getting the knots out of it. "Can I come in," with no response, the girl opened the door and she recognised the face.

She put her thumb up from her fist and moved from her wrist to her thumb from side to side, asking Ollie if she was finished. Ollie replied by pulling her hand into a fist and moving it up and down at the wrist.

"You aren't deaf, you replied to us before at the park so something happened to make you not talk," the girl Ollie recognised as Aggie, stepped in and closed the door, taking the brush from Ollie and getting the tangles at the back.

"My brother is deaf," Aggie started, "He has been since he was born so I had to learn sign language to talk to him. I love my brother but it's hard to talk to him a lot of the time because of it. You aren't deaf, you sign like it's robotic," she gently nodded her head, taking the brush from Aggie and putting it down. "You have learnt sign language? Do you speak anything else?" she nodded. "Why won't you talk?" she didn't reply, just averted her eyes from Aggie's and hid the tears that were starting to form in her eyes.

'Why won't you talk?' Aggie asked using her hands to communicate.

'I can't,' she relied, refusing to say anything else if any other questions were asked of her.

She could remember talking to someone one day, she spoke a language that she couldn't name and every word she spoke to the deep voice had her heart beating faster. That was how she knew what rain smelt like; he was the reason she knew what rain smelt like at the beach and at the forest.

That smell was something she never wanted to forget and she was determined to find the man that had given her the strength to carry on and live each day so she could one day go and find him.

"I'll leave you to it. I've left some food out in your room in case you're hungry. You look like you haven't eaten in years," Aggie left the bathroom with a small smile, seeing that she was in pain with company.

she sat down in her room, dressed in a pair of black leggings, a white singlet and a knitted cardigan to keep her bare arms warm.

On her new bed sat a plate of toast with butter on it, orange juice, apples and pears. The range of food was something she hadn't seen in a long time and it warmed her stomach to know that there were people out there that cared.

she wished she could know if they were looking for her, if they still cared about her, remembered her, any of that because if she knew, she could know just how hard she needed to fight and just how much she wanted.

Even if they weren't looking for her, she wanted to see them again and she promised herself silently that one day, she would find them.

* * *

A diary lay next to the bed, being lit by the yellow light of the lamp in the bland room with white empty walls. Scribbling and drawings lay inside book, showing scenes that had run through her mind when she had slept.

Determined to remember as much as she could, Ollie had started keeping a diary, just in case what came up was a memory that she could play with and bring back her past into the forefront of her mind.

The drawings inside the book were of waves hitting the sand; the pencil in which she had drawn them in was smudged a little with tears as Ollie drew it down. Words surrounded the picture too; *beach, love, dress, old, family, friend, sister, leaving, home, life, caring, laughter.* A few of the words were written in bold, and highlighted, screaming to Ollie that they meant something else to her, they had a deeper meaning to her that she just had to discover.

Other pages had faces with long hair and no facial features, another drawn picture was a man with his back to the page and a surf board under his arm, looking out at the ocean as waves rose far out. The longing he felt to be out in those waves were so powerful to Ollie as she drew the picture, so powerful she was reduced to laying in bed, her mind spinning with emotions she couldn't register.

The book lay open, being lit up by the shaded lamp as Ollie slept, her head resting on the fluffy pillow as her eyes were closed, hiding the glowing eyes of the full moon that scared Ollie. She still didn't understand the power within her, but she felt as though it meant something, something she had forgotten about a long time go as she lay dreaming in a bed that she felt was too soft and too comfortable.

He watched the stage as girls moved around it in barely anything on their bodies but a small pieces of fabric. My eyes begged me to lay down and close them so they could sleep but before I could think about it again, a hand wrapped around my upper arm and pushed me on stage, letting me start dancing in the way I knew best.

I didn't want to go on stage and dance, I wanted to pretend I had a normal life, pretend that this wasn't happening and that my parents cared about me, but I knew it wasn't true so I just had to do what I did best to avoid any form of conflict within the family.

Other girls were on the floor, dancing around men while I stood on stage, moving my hips from side to side as I walked to the pole and wrapped one leg around it, letting it hold my whole weight and dropping my body back, showing off my strength and flexibility. Roars erupted from the crowd, begging me to continue dancing on stage.

I could see him in the back of the room, hidden by the shadows the bad lighting in the under ground club. Another man, a taller man, stood next to him, chatting to him about something that I assumed concerned me as they kept watching me dance, getting money tucked into the straps of my underwear and thrown at me, making it harder and harder to walk around on stage in the six inch heels that I had been forced to wear.

I had a pink bra on, pushing me up as I moved and black thin underwear, covering everything I wanted covered. I could feel myself starting to slowly sweat as the makeup he had put on my body to cover the bruising started to drip away.

Fearing what he might say, I walked off stage, swaying my hips and moving my body in a seductive way leaving them wanting more as she went behind stage to fix up the make up that was covering her body. The lady behind stage helped me, aggressively getting me ready to go back on stage to get dancing again.

Men cried out as I got back on stage, men grabbed at my ankles, grabbing me and trying to get a piece of me. One man grabbed my ankle tightly and pulled me, bringing me down and smacking my head against the stage.

Everything was black as she opened her eyes; the only form of light was the moon that was shinning through a crack in the window of the curtains she had closed before she decided she needed to get some sleep.

The moon showed her how much she didn't remember, she had seen in the mirror before she went to sleep that her deep blue were glowing, staring back at her like a pool of water. She couldn't remember why they did it but she knew it was for a powerful reason.

Something she could remember was the girl with short blonde hair and the stories she had told her; the stories of things she had called 'Mystics'. Mermaids, Werewolves, Fae, something along the lines of a Banshee, all the words came flooding back to her as she lay in bed, her mind suddenly wake.

She pulled her notebook from the side table and grabbed the pencil she had with it and started writing everything down about the short blonde girl and the 'Mystics' she had told Ollie about.

Writing the names of the creatures down, she started to imagine what they would look like, drawing a mermaid in her notebook along with a beautiful ghost like creature that transformed when she screamed, a wolf with light crystal eyes and the blonde girl, still looking at her back, with wings coming from her back, four feather like wings coming from her shoulder blades as she hovered in the air, showing off her magic with a light aura around her, telling her that she was pure.

She could see faded colours around the people that were putting her up, all were very light colours and the meanings just came to her like the sign language had. They were pure people with kind intentions and only wanted to help her, something she wasn't used to and it was going to be hard for them to still gain her trust after everything she had been through.

It wasn't going to be easy from here on in, but she was going to fight for it so she could find out about her life and get Red Eyes, Dark Eyes, Gold Eyes and Ally, they can't get away with what they had done, to her it just wasn't fair if they did. There had to be some form of justice in the world for everything that be bestowed upon her up to this point.

'My name is,' she paused, trying to run through her memory to find out what her name is, *'I live in,'* again she drew a blank, but that wasn't going to deter her. *'My sister is. My mother is. My father is. My best friend is. My boyfriend is.'* She wanted to know the ends to all of those sentences.

'I was a student,' the answer surprised her, she didn't expect to answer her own question, so she wrote down the answer and question and tried

to think of other answers to the questions she had asked but her mind drew a blank.

'I was eighteen,' again she wrote down the answer to her own question. It was obvious to her that every answer was from the answers were, 'I was' so she wasn't a student anymore and she wasn't eighteen anymore, all her answers were in the past.

The thought of finding this out had her heart beating faster as she watched the moon move around from one side of her window to the other, slowly telling her that morning was just around the corner and that, to her, meant another day of self-induced solitude as she tried to remember everything that had happened to her.

There was a small sized TV in her room that she usually played a movie on while she tried to remember if she had seen it before.

The TV started and a menu popped up, asking if she wanted to play the movie or go to scene selection. Play was clicked before a black and white video started playing, women and men dancing on the screen were shown before in slanted pink writing *Dirty Dancing*.

The scene looked somewhat familiar to her, but she just couldn't work out if she had seen it before or someone had told her about it, the old looking film was very comforting to her, the old style of the movie was very warming to her.

She walked around the school, dressed in a pair of black leggings with a black zip up jumper to keep her warm. The girls were in class; all doors of the rooms were closed with only a window to show them what was in the hallways. The boarding school was a very odd experience, sleeping in the same place that you went to school seemed rather silly to her.

Walking past one of the classrooms, she saw Nora teaching English to some fifth years. She recognised Aggie sitting in the class and knocked on the door.

'Can I join?' she signed to Aggie.

"Can she join us?" Aggie asked Nora.

"Of course," Nora allowed her into the room, handed her a pen and book and pointed to the empty seat next to Aggie. "You can sit there. OK, now back to what we were talking about. Conflict is seen in everyday life, it is something that is seen in all countries and in all walks of life with religions and parenting thoughts and the way in which people decide to live their life," Nora started writing a few things on the white board behind her and everyone in the class started taking notes.

"We're going to be studying the book The Rugmaker of Mazar-E-Sharif as it demonstrates a conflict within a land and religions," Nora handed out the book, giving one to her as well.

Flipping through the book, she could see it was about a refugee trying to escape life in Afghanistan and come to Australia. That word, that word meant something to her, she couldn't remember what but the word Australia had a meaning to her, it had her heat racing as she looked it over, trying to think of where the country was.

"Afghanistan is in the Middle East and Australia is below Indonesia, a Westernised country below Asia," Aggie leaned over and explained to her as she saw confusion written all over her face. "Do you remember where you are from?" earlier the day before she had explained to Aggie that she didn't remember much of her life before, not her name, how to speak and where she had come from. Aggie had been trying to jog her memory; help her remember where she was from.

"Aggie," Nora warned her student.

"Sorry, Miss, I was trying to see if she remembered anything," Aggie explained.

"Do it when I'm not teaching," Aggie nodded her head and kept it down, writing the notes from the board in her book as Nora continued teaching.

At the end of the class, Aggie walked out with her on one side and another girl on her other side. She had introduced her friend to her as Logan, another fifth year in her English class.

She liked Aggie, she thought she was really nice and easy to communicate with, with what she could remember of her sign language, still too scared and scarred to talk, especially about what had happened to her in the hellhole she hated calling upon in her memory.

She also liked Nora, she seemed really kind and caring as she went about her duties, teaching students, trying to further their education and further them in their worldly experiences so they became better citizens, to her it was a very noble cause the Nora was embarking on, something she wished she could do one day to make a difference in someone's life, even if it was only one person.

Lacy sat in the car, watching the scenery move past her, the bushes, the cars, the ocean starting to creep up on them. Lacy was in the car with Jason, Nuru, Matt and Ain. In the other car behind them were Jay, Harry, Liam, Martha, Sarah and Polly. They were all heading to Lacy's old house, they hadn't ended up selling it so it was free until they did, so Lacy and everyone were able to stay at her old place.

It was something Lacy was looking forward to, seeing her old place, the house she had grew up in. Jason had never been to her old place, so her was excited to see her room, but aside from that Lacy really wanted to go to The Local everyday for a week, to see if Ollie would show up, to see if she had remembered, to see if Ollie was ever going to come back into her life.

"Lacy, you have to understand, she might not come," Jason rested a hand on her thigh as he drove through Saint Louis.

"I know, but I have to have hope, because if I don't then no one will, you all think she got away and is dead somewhere. I know she isn't dead, I know she is somewhere, waiting for us to come and find her," Lacy explained, trying to keep her hopes up, but at the same she knew she had to keep level headed in her hopes because who knew what was going to happen and Lacy couldn't stand disappointment, not again.

"So are we gonna unpack and then just chill? Or what?" Matt interrupted the silence in the car as they grew closer and closer to Rosewood.

"I'm going to go for a walk around town, people can do whatever they want," Lacy turned down the music and unwound her window letting the fresh air pierce the car and cool down her warming cheeks.

"Cool, I want to take Ain to the pool and then to Saint Louis to check out the beach and show her the shops," Lacy heard what Matt was saying but she wasn't really listening as they pulled into the familiar street she and Matt had left behind not long ago.

"Have you spoken to Cruze?" Lacy asked Jason as he stopped the car and Matt and Ain fell out, ready to stretch their legs and explore the old place they hadn't sold and Ain hadn't seen before. She was curious to see where Matt had grown up.

"No, not since he left but I'll give him a buzz when we're settled," Jason got out and unclipped Nuru from her baby seat, trying to ignore the nagging feeling that was pulling him down at the fact that he was lying to his mate, his best friend, the other half of his soul.

"Jason, they've been there for a week and he's your best friend; why haven't you spoken to him and why won't you explain it to me. I can tell you're holding back," it was just a feeling Lacy had but she was pretty sure it was the mate bond that was letting her know and she didn't like the feeling. She didn't want to hear it or be bothered, knowing her mate was lying, "You know what? I don't want to hear it," Lacy grabbed Nuru from Jason and walked inside, closing the door behind her and leaving Jason to get all the bags from the back of the car by himself.

"Hey, Lac?" Lacy let Nuru walk around as Matt entered the room.

"Yeah?"

"I know you'll find her, but if you don't can you please come back?"

"What do you mean?"

"We used to have so much fun, you used to laugh, you used to enjoy life and joke and now you just sit on the balcony and I don't know what to do to make you happy," Lacy hadn't realised just how much of a toll this was taking, not only on herself but on her family too. She could understand why Jason was a little pulled back now and why Matt spent a lot more time with his mate then she did with hers.

"I'm sorry, Matt. I'll be here for you, I really will."

"I know you're trying, but you need to come back to us, not just me but Jason as well. He misses his easy going, funny mate."

"You two are close aren't you?"

"He's my brother, of course we are," Matt entered the kitchen and grabbed a glass, filling it with water.

"I love you, Matt. Just remember, you need to stay as pure as the Virgin Mary before she fell pregnant."

"You know they call her 'Virgin' Mary for a reason yeah?"

"Doesn't mean I have to agree with religion. I can have my own opinion," Lacy poked her tongue out at Matt.

"But you have to respect what others believe."

"I do."

"No you don't."

"Yes I do."

"No you don't."

"Yes I do, now just accept that I'm right because I'm older then you and you're always wrong because you're a boy, so deal with it," Lacy filled her own glass with water and without warning, threw it at Matt, "As I girl, I would've seen it coming," Lacy jumped out of the way when Matt threw his water at Lacy. "See?"

"Go jump in lake," Matt poked out his tongue this time.

"Go eat your own vomit, now if you don't mind, I have an aunty to call so I can get to the bottom of this and then it is on to the end of the world to walk around the dark abyss," Lacy struck a superhero posse and ran away from Matt towards her room so Matt couldn't get her.

Walking into her room, Lacy saw just how little it had changed and just how much she missed it in Rosewood. She could just imagine what Ollie would say to that comment.

'It's because people never really change, at least not on the inside and if you want to remember something, it will remain the same because your memory will preserve it that way,' Lacy rolled her eyes at the comment.

"Good one, Ol," she snorted, going into the ensuite to freshen up for her walk after she called Arabella to find out what was really going on over in the land of the misfit children, or better known as England.

Her phone buzzed before Lacy could call Arabella and she dived to pick it up, curiosity getting the better of her.

"Hello," there was no caller ID on her phone, just a number that looked like it was from another country.

"Lacy?"

"Speak of the devil, I was just about to call you and have a little chat," Lacy sat down on Ollie's old bed and rested her back against the coloured wall. Lacy remembered when they screwed the wall up, painting the other walls and getting paint on the white wall, then decided to leave it with splatter marks all over it.

"Yes, well I thought I'd let you know we're with the infamous Becca, Aviva's daughter," Arabella had such a soft voice.

"You know you haven't explained why you left, just that there was little bit of pack business over in the UK, care to tell me the details?" Lacy tapped her fingers against her leg, her body shaking with nerves.

"We didn't want to tell you before you left because we were scared you wouldn't go back."

"To Rosewood? Ara, what happened?"

"We have heard news from Becca that while she was kidnapped, she saw Ollie and we want to make sure that she doesn't go back to Rosewood and we miss her," Lacy's mouth dropped. "We're here to see if we can find her, to see if she has left a trail for us to follow."

"Are you freaking kidding me? You kept this from me?" the pain and fire in Lacy's voice as she yelled at the phone was breaking her own heart. She couldn't believe that this was kept from her. "Why the hell didn't you tell me? Of course I was going to come here because I know she'll remember it!"

"We had to make sure, I know you are hurt and upset . . ."

"Understatement of the year!"

"But you need to understand why we did it. We held Jason under oath of the pack," Arabella continued, ignoring Lacy's outburst, but she interrupted again.

"Jason knew? He knew and he didn't tell me? Fuck the oath of the pack, I'm his freaking mate, he should be able to tell me everything. This is some messed up shit; I hope you understand that," Lacy had jumped off the bed in anger and was now pacing the room, weaving between the beds as she spoke angrily into her phone.

A knock on the door threw Lacy off and she turned to open it, only to reveal Jason.

"I can explain," Lacy slammed the door in his face, angry at everything that had happened.

"I don't want to hear it, Jason, screw the pack oath, I'm your bloody mate and I'm the one you are meant to share everything with; no matter what! At least that is what you said at our Bonding, or was that all a lie?" Lacy screamed through the door, the phone still pressed to her ear as she screamed at her mate on the other side of the door.

"Lacy, please understand," Arabella spoke through the phone, trying to calm her, "We forced him to stay quiet."

"I don't give a flying sack of crap, Arabella, I'm his freaking mate!" Lacy hung up the phone and threw it at her bed. Jason opened the door, hearing it hit the floor scared that Lacy had hurt herself.

"Lacy, please let me talk to you."

"Give me one good reason why."

"Because I'm your mate."

"Don't try that with me, don't even try that one because you didn't seem to believe it when you were keeping things from me."

"I didn't have a choice, once you are under pack oath, there is no turning back unless your Alpha's change their mind and let you speak against the oath, Arabella let me once she told you, but no one else is to know," Lacy stared at Jason with narrowed eyes.

"I am your mate."

"And I love you, you are my other half, but my Alpha's, our Alpha's, become God and that I can't change. They have powers over the pack, something they don't use often," Lacy didn't want to believe what Jason was telling her, she didn't want to understand, it would have been so much easier if could just stay mad at him and not believe him, but everything Jason said screamed the truth at her.

"I believe you, but that doesn't mean I'm happy with you," Lacy pouted, her arms crossed over her chest and her bottom lip out.

"I can deal with that so long as you believe me and understand the position I was put in. I only wanted to keep you safe and I only wanted to make sure you were going to be OK and you were going to be here. You have been so distant from me, from everyone, and we just want you happy again."

"I'm happy, I'm just not expressing it the same without my sidekick because I don't know how, but I'm learning. Ollie was the yin to my yang."

"So what am I then?"

"You are the other half of my soul," Lacy shrugged her shoulders, "You know I love you but I'm not good with words, not like you are."

"I Google a lot of things like the poems I write down for you and leave around the room."

"I knew there was a secret!" Lacy jumped up, pointing her finger at Jason accusingly. "I should so start doing that, I feel lousy when I can't come up with those words."

"You are pretty lousy when you don't think to Google those types of things," Jason nodded his head.

"You suck! You're too old to know about Google and how to use it," Lacy threw a pillow at Jason, running out of the room, knowing that her was going to come running after her, pillow in his hand stalking Lacy like she was his prey, something to hunt.

Lacy could see his light brown eyes were glowing as she emerged from her room, narrowed glowing eyes as he saw Lacy sitting on the couch, trying to act natural so she wouldn't draw attention to herself.

"Lacy," Jason sang her name in a very off key voice.

"She's unavailable to make your call at the moment, please a message after the beep. Beeeeeep," Lacy robotically said hiding her face in her hands.

"Don't try and hide from me my love."

He watched m; he stared at me. I knew those eyes; I knew the colour and I could see them watching me in the dark, the shades not being able to hide the glow that sat behind them.

Why was he watching me, I had only seen him a few times in the background of the club but now he was closer to the front, almost like he wanted to remember every inch of my body, remember every curve. An unnerving feeling overtook my body as he sat in the front, watching, staring. Memorising.

Chapter Twenty-Five

Defeat Is Not The Worst Of Failures. Not To Have Tried Is The True Failure

SHE CLOSED HER eyes, letting the wind blow her hair behind her, moving each stand as it made the hair dance behind her. She opened her mouth, begging some words to come out but they still managed to evade her, leaving her feeling completely helpless and foolish.

How could you forget something that seemed like second nature to everyone else? How could it just leave you, letting you feel as though you have failed life, like you haven't been a true person? All those question floated through her mind as she sat, cross-legged, on the green grass outside the school.

It was late December, Christmas was soon approaching and she was left not even being able to say 'Merry Christmas' and 'thank you' to those that had given her a home when she thought everything was lost.

"I, I, I," the stutter was pushed out of herself, like she was being punched in the gut to get the words out. Even just stuttering was like climbing Mount Everest to her now. She couldn't believe she was able to even say that. The meaning didn't escape her like she thought it would.

"I," she tried to push out more words, "Am," they were slowly coming to her one by one.

"You are worthless."

"Please don't."

"No one wants to hear what you have to say, you are worthless," he breathed down my neck, holding me by the collar as he held me against the ground.

"Please," I begged him. I begged him not to do it, I begged him to just leave me be and let me live like I need to, let me do as he asked and then get out of his way. I didn't want this to happen but I knew he did.

"You've done this to yourself," before I could beg him again, my whole face was submerged in water. Bubbles started to surround me as my eyes stayed open under the clear water.

I couldn't breathe, I couldn't move, I was his own personal punching bag and he enjoyed making me suffer and beg for mercy.

"I am worthless," the words were forced with no emotion in her voice. There was something scary about saying her first words again, something that had her heart beating faster as she sat, her eyes still closed, trying to become one with nature.

The more she fell away from herself, the more she could feel herself being able to get strength and get the force to talk, to say words again, even if there were no emotions in them.

"My name is," that one question still seemed to disappear from her mind; she hadn't been addressed by it for so long that her memory had just tossed it out, replacing it with other useless details that she felt were taking away from what she really needed and wanted.

"I do not sister. I have best friend," she had thought that a long blonde headed girl was her sister but it turns out to her that she was her best friend. It warmed her heart that she had had someone so close to her that they were like sisters, so friendly and always laughing with each other.

She got up from where she was seated and walked towards the large building in which the rooms and classrooms were. She was excited to slowly talk and to slowly thank Nora, Donalda, Aggie and Mabel.

The door to the kitchen was quite large, allowing the kitchen staff, who were like teachers when it came to baking as a class for the fourth and fifth year students. She entered through the door, trying to be as quiet as possible as an exam was being taken by a few of the third year students.

She made her way to Mabel's office where she knew Nora and Donalda would be having a chat during their free periods they had off. She was excited to just say thank you to them.

She knocked on big oak door that stood before Mabel's office, the door seemed to intimidate her a lot, like she was going in to be questions about something she didn't know about but knew she was going to be found guilty.

"Come in," She opened the door to see Mabel, Nora and Donalda all sitting around a coffee table on couches, chatting happily.

"Good to see you," Donalda smiled and tapped on the cushion next to her, asking Ollie to sit down and join them, even if she didn't have any input. They all wanted to make her feel as at home as possible.

"How are you?" Nora asked, expecting a hand movement meaning good.

"Good," she spoke, all three women stopped and stared at her, making her feel like a crazy person as their eyes widened in surprise.

"Um?" Nora's mouth started moving up and down like a fish breathing.

"I tried. I can little," her words were disconnected and emotionless still, but they were words and that was a lot better then what she had been doing for a while. "Thank you. I say thank you," Ollie spoke.

"There is no need for thank you," Mabel started, moving over to sit next to her, "You have been a pleasure to have and we'll help you until you no longer need us and even then I think we have found you a place here if you would like to take it up," she looked at the three with a wide smile on her face. "Do you remember your name? Do you remember anything? Aggie says you have lost a lot of your memory."

"No."

"Do you want us to make you a name?" Mabel stood up and grabbed her laptop so they could go searching on the internet to find a name that would best fit her. Getting a nod from her, Mabel started searching through different websites.

"Something meaning beautiful," Donalda said.

"Ella?" she turned her nose up at that name, "Keva?" another no, "Orabelle? Yedda? Lindi? Lillie? Adara? Ligia? Nani? Adah? Alaine?

Annabel? Annabella? Addien? Addiena?" the names came pouring out as Mabel read through the names that came up on the page Mabel was looking at.

"I like Nani," Donalda smiled, taking her hand as support.

"Orabelle or Orabella?" Nora suggested.

"Addiena?" Mabel continued to keep her eyes on the screen as she read through other names. "Isa means strong, Orianna means golden?" the three turned to her to see what she liked.

"Nani, Orianna," was her only response as she tried to think of which she thought would suit her better. "Nani," she smiled. "I like Nani," and that was how Olyanah became known as Nani.

"Nani it is, it suits you. Now we have a job offer for you if you'd like?" Mabel closed her laptop and waited for Nani to nod to tell her to continue. She liked the name Nani, she felt as though it suited her as much as a name could, but she knew it wasn't her real name and she couldn't wait until she found it out, but for now, Nani would have to do as her name.

"Yes?"

"Would you like to teach sign language to the fourth and fifth years? Even with limited English you'd be able to teach them, things like yes, thank you, no, all of those types of things," Donalda explained.

"Sound fun," Nani smiled at the idea of doing more with her day. She knew her English wasn't very good but she could deal with it and slowly it would improve, so she hoped.

"Well you can start after the holidays in a few days."

"A few day?"

"Yes, the holidays will be here by tomorrow, a few students will go back to their parents and other will stay here with buses going into to town through the public transport but they are still our responsibility. If you'd like you can go into town, Aggie and Logan will be staying here and a few of the other staff too, all of us will be staying too and we are more then happy to take you into town as well," Nora stood and got Nani a drink.

"Yes please, town," Nani was quite excited to go into town, explore the place that surrounded where she had been staying.

"Sounds good. Well, Nora has a class now but why don't you go sit in and you might be able to improve on your English and also learn a few things on teaching," Nani nodded her head at Donalda and stood with Nora.

"Thank you," Nani smiled, bowing her head a little with respect. No one around her had bowed their head in respect but it just felt right to her, felt normal to do it. "Now we go?"

"Yeah, come on, I've got a few spare books you can have in class so you can write everything down," Nani nodded her head in appreciation.

"Room first?"

"Yes, that's fine," Nani smiled, bowed her head slightly then walked off towards where her room was so she could grab her own book and write down what she had remembered in the garden about the man trying to kill her, drowning her in a few inches of water.

Nani made her way back to the classroom she knew Nora was going to be in, Aggie was also in the class and her friend Logan which put Nani at ease because she was going to know someone and she was going to be able to have someone to sit next to in the classroom.

She entered along with everyone else, taking the same seat as a few days before, waiting for Aggie and Logan to enter so she wouldn't be sitting by herself. Aggie and Logan entered last, walking over to sit next to Nani.

"Morning," Aggie greeted Nani.

"Morning," she replied, getting wide eyes as a response.

"You can talk?"

"Little."

"How?" Nani just shrugged her shoulders, she had spent so much time trying and yet she was too scared, but sitting by herself in that garden, being one with nature helped her not to be scared and see how much she needed to thank those who had helped her.

"This is so cool," Logan commented with a large smile.

"Yes," Nani responded, "Nani," she pointed to her chest, indicating that was her name.

"So Nani is your name?"

"No."

"For now though? Until you can remember it?" Aggie asked.

"Yes."

"How brilliant, it's lovely to hear your voice. I am sure we will get sick of your talking soon enough," Aggie winked before giggling a little with Logan and then quieting down as Nora started her class.

"OK, so we have Nani here again. She has limited English as she has only just started talking again," everyone knew Nani's story and they were quite good about it, trying to make her feel as much at home as possible, "She is going to be sitting in to help her, and then next term she is going to teach sign language to fourth and fifth year students, so that will be you as well," the class broke out in chatter, whispered from side to side as they absorbed the information that was being thrown at them.

"I want you all to help Nani out as she is still new here and still not one hundred percent well. It will be your job to help her out as she teaches you and to be the best you can be. For the first few lessons we will have someone sitting in to help her out. Now, it is time to start our lesson. I hope you have all read the first few chapters because we are going to start on them, explaining what has happened and the meaning of it, along with the conflict that is very deep within the story," Nora turned around and started writing a few things on the board before getting down to the lesson they were starting today.

"Three years ago, you two went out to the footy field while they were practicing and flashed them!" Jay burst out laughing as Lacy blushed a little but smiled at the fond memory.

"The school was buzzing with the news for weeks," Martha giggled. "You two were like the Hocus Pocus sisters, always getting into trouble and just about getting out of it every time. I'm surprised Davis didn't call you into his office more often."

"He was probably off shagging someone, too occupied to care," Lacy laughed, grabbing Jason's hand that was dangling over her shoulder.

"God, no wonder he was always absent, he was probably getting his freak on because he was too busy studying as a kid," Liam rolled his eyes, "Davis was always a weird fella."

"What do you mean?" Lacy looked around the group, curious to the underlying meaning.

"Davis is one of us, and Jane is his mate," Jason rubbed Lacy's shoulder as he spoke, "I know you don't like Jane and Greg, but if I have to be honest, Jane is a much nicer wolf than Greg, he always seemed hidden, kept to himself whereas Jane was a bit more open but she can easily be sucked in to manipulation easily."

"So you're really going to sit there and defend them?" Lacy was shocked and disgusted.

"No, what they have done is unforgivable, whatever that may be, but Davis was never apart of our pack and Jane has now left, ready to start he new life with her mate."

"And where is Greg?"

"He's with another pack too."

"Don't you lie to me, Jason," Lacy crossed her arms and moved so that she could look at him in the eyes and show him just how mad she was that he was going to try and lie to her again after everything.

"We aren't sure, we think he went to another pack but you can never be sure until we have the evidence," Jason played with Lacy's hair as he spoke, trying to take his mind off what he was saying and what her reaction might be.

"So that psycho could be running around?"

"Yes, he could."

"That has to be some kind of a joke right? How can you not be scared about this?" Lacy looked at the group with wide eyes. "I don't even know the extent of what he did to her and yet I can already tell you that he is a bad person. I get a vibe from him and I can tell you, it isn't the warm and fuzzies that you get when you see a cute little puppy," Lacy rolled her eyes.

"We can't do anything, this isn't our real territory, we only have jurisdiction in Egypt. We can't keep going around looking for someone who is no longer part of our pack," Harry butted in, taking Lacy's focus from Jason to himself.

"That you know of."

"He hasn't shown up in two months, that means we stop looking and he is no longer apart of our pack. It is our law," Harry explained.

"Screw your law because I used to live here and I know he was a real bastard to my best friend and I think that you should keep looking because if he is out there, I don't trust the world," Lacy was quite forceful with her words, letting the group know exactly how she felt about what was going on.

"Lac," Martha strolled into the door.

"Martha, what's up?" Martha and Polly had been doing something for Aviva and Winslow before they were able to meet up at The Local with the rest of the group.

"We have some news for you," Polly pushed Jason and Lacy along the booth and sat down, Martha sitting next to her. "Some news that I feel as though you all might find very interesting."

"It will tickle your bellies like no fingers ever have before," Martha winked, letting the group laugh at the joke.

"It's news about England."

"Will you two shut up and stop being so vague about everything. Just tell us what you know!" Lacy cried, shutting everyone up, waiting for Martha and Polly to tell them what was going on.

The sun shone down, breaking through the thick trees to provide those living underneath a form of light and warmth. It lit up everything that had a reflective surface; glass hanging off tree branches, mirrors on the tree trunks.

Not all things that have been written down about Fae and Elves are true, they have kept some things close to the facts, but by the Fae's orders, they have changed a lot of things too. They were mysterious peoples, making sure that they were still one with nature and showing that they respected the land they lived with.

"Aviva, how lovely to see you again," Arabella embraced Aviva in a hug.

"Winslow," Enakal put out his hand and hugged Winslow while shaking his hand as well. "It is brilliant to see you again, I have missed your companionship and company over the years," Winslow nodded his head in agreement.

"You have been very much missed on this side too, my friend," Winslow smiled, letting go of Enakal's hand and embracing Arabella in a hug. The long time friends had missed each other and now that they were seeing each other again, it was a very lovely time to catch up but also to find out what had happened to Ollie to save their world.

"Now, I feel as though we should reminisce about the past," Aviva directed the two Alpha's inside and let them sit on the couches. "But I think we should get down to business long before we start chatting like old friends," Arabella and Enakal nodded their heads, eager to get started on finding their missing daughter.

"What information do you have?" Enakal asked, taking Arabella's hands in his, letting her feel as though he was here for her, which he was, but sometimes he felt as though he needed to reassure her.

"We have no new information other then what was conveyed to you on the phone and we have been waiting for you before we go back and have another look at the building to see of they are still in chaos," Aviva waved her hand over the coffee table between the couches and soon a pot of tea and some tea cups were sitting there.

"Magic, I love it," Arabella laughed, clapping her hands.

"We have been training our troops and now I feel as though we are ready when you are to go and find your daughter," Winslow smiled, grabbing a shell with a hole on either end and blowing on it. "They will be waiting outside soon for our orders."

"Thank you," Enakal felt as though those two words didn't express the true thanks he had towards his long lost friend and the Seelie's for what they were going to do to help find his daughter.

"We will take you to the place, flash you all there and you can see for yourself and get the people responsible."

"Again, I thank you, old friend," there were noised around the small lounge room in the cottage and soon Becca emerged from upstairs.

"Becca, I would like you to meet Enakal, Alpha male of the Egyptian pack and Arabella, Alpha female of the Egyptian pack," through her books, Becca knew how to act around Alpha's and Werewolves and bowed her head slightly, exposing her neck in submission and respect.

"It is in honour to meet you," Becca smiled, "I only wish the circumstances were better."

"As you, yes, if only we were able to converse in a much more comfortable environment, but I'm afraid we will be occupied with trying to find out Ollie," Arabella spoke while going over to hug the girl, letting her know that she accepted her thanked her. "We would like to thank you for helping our daughter and giving her hope. You have taught her so much and we can never repay you for that," Arabella held Becca out at arms length.

"Ollie was an awesome, beautiful and funny girl. Through everything she managed to laugh and make jokes and she took it all well, at least as well as you could expect," Becca smiled as Arabella let her go and she was able to shake hands with Enakal.

"Becca, would you please address everyone and let them know what is going on?"

"Sure, father," Becca walked out side, hovering with the small wind around her moving her white chiffon dress around.

"She is a beautiful girl," Arabella smiled as Becca closed the door behind her.

"An honest angel," Aviva agreed.

"OK, so the four-one-one is basically that we have the Alpha's of the Egyptian pack to flash with us back to the building and then see if we can capture those bastards and find Ollie," Becca hovered high above the Seelie as she spoke, trying to be as humorous as possible about the situation to set everyone at ease.

"How long away will it be before we leave?" a Fae cried out, raising herself as she asked the question.

Becca shrugged her shoulders, "I'd say from not to a few hours. I don't know too much about that, only what is going on. Alpha Enakal, Alpha Arabella are here with their Beta Cruze, Ollie's mate, their second Drake and their fifth Brent with Alpha Arabella's sister Sally and her mate Charles," Becca recalled the names her father had told her.

"They are all here?" the same Fae asked.

"Yes, they want to find their Princess, their daughter, their friend and their niece. I can promise you they have permission to be here and they are not here to fight, they want to work as one with us. We are to help them out and act appropriately. We have not fought with the Wolves for many centuries and I can promise those who do fight against them will receive a consequence fitting with their crime," the statement was strong and everyone nodded, understanding the message.

"Becca," Winslow, Aviva, Arabella and Enakal emerged from the cottage along with the rest of the pack they had brought along. "We're ready."

"OK, everyone partner up again and we can flash back," Becca walked over to a tall wolf with sandy coloured hair like he had spent a lot of time in the beach sun.

"Becca," he nodded his head as a sign that he knew who she was.

"You are?"

"Cruze, Olyanah's mate," Becca smiled at him.

"You look exactly as Ollie explained to me."

"How did she explain me?" curiosity was clear in his voice.

"She said you were a surfer and that you smelt like rain, I don't get the rain thing but the surfer thing I can see."

"It is because she is my mate, she can only smell that smell on me," Cruze wasn't smiling like Becca had expected at the sound of his mate, just keeping a blank face and no emotion in his voice.

"She couldn't remember too much though. I don't know what they were doing to her but she was pretty beaten up and seemed like just thinking of everyday things was hard for her," Becca knew this wouldn't help but she hoped it would give Cruze some drive.

The day Ollie had been taken from the shared cell, she had started having problems with her speech and she looked as though things were starting to confuse her, like what they had been giving her and doing to her was only just kicking in.

"Just flash," he spoke harshly, putting out his hand so Becca could take it and flash the two to where everyone else was waiting for them, Fae shrinking and Wolves and Elves getting down to army crawl again towards the dot in the distance.

Cruze's heart was beating as he thought about the fact that he might be able to see his mate again. He felt so nervous and so ready to kill whoever had taken his mate from him and for everything that had done.

He liked Becca, she clearly had known Ollie, but he didn't want to talk to her or have her touching her because she wasn't his mate and she had told him that Olyanah was starting to forget things and that whatever they had done to her had caused this.

He had told Enakal that when they got their hands on the people that had done this to Olyanah, they were to die at his hands, no acceptation.

"You look beautiful," my hand moved down her cheek, feeling her soft skin under my rough hand. "So, so beautiful," I could feel under my hand a hot blush overcome her cheeks at the compliment.

"Stop it," she laughed, trying to hide her blushing cheeks from my crystal eyes as I wanted to soak up every feature of her beautiful face. I knew she would be gone soon, trying to see the world and it was going to tear my heart away but I knew she had to do this or else she would never content with out lives.

"Cruze, you need to be on your game," Becca's voice floated through the wind and landed on Cruze's ears, making him jump a little as he crawled, shaking the tall, tall grass around him. "Cruze!" Becca scowled him.

"Sorry," Cruze closed his eyes, trying to remember why he needed to be quiet and focused as he crawled through the tall grass towards the place his mate had been. He was hoping that he might be able to detect that lavender and old book smell in the air and then he could follow it and find his mate, wherever it might be.

"We will find her, I know we will and she is never going to give up. From what I saw she was so strong, maybe too strong and she'll never stop trying."

"I know."

"She's lucky to have you in her life and as her mate. I know one day you guys will Bond and then you will be the happiest mates in the world," Becca and Cruze were at the front of the group, chatting between each other quietly so that they wouldn't be heard by anyone else.

"She's lucky to have met you too. I know she's strong but sometimes that means that she is pig-headed and won't give up. She could be gone, far away and that is a problem for us. I can't feel her anymore and that scares me so much," Cruze meant every word he spoke. He hoped that he would be able to get Olyanah back in contact with Becca when she was found and the two could continue a friendship because Becca had done so much, making sure that Olyanah never gave up hope.

"Like I said, she is lucky to have you," after that, Becca and Cruze stayed silent as they made their way closer and closer to the building that Becca had once been held as a victim.

"You OK?" Cruze asked, his deep voice echoing around the tall grass.

"Yeah, I'll be fine."

"You sure? We can stop and take a break if you need," Cruze watched as Becca made herself a little taller and looked to see just how far away they were.

"All need to stay quiet," Becca forced her voice around the wind so that all the Seelie and wolves would be able to hear her. "We aren't far away," with that everyone fell silent, leaving an eerie feeling fall over the group.

Cruze didn't like the feeling but he knew he would have to run past it if he wanted to get there and try and find who had taken his mate from him. There was so much anger and so much pain building up inside of him that Cruze didn't know how to release it anymore, the only way he could think was to kill those ho had taken his mate from him and watch the air leave their lungs.

"We're here," Becca announced quietly to everyone.

Chapter Twenty-Six

We're So Happy Even When We're Smiling Out Of Tears

NANI STOOD IN front of the big oak tree in the large backyard, her back leaning against the tree, letting her feel one with nature. She wasn't sure believed you could be one with nature or anything of that kind but she actually did feel as though the tree was providing her with a certain type of comfort.

The wind blew through, releasing her from the grips of the sun that the Scottish summer was bringing down on her. *'Why is it always windy here?'* Nani asked herself. She found that she was able talk quiet normally in her mind but had trouble when it came to forming the words and sounds with her mouth.

With everything that was going on, Nani felt as thought something was missing in her life, as though she still wasn't complete and something still wasn't right in her mind. She knew that her name wasn't her real name and that her life wasn't her real life and that hurt her very deeply. Nani only wanted to be back in her old life, she only wanted to have her old life back, whatever that was and it cut her that she couldn't remember many things from her old life, nothing that she found too important anyway.

All the information that she had gathered she had thought was very silly and none important but she knew that if she had either of the blonde girls looking at it that they would know what was going on. There was a nagging feeling that they would know what was going on and that she should know too but everything had been lost in her attacked memory.

"Hey, Nani," Nani looked up and saw that Aggie and Logan were walking over, sitting down against the tree next to her, one on either side.

"Hello," Nani greeted them with as much of a smile as she could manage at the moment.

"How are you?" Logan asked looking around as everyone enjoyed the sun on the Saturday. The weekend had everyone buzzing, excited that they didn't have classes for two days.

"Sad."

"Why?"

"Missing home."

"Do you know where home is? Can you remember?" Aggie asked, none of the three girls looking at each other, just watching the yard and the interactions between the different groups that were outside.

"No," there was a group of fourth year girls that were sitting in a circle on the grass, all had phones in their hands not looking at each other or having any form of social communication. It saddened Nani that those girls weren't able to have a proper conversation, something they were taking advantage of and not using the gift they were given.

"Any ideas at all?" Aggie asked. There was a week left of school and then holidays were coming, Nani was hoping to explore the country a little, maybe then she would get some sort of an idea, but she wasn't going to do it alone.

"Warm," Nani remembered warmth of the sun all the time. "Beach?" The only reason Nani thought there was a beach where she had lived was because of the back of the man she had drawn and the fact that she could remember the smell of rain in a forest near a beach and to her that wasn't just something that came from no where, there had to a source that the idea of the smell came from.

"We can work on that. Maybe look at the warm places by a beach?" Aggie started getting excited.

"We can start researching in the holidays and then we can look up photos and see if you recognise the place," Nani nodded her head with a large smile on her face.

"I like here but not like home," Nani tried to explain her feelings but she felt like she didn't do a very good job.

"Nothing is like home, don't worry. We'll get you home one day," Aggie and Logan hugged Nani from both sides. "We know you'll try when you start teaching but we also know you're going to leave at some point, but I hope you stay in contact with us. You're a pretty cool girl," Logan winked.

"Yeah, we'd hate to lose you but we'd also hate for you to not be happy," Aggie added happily.

"Yes. Contact," Nani agreed shortly. She liked these two girls and the teachers as well, getting along well with them, as well as she could but like they said, nothing was like home.

"Good, because I don't want to lose contact with you. We'll give you our numbers and you can call us when you think you are close to home. How long do you think you are going to teach here?" Nani shrugged her shoulders, not sure how much she would get paid for her teaching so she would be able to travel and find where she was from.

"Well, we can have a chat to Mabel and see what she says. Maybe only a term because then you'll be able to get going soon," Logan suggested.

"Sounds good to me. We can talk to her in the holidays?"

"And we can ask about pay," the girls started rattling off ideas of what they could do to help Nani find her way back home.

"Thank you," Nani smiled, thanking her two new friends.

"That's what friends are for," Aggie laughed with a smile, winking at the same time as Logan.

Light flashed around, blinding her as she walked aimlessly in the desert that looked so foreign to her. Her toes sunk into the yellow sand, tickling her skin with each timid step.

The harsh sun started beating down on her skin, warming it up and burning it, turning the natural colour an unnatural red. The pain of the burn wasn't there; there was no pain, no feeling, and no nothing almost like the red was painted on, not burnt from the hot rays of the sun.

"You look good," she turned around, seeing the back of a long blonde haired girl looking over a lake. "Different. You used to have different hair; it was shorter and thinner. It's been almost a year, you know. I miss you but you look different," she didn't know what to reply to that, she didn't even know if she truly knew who the girl was, the long blonde hair was somewhat familiar but other then that she didn't know much.

"Who are you?" Nani surprised herself by speaking in coherent sentences, actually making sense.

"You don't remember me?" there was pain in the blonde girls voice.

"I don't remember your name but I remember you."

"Then why won't you look at me? Why won't you get me to turn around so you can see me?"

"I want to see you. I remember you. I remember your hair."

"Only my hair? Do you know how many people in the world have my colour hair?"

"Please, turn around," she started begging the blonde girl, tears falling from the corners of her eyes. "Please, please turn around. Please, please."

She woke up in a pool of her own sweat; fear coating her skin and wetting her body as she panted from the fear that her dream had provoked. Why couldn't she remember? Why? It was so painful for her to not remember, there were so many answers in her dreams, she just had to get past the bad part of her dream and remember.

Sitting up in bed, Nani started writing down what had happened in her dream; drawing the scene she had seen so realistically in her mind that she had lived through. She wanted the blonde girl to turn around, she wanted her to reveal herself but Nani knew she wouldn't for a long time and she didn't know if she could deal with this for too much longer.

Imagine the answers she could achieve if the blonde girl turned around and showed herself, spoke to her properly and stated who she was. There would be so much pain lifted from Nani's mind if it ever happened.

Nani got out of bed after she finished drawing and writing everything down. She pulled an old fashioned black coat around her white silk pajama, warming herself around the old brick building.

A few fires were on in the main rooms that were once living rooms but other then that there was on heating in the old castle that had been converted into a schoolhouse. Whoever had once lived here would have had to be incredibly rich to have so many rooms, such a garden and still be able to have a brilliant landscape with history everywhere.

Nani admired the worn brick as she walked, running her hand along, feeling the rough texture beneath her soft, scarred palm. So many different things to see and touch and experience in this building, so much history hid beneath the walls.

Nani was so curious to know who had lived here and what life they had lived. If they enjoyed the rich life or if they wanted to change the world. If they were nice people or just there to exploit those who didn't life the same life as they did.

Nani sat in Nora's last class for the term, listening to what she had to say and how she taught but her mind was on the dream she had the night before. She was watching the scene unfold again in her mind, imagining that she wasn't in the classroom but back in that unknown desert that was haunting her.

Nora spoke loudly, trying to get the attention of everyone in the classroom when she noticed that Nani was distracted. Her deep blue eyes were glassed open and she was staring into space thinking about something that had nothing to do with what they were doing in class.

Nora felt so sad whenever she saw Nani, feeling the pain she must be going through having no memory of her former life and having to life with strangers after whatever it was she had been through.

Everyday Nani managed to wake up surprised Nora. She didn't know if she would be able to after everything and yet the strength of Nani managed to surprise everyone everyday.

There was a smile on Nani's face, Nora noticed, as she dreamt about whatever was running through her mind. She had noticed long ago that her mind was like a jumping spiders web of thoughts.

"Nani," Nora set the class some work and walked over, bending down so she could talk to her at eye level. "How are you finding things?"

"OK."

"Not too hard?"

"No."

"Do you want to make some plans for the holidays?"

"Yes. Please."

"OK, meet me in Mabel's office after class and we will talk to her about plans we can make. I am sure Logan and Aggie will like to travel with you and then Donalda and I are more then happy to as well."

"Thank you," Nora went back to her seat, watching the poor girl again with sadness caught in her throat.

An eerie silence filled the group as they emerged from the long grass, all in their true forms as nature had intended. The silence and confusion fluttered through as everyone looked at each other twice, wondering what was going on. There was no commotion, no chaos as remembered, just silence.

The chaos that had once been there was gone and in its place, left a feeling of pain, sorrow and emptiness, like the people that had been kept there were leaving their messages in the wind, letting those who came near by not to enter; to save themselves from the horror inside.

"OK," Aviva moved up to the front of the group with Winslow holding her hand to keep her safe and keep her near him. "It was so much busier last time, so many more people," Aviva looked around the building, her eyebrows furrowed in confusion.

Cruze slammed his fist against the outside of the building in anger, frustration and pain, tears were forming in his eyes at the thought of never being able to see his mate ever again but he refused to give up, not now.

"OK," Becca resized and looked around. "Who wants to go exploring?" a devious smile playing on her perfect lips.

"Becca, no," Winslow let go of his mates hand and rushed over to his daughter, a hand on either shoulder so she would listen to him.

"I don't want to hide, father, I want to go in there and if they have left other girls then we are going to help them. Got it. I won't be alone. We can go in a few groups so no one is alone but I'm going in there with or without you. Fear is not something I want to live with for the rest of my life," Becca stood tall, hovering a few inches above the ground so that she was eye to eye with her father.

"You are to go with Cruze, Enakal and Arabella," Winslow conceded, letting his daughter go into the place she had once called the dungeon of hell.

"Why not you?"

"Because I do'nt think I will be able to deal with you leading us and maybe getting yourself into trouble. The less I know the better," Becca nodded her head and the large group of about two hundred plus divided into groups of six with thirty-five in each group.

Becca led the group with Cruze, Enakal, Arabella and the other wolves along with some Fae and Elves. The walked inside and into the room with the stage at one end, the room she managed to escape from the day they let their guard down.

The memories hidden in the walls haunted Becca, she could hear the screams of other girls echoing around, bouncing off each wall as she spun around to get her bearings. She knew the room, not well but she knew it, and she had to work out the way she had come so she could follow it and go back to the room she was kept in. Maybe Cruze would recognise the slight scent of Ollie if there was a scent there and they could follow it.

Finally deciding to go back out the double doors, Becca led everyone behind her as they looked around in awe at the building. It was clear it was once a hospital building and before that a large manner that had hosted many gatherings and parties long, long ago.

Becca took a left and a right, slowly the sun was starting to fall, leaving her with the normal dark feeling that she had gotten used to while she was here, held against her will.

"Where are we going?" Cruze walked next to Becca, determined to keep her safe as Winslow had asked of him.

"To my room," Becca shrugged her shoulders as they came to an intersection. Right was down a very dark hallway and left led to a door that Becca assumed went down stairs to where there were no windows.

"Which way?"

"Right, I never went downstairs, we can go down later but I know I've seen the door before," the group started following Becca again, guided by the bright white light she was letting off with her body like a torch.

"Do you know where Olyanah was kept?"

"No. They took her away one day and I never saw her again."

"I'll kill them," Cruze's teeth grinded together as he thought about the pain his mate went through and the fear she was probably feeling now.

"I'll help. You know she thought about you but slowly the poison started to take over. I think they wanted her to forget so she wouldn't go home."

"What poison?"

"They tied her up with chains to the roof so she was dangling, only her toes touching the ground. The chains had poison on them, weeping into her open wounds so that it went straight into her blood stream. It was like they were giving her a slow stroke and killing her memory," Becca remembered the time they were in the cell she called home and a few days before they came for Ollie her mind started dropping. She started forgetting things and her speech slurred, new information was kept for a time but old information and memories were gone, like she had never lived before the time she was taken.

"I'll kill them," Cruze repeated with narrowed glowing eyes, making his crystal eyes look like they were white.

His breathing was deep and heavy as he thought about just how he would rip their heads off and watch the light leave there eyes just as it would have when they were attacking Olyanah day after day, night after night. He could see the blood dripping from their wounds and that was what spurred him on.

"Like I said, I'll join you," Cruze was thankful Olyanah had met such a strong girl like Becca.

Winslow followed his mate, holding her hand and guided by her glow as the rest of their search party followed too. All the cells they had looked in and seen had no one in them, it looked like it would've years ago before it had ever been occupied.

Paint peeling of the walls and metal slowly rusting was a common sight now as they turned right then right again down a hallway. Winslow was decked out in old warrior wear, a metal chest covering and a dark cape tied to the shoulder blades and down his back showing his statues as the King of Elves.

"This looks like hell," one of Winslow's most trusted, noble and strongest Elf Warrior, Dominic walked up behind him, speaking under his breath just in case. Dominic had appeared once Becca and her group had gone inside, he had been going around the building to check it out.

He had also been on a mission for the past few weeks, keeping him away from the Seelie and the forest they lived in.

The Seelie were having troubles with the Tree Nymphs and Dominic had been asked to find out why while keeping a deep cover.

He had turned up in the same gear as Winslow but with a light brown cape around his shoulder, meeting on the shoulder blades as well. The light cape made his dark skin look darker and his dark dread locks were tied back a little to stay out of his eyes.

Dominic had honey coloured brown eyes that showed just how strong of a warrior he was and just how loyal and caring he was for the Seelie he lived with and fought for.

"I didn't imagine a five-star building," Aviva winked at the Elf.

"Yes, but the outside is much nicer then the inside."

"You can't judge a book by its cover, have I taught you nothing?" Winslow asked, shaking his head and sighing.

"I apologise," Dominic bowed his head as a sign of respect; unlike the wolves he didn't bare his neck in submission.

"Now stay quiet, we're too keep a good look out not just for Olyanah but also for other girls that have been victimised by these horrible people that we will find one day," Winslow spoke low but again let the wind carry his voice to the rest of the group that were following him.

The group stayed quiet as they walked, reaching an intersection, if they turned left there was a door and if they turned right it led to a dark hallway. Deciding upon the curiosity within him, Winslow went to open the door.

The doorknob rattled under his hand but didn't move, leaving the old wooden door in place. Looking at his mate, Winslow smiled as Aviva stared at the door, setting the lock on fire and melting it then stopping the fire so they could enter.

"Always one to be there when I need you," Winslow smiled, taking his mates hand and pushing the heated door open, revealing a set of stone stairs going down into a basement. The stairs wound around a stone pilfer in the room.

"Ready?" Aviva asked with a cute, innocent smile on her lightly purple painted lips.

"Always," Winslow took the first step and started walking down, his footsteps echoing around the walls, hitting his ears again. The Fae didn't make any noise as they hovered, the only noises from the Elves as they kept down and tried to minimize the noise their shoes were making.

The end of the stairs opened out into a dimly lit room with luminescent lights beating down, hurting the sensitive eyes of the Seelie. Winslow led the group, looking into each room that was covered with bars instead of doors like a prison cell.

"This places looks horrible," Aviva shuddered as they walked along, the cells stopping and a single iron door appearing. Dead bolts were on the outside, clearly locked tight with a key, stopping people from getting in and whatever was inside, getting out.

"You know I'm going to ask you to open it but I want you to stand back because we don't know what or who is inside," Aviva nodded her head, obeying her mates orders along with the rest of the group that had come along to explore the building with their King and Queen.

Aviva closed her eyes and moved her hands, chanting in her head in Latin as she started trying to open the door. The lock moved around, tempted to obey the Fae but unable to for some unknown reason to those watching. She tried harder, trying a new chant to open the lock but still nothing happened inside her to let her know that the chant and spell was working.

"What's happening?" Dominic asked, staring at the rattling lock, soon it went limp, not unlocking from the position they had first found it in.

"Someone's cursed it," Aviva opened her eyes and furrowed her eyebrows, trying to work out what to do to lift the curse on the lock. "I need everyone to stand at least three metres away," she announced, a plan coming to her mind. "The further the better," the sound of feet shuffling echoed around as the group moved back, Aviva, Winslow and Dominic standing in the front of the group.

"What are you planning?" Aviva didn't have time to reply to her mate as she closed here eyes and started chanting to herself to get ready for what she was planning. Opening her eyes she smiled as fire shot from her hands, moving around in a straight line like a snake.

The fire hissed and spat as it moved closer and closer to the lock, weaving its way around like a snake would if it were slithering around. The snake fire hit the lock with such force that a fire ball exploded into the door, pushing everyone, but the three in front, back into the wall.

Aviva, Winslow and Dominic stood tall and strong as they waited for the fire to clear and the smoke to disappear so they could see if it worked. Smoke moved around slowly, not clearing as fast as Aviva had hoped but clearing nonetheless.

Once the smoke was gone and the heated wave left their bodies, Aviva stepped forward, using her light to shield her from any damage. She looked at the lock and smiled to herself before turning and giving her mate the thumbs up so he knew it had worked. No one else was able to withstand the heat that still encased the one metre radius that had been hit by the fire.

"Only you would be able to burn a cursed lock open," Winslow smiled as Aviva continued forward to she could see what was inside. Winslow smiled with utter pride as he watched his brave mate walk forward, fearless of what lay on the other side of the door, only wanted to help those that needed the help.

"You have to see this," she called over her should, utter fear and pain laced her voice, causing her mate to run towards her to make sure she was kept safe from whatever was inside.

"What?" he pushed through the slow clearing smoke and his eyes widened as he saw what was awaiting them on the other side of the locked iron door.

Chapter Twenty-Seven

All It Takes Is One Song To Bring Back A Thousand Memories

NANI LOOKED AROUND the room, admiring the posters that were on the walls, posters of bands she had never heard of and of actors that she had never seen. Movie posters were on the walls too, but Nani had no idea what there were or who was in them.

"I made this about a year or two ago," Aggie walked around the room, a device Nani had never seen before in her hand. "It's really old but whatever, it'll do," the holidays had come and gone and Nani had been left in the building spending time with Nora, Donalda, Aggie and Logan.

Plans of travel hadn't eventuated and she studied in her time when she was by herself. The school had a large library with a fire crackling, something she enjoyed very much, and even the solitude was something she liked.

Nani had had a chance to explore the building and find hidden rooms and passages that no one knew about. She had been able to have time to herself, constantly giving herself a headache trying to remember her old life to write down and see if she could find out where she was from.

The little she spoke showed no accent and no one was able to discern where she was actually from and what area she had grown up in.

"Old?" Nani asked with a question, eyebrows furrowed in confusion.

"Yeah, like two or three years old," Logan was lying on the floor, head resting in the palms of her hand and legs up like she was kicking something invisible. Logan watched Aggie walk around the room, her eyes sparkling as she watched her friend clicking on the electronic device.

"Some are older," she explained with a shrug, rolling over onto her back so she could look at Nani while explaining. "More then a few years, maybe ten but the older they are the more classic they are," she laughed a little before flickering her eyes back to what Aggie was doing. "Come on, Ag, what're you doing, showing a turtle how to use it?"

"Older first," Nani requested, sitting on the edge of the bed with her hands resting in her lap and her legs pulled up in Indian styled crossed legs, a smile plastered on her lips as she sat in the room enjoying the banter between the two that looked so natural and easy.

She knew they had been friends for a very long time and it showed in the way they interacted, the way they laughed, spoke and the easy banter as well. She wished she had something like that, a friend that was so much like a sister, a best friend that she could love and that would love her.

"Older it is," Aggie pulled something from her bag on the floor and plugged the device in, pressing a few buttons and soon music came pouring out of the speakers, something Nani had never seen before. Music started playing from the speaker, different instruments that Nani couldn't recognise.

The new technology she was always being introduced to was something that had her head spinning. It confused her how such things could exist when she couldn't really remember much of anything.

"My milkshake brings all the boys to the yard!" the song started, causing Nani to let her legs crash down onto the ground and sit up straight. Her deep blue eyes widened as she heard the song continue. "I can teach you, but I have to charge," the more the song went on the more Nani tried to calm her beating heart but nothing was going to calm it.

"Nani, what is it?" Aggie asked, pausing the loud song. "Are you nervous about tomorrow?" Nani was going to start her first day teaching tomorrow and she was quite nervous, along with feeling as though every second her confidence was leaving her and that she couldn't be able to do it.

Aggie and Logan were going to be in her class and Mabel had asked them to help her out if something was to happen that would cause the class to erupt into uncontrollable chatter. They had been warned that Nani would be their teacher and to be nice to her as she was just getting back on her feet.

"Nani?" Logan asked, as she stayed quiet. "You know we'll be there tomorrow right?" Nani nodded her head before rushing out the door and towards her own room that was at the other end of the long stone hallway that was lit up with very dull lights that had probably been installed a long time ago.

"Nani!" her name was called from the hallway but she continued, not being deterred.

Reaching her room, Nani grabbed her notebook and started writing down what had just happened and what she had seen in her mind when the song started playing in Aggie and Logan's room.

A knock on her door pulled her from her mind, but she kept writing as she walked to open the door to reveal Aggie and Logan looking scared and worried about her storming out.

"Nani, what's going on?" the two entered and sat down on the single bed in the room while Nani sat at the desk like table and finished what she was doing.

"I remember little," Nani called them over and showed them her book that she had so far kept to herself. "Little," she explained, pointing to what she had just written down.

Aggie and Logan stayed quiet as they read and saw what had been written down and drawn. There were so many different things for the girls to take in as they looked over the pages.

"Wow," Logan finally spoke up, taking the notebook from Aggie's hands and staring at the drawing Nani had just completed.

"You did this?" Aggie looked over Logan's shoulder.

"Yes."

"And this is what you remember?"

"Yes."

"Why haven't you followed it yet?"

"Money."

"Well you'll probably only have to work for a term before you get the money to try and find your way back home, but like we said; you have to stay in contact with us, there is no way in hell we are letting you get away like that," Logan laughed, giving Nani the book back and sitting on her bed with a softly amused smile on her face.

"Yes."

"OK, we are allowed to tell anyone or is there a 'keep our traps shut' situation?" Aggie asked, Nani just shrugged her shoulders, not really knowing what to say.

"OK, I think Mabel needs to know, Nora and Donalda too," Logan conceded.

"I agree," Aggie nodded her head.

"OK," Nani agreed, not really minding, just excited that she was able to remember something so big in her life. She had no idea that hearing one sing would be able to bring up so many memories.

The song had made her think of the long blonde girl and how close they were and that she would often embarrass Nani, and that song. The song had something to do with the embarrassment, something the long blonde girl used to torment Nani with a smile on her lips and a laugh echoing in her mind.

"You miss her?" Aggie asked.

"Yes."

"You'll find her, I have faith that you will."

"Thank you."

"And you know, anything we can do to help, we'll do," Logan added, trying to make sure Nani knew how much support she had here already.

"Thank you."

"And we don't want you going off without money, Mabel can help with that," Nani started shaking her head, "You'll be working for it, don't worry," Aggie assured the quiet girl in front of her who had transformed a lot since she had first found her in the park, sleeping on a bench and covered in dirt, scared of the world around her.

"Thank you," Nani smiled again, appreciating everything they were doing for her.

"What are friends for?"

Nani sat in a cool blue chair, laying her head down and keeping her torso straight and still so the needle wouldn't pierce any skin that wasn't meant to be pierced. The shiny needle glittered in the bright light of the room as the woman moved around, getting everything ready like she had probably hundreds of times before.

"Just lay still," she instructed and Nani tensed her body. "Relax," the woman smiled kindly down at Nani, putting her at ease straight away. "Good," something pierced her skin quickly and painfully, making Nani wince before the pain went away and the woman smiled.

"Done?"

"All done, just stay lying down for a few seconds so you don't get too dizzy when you stand up and faint, OK?" she nodded her head. "Good. I followed the old line where you used to have it pierced so it shouldn't be too uncomfortable but there is a line of scar tissue which is probably the result of it being pulled out, am I right?" Nani nodded again. "OK, just be more careful this time because the more it gets pulled the harder it'll be to stay in," Nani took the care sheet from the woman and left, her mind feeling clear and her heart happy at the feeling of the belly piercing being back in her belly button.

It was as though something had been missing and now a piece of the puzzle had been adding, slowly getting to the complete product that Nani was aiming for. Everything was slowly starting to make sense to Nani; she was slowly putting all the pieces of the puzzle together a picture forming in her mind of what it should look like in the end.

"Come on, we need to talk to the teacher now," Aggie decided for the group, getting up and taking the notebook from Nani before ushering them out and towards Mabel's office.

"Now?" Nani asked, following along obediently.

"Yes, now. The quicker they know the better. You start tomorrow so it is only fair that they know as soon as possible," Logan agreed with Aggie, making the point for her friend.

"OK," Nani conceded, following the two girls through the hallways and towards Mabel's office.

Nani stood at the front of the class, ready to start her first lesson of sign language to the fifth year students. Donalda was at the back of the class to make sure that everything went smoothly, while Aggie and Logan were sitting at their desks, giving Nani the thumbs up and waiting for her to start teaching.

"OK, Nani," she pointed to herself, letting the class know her name. "This sign language," Nani explained. "Start slow," Nani turned around and started writing something on the white board behind her.

Yes. No. Thank you. Please. Were all written on the whiteboard, Nani pointed to the *Yes* and made a motion with her hand.

"This, yes," Her hand was in a fist and moving up and down like a head. "Copy," she asked the class and they all copied her action, saying yes to her request and doing as she had asked. Turning around, Nani started writing on the whiteboard again.

Once you enter the room, you are to use the things you have learnt. There will be no talking when asked a yes or no question, Nani wrote, letting the class know that she wanted them to learn as much as possible and it was easier for her to talk when she wrote on the board.

"Understand?" the class used their newly learnt 'yes' to reply to Nani's question. "Good," and she got to work, teaching them the other three words and a few more, making sure she went back to them so they wouldn't forget.

Once the class was over, Nani was filled with a sense of accomplishment at being able to teach a class and being able to control them. At the end of the class Nani thanked everyone, letting them know that she really was thankful for their listening to her and helping her teach for the first time in her life, that she could remember at least.

"What was in there?" Becca sat with her legs crossed, Indian style, on the green grass outside her cottage home in the English forest. The Egyptian pack wolves were there as well as a few warriors, Fae and the King and Queen.

They had started telling everyone about a mysterious room that had found in the basement, something that had scared them and forced them to call everyone back to the forest the Seelie chose to live in and stay away from humans. There was a buzz about the group as they waited for Aviva or Winslow to answer.

"I don't know how to explain it," Aviva started, waiting for Winslow to take over and describe what they had witnessed.

"It was a room, no windows, with a single light bulb hanging over a stone bench. The bench had chains on it, like someone had been held there, unable to move. The room, well to better describe it would be dungeon. There were tables filled with devices that looked from the medieval times, torture devices," Becca could see Cruze visibly shaking with anger as he heard what Winslow was saying, knowing that Olyanah had been in there. It was a feeling he had and it broke his heart knowing he hadn't been there for his precious mate.

"It was pretty dark but you could see the blood on the floor and on the devices that had been used. I remember when King Henry the Eighth was in power and the way he acted to the church and how he severed the country from the church, along with his wife's arrest and death," Winslow reminisced, "He was a harsh man and the devices I found in the dungeon were pretty similar."

"So she was tortured?" Cruze asked, standing and pacing around the group.

"We don't know that," Becca tried to assure him, "We don't know Ollie was in there, there's no proof, you need to have hope," Becca tried to calm the angry Beta but there was no way she could do that, not now.

"We don't know?" Cruze cried out in anger, "Of course we know! Of course she was in there and of course they were trying to weaken her, don't be so stupid and naive," Cruze yelled at Becca.

"Don't threatened my daughter," Winslow rose to his feet and stared at the Beta, challenging him to raise his voice at the Princess of the Seelie again.

"She must learn that everything is not all roses and cupcakes!" Cruze had a calmer voice but he was still quite angry as he spoke.

"Not all roses and cupcakes?" Becca stood, hovering so she was able to be at eye level with Cruze. "I was kept in the same place as your mate, my friend, and I was abused. Maybe not nearly as much as her but I was hurt nonetheless, so don't talk to me about roses and cupcakes because you don't know what it was like in there. No food, no water and beatings all the time," Becca stared at Cruze with narrowed eyes. "I'm the only one who knows what she went through and as far as I can tell, I'm the only one that was truthful with her, telling her about Mystics and what we're like," Becca stormed off, entering the old English cottage.

"You may have crossed a line there," Brent didn't make eye contact with his Beta as he made the comment. Cruze rubbed his eyes with his hands before running his hands through his messy hair.

"Please, I apologise," Cruze turned to Winslow and Aviva.

"You don't have to apologise to us, it's Becca you have speak with," Cruze nodded his head, leaving the group and going up to Becca's room in the cottage. "Becca," he knocked on her door, speaking in a soft voice so she knew he was here to say sorry, not pick another fight.

"Cruze," she opened the door, a calm look on her face.

"I'm sorry. I forgot that you were in there and I forgot just how hard this is on other people, not just myself," Becca let Cruze enter her small room and he sat on the bed, resting his head in his hands.

"You miss her, that's clear," Becca sat next to Cruze, not touching him because she knew just much a female touch would set him off again because it wasn't his mate.

"I don't know what to do, I miss her so much and I love her so much but how am I meant to deal with his and still be the strong Beta my pack needs. Everyday I lose more and more hope because I can't feel her; I can't smell her. I don't know what to do anymore because the mention of Olyanah has my heart racing and my palms sweating. How am I meant to keep going like this?" there was so much pain and despair in his voice, Becca didn't know how to deal with a broken wolf, let alone a broken Beta.

"Go for a run, clear your head and then come back and we'll talk then," Cruze nodded, thanking Becca before leaving her room and going outside.

Cruze picked up speed as he ran, weaving through the branches of the trees before jumping and changing into his wolf form. Every step was quiet as it hit the forest ground, breaking leaves and twigs with every step.

Cruze stayed crouched down as he ran, letting the wind push through his fur and cool his skin. The force of each stride had a new sense of hope and thrill running through his veins, his wolf letting the man know that his mate was out there and waiting for him to go and save her, go and find her so they could be together; in every way mates should be together.

Cruze loved the feeling of being in his wolf form, he loved the freedom he had and the power. His eyes caught onto every movement in the trees and fur let him feel the wind as it ran through each strand. The senses he had as a wolf always had his heart thumping against his ribs and a smile forming on his wolf lips, pure joy filling his body with each stride and each metre he gained on through the forest, not losing his breath as he ran.

"We have to go," Arabella sat on the edge of the bed they were sleeping in. The bed and room were in a small spare cottage with a few other wolves in the same cottage as them and the others in another spare cottage.

"What?"

"I love our daughter but we do have another daughter and she isn't here. I know she will come back to us, I just know it but Nuru needs us and we have to go home to be there for our pack," Arabella took her mates hand and squeezed it, letting him know just how much she needed to go back home.

"Are you sure?"

"Yes."

"OK, we'll pack tomorrow and we'll go home soon. I promise you that."

"Thank you," Arabella stood up and pulled her mate up with her, pulling him in for a warm and passionate kiss that she had needed for a long time. Feeling her mates warm arms around her waist was a feeling Arabella had missed for a while.

Enakal had been so pulled back since they arrived and since finding out that the building was empty, no sight of their daughter. It had broken his heart and since then he had pulled away from his mate a little too much for Arabella's liking.

"You are such a liar!" a giggle escaped her lips as she yelled, throwing a pillow across the room.

"How?"

"You so didn't do that!"

"Yes I did!"

"You can't even show me the scar, therefore you can't say you did it because you clearly don't have the proof," Lacy stared at Jason from the opposite couch, another pillow in her hand as ammunition.

"I have the scar but I can show you tonight, not now."

"Why tonight?"

"Because it is a proven fact that women love scars and if I show you tonight we might be able to have a little more fun," Jason winked at his mate but Lacy only rolled her eyes and laughed.

"Well that might be proven tonight, or it might not be. We'll just have to see what'll happen," Lacy got up from her couch and walked into the kitchen to get something to eat for the two.

"It will won't it," Jason laughed.

"Want something to eat?"

"Yeah."

"Well what then?"

"Food?"

"You are such a pain, sometimes I just want to hit you," Lacy cried out, trying not to laugh so Jason would know she was trying to be serious, which didn't happen very often between the two.

Since being in Rosewood, the two had grown so close, they had just fallen more and more in love as they days went on and friendly banter was something that happened every minute in their relationship.

They were never alone and had very similar thoughts a lot; the main topic of their conversations had been children recently. Jason had explained to Lacy that although they were two species crossed, conceiving was somewhat difficult depending on the lineage of each partner.

Jason knew Lacy was OK because her parents had conceived, but Jason didn't know too much about his history so he was going to do some research when they got back to Egypt. If he was going to have trouble then it wasn't impossible, just very difficult to have a child and more then one would be a miracle.

Lacy walked back into the room with a plate full of food for the two as they put on a movie. Lacy wasn't in the mood to be lectured about her mates bad genes and just wanted to enjoy being with him, having his arms around her and enjoying his touch as they sat comfortably without having to always talk.

"Lac," Lacy groaned, knowing the tone all too well.

"Don't start, not now. Just enjoy the moment, please," Lacy was ready to get on the ground and start begging Jason.

"You don't even know what I'm going to ask."

"I can take a pretty good stab in the dark when it comes to you, baby. You aren't all that good at covering your emotions with your voice when it comes to me," Lacy pointed out with a devilish smile.

"Well, I wasn't even going to talk about that, I was going to ask if you wanted to go for a run in the moon light, enjoy the beach and forest and just go for a run. But if you want to talk about that . . ."

"Run, sounds good," Lacy cut in.

"Good."

Lacy shed her clothing as she took a step running, falling to the ground as she went from human to wolf in a matter of seconds, something Jason had been helping her improve on.

The feeling of being in her wolf form was so exciting and wonderful, like seeing the world from a whole new view and having Jason by her side running with her was the icing on top of the cake.

She felt so free and so alive as each stride took her closer and closer to her goal and reaching the end of the forest. Every stride hit the ground with such force but no noise from her paws, no noise as all as she continued to see the world in a new way from her amazing sense that had slowly been developing.

Every leaf, every water droplet, every stick on the ground could be seen in detail by Lacy. The sight helped her dodge branches like she was dancing with nature as she moved along the forest floor along with her mate.

Jason shot images of the beach dark at night with the full moon reflected in the water, surrounded by different sized stars. Lacy knew where Jason was going with this and it only served to spur her on to her to the end destination quicker. Being able to get to the Saint Louis beach with her mate and swim in the moonlight sounded like the most amazing idea she had ever heard.

'You are such a dog,' Lacy send Jason a wink along with the message and heard a literal bark of laughter from her right.

'And you are such an amazing tease, how about we revisit old memories?' the suggestion in Jason's tone wasn't lost on Lacy and it sent a shiver running down her body as she run fast and fast, keeping up with her fit mate.

'Ah, Memory Lane, how I have missed you,' she joked, sprinting ahead of Jason as she saw the opening of the forest, showing the beach she had pictured. The moonlight was so bright and so warm Lacy couldn't help but feel so at home and so alive as she ran, stopping at the sand and changing quickly back to her human form, covering her naked self with her hands.

Jason changed next to her and looked out at the water, remembering the times he and Cruze would go surfing, sitting on their boards out in the ocean and talk about finding their mates and what it would be like.

In all their talks, Jason never imagined it like this, he never imagined it to be so fulfilling, like a part of his soul and heart had found their way back to him.

"You are beautiful, so beautiful. Please don't cover yourself," Jason pulled Lacy in for a hug, letting her know just how beautiful he thought she was and that it broke his heart because she didn't believe him. "Did you know Plato's, in Greek mythology, thought that all humans were born with four arms, four legs and two heads. Zeus feared their power so he cut the humans in half, letting them wonder around for the rest of their lives trying to find their soul mate," Lacy watched Jason talk about the old theory.

"Do you believe it?" Lacy cut the silence with her question.

"Yes, I believe in soul mates as it has been proven to me time and time again, but do I believe we were more then one person? No. That is not what I believe to be true and not what Anubis has taught me."

"Maybe Anubis isn't the only one you should believe?"

"How do you mean?"

"Well, Anubis did create Werewolves, that much I know and believe, but who created the others? Who created the Banshee's and the Vampire's and the Fae and Mermaids and the rest of them? Who created them? Because I don't think Anubis created all the Mystics," Lacy rested her hands on Jason's chest. "Just think about it OK? I'm not asking you to believe it, I'm just asking you to think about it," Lacy wriggled out of her mates grip and ran towards the water, calling out to him to follow her.

"Wait up!" Jason cried, chasing after his mate but his mind on what Lacy had just said to him. He had asked Lacy to think about it when he told her about Werewolves, not to believe him straight away because it would be a shock to the system, but to just think about it and see what she thought.

So much alike the two were, their minds were so in tune all the time and that was something Jason would never give up on. He loved his mate and he never wanted her to leave him, he hated that Cruze was without his mate but he was so thankful that Lacy had escaped.

"Come here, my beautiful mate," Jason reached Lacy treading water in the ocean, being taller he was able to stand easily, and wrapped her up in his arms, place warm, soft and passionate kisses all over her mouth, jaw line and collar bones until he couldn't wait any more.

Lacy jumped in the shower, enjoying the warm water as it ran over her cool body, warming up the blood that was travelling in her veins. The fresh clean water was refreshing, more refreshing then the salty ocean water she had been in earlier.

Jumping out of the shower and plaiting her hair, Lacy went out to join everyone watching a movie in the lounge room. A few were on the ground while the couches were all covered with bodies trying to enjoy the movie, Crazy, Stupid, Love.

Lacy loved the movie, she loved how Emma Stone reminded her of Ollie and the fact that whenever she watched the movie, she was able to feel hope that Ollie was out there and out there alive. It was the first modern movie Lacy had shown Ollie on schoolies and it fascinated her.

Lacy could remember the way Ollie sat watching with such intensity as she tried not to analysis everything that was happening on the screen and just enjoy the romantic comedy.

"I feel better now!" Lacy sang as she walked into the room looking relaxed and ready, trying to hide her emotions. She knew Jason would feel her pain but wouldn't say anything, not in front of everyone at least.

"Good shower?" Ain asked from the ground. Lacy nodded taking a seat next her with Jason on the cushion behind her, seated nice and high on the leather couch.

"One of those ones that just washes everything away."

"Lacy, I have to ask you something," Lacy pulled her pajama top over her head and crawled into bed, resting her head on Jason's chest, waiting for him to talk again and feel the vibrations of his body. "We've been here for a few weeks now, almost a month. Christmas has come and gone two weeks ago and you haven't seen your parents since we left. The others are heading home, we need to too."

Lacy closed her eyes, trying to hold her emotions in as she thought about giving up on Ollie and giving up on trying to find her. She couldn't imagine what was happening to her best friend and tried to avoid it often because she was scared of the images that might go floating through her mind.

"We aren't giving up on Ollie, we'd never do that but your family needs you home, our pack needs us home and Nuru misses her parents. Please just say yes and I promise we will come back here every year at the same time to honour Ollie and one day find her."

"Find. But we better come back every year," even agreeing to what her mate was asking was killing her, breaking her heart as she thought about her best friend and everything they had been through.

"Thank you, I promise you we will; no matter what. This also gives us a chance to look at my family tree," Jason hinted.

"Don't get started with me," Lacy groaned, moving so she was resting on her elbows and staring into her mates brown eyes.

"I just want you to be prepared because I want to give you the world and I know just how much you want children."

"Jason?"

"Yes?"

"What happened to your parents?" the topic of his parents was something Jason avoided talking about, something he had learnt from Cruze when they had lost their parents so young, giving them a bridge to each other and letting them start a friendship together as more then pack mates.

"That is a story for another day, my beautiful little wolf," Lacy could see Jason's eyes were glasses over as he answered her.

"OK, but we will talk, yeah?"

"Of course."

"OK. When are we going to leave?"

"Tomorrow night."

"Wow, you wolves really don't like to waste any time do you?" Lacy laughed awkwardly, trying to break the tension that was in the air.

Lacy felt as though whenever she brought up the topic of his parents, Jason seemed to shut down, build his walls again. Lacy wanted to tear those walls down and see what was waiting behind them, let her mate know that she was there for him and she would love him no matter what.

Resting her head on his chest again, Lacy closed her eyes and begged for sleep to take her away so she could see tomorrow and be in a new day. A day where she would be going home and seeing her parents and be there for her pack as they needed her to be.

Chapter Twenty-Eight

To Awaken Alone In A Strange Town Is One Of The Pleasantest Sensations In The World

THE SOUNDS OF birds tweeting could be heard from every step on the grounds as the soft wind carried the music sound to people's ears, letting them embrace nature and everything it entailed.

A crowd of women, ladies and girls were all gathered around a black car with tinted windows at the front of the grounds in the driveway that would've once been the road for horses with carriages and carts trailing behind, behind moved by their powerful legs.

Tears were being spilt as they hugged a dyed red haired girl. Her hair was pulled into a French twist with a piece of fabric around her head to keep the thick red hair off her face and out of her eyes.

"You have a good time and call us and let us know what happens," Mabel pulled the girl in for a hug,

"Make sure you call us!" Nora yelled with a smile on her face at her new friends departure.

Calls of 'Goodbye' and 'Have a good time' and 'Don't forget to call' were being yelled at Nani as she made sure she had everything and hugged all of her new friends goodbye and thanked them.

Everyone could see the progress Nani had made since arriving at the boarding school in Scotland. She had started talking after a while and even got the confidence to teach sign language in front of a class, getting them to have the basic communication with those who were unable to talk like everyone else.

Slowly since she started teaching, her speech had gotten better and better, although still being broken and a little awkward, Aggie and Logan were able to discern where they thought she was from and have easier conversation with her.

"Make sure you send lots of photos!" Logan and Aggie yelled out at Nani at the same time, making everyone erupt into a chorus of laughter.

"I will. Goodbye and study," Nani called out as she stepped into the car with the driver in the front and closed the door, waving out the open window as the driver pulled out and headed towards the airport.

It had been a long road to get here, eight weeks of working and trying to organise a passport when she didn't even know what her name was or anything about herself aside from the fact that Aggie and Logan thought she was Australian, which was where she had decided to start her travel of finding herself, who she really was and who she knew.

So much was riding on this and so much was riding on her shoulders to find out where she really was and where she was from.

The thought of not having anyone and all her memories being nothing but lies had haunted Nani for a long time, keeping her up at night since she had booked the ticket a week ago.

Watching the still unfamiliar country side roll past as the man drove her to the airport left Nani with an uneasy yet familiar feeling in her stomach as the car rolled along further and further towards the airport.

"Excuse me?" Nani sat forward in the backseat and grabbed the attention of the driver.

"Yes, miss?"

"How far to airport?"

"Not long, maybe twenty minutes. Is everything OK?" he seemed like a nice man but Nani had learnt not to trust people the hard people way and being in a car with a strange man was setting her anxiety off, making her shake and have shallow breathing.

"Yes, thank you," Nani sat back in her seat and tried to calm her beating heart as she pulled her notebook out and started writing down the feelings she was feeling about going to the airport.

The only way she was able to calm herself down was by flipping back a few pages and reading what was written on the page that had the man sitting on the beach watching the waves.

Around the picture were words about a certain smell, the smell of fresh rain falling in a forest that sat on the edge of a beach. Nani could smell the droplets hitting the leaves of the forest and gradually moving around to the beach where the sand turned into a mud like substance.

The rest of the drive went quickly and so did the flight to the Northern Territory, Australia, the one place on the map that seemed to make Nani feel the most nervous and excited at the same time, so many things were going through her head, so many different feelings Nani didn't really understand.

The plane arrived in the afternoon, leaving Nani feeling exhausted and run down as she walked outside and was greeted by the warm Australian sun, something she had been missing while she was in Scotland.

It was a nice feeling being in the sun and being able to breathe fresh air for the first time in a while. She had been in a plane for so long that she had forgotten what fresh air smelt like and smelling it in Australia it had a different smell then Scotland had, a smell she had grown used to but the smell in Australia was familiar to her as she walked to the taxi rink where she could get somewhere.

A few names were written down in the notebook and it was up to Nani to figure out where she was going to go. She had a map out on her phone that Mabel had given to her as a gift, Nani slowly typed a few letters into the directions and when it came up with no location she typed another word in to see if that was a place she could go to.

Finding a name in her notebook that was recognised by the map program and Nani stood up with excitement hailing down a taxi so she could tell them where to go.

"Where?" the taxi driver asked with furrowed eyebrows as Nani told him where to go from the back seat, her heart beating erratically again at being in a confined space with a man she didn't know.

"Saint Louis," Nani got the map up on her phone and showed the man.

"Oh, OK," he typed what was on her phone into his GPS and started the car. Nani watched out the window, trying to see if she could recognise anything or if anything would come back to her.

Before she knew it, Nani was paying the taxi driver and thanking him for taking her so far out; it ended up being about forty-five minutes to get out to the Saint Louis beach.

There was nothing jumping out at Nan so she decided to go down to the beach and sit down, hoping something would come to her while she was looking at her notebook. There were so many things written down it was hard to make sense of everything.

The one page Nani kept flipping back to was the one with the drawing of the man sitting on the beach watching the waves. There was something eerily familiar about the image now as Nani walked down to the beach that was filled with people enjoying the warm February sun.

Students were back at school but that wasn't stopping them from enjoying the sun, Nani could see some skipping class to come down to the beach so they could go for a surf and just lay in the sun before it started getting too cold.

Nan reached the sand and threw her shoes off, picking them up in her hand so she could walk along feeling the grains between her toes with each step. The feeling was beautiful and when Nani was happy she sat down in the sand and pulled her bags up next to her so she could get some things out.

Pulling out her pencil case so she could write a few more things in her notebook, everything she was feeling and everything she could see. Drawing what was in front of her as the people moved around and the waves crashed down on the sand foaming white as they hit.

Nani pulled out her phone that Mabel had given her and took a photo, sending it to Aggie, Logan, Nora, Donalda and Mabel so they knew she was here safely and enjoying the beautiful view Australia had to offer.

Aggie: Looks amazing! I can't wait until we go and we can see you there too.

Logan: I'm coming as soon as I get out of this place.

Aggie: Logan and I'll be there in a few years, don't worry about that.

Mabel: Looks wonderful, warm and sunny. Enjoy your time there and try and find out who you are. We miss you.

Donalda: Stay safe!

Nora: Make sure you're safe and good to see you're trying to find who you are.

Nani smiled at the messages from her new friends; thankful that they were the ones to find her and that they had taken her in and accepted her as their own. It was a feeling Nani had never felt before,

She walked around the town, rolling her suitcase behind her on the smooth pavement. Each shop had an end of summer sale or winter arriving sale. The money people had to buy the clothing astounded Nani, she would never be able to afford the clothes in the nice shops.

Everything looked so fancy to Nani, something she wasn't used to. The boarding school had been very minimal or very personal not made in bulk so everyone had the same thing and looked the same trying to look different from each other.

There was a hotel up at the plaza of shops that were in Saint Louis, Nani made her way up to the hotel and waited, hoping that they would have a room for her.

Luckily they did have a room for her, the perfect cheap room Nani decided as she walked into the minimal beach hotel styled room with blue, yellow and white accessories everywhere.

Nani unpacked her bag, taking the little clothing she had and folding it neatly on the table that was meant to be used as a desk, leaving space so she could write and draw when things came back to her.

Nani lay in the bed of the hotel that night, wishing she was with those who loved her and not feeling like she was alone in the world again. She didn't want the new friendship she had found, instead she wanted the friendship she had written about in her notebook, the friendship that was like a family relationship to her.

Closing her eyes, Nani started to fall asleep, dreaming about a life that she missed and a life that she had forgotten in another world, a world that she missed like she had never missed anything before.

There was a soft mist covering the familiar place I had known so well as a child, the playground stood lifeless in the dark light that was being let off by the barely there moon. Everything I had known and known for such a long time was slowly fading into black and I knew I could no longer bury my head in the sand. I was not going to let them push me around; not for my last few weeks of school.

I would be gone soon and then I would never have to see them again, I would never have anything to do with them again and that was going to be the best day of my life; the day I forget about them.

Nani woke with a start, scared of everything she had remembered or seen in her dream. Everything seemed so real, so true and yet there seemed to be a little bit of doubt in what she had dreamt, like she wasn't really dreaming, more so reliving a memory, a memory she wanted to forget and had tried hard to forget; like everything else in her life.

With her palms sweating and hr mouth feeling dry, Nani changed into a pair of leggings and a grey jumper before grabbing her phone and wallet and heading out the door in need of some fresh sea air.

Nani wanted to soak up the beach lifestyle and she thought going for a walk at the crack of dawn was going to help with that and help her clear her head as well. The dream was haunting her and she was trying to remember where or when it had happened, every step she took towards the neighbouring town of Rosewood had her getting her hopes higher and higher, feeling as thought she was getting closer to what she wanted to see.

"Oh my god," Nani stopped dead in her tracks with her eyes wide open and head tilted to the side in disbelief. It was almost as though this was a sing from the universe telling her that this is what she had been looking for.

In front of Nani stood an old looking playground that had probably been used for years, but there was something about this playground, something Nani felt as though she should know.

Shaking and her head telling her to stop and go back, Nani walked over to the playground and onto the platform where the slide went off. Looking out onto the pathway, she could see houses lined up, people living their perfect lives in them with their perfect families. It hurt her inside that she couldn't remember if she had had that life, but something deep inside told her that she had never had a perfect life, in fact she'd had the opposite.

Nani rested her head on the top of the slide, opening her eyes to see a tiny engraved detail on the red plastic slide, something that shouldn't be there.

Lacy and Ollie forever best friends.

Whey were those names familiar? Did she know those two girls? Were they her friends? Did they still live here? How long ago had it been carved? Question after question filled Nani's mind as she ran her hand along the engraving, sending a shiver down her spin and making her jump off the playground, scared for the feelings she had just uncovered inside herself.

Who knew what she was likely to remember and without her notebook with her, Nani didn't want to remember a thing.

Tears started to prick to her eyes, rolling down her cheeks as she turned her back on the playground she was sure she had seen before and walking into what she hoped was town so she could get some breakfast into her stomach and then make the two hour walk back yo Saint Louis to write everything down.

Nani refused to forget what she had seen, she refused to forget the feelings that were floating around inside her stomach, her mind and her heart as she made it to the local strip of shops in Rosewood.

There was a line of shops opposite a car park, the one that caught Nani's eye was the 50's styled diner with booths filled with school kids getting breakfast on their way to school, making sure they were ready to start their day.

Stepping in, Nani waited until someone came up and greeted her, taking her to a booth that was away from the school kids. The young girl in a poodle skirt and white top, rolling around on roller blades, handed Nani a menu, showing her everything they offered for lunch.

"Excuse me, may I take your order?" Nani looked at an older man looking at his notepad, he wasn't wearing the same uniform as the other men working at the diner so Nani guessed he was probably older and more superiour then everyone else.

"Pancakes, maple syrup," Nani ordered, trying to sound polite with her broke and somewhat rude sounding English.

"No problem."

"Thank you," the man looked up to take them menu from Nani before stumbling back a little with wide eyes that looked as though they were going to fall out of the sockets.

"Ollie? Is that you?"